Another clap of thunder, coupled with a bright flash of lights, wrenched me back to consciousness.

The power was back on.

Struggling to my feet, I leaned against the sink, using it as a support. My hand slid along its porcelain edge, leaving a wet trace of . . . was that *blood*?

A chill skittered down my spine. I'd been here before. Several times before I'd had nightmares of the mortuary. The smell of blood, of death, of—

Suddenly, I didn't want to turn around. I knew there was something behind me and it wasn't a vacant embalming table. I could smell it.

Closing my eyes, I turned, my movements deliberate, my hands clutched into fists, the drying blood tacky against my skin. I didn't want to see, but I had to. I made myself open my eyes.

The once-empty table now held an occupant. It was definitely Marty. And he was most definitely dead. This was exactly like my dream. Only this time—

A pounding on the hall door tore my gaze from the scene. The lights flashed again. I blinked and shook my head, darting a glance across the room.

Everything was the way it had been. The embalming area remained in shadow; no body lay on the empty table.

Tur
Matters of

D0035135

Praise for
MARIA LIMA
and
MATTERS OF THE BLOOD

"A fast pace that never lags, suspense to keep the reader turning pages, paranormal beings including shapeshifters and vampires, and a personality of its own. . . . It's a complex plot with the requisite twists and turns of a mystery, the passion of a paranormal romance, and the unearthly elements of urban fantasy."

—SF Site

"An absolutely spectacular addition to the paranormal landscape. . . . Novels of this caliber are few and far between. . . . A classy, teasing tale. . . ."

—BookFetish

"Dark, seductive, and bitingly humorous. . . . This is one paranormal super-thriller you should 'bump' to the top of your to-be-read pile."

—Heartstring

"A great page-turner. . . ."

—The Bookshelf Reviews

"An excellent book, readable and gripping with varied characters, an interesting plot, and a great setting in small-town Texas."

—Curled Up With a Good Book (5 stars)

"Keira Kelly kicks butt. . . . A supernatural mystery with guts, brains, and soul. . . . Hot action and spicy romance with a biting sense of humor."

—Dana Cameron, author of *Ashes and Bones*

"A pleasure to read from the first page to the last."

—*CrimeSpree* magazine

"Funny, sexy, mysterious, and lots of fun to read."

—Nancy Pickard, author of *The Virgin of Small Plains*

MATTERS
OF THE
BLOOD

MARIA LIMA

POCKET BOOKS
New York London Toronto Sydney

Pocket Books
A Division of Simon & Schuster, Inc.
1230 Avenue of the Americas
New York, NY 10020

This book is a work of fiction. Names, characters, places, and incidents either are products of the author's imagination or are used fictitiously. Any resemblance to actual events or locales or persons, living or dead, is entirely coincidental.

This Juno Books/Pocket Books paperback edition September 2009

JUNO BOOKS and colophon are trademarks of Wildside Press LLC used under license by Simon & Schuster, Inc., the publisher of this work.

POCKET and colophon are registered trademarks of Simon & Schuster, Inc.

For information about special discounts for bulk purchases, please contact Simon & Schuster Special Sales at 1-866-506-1949 or business@simonandschuster.com.

The Simon & Schuster Speakers Bureau can bring authors to your live event. For more information or to book an event, contact the Simon & Schuster Speakers Bureau at 1-866-248-3049 or visit our website at www.simonspeakers.com.

Cover design by Stephen Segal

Manufactured in the United States of America

10 9 8 7 6 5 4 3 2 1

ISBN 978-1-4391-5674-2
ISBN 978-1-4391-7543-9 (ebook)

Dedicated to the Evil Enablers:

Dina S. Willner

Maryelizabeth Hart

Carla Coupe

You put me back in touch with my inner fangrrl.
It's *still* all your fault . . . Thank you kindly.

ACKNOWLEDGMENTS

It takes a village . . . or in this case, many villages . . . many people without whom this book would not have been written and I thank each and every one of you. Of course, if I detailed the lot of you, this list would be longer than the book. Please know that each of you holds a special place in my heart.

That said, there are some that deserve a shout-out:

• First and foremost, my family both virtual and non— my parents, my sister Laura Condit, my brother-in-law Ken, all the Buds—Tea, Buffy or otherwise. Without you, this would still be a dream.

• My unofficial critiquers who helped me over more than a few bumps in a long road: Partner in Crime Donna Andrews, Second Twin Carla Coupe, the Evil Doctor Dana, Enabler Dina and my lovely "twin," Elaine Yamaguchi.

• Lonnie Cruse, whose knowledge of the funeral industry saved me from a most embarrassing gaffe.

• An extra-special thank-you to Jan Burke, Charlaine Harris, and Jerrilyn Farmer—who many times kept me going when the going got way more than rough.

Muchisimas gracias.

CHAPTER ONE

I KNOW THE DEAD and the dead know me. Not a personal choice, mind you, just the result of being born into a family of necromancers. It's in our blood, so to speak. Not that I am one—not yet anyway. It's more that they needed someone to learn the family business. So instead of more practical training, I learned how to deal with death.

Two years ago, my entire life changed and I ended up more or less back where I'd started—the heart of Texas Hill Country in a small town called Rio Seco—babysitting a whiny forty-year-old mortician cousin whose idea of fun was to call me at the ass crack of what-the-hell-time-is-it, a couple of hours past my usual dawnish bedtime, and beg for money. Okay, I had it and he didn't, but all I wanted from him was a little respect—you know, the stuff Aretha sang about. My cousin had plenty of respect for his clients (actually, for their families who were paying for his services) but not for me. Marty Nelson would always bitch to me about his dead-end (pun intended) job, his life (mostly useless) and his lack of funds (eternal).

Enduring two years of boredom, near-solitude, and conversations with a man with whom I had less in common than a family pet wasn't what I'd imagined. Okay, so I had made this choice. What can I say? At the time, it sounded easy. I hadn't bothered to consider the consequences, imagine the future and recognize how unspeakably bored I would become. Marty certainly didn't make it any easier.

Then things started changing. Over the past couple of weeks, I'd been blessed with my own personal nightmare freak show. Lifelike dreams, crashing into my REM cycle with an overwhelming assault of vivid Technicolor, surround sound and Smell-o-vision. I spent years as Death's assistant and now those years were coming back to haunt me . . . not with guilt or accusation, but in nightmares full of pain, fear, violence and a hell of a lot of blood.

That was the part I kept wondering about. Clan deaths were rarely violent, at least in the last century or so. Nowadays, when our folk died, it was by choice, not by chance. I wasn't sure where all this was coming from, maybe it was just my own sick psyche dealing with the so-called facts of my life.

This last one was the worst so far. Even the bright mid-afternoon sun couldn't chase it away. I still tasted blood, tasted death. The rich flavor of life bleeding into lifelessness hovered at the back of my throat, covering my tongue with that morning-after-the-night-before fuzzy coating that makes you run to the nearest toothbrush and giant bottle of Scope.

I could still remember every last bloody minute of it.

I ran. Faster than I could ever remember running, my feet passing smoothly over rough terrain, my body automatically turning, avoiding rocks, cacti, and stumps of dead mesquite dangerously spearing the still night air. As the pale light of the nearly full moon blazed my path, my night vision adjusted automatically.

I could smell them in front of me. Hot fear-scent mixed

with the exhilaration of the chase. This was what I wanted, what I needed.

Two hunters ran in front of me, staying in the shadows so I couldn't see who they were. No matter; after they fed, then I would.

I lunged forward, impatient now to reach my—

The smell slammed into my nose as I heard their prey fall, one body, then another. My gut roiled in agony, anticipation.

Blood. Lots of it. Where were they?

Fog clouded my vision. My senses shut down as the blood spoor became my only focus. I broke through the bushes, branches scratching my face, my arms, my body, pain receding into the background. There they were— ahead, in a clearing just by the lake, next to the homey picnic benches scattered throughout the small area.

Two of them, torn and bleeding. The rich scent teased me, luring me over. I looked around. The hunters were gone. Long gone. No one was there but the dead . . . and me.

I stepped closer. Two deer, small, defenseless, spotted bodies too small to escape the things that chased them. I reached down, my hand operating independently of my conscious brain, my body taking over, knowing it needed—

I screamed as I realized that the bloody corpse nearest me wasn't a deer after all.

It was my cousin, Marty.

SOMETHING BUZZED at my hip and my hands jerked the wheel. The Land Rover's right front tire slid off the road onto the gravel shoulder, kicking up dust. I recovered, steering back on to the road.

Holy crap. I really had to stop thinking about this,

especially while I was driving. Maybe I should try to adjust my sleep cycle and sleep at night, like normal people. Yeah, right. *Normal*. Ignore the obvious.

The buzz-tickle came again—damned cell phone. Would I ever get used to this thing? I fumbled it out of my pocket while steering one-handed, and answered. "Hello?"

"Keira?"

"Hi, Marty." Great. I should have looked at the caller ID before answering. Who else would call at three P.M.—early for me—but my charge, my responsibility, the reason for my dissatisfaction and the frequent star of many of my recent nightmares? Of course, the dreams of his death might just be the product of my jumbled mind sorting out not-so-cousinly feelings. Could just be a bit of scary wishful thinking. After all, two years was twenty-four months too long to be riding herd over a man only three years my senior, especially one as annoying as my cousin. After this last set of dreams, though, I was considering changing my analysis. These nightmares weren't fodder for a shrink's couch. They'd send any would-be Freud screaming.

"Are you busy?"

Busy trying to not freak out, but otherwise, not really. Can't say "busy" describes my life these days.

I pulled over to the side of the road so I could concentrate on talking to him. I didn't like to talk while driving the narrow, winding back roads.

"Not exactly. What's up?"

He paused, as if my question was too hard to answer.

"Keira, I'm sorry, I know you hate to be called early, but . . . uhm . . . I sort of need . . . I've got . . ." A sigh and another pause followed.

An armadillo waddled across the asphalt, its leaden progress hypersonic compared to the conversation I didn't actually seem to be having. The silence stretched. I could hear Marty breathing, but no words.

I finally spoke, unwilling to sit watching armadillos avoid becoming road decor any longer.

"Marty, what the hell do you want? I can't do anything if you won't talk to me."

Closing my eyes, I leaned back in my seat, holding on to my temper. I could feel it rising, an almost automatic response. Deep breaths, Keira. Slow, calming breaths. It didn't pay to get angry with Marty. He never really noticed.

No doubt his skinny, balding self was now sitting behind his previously owned pressboard desk, the very picture of a respectable mortician in a baggy Men's Wearhouse three-piece suit while I sat here like an idiot in my vintage Land Rover Defender waiting for him to tell me something that mattered. It never mattered to me—only to Marty and his overbearing sense of self-importance. The fact I'd been "assigned" to him couldn't help his misguided illusions of grandeur.

"I think I'm in trouble," he finally whispered. Marty's voice sounded hesitant.

"How much is it this time? Another security door? The latest and greatest embalming machine or whatever?" At the beginning of this particular month, he'd needed to pay his property taxes. The week before that he didn't have enough to cover an overdue invoice. Two days before that . . . well, it was always the same thing. Just a couple of weeks ago, I'd paid for a state-of-the-art security door after another phone call, during which he whined for the better part of a half hour and then gloated over his nifty new toy, an electronic door controlled by a security touchpad. Expensive high-tech protection. Just what a small town mortuary run by one guy and a part-time receptionist needed. As always, it had been easier to write the check and pay the invoice. If money could buy a little peace and quiet, then so be it.

"No, it's not—Keira, I . . . can't . . . Shit. I need you to come over." He sounded exasperated, a change from his usual pity-poor-me-I-need-money whine.

"Excuse me? Come over? *Now,* before I eat breakfast?"

"I really need you to come over here, Keira."

"Why—the door break down?" I couldn't help it. I'd not only paid way too much money for the thing, I'd also had to pay for the special technician to come in from Austin and re-install the door after Marty's local bargain guy messed it up.

"Look, I really need to talk to you. It's important. But I can't talk right now, and not on the phone."

The last words were more breaths than actual words, as if he were trying not to let someone overhear. Who, I had no idea, since the receptionist was older than God and almost as deaf as Marty's clients. She was unlikely to be there at this hour anyway.

Damn it, if I avoided him now, he'd keep badgering me with phone calls and voice messages until I gave in anyway. But I gave it one more shot.

"Marty, can I call you later, after I get some food in me? I just got up."

"Yeah, I guess," he said, reluctantly. "But don't call, just come by when you're done eating. I have to see you in person, Keira." He hesitated, then continued. "This is family important . . . blood important. Please."

Bloody freaking hell. I hated this already and I didn't even know what it was about. I'd let the words sway me, but I knew his tendency to exaggerate. Last time he'd sworn it was a family thing he'd been scared he'd gotten his then-girlfriend pregnant. He wanted money for an abortion. She wanted the baby and a husband—turned out to be a false alarm. A few weeks later, she moved to Dallas with a new guy. Marty kept the money and bought a new suit. That was eight months ago. I told him then that if he ever invoked the family again when it was a personal problem, I'd call in said family. Why did I think he'd listened?

"I'll be there as soon as I can, Marty. Don't get your tighties in a wad. Let me eat or I'll be more than useless."

I took a breath. If this *was* serious family business, he wouldn't want to wait.

After a short pause, he spoke again. "I'll wait. And, Keira . . ."

"Yes?"

"Thanks."

The odd flat silence finally penetrated as my brain processed the fact that Marty hung up. He'd said both "please" and "thanks"—two words that I'd rarely heard from him over the past two years. Hmm.

I tried to ignore the distant alarm bells clamoring in my head as I pulled back onto the road. Damn it. It really wasn't Marty's fault that for the past several weeks, I'd woken up either just before or just after dawn with shrieks still echoing in my ears. It also wasn't his fault that until this last one, most of the previous nightmares involved his screams, his blood . . . and that somehow, for some bizarre reason, I felt guilty about it.

Okay, maybe not so bizarre considering what was happening. To me, not Marty. I had no idea what he was going on about. After two weeks, I'd finally figured out at least part of what was going on with me. The nightmares were just a small part of it. The paranormal floodgates had most definitely opened, the psychic horses had gotten out and my personal Elvis had finally left the fucking building.

I should have known, especially after the past few visits from the nightmare fairy, but ignoring the signs was far too easy. Ignoring wasn't going to help now.

I saw it in the mirror this morning. It was most definitely there, slipsliding behind my eyes: a hint of darkness, of *other*.

It really wasn't all that noticeable. I don't suppose it wouldn't stop any presses or even a casual passerby. At first glance, I looked normal, human. But I'd always known better. I was Changing—twenty years too early and with no one to guide me—coming into my full powers as a family member. Well, I always was GDI (god-damned independent) and (according to my instructors) advanced for my age group. Guess I'd have to live up to that reputation now.

Meet Keira Kelly: not-such-a-child prodigy. Height: Five feet, ten inches. Eyes: Gray. Hair: Black. Likes: Old movies, good books and great wine. Trained as: "Escort," temporarily on leave. Talents: Clairvoyance, farseeing, necromancy—a lovely smorgasbord of supernatural powers and things that go bump in the night.

I left off shapeshifting, since it would be overkill to state the obvious.

CHAPTER TWO

DESPITE MY DISTRACTIONS, I made it to my destination without having an accident. Not hard to do in Rio Seco. Our idea of heavy traffic was more than one vehicle approaching the four-way stop at the same time. Yeah, "the," as in "there's only one." One main intersection marking the center of what we called "town." We were so small, we not only didn't have a Dairy Queen, we didn't even have a football team. In Texas, that's tantamount to heresy. No worries on our end, though; it helped keep us out of the limelight.

Places like ours still exist in parts of the Hill Country. Some towns, like Luckenbach or Fredericksburg, hang on due to tourism. Others are supported by some local product, usually limestone or cattle. Then there's most good ol' boys' favorite "product"—hunting. Rio Seco had only a few small ranches, our quarry closed more than twenty years ago and—despite the occasional SUV-load of family out wandering the Hill Country for lack of anything better to do who stopped here because they were lost or needed to pee—we didn't do tourists. We existed for the seasons: dove, quail, javelina, turkey and the most popular: deer.

Whitetail season opened in a couple of weeks for general hunting. Bow hunting season was already in progress, but we don't get much of that around here. The town itself didn't do much direct business with the hunters, but the residents of the county, mostly ranchers with lucrative leases, did.

I crossed the parking lot of the small strip center that was pretty much all there was of beautiful downtown Rio Seco. A small silver-haired woman holding a couple of cups of coffee stood just outside Bea's Place, our only retail food establishment. I was there for fuel: caffeine, food and a quick gabfest with my best friend (and the café's owner), Beatriz Ruiz.

"Hey, Greta," I called to the woman, smiling as I approached and trying to keep a neutral tone. Hard enough to keep my regular secrets from the locals without anyone noticing this Change business, too. Would she see anything different about me? Marty hadn't noticed, but then we'd only spoken on the phone. Besides, he was preoccupied with whatever it was he was caught up in.

"Good day, Keira." Greta Nagy returned my smile with one of her own. Good. She sounded like she usually did. I guess that meant I didn't sound any different, even though my brain was still buzzing.

"How you doing?" I asked. "That a new outfit?"

"Yes." She preened a little, showing off the snazzy silver-gray track suit, the uniform of choice around here for women of a certain age. "Thank you for noticing."

A bit over seventy, Greta and her slightly more senior brother owned and operated the deli/convenience store that made up most of the right-hand side of the L-shaped center. The café anchored the far left of the strip. A laundromat, video store and a real estate office made up the rest. Not much town here, but I loved every square rolling foot of it, despite my apathy of the last couple of years.

"Since it is the middle of the afternoon, you must be having breakfast," Greta asked.

"Nothing like Bea's breakfast tacos and coffee to wake a person up." I smiled. My stomach made the appropriate accompanying noises.

A glimpse of movement at the corner of my eye caught my attention. Greta's brother was in front of the deli, loading the store van with what looked like cases of wine. He carried them almost effortlessly, with the smooth moves of a much younger man.

I turned back to Greta. "So, how's Boris doing?"

She grimaced a little, but kept her polite tone. "He is better."

I heard the uncertainty behind the words, not completely masked by her matter-of-fact delivery.

"No more problems, then?"

"A few nightmares, but he is better. I will let him know you asked, thank you."

With that, she smiled and walked away.

I watched as she handed him his coffee. They were too far away for me to hear anything, but as he took a sip, he wiped his forehead with a red bandanna and looked over at me, a strange expression on his face.

I waved a "hello" and walked into the café.

Poor man. I wasn't the only one having nightmares. Boris had mentioned he had horrible nightmares, sometimes so terrible they affected his health. Were they as bad as mine? Maybe, except his were based on reality; mine only seemed like they were.

Last time I'd talked to Boris, a few days ago, his usual tan was faded and his eyes were sunk into his wrinkled face, making him look much older than his seventy-odd years. Normally he was as fit and as physically able as his sister or more so. Perhaps he was better, as Greta said but, knowing Boris, he probably figured lying to his sister, pretending the drugs helped, was better than continuing to go to doctors who could never really cure what was wrong. Doctors cannot make the past go away.

I'd only seen the numbers tattooed on his forearm once, but I knew what they were. Greta had her own set. Neither of them ever discussed it, but I knew enough to recognize the symptoms of trying to forget. I could relate to having memories that needed to stay hidden.

I crossed the floor of the café. Before I could order, Bea's nephew, Noe, handed me a giant mug. Coffee: hot as hell, sweet as love and white with real cream. I took a deep gulp of the hot liquid and silently blessed the boy for anticipating my order.

"Thanks, Noe," I said. "Can I get my usual?"

He nodded and rang up my order.

I was putting my wallet back into my backpack when a deep voice behind me muttered, "Strange doings at the Wild Moon."

I turned to see Boris standing just inside the door of the restaurant. He wiped his hands on his bandanna, then placed it carefully in his left back pocket as he approached. He walked up to the counter and I watched him pull two packets of sweetener from a small bowl and place them into his shirt pocket, then pat the pocket as if to make sure they were carefully tucked in.

Boris wore a male version of my own outfit: jeans, hiking boots and a plaid cotton flannel shirt, worn open over a T-shirt. His was crew necked with short sleeves; mine was a tank top, but both were standard Hill Country gear. Most local guys wore their shirt sleeves rolled up, even in winter, but Boris's sleeves stayed tightly buttoned over the telltale numbers on his arm.

"Hey, Boris."

He did look a little better, less faded than the last time I'd seen him, but I could still see the strain in his eyes.

He nodded, a grim expression on his face. "I was there this morning," he said.

"There where?" I asked.

"At the Wild Moon."

Once a local hunting ranch, the Wild Moon had closed about thirty years ago when its absentee Houston owners abandoned it after their oil stocks tanked. The bank that held the note couldn't unload the place, so it had been left to decay, becoming the playground for the county's adventurous teenagers who liked to trespass. Its nearly two thousand acres also provided a great happy hunting ground for members of my family who preferred to hunt the old-fashioned way—chasing down their prey before they killed and ate it.

A couple of years ago, not too long after I'd come back home, all that changed. Some unknown outsider bought the place and started renovations.

I hadn't heard the Wild Moon was open for business, but it was possible. Although the ranch was located only a dozen miles outside of town, none of the locals ever went out there. Residents here had grown used to the fact that guests at exclusive ranches for the rich and shameless rarely left their pampered lives to shop at the Video Hut or lunch at a small town deli. No matter—for the most part, we didn't bother them and they didn't bother us. I figured this incarnation of the Wild Moon was just another way for outsiders to not spend money in town.

Boris took out his bandanna again, his hands restless. "You haven't heard then?"

"Heard what?"

"Two children, young people. They found two dead

deer. By the picnic grounds at the lake. Bled. Mutilated."

Oh, that was just freakin' dandy. Unless Boris had a
direct line to my twisted psyche—which he couldn't—
evidently what I'd experienced were more than just
nightmares; they had some connection with reality.
Nightmare Visions Are Us. Welcome to the Clairvoyance
Club—another byproduct of my wonderful weird heritage.

But, wait—something didn't quite match my bloody
dreams.

"What do you mean, 'mutilated'?" I asked. "Like the
cattle in those horrible UFO stories?" Maybe I was wrong,
maybe it was just—no. I wasn't wrong. I knew I wasn't
wrong. The memory was too real, too fresh in my mind.
This could *not* be a coincidence. Or could it?

Boris shook his head as if to dislodge the memory.
"Someone took the heads." He sounded tired, raw.

Now that was an interesting twist. When I'd—

Okay, I'm not wanting to remember that part right now,
but I do know the deer were intact in my vision. Dead, yes.
Bled—well, yeah, as part of the feeding. But they had not
been headless.

Boris continued his story. "I was just making morning
deliveries to the Inn. Then there was the shouting."

"Deliveries?"

"Yes. They are stocking up, I think. Open for guests
now. Been taking supplies out there every day before
breakfast. Most afternoons just before dark. I order wine
and other things for them. Deliver it. Business is good."

The last word came out as "goot." Neither he nor Greta
had much of an accent but, every once in a while, traces
in their speech were reminders they hadn't always been
Texans.

Boris glanced past me. I looked over my shoulder

to see what he was looking at. No one was near. A few customers sat in booths to our right, nobody I recognized offhand. Probably daytrippers. Boris wiped his face with his bandanna, as if just the telling of his tale upset him. "Those poor children. It was terrible. The blood was gone, the heads . . . terrible."

"Did *you* actually see the deer?"

He nodded, and leaned toward me, whispering faster, as if the faster he spoke, the easier the words would be to say.

"When the manager went to look, I followed. I saw the bodies. The death." He shuddered a little and stuffed his bandanna back into his pocket. "There is evil. It is not safe, Keira. He doesn't know. Tell him—"

The brass Indian elephant bells attached to the café door tinkled behind me, announcing a new arrival.

Boris could see whoever had just entered. His eyes widened and a look of horror spread across his face. He shut his mouth, pressing his lips together.

I whirled at his reaction, nearly dropping to a defensive crouch before I saw it was just Greta coming through the door. She had a peculiar look on her own face. Her mouth smiled, yet something else swam behind her dark eyes, something that could almost be anger. I'd never seen any strong emotion from her—at most a gentle lift of the corners of her mouth as if slightly amused.

"Boris, did you get what you needed?"

Greta's words were flat, juiceless, completely without inflection, as if each word were printed on a piece of paper from which she read.

I tightened my grip on my coffee cup, my adrenaline surging just a little as I sensed her tension. I reinforced my mental shields. I did this naturally, without thinking. My barriers were a part of me; the first thing I learned during my early years—how to hide in plain sight. The emotions of others couldn't get in; mine couldn't get out. Survival training at its finest.

But Greta's silent agitation wasn't directed at me. She approached her brother and took his arm. He grimaced as her fingers dug into the cloth of his shirt, but didn't remove her hand. There was more than tension there. Fear maybe? I couldn't tell by just watching them and I wasn't prepared to do more than look with my eyes.

Maybe that's all this was—fear, worry that Boris was descending back into his own private mental hellhole, triggered by what he'd seen at the ranch. I didn't want to upset him any further, but it did bother me that Boris seemed to be trying to warn me in the same breath he used to speak of the Wild Moon and mutilated animals. Who did he want me to tell—and what?

Before I could say anything, Greta spoke.

"We need to go now, Boris. Let Keira have her breakfast." Her voice still sounded strange—strained, as though she were forcing out the words, making herself act normally. She turned and practically dragged her brother out the door with her. As they exited, Boris shot me a despairing look.

STILL A POPULAR HANGOUT after more than fifty years, not much ever changed about Bea's Place, not even after Bea took it over from her parents ten years ago. She was still single, like me; we had been friends since nearly forever.

As a feisty eight-year-old and the only child of aging parents, Bea took me under her wing, determined to befriend the pallid, scared and semi-motherless seven-year-old with bushy black hair, pale gray eyes and a funny accent.

Thirty years later, I'd lost the accent and tamed the hair, but still had the same pale eyes and best friend. Bea was the one person in my life whom I could count on to be there for me without an underlying agenda. My family always had ulterior motives for everything. Bea did things out of the goodness of her heart and for friendship. At least some things never changed.

And some things most definitely did not stay the same. The string of brass bells tinkled again; the café door swung open and my day got even more complicated.

Beige Stetson poised on his once very familiar head, Carlton Larson, acting county sheriff, stood in the doorway, his handsome face serious as a funeral. Nearly six-five, and with a build to match, he'd always tended to overwhelm a lot of things, not the least of all—some fifteen years ago—me.

I spoke first, hoping my voice would stay steady and friendly. "Hey, there. Welcome back."

I succeeded.

"Well, if it isn't Keira Kelly," he replied, his deep voice rumbling throughout the restaurant. "Been a while. Good to see you."

He seemed just as calm as I was pretending to be. Good sign. Last time we'd been in the same room together, sparks flew, and not from passion. We'd both lashed out. Me to wound him, him in anger—cut too deep, not wanting to hear what I was saying. I'd still wanted to be with him then, but not in the way he'd wanted. Not forever, because that was impossible.

Flirtation at twenty-two became an affair at twenty-three. Then one morning, nearly a year after our first date, I woke up and realized he really meant what he said the night before about the whole white-wedding-and-matching-appliances-from-Sears thing, and ended it. No looking back. No other options.

A couple of months after that, just long enough to go through the application and admissions process, Carlton left Rio Seco to join the San Antonio PD. I'd beat his exit by five days and five thousand miles.

I'd beat him back, too—by just under two years. Except . . . unlike me, he brought back a hell of a lot more baggage than he'd taken away. He was married and had children.

This was the first time I'd seen him since he'd returned a couple of weeks ago. In fact, it was the first time I'd seen him since I'd left.

We stared at each other, appraising, the silence acknowledging every single one of those thirteen years. He'd trained to become a cop. I'd trained to become . . . something else. As far as he knew, I was still the same unemployed trust-fund baby as before. The trust fund still existed, but my job description was totally different—and nothing he would ever find out about.

I took a sip from my cup, taking a moment to taste my feelings as I tasted the rich flavor of the coffee. As I swallowed the hot liquid, I began to relax. His voice once charmed the pants off me—literally—but there was no more charming here. Everything I'd ever felt for him was most definitely in the past tense. Lover: as in *former.* These worn blue jeans were definitely remaining firmly on my body. Thank goodness. Not that I'd be opposed to some horizontal exercise, but definitely not with him. Not now, not ever again. Especially not now.

"Just getting breakfast." I smiled the polite smile of

I-have-no-clue-what-to-say-right-now. "So, what's new?"

Carlton took off his hat and ran his fingers through his thick, short-cropped brown hair. He still didn't show any gray, even though he was a couple of years older than me.

"Want to sit?" He strode over to the nearest empty booth, put his hat on the tabletop and motioned to the seat across from him.

As I slid across the bench, Noe came over and dropped off my food without a word. He set down a full glass of tea and several packets of sugar in front of Carlton, then returned to his post at the cash register.

I watched Carlton perform a routine I'd seen countless times. Tap the packets together to line them up, tear them all open at once and dump too many teaspoons of sugar into his glass. The long-handled spoon clunked against the plastic as he stirred.

"Still drinking sweet tea?"

Carlton chuckled. "Yeah, still."

I took a bite of my bacon-and-egg taco dripping with salsa. Heavenly. I sighed and settled in to eat, just like it was any other day. I was good at pretending.

"You look good," I ventured, talking around a mouthful of food.

The years away from Rio Seco had etched Carlton's face. Fine lines defined his deep brown eyes, a few extra lines on his tanned forehead enhanced his good looks. He'd always been a candidate for Marlboro Man ads, even more so now that he was older and more settled into his features. He even made the cheap brown polyester uniform he wore look good. Not a mean feat.

"Thanks," he said. "Good genes, I guess." He picked up the spoon again, stirring and staring at me, a puzzled expression on his face.

"You know, it's really amazing, Keira. It's been too many years to count and you haven't changed a bit."

"Good genes," I repeated and took another big bite of my taco.

"How's your family? I heard they moved to Canada."

Sure did. Lock, stock and grimoire. Everyone from my great-great-grandmother on down to my brothers and once-local cousins. Everyone but me and Marty.

"Can't keep a secret in this town," I joked. "They're in British Columbia. Doing great. Dad enjoys the hunting."

I returned his query, lobbing the conversational ball back over to Carlton's side of the court.

"So, speaking of family . . . Carol and the kids getting settled?"

"They're fine."

Carlton put down his glass with a small thump, sloshing a bit of the tea over the side. As he mopped up the spill with a paper napkin, he changed the subject. "What have you been up to?"

Score a point for me in the I-don't-care game. It obviously bothered him to talk about his wife with his former girlfriend.

"Just breakfast," I said, with a shrug. "Still not so much into the cooking."

The smile crinkled the corners of his eyes and he inadvertently echoed my earlier thought.

"Some things don't change, do they, Keira?" He spoke softly.

Well, not exactly.

I knew the Change wasn't obvious since none of the people I'd talked to earlier had noticed. There was no neon sign above my head or anything, but oddly enough, it would've been nice if someone noticed something, anything. Someone could ask me if I was feeling okay or even—

Damn it. I didn't really know just what I wanted. It was kind of like getting your first period. You didn't want to talk about it, but you wanted everyone to know you were a woman. Maybe not the best analogy, but it works for me. This was a major rite of passage for me, but no one other than my clan really understood what it meant, and they were all in Canada or other parts of the world. Which actually is a good thing most days. It means they stay off my back. But today, I wanted to be able to share with someone who understood.

I looked at Carlton. He'd known me so well back then, or so he thought. He never knew me, what I really was. All he ever saw was a girl who'd broken his heart. I hated it, but I did what I had to then. No regrets.

"So what's been happening?" I asked, bringing us back to the present and to safer ground.

His face tensed, the smile was wiped away in an instant.

"I suppose you've heard about what happened out at that ranch. Up to hearing the gory details?"

I put down the remains of my taco, my appetite waning as I slowly wiped my hands on a paper napkin. I couldn't meet his gaze. "There are gory details?"

I should have known that they'd called out the sheriff.

"Pretty nasty details, actually. You sure you're up for this, you look a bit—"

"I'm fine," I said, cutting him off. The nasty details were what I needed to hear. I wanted to know more.

He frowned, but continued. "Out at the Wild Moon— its outskirts, really. Got the call before dawn. A couple of kids took a walk down on the Point after an all-night party out at the Bar-K dance hall. Probably went to make out by the lake. You know how dark it is out there."

Another smile zipped across his face, a flash of the old twinkling eyes peeked out at me, before the seriousness returned.

I smiled back out of reflex. Oh yeah, I knew how dark it was out there. Nights out at the Point, by the lake. Nights spent with Carlton, doing things that might get a person arrested for trespassing and more—except his daddy had been the law back then and we'd had the arrogance of youth.

He kept talking, his big hands folding and re-folding a paper napkin.

"They literally stumbled across the carcasses. Two Sitka deer bodies."

"Do you know who did it?"

I wanted to see what he'd say. There was no way he could know that the hunters weren't human, but someone else had mutilated those deer . . . and my bets were on the mundane.

"Not a clue. Anyone can sneak out to the Point. I don't know if you've seen the ranch since the renovation. Most of it's fenced now, some even game-fenced, but not all the way out to the lake. I think it has something to do with an easement or something. Right now, my guess is poachers. Some out-of-town fools with more money than sense trying to get out of buying a license or getting a jump on the season. Even so, I can't put my finger on why these deer."

"Why not?"

"Sitka aren't much good for trophies in any event, and these particular ones were young. Not much meat, not much in the way of a rack."

Young deer. Not a bad choice for hunters chasing prey

on foot. Hunters not interested in meat or trophies, just blood, the exhilaration, the bliss of the chase followed by the capture and the kill. Small animals, almost too easy to find, to follow under a hunter's moon, full and bright.

I never saw the predators' faces in my dream, didn't see their real forms. That part of my memory was hazy, wrapped in shadows. Clear as dirty ice. Deliberately? Something else I didn't know.

Carlton spoke again, eyes almost closed as if telling the story tired him out.

"Keira, there is something else that really freaks me out—something that makes me sick to my stomach."

I turned my attention to him, reinforced my mental barriers, and placed my hand on top of his. The energy that radiated from his body flowed over and around me, as I tried not to notice the distraction. Most humans emitted some kind of "noise," but Carlton's anxiety increased the sensation, so that it felt like the hum of a high-tension wire sizzling against my skin.

He looked around, as if to see who was nearby. Most of the tables had emptied by now. It was getting late. No one sat within earshot. Even so, he dropped his voice to a pitch so low that even I almost had to strain to hear it.

"When I said trophies, I meant it. They weren't field dressed and pieces left behind—the heads are missing."

He paused a moment, then continued. "Gone, hacked off, brutal. I can't help but think this is something more than just poachers." He dropped his head and wouldn't look at me as he whispered. "What if we have some sort of satanic cult around here?"

I pulled away.

"Shit, Carlton, you're not serious?"

Shielding my emotions was one thing, but maintaining

my control would be harder if I were touching him. What was he doing talking about cults instead of poachers? I tried to control my breathing, the irrational panic I felt building. Crap, crap, crap. Not good. Too many childhood stories racing through my mind. Persecution, being hunted down, treated as Enemy. We weren't, but it was too easy to call us "cult," or worse.

"Carlton, you can't possibly believe that."

As far as the general public was concerned, my people were nothing but rumor and superstition. Fine by me. I'm not so ready to wave that particular pride banner, thank you very much.

Unfortunately, stupid imitators and wannabes kept enough rumors alive to leave just a tiny bit of doubt in people's minds. Just enough to make me worried in this kind of situation. I was not in the mood for another Inquisition. Torquemada may have been right about one thing, we were pretty much all heretics, but I wasn't going to burn at anyone's stake. Not even a symbolic one.

"I can't really believe in any of that stuff, Keira," Carlton admitted. "But what if some group's gotten into voodoo or Santeria or something like that? We may be a small town, but you know how many new people are moving out to the Hill Country. Maybe somebody's into animal sacrifice or something. You wouldn't believe some of the weird-ass cult shit I saw in San Antonio."

"Come on, Carlton, are you listening to yourself?" I fought to keep my voice from rising. "Nothing's changed around here. We're still in the middle of White People Central."

No shit. We were Texas' answer to Wonder Bread, mayo and Baptist church Sundays. This part of the Hill Country had been settled by conservative German immigrants. The closest thing to a cult was a little charismatic Christian church across the lake. No practitioners of Voudoun there, just a bunch of folks who like to sing loud hymns and testify about Jesus to unsuspecting campers.

"Next you'll be blaming the deer mutilations on the Chupacabra." I smiled weakly, and poked him in the arm. Nudge, nudge, wink, wink. Take the hint, Carlton.

Just because last night's hunters fed on blood didn't mean they were unnatural—just some kind of preternatural creatures whose identity was best left hidden from the mundane world. There *had* to be a run-of-the-mill explanation for the missing heads. Something explainable by normal human means. Some local boys maybe, running across a couple of dead deer and thinking it was funny to steal the heads. Had to be something like that.

"I know. I know," Carlton laughed, a little of his usual humor coming back into his soft brown eyes as he visibly relaxed. "I'm just grasping at straws. I don't believe in all that junk anyway. Too much like tabloid TV."

I had to stop myself before I said something I regretted. The part of me that wanted validation wanted to speak up. *Not* a good idea. I settled for changing the subject.

"I heard the ranch is open for business. Have you talked to the guests out there?" I asked. "Maybe someone saw something."

"Come on, Keira, cut me a little slack. I did try." Carlton sighed. "Those folks out there keep your kind of hours. Seems there was an all-night party or something—most of them are still sleeping it off. Hell, even the owner isn't available to talk to me."

"Who *is* the owner? All I heard was that it was someone who was not from around here."

He shrugged. "Don't know much. I talked to Kevin Hilton a couple of hours ago. His brother-in-law, Alan Richards, brokered the sale. Alan's out of town, but Kevin remembers the guy who bought it was from England, looking for an investment. Bought the place a couple of years ago, then sank a ton of money into it for renovations. Hired a bunch of outsiders to do the work. Hell, they're not even hiring locals now that they're open."

"So what's their deal, some sort of dude ranch or something?"

"Looks like. A bunch of spoiled European snobs, I'm thinking. The place looks expensive. But there wasn't a soul around. The only person I saw was the day manager. Nice enough, but no damned help to me. I haven't met the main guy yet, but the manager said he just moved on site."

The strains of a digital rendition of *Toccata and Fugue* interrupted. Crap. That setting wasn't any better than "vibrate" mode.

I pulled my mobile out of my backpack, glanced at the ID on the screen, then put the still-chiming phone back into the bag.

"You going to answer that?" Carlton asked.

"Nope," I answered. "It's Marty. I'm already going over there, so he can just wait."

"I take it he's still as much of a pain in the ass as he always was."

"That's putting it mildly. It's always something with him—usually money."

"He asks you for money?" Carlton sounded surprised. "I thought the funeral industry was pretty recession proof."

I shrugged. "I imagine so, but you know Marty with the spending."

"You still bailing him out?"

"I still do," I admitted. "Someone's got to watch out for him."

That someone being me. Clan by birth, but not by genetics, Marty was a biological anomaly. I may be half-blood, but neither of my halves were human—couldn't be. Biologies weren't compatible.

Somehow, something in Marty's chromosomes was defective, at least to our way of thinking. Some mutation caused by who-knew-what made him powerless and fully human, a reverse X-Man. In less enlightened times, he would have been dumped at birth and left to die. Instead, he'd been allowed to live, but as an outsider. His own parents abandoned him. He was raised by an uncle and taught the funeral business. Uncle Damon was a necromancer who'd translated his natural talent into an acceptable mundane career. Marty took over the business when the family left. The clan decided that Marty could run the place, even without talent or powers. I'd always figured they'd thrown the human dog a bone.

I was the dog sitter left holding that particular leash.

My one and only job now was to make sure Marty didn't get into any trouble—interpret that to mean "embarrass the family." Not that any of them were actually concerned with his welfare, just with the possibility that he might do something stupid and drag them into it. Unfortunately for me, Marty's lack of power seemed to translate into a distinct lack of sense, common or otherwise. My dear cousin appeared to enjoy getting into messes. I hoped that wasn't the case now. I did not want to get on the wrong side of my double-great-grandmother.

"Well, enjoy," Carlton said, still chuckling. "Thanks for the company. I'm heading back over to the ranch. Maybe I can convince that manager to roust the owner so I can get some questions answered."

He paused as he slid out of the booth, his gaze catching mine. "It was good to see you again, Keira. It's always nice to see old friends. Check you later?"

Old friends. I suppose you could call us that. Had a nice ring, false as it might be. Former lovers never really translated into friends. Too much muddied water under that particular bridge.

I smiled back anyway, willing to keep playing this role for now. Made things a lot easier.

"Sure, later," I said and watched him leave the restaurant.

I was glad he was happy. He deserved it. I was equally as glad that the attraction was over. No anxiety, no thump of jealous heart. Maybe Carlton and I wouldn't be the best of buddies, but we could exist in the same small town without emotional angst. Things were looking up. Sort of.

I sighed and looked at the clock above the cash register. It was nearing four-thirty, but I could definitely use another cup of coffee before facing Marty. My version of "soon" wasn't going to be the same as his. Tough. He'd live and all his clients were already dead.

CHAPTER THREE

"SHERIFF-MAN MAKING googly eyes at you again, *m'hija*?"

Bea slid her petite curvaceous figure into the seat Carlton had just vacated, cradling a large coffee mug in one small hand and carrying a full pot of coffee in the other.

"That's *so* not even close," I said as she topped off my mug. "You know that's long over. He was telling me about— Shit, Bea, are those two working here?"

The two stupidest criminals in the county had just walked through the kitchen door, out into the main café. The brothers stood behind the counter, side by side, sleeves rolled up past their elbows baring overly pumped armloads of tattoos. I watched as they served themselves coffee.

Dusty Albright, the elder of the two by ten months, glanced in my direction. He'd probably heard me. The place wasn't all that big and I hadn't exactly been quiet.

His dark bushy eyebrows contrasted with his neatly shaven head. He turned to face me, and I saw he held a chef's cleaver in his left hand, caressing it with his right as if it were his favorite toy, or worse, an intimate body part. His near-twin, Derek, stood silently beside him, no expression on his face.

Wonderful, the two town idiots wanted to play the "whose dick is bigger" game. Any other day, I'd have been happy to just avoid them and concede the match, since I didn't have any manhood to wither, but Carlton's information had already put me into a mood.

I stared straight at Dusty's muddy-colored eyes, keeping the lines of my body loose and relaxed, even though I did cross my arms in a sort of warning to back off. In my opinion, people like the Albright brothers should be treated as if they were unfamiliar animals, with caution and a little aggression—just enough to assert yourself, without appearing to be a direct threat.

I had no idea what set them off, as far as I knew I'd never done anything to them. Considering the fact they'd both just gotten out of jail, it was probably just that I had the balls to look at them without permission. In high school, Dusty had beaten a kid nearly to death for standing in front of his locker. My cousin had often been their unwilling victim.

The silent pissing contest continued, neither Dusty nor I allowing ourselves to look away. What he didn't know was that I was perfectly capable of staring like this indefinitely— for hours without getting tired. Predator genes.

Bea broke the edgy silence. "Go back to the kitchen, boys. Dusty, you need to finish chopping the vegetables. And Derek, weren't you finished with your shift?"

Dusty licked his lips and gave me a smirk, punctuated by him mimicking a kiss. Without a word, but with widening grins, the two turned and passed through the swinging doors out of my sight.

I stared at my friend across the table, not sure what I wanted to say.

She looked down, delicate fingers stroking the sides of her coffee cup. With a sigh, she looked back up at me and crossed her arms.

"I know . . . bad idea, but I needed help and they needed a job to satisfy their parole," she explained. "I'm running out of options, Keira. I hate the fact I had to hire those bozos because no one else applies for work. I can't compete with all those resorts opening up."

More proof that progress wasn't necessarily always good. Until a few years ago, Rio Seco had enjoyed the anonymity of a small town buried in the depths of the Hill Country. But the sprawl of the cities kept inching its way in our direction as more and more people discovered the great location. Besides the Wild Moon, two other resort ranches had opened for business over the last couple of years. The Wild Moon might not hire locally, but the others did.

Rio Seco was still pretty much the back of beyond, but "beyond" was becoming a much smaller place, which was the main reason my family packed up and left. Too hard to keep ourselves hidden.

"Hell, even my own relatives won't work for me anymore. The only reason Noe's still around is because the other places don't hire minors. The minute he turns eighteen, he's out of here."

"Don't worry," I said, trying to cheer her up. "I'm sure that after the excitement of working for a new place wears off, some of them will come back."

"I hope you're right," she said. "I'd hate to think I was stuck with those two idiots forever. Not that I think they'll be here longer than a few months. I just hope they don't clean me out before they go."

I laughed. "Maybe they'll leave you alone anyway. After all, you don't sell candy bars or T-shirts."

The last time either of the Albright brothers had spent more than a couple of months in any one place had been their recent jail stint, and even that had been cut short when they'd been released under a new statewide leniency program. Of course, their crime had been pretty minor. They'd tried to hold up the band concession booth at a nearby high school football game. Truly brilliant, considering that county deputies always attended the games.

Bea grinned back at me. "You may be right, girlfriend. But I'm not holding my breath that they'll stay long enough for me to find more help."

She shrugged and pulled the pencil out of her hair, sending it tumbling to her waist, black, thick and shiny. Miss Clairol was not making any money off Beatriz Ruiz. Of course, I wasn't contributing to their profits, either, but that was different. By my family's reckoning, at thirty-seven, I was barely out of adolescence.

"All done. Your turn."

"My turn what?"

"I've known you too damn long, Keira Kelly," Bea said. "I can see something's up other than you seeing Carlton again and the two idiot brothers working for me. You look tired. Are you okay?" She frowned at me, worry lines creasing her forehead.

I let out a sigh, a little relieved. Bea noticed something off kilter. *Now* I could talk about it. This wasn't as good as sharing with family, but it would work . . . for the short run.

"Yeah, I guess you could call it 'okay,'" I said. "Notice anything different about me? Something not quite usual . . . something that's *changed*?" I emphasized the last word.

She narrowed her eyes and stared at me silently. Her eyes flicked up and down as she searched my face. As realization dawned, she leaned forward and dropped her voice to a whisper.

"Change? No shit, already? I thought you said none of that happened until you were in your fifties."

"Lucky me, I guess. I suppose I get the early bird prize . . . so to speak. You heard about the animal mutilations out at the Wild Moon?"

She nodded. "We all heard. Pretty damn sick. Oh, hell, was that what Carlton was talking to you about?"

"Well, yeah, except that's not really the problem, Bea. I already knew."

I drank down the last of my coffee. "I had the great good fortune to dream the whole thing before it actually happened . . . or maybe even during."

Bea didn't even blink. "A vision?"

"Maybe, I don't know what to call it. These last few weeks have been hell. I've had death dreams, blood dreams. I even dreamed that Marty was dead. But this dream . . . the whole thing was way too real, just like I was there watching the deer get hunted and die."

I pushed the empty mug away from me. "Bea, I not only saw it. I was a part of it. I even tasted the blood . . . and I wanted to." I didn't want to tell her the last part . . . about the deer body turning into Marty. That wasn't prophecy or a vision; just my own sick subconscious playing tricks . . . wasn't it?

"Damn, and I thought *I* had problems." Bea relaxed and smiled at me, trusting in my self-diagnosis. "So what happens now? You've never really told me."

"I never told you specifics because I didn't expect to have to deal with it anytime soon," I said, shrugging. "Mostly, I just wait. Not much else I can do. I might have more visions, short spells of power bursts or any combination of symptoms. Then after a few weeks, it'll all be over and

I'll settle into one talent. Probably shapeshifter since that's what my brothers are."

I had my mental fingers crossed. I hoped I wasn't underestimating this. One of my aunts described the experience as being like a real-life role-playing game. The multi-sided die would be tossed down a long narrow path, bouncing and skipping its length. Each side was another manifestation of power and Fate was the Dungeon Master. Every time the die turned and a number flashed into view, some talent would manifest itself, then another and another until, eventually, it came to a halt at the end of the lane with only one face pointing upward. The power "showing" was your lifetime talent.

"Symptoms?"

"Nothing bad, really," I said. "When Aunt Jane went through this about twenty years ago, I barely even noticed. Every once in a while she'd go into a mini-trance and make some prediction about the future. She had a couple of episodes of telekinesis, too. She could float pencils. But nothing of consequence."

"So, what is she now?"

"A healer. Symptoms don't necessarily mirror your inherited talent. We don't really know why." I laughed a little, trying to ease both of our minds. "Don't worry, it's never fatal."

That was the understatement of the century. What was the opposite of "not fatal" anyway? Oh yeah, "immortal," or near enough. Not a bad trade-off, but sometimes the price was a little high. I was afraid mine was going to be higher. Thirty years of living in mainstream human culture didn't necessarily prepare me to handle this on my own. But I sure as hell wasn't yelling for help—not just yet.

"This whole thing's a big pain in the ass for me right

now," I said. "Usually, when the Change comes on, you spend time with family, but the last thing I want to do is go back to the smothering bosom of the clan."

Bea raised a perfectly plucked eyebrow, giving me that "don't mess with me" look.

"I'll be fine," I insisted. "They obviously think I'm better off here as Marty's watchdog." I stopped talking, turned in the booth and leaned against the wall, not wanting to meet Bea's eyes. There was something else I wasn't telling. I hoped she wouldn't remember that part. I'd shared the story of my heritage years ago, just before I left for England, after my breakup with Carlton. She'd swallowed hard, looked me in the eye and basically accepted everything I told her. Not surprising, she'd spent enough time at my father's house to notice things we normally didn't let outsiders see. By the time we were in our early twenties, she'd become an adjunct member of the family.

"But what about the Inheritance?"

Shit. She remembered.

Only one person in a handful of generations inherited *all* the abilities and powers of the clan and was therefore destined for greatness, yadda yadda . . . blah blah blah. Chosen One and all that. This may not be *Buffy the Vampire Slayer,* but our genetic Texas Lotto winner was just about as lucky . . . or as cursed. Whoever became the heir got to play politics for the rest of his or her extremely long life—or as long as she or he could stand it. Trouble was, you couldn't just abdicate. There had to be an heir ready to take the position.

My father's great-grandmother, Gigi, currently held the post, and there was no heir in sight. Not that it was a problem, she loved being in charge. In fact, she really wanted the position to stay in our branch of the clan, but there was no guarantee the next leader would come from our particular line. Even so, genetics being a powerful thing, my family was willing to play the odds. At the very least, I carried half my father's genes—genes that could be passed on to a future leader. Making babies would be right up there on their list of Things for Keira to Do, but most definitely not on mine. Bea knew I was expected to rejoin the family when I began to Change. I wasn't going.

"Bea, I am not ready for this. I'm too damn young to start playing the politics and breeding game."

"They're not going to come here and drag you there if you don't want to go, are they?"

I smiled. "I don't think it's likely, but better safe than sorry. I'm not telling anyone. You know how Dad is. He'll start begging and appealing to my better nature or whatever. It's bad enough that I keep having to deal with the consequences of Marty's short leash; I don't want to have to mess with clan politics for a long time yet."

"They haven't changed their minds about him?"

"Nope. And they aren't likely to. All I ever wanted was to stay here and be left alone for a little while—instead, I got stuck with Marty. I never told you this, but I even asked if I could donate part of my regular trust allowance to him."

"Would he have taken it?"

"Oh, please, what do you think? I was counting on it. Then he could do what he always wanted—leave town. That would get me off the family hook. But for some reason, Gigi had a conniption fit. My guess is that she doesn't want him loose. He knows too much, hates us too much to be trusted."

I brightened a little as something occurred to me. Considering my new circumstances, I just might be able to free myself of Marty duty for good, maybe turn it over to some pre-changeling who needed a job. My spirits fell again as I realized what I'd have to do to reap that particular benefit. It would mean going home . . . not Rio Seco home, but clan home in Canada.

Not an option at this point. I preferred Marty's whining to Gigi's wrath, any day. At least I could pretend to ignore Marty. Ignoring Gigi was neither safe nor recommended.

Bea laughed. "Damn it, girl, I've always known your family life was interesting, but this is too much. I'm so glad I'm just a lowly human with mundane problems like making a living, paying my bills, hiring ex-convicts."

"Yeah, I guess I'm just living in interesting times."

I really wouldn't trade my abilities for anything, but I'd certainly give up some of the intrigue that went with them.

Bea picked up her coffee cup and took a sip. "And I suppose I need to get back to my own problems. I need to check to make sure Dusty's chopped up the veggies and not his brother."

She looked back over at me. "You are going to be okay, *m'hija*?" She made it more of a question than a statement.

"I'll be fine," I said as I stood up. "I really should run. Marty's whining that he needs to see me and I want to get over there and out before dark. We still doing the chick flick thing later?"

"Who's on the short leash? Baby Cuz yells for you and you're going out to pull his bacon out of the fire again?"

I shrugged. "Yeah, well, what can I say? If I don't go, you know I'll hear about it for days. He's saying it's family related and you know what happened last time."

"Yeah, but he's not dating anyone, is he?"

"Not that I know of, but who knows with Marty?"

Bea grinned. "So true." She drained her coffee cup and

stood up. "Okay, girl, I'll see you later. Bad movies and good munchies it is. You get wine?"

"Yep, stocked up a couple of days ago." I headed out the door with a wave. "See you when you get there."

I noticed Dusty Albright standing alone at the counter as I left. His gaze was a tangible weight on my back as I crossed to the exit. I couldn't help shivering as a low snigger followed me out the door.

CHAPTER FOUR

FAT DROPS OF RAIN splattered my windshield as I pulled into the back lot of Nelson Funeral Home some twenty minutes later. The perfect weather wasn't all that perfect anymore. Typical. Weather around here changed more often than I changed my mind. I'd have to hurry if I wanted to get home before the storm hit. I figured I had about an hour. Maybe, with luck, I could be in and out of the mortuary in a few minutes.

Luck. Fate. Yeah, right. Life's a bitch, and then you have to deal with your relatives.

I parked near the rear service entrance, under the carport roof, next to the hearse and the mortuary van. My Land Rover Defender was most definitely out of place, adding an almost lighthearted note to the ghoulish lineup. I smiled to myself remembering Marty's reaction the first time I'd parked there. He'd wanted me to move the car. He said it was because it looked bad to have such a frivolous car parked next to the hearse. He was just jealous, because he couldn't afford one, too. I kept parking there to piss him off. It always worked. It's all about the small victories.

TO GET to Marty's office and the front of the building, I had to walk through a couple of storage areas, past caskets and urns and things I never inspected too closely. I might know Death better than most, but I never liked the tangible evidence of it. Besides, humans made such a fuss over it all, spending too many hard-earned dollars on overpriced trappings. I liked our way of dealing with it better—we mostly didn't.

My clan doesn't die of natural causes. We can't catch diseases. Short of being beheaded, having our hearts ripped out, or total exsanguination, we survived just about anything. Death is a choice for us. Sometimes, after centuries of life, the only thing left to experience is the absence of it. Some choose to die sooner than others. Thus my original job as Escort—Death's little assistant—a sort of Keira Kevorkian to the supernatural. Weird, but it was what I did. Trained at my uncle's knee. I was good at it, too. A natural empathy for the dead ran in my branch of the family. Even those of us who became shapeshifters still understood the dead better than most. The only one without said affinity? Yeah, Marty.

As I turned a blind corner just past the storage room, I smacked straight into a body. Only this one was alive and walking—or at least had been until I knocked into him. He grabbed both my arms and turned me to the side.

"Watch where you're going," he growled and kept going past me without stopping.

For a moment, I didn't recognize the stocky figure. He was so out of place, I had to do a double take for my brain to register his identity.

Derek Albright didn't stop walking and was soon out of sight. Confused, I paused for a second before running after him.

I caught up to Derek in the storeroom. He was squatting down in front of a mini-fridge, just closing the lid of a small plastic Igloo cooler that was on the floor in front of him. The cooler had definitely seen better days. Its white lid was mostly gray, a few reddish brown smears dirtying the torn KAJA-97 and Red Man stickers. I caught a glimpse of a couple of Mason jars inside before he snapped it shut.

"Hey, what are you doing?"

"Working," he said, abruptly, and stood up.

"What?" I was stunned.

"That's right," he snarled, "I'm working for your piss-ant little cousin—seems he needs my help." His smirk matched his tone of voice. "Daytime at the café, evenings here. Ain't that just grand?"

Oh yeah, grand and totally dandy. It wasn't bad enough I'd had to play chicken with his brother earlier, now the younger of the two macho morons needed to cluck and shout. What the hell did I ever do to deserve this?

I stood my ground, meeting his stare and absently noticing that, despite everything, he cleaned up fairly decently. Out of his chef's whites and into the standard good ol' boy uniform of jeans and boots, he was almost respectable in a cheap-trailer-park-shiny-pants sort of way. Even so, he still couldn't hide the fact that he was uncomfortable. The knuckles on Dusty's hand had turned white as his grip on the cooler's handle tightened.

"What are you, chief mourner?" I asked sarcastically, still blocking the door so he couldn't leave. "I don't suppose you'll tell me what you do for my cousin?"

"No, Miss Smarty-Pants," he said, mimicking the name-calling he used to do in school. "I work for him—not for you."

"I don't imagine you'll tell me what's in the cooler?" I said as he neared.

"Barbecue sauce."

"And you have it here because . . . ?"

"Because I feel like it."

Oh lovely, such scintillating conversation.

"So, where's Marty?" I asked.

Derek shrugged. "Had to go out."

"Out? In what?" He obviously hadn't taken either of the business vehicles. Both were still parked out back.

He shrugged. "Dunno, his car, I guess. Got a call. He'll be back." He glanced at the cheap plastic watch on his wrist. "I gotta go. Get out of my way."

Derek moved toward me, bulky body looming. He wasn't much taller than me, but his shoulders were easily half again as wide as mine.

Before he could push me aside, I stepped back, causing him to break stride and nearly stumble. He grunted and left through the back door, letting it slam behind him.

Bloody hell. This was just great. Marty wasn't here. But he'd be back. Yeah, him and the Terminator—and me. I was *not* sticking around. A rumble of thunder echoed in the near distance. Time to leave my dearly departed cousin a note and be just as departed. He could call me later and come by my house if he still felt the burning need to talk.

When I opened the service hallway door that led into the main reception area, I realized something was wrong— well, not exactly *wrong,* more like *not right.*

I hadn't been to the funeral home in a couple of months, but the last time I visited, the place resembled a dilapidated Edward Gorey mansion, just like it had all my life. But now, it looked like the "Trading Spaces" crew had been let loose with a ton of money and a hell of a lot more taste than they'd ever shown on television.

Walls once covered in gloomy paper and dark paneling were now painted soothing shades of beige and sage green. The oppressive moth-eaten furniture was gone, replaced by plush overstuffed chairs and an equally plush sofa, all color-coordinated with the new brighter color scheme.

Tiffany-style lamps flanked the elegant seating area, casting a warm, almost inviting, light.

This most certainly didn't track. Either there had been a whole hell of a lot more dead bodies in Rio Seco County recently or my cousin had finally hit the winning Lotto numbers. I doubted the latter, since I'd be the first one he'd gloat to . . . and I didn't actually know much about the former. I never read obituaries.

The decorating hadn't stopped at the reception area.

I sat down in the still-shiny-new executive chair in Marty's office, my hand automatically stroking the smooth mahogany leather. A new Euro-style oak desk and file cabinet dominated the center of the small room; a couple of leather guest chairs added an additional grace note. Forest green pleated shades covered the windows, complementing the delicate fawn of the new Berber carpet. Okay, all this was way beyond Marty's budget, no matter how many overpriced funerals he'd performed.

So much for leaving a note and taking off. I had to know how he could afford this. Marty had never computerized, but I knew he kept comprehensive paper files. I opened one of the drawers in his desk to see if I could find anything.

It didn't take long for me to realize that the subtle lighting of the room might be fine for comforting a grieving family, but lacked the right number of lumens for comfortable reading—or snooping. I leaned over to reach the switch of the floor lamp that stood next to the desk. Nothing happened when I pressed it, even though there was a bulb under the shade and it looked new.

It didn't take long to discover the problem. The lamp was plugged into a power strip to the left of the desk. A couple of other cords led to a calculator and to an electric pencil sharpener. The strip wasn't plugged into the wall socket. Easily remedied.

A few seconds and a couple of sparks later, all the lights in my cousin's office went out. The hall lights were still on, so I must have just tripped a breaker.

Double damnation and hell. The breaker box was located in the one room in this building I really hated. I could ignore the problem and pretend I didn't know what happened—which would result in my totally non-handy cousin calling an electrician and paying outrageous rates—or I could swallow my distaste for the room and take care of it myself. Guilt won out over aversion. Besides, an electrician might cost *me* money.

I unplugged the offending strip and headed to the prep room and the breaker box.

The prep room was located at the far back of the building, just past the rear service entrance where I'd originally come in. Access to the room was through the infamous security door.

My cousin shared the key code with me when he'd shown off his purchase, making me try it for myself, preening at the overwhelming coolness factor of having this high-tech door, never once thanking me for paying for it. Typical.

I punched in the code, half-hoping Marty had changed the combination in his quest for better security. It would have given me an excuse to just leave and not worry about the breaker, but I wasn't that lucky. The lock clicked and I pushed the lever down to open the door. I checked to make sure there were no occupants before I stepped through. I didn't think there would be. Unless Marty was working on someone, any bodies would be in the mortuary refrigerator.

The door slammed shut behind me as a massive boom

of thunder shook the building, catching me by surprise. I could have sworn the storm hadn't been that close. The overhead lights flickered once, twice. I held my breath. Another crash sounded and all the lights blinked out, plunging me into a darkness so complete, it was almost solid. There were no windows to let in even the weak light of the rainy evening. With no light at all, even my better-than-human night vision couldn't help.

Shit. Now what?

The room suddenly felt oppressively small, even though I knew it was more than thirty feet to the opposite wall and at least twenty across. It wasn't the complete blackness that bothered me, but the aura of profound sadness permeating the entire building was stronger in this room. Its patina coated every wall, every fixture, pressed against me, seeped inside—shadows of sorrows past and present, reminding me of the fragile mortality of humans. The funeral home had been operating for nearly a hundred years. That's a lot of bodies, a lot of grief. Right now, I felt every single bit of it. Just another side effect of being who I was. My special bond with the Reaper enhanced any emotions associated with death.

I really was locked in. My futile pushing against the crash bar did absolutely nothing. Sure, an electronic lock with no electricity would shut down and keep people *out,* but shouldn't it still open to let someone trapped *inside* out? Damn my stupid cousin anyway. I'd lay any bets he took the money I gave him for the reinstallation and spent it on something else. I'd never seen that particular invoice, just given Marty a check.

I stood still, trying to decide what to do, when suddenly the scent of life came to me, faint behind the scent of old death—a gentle whiff, quiet on the still air. My nostrils gathered it, my brain processed it, and the knowledge stunned my awareness.

Holy hell. There was something else in here with me . . . something or someone. I couldn't identify it. A scent of blood, but not of spilled blood. This blood was still circulating, nourishing someone's body, making a heart beat. Doing what it was meant to do.

"Hello?" I called out into the silence, my words vanishing as if swallowed by the absence of light.

Living energy stroked my skin, dancing along it as if I were touching one of those lightning balls sold in novelty stores, creating crazy patterns in the back of my eyes. I still couldn't see in the pitch blackness. I cautiously lowered my shields and reached out, trying to feel whatever else was there. A flash of brilliance and then there was nothing.

ANOTHER CLAP of thunder, just short of a sonic boom, coupled with a bright flash of lights, wrenched me back to consciousness, my eyes blinking away the brightness. The power was back on.

My stiff muscles ached with the effort to sit up. For some bizarre reason, I was lying on the floor. Last I remembered, I'd been standing up, thinking that someone else was in the room with me. I turned to look around and groaned, the sound loud in the silent room. My head pounded with pain, my pulse beat in time with each throb.

Struggling to my feet, fighting the nausea that swirled through me, I leaned against the sink, using it as a support to help me up. My hand slid along its porcelain edge, leaving a wet trace of . . . was that *blood*? Every muscle in my body tensed. Both my hands were coated with red.

Slowly, I raised them to my face and took a careful sniff. I knew instantly the blood wasn't mine. At first, that was a relief, but then I realized it had to belong to someone else.

Wait. A sink?

I froze in place as I recognized my surroundings. Instead of being near the entry door, I was on the other side of the room in the embalming area. I couldn't remember having walked there.

A chill skittered down my spine; invisible frozen fingers brushed my skin, as if in warning. Oh, no. This wasn't happening. I've been here before. Several times before. In my nightmares. Before the hunting, before the deer, I'd had nightmares of the mortuary. The smell of blood, of death, of—

Suddenly, I didn't want to turn around. My hands gripped the sink. I knew there was something behind me and it wasn't a vacant embalming table. I could smell it. Fresh, still warm, its tang filled my awareness, calling something deep inside me. The pull of the blood threatened to take me somewhere I wasn't ready to go. It's always about the blood, the red pulsing liquid flowing through my veins. My aunt's voice slid through my memory, remembrances of lessons learned, lectures committed to the subconscious. Blood and flesh nourished many of my family, my branch is mostly hunters, predators. The need, the urge to see what made the smell begged me to turn, to track down the source.

I held my breath, needing to shut it out, to stop breathing in the scent. I didn't want to go there, but it didn't matter. I didn't need to breathe to sense it. Closing my eyes, I turned, my movements deliberate, my hands clutched into fists, the drying blood tacky against my skin. I didn't want to see, but I had to. I let myself open my eyes.

No. This could not be real.

My brain refused to process the scene. The once-empty table now held an occupant. It was definitely male.

It was definitely Marty. And he was most definitely dead. A drainage tube jutted out of his jugular. His life's blood dripped to the bed of the table, snaking a bright red line across his nude body, across the stainless steel and into the drain below, as if he were no more than another client, another corpse to be embalmed. This was exactly like my dream. Only this time—

A pounding on the hall door tore my gaze from the scene. The lights flashed again, seconds of darkness followed by the brightness of their sudden glare. I blinked and shook my head to clear the cobwebs, darting a glance across the room.

Everything was the way it had been. The embalming area remained in shadow; no body lay on the empty table. I was still at the entrance. My hands were clean. Nothing had changed. What in all the levels of all the known and unknown dimensions of hell had just happened?

"Keira, open the door!" Carlton's voice boomed from the other side. "Keira, are you okay in there?"

I wasted no time pushing the crash bar. This time, the door opened, right into Carlton, whose hand was lifted as if ready to knock again.

"Whoa, buddy," I said, putting my hand up in front of my face. "Watch out." I stepped through and let the door close behind me, shutting away the vivid scene that didn't exist.

"Are you all right? I saw your car out back. I knew the power had gone out around here." He looked a little sheepish. "I came in to check on you."

Without answering, I walked away, down the hall to the reception area. I needed to put a little distance between myself and that room. Carlton followed me.

I dropped into one of the new chairs lining the wall and

stroked the softness of the fabric, trying to ground myself with the tactile sensation.

"I'm fine, Carlton. What brings you out this way?"

I tried to sound normal, to keep the sounds and thoughts gibbering at the edges of my brain from coming out of my mouth. Whatever had just happened back there, whether waking nightmare, vision, or whatever, I wasn't ready to share. Never with Carlton, maybe not even with Bea. It may seem silly, or bizarre, but in my reality, words were power. If I talked about what I'd just seen, it might give it substance, make it come true.

The sheriff moved closer to me, squatting down in front of the chair, moving with a grace that belied his size. He rested a hand on either arm of the chair. The cloth of his uniform slacks stretched tight across his thighs, reminding me of my long ago attraction. He moved so quietly and softly for such a square and solidly built man, comfortable with his size, his knowledge of self. I'd run across few men who were so self-assured, so aware of who they were and their place in the world, never clumsy or awkward—only one other had been human.

"I actually came out this way to talk to your cousin," he said. "I take it he's not here?"

"He's not," I replied. "He was gone when I got here. About . . ." I grabbed Carlton's wrist to better read his watch. "Shit, about three hours ago," I said, letting go of his arm. I'd lost time in there. That wasn't a good sign.

"You've been waiting for him for three hours?"

"Yeah, I promised I'd come talk to him." He may not believe me, but what the hell else was I supposed to say?

Carlton's face was level with mine. He nodded, as if distracted, and slid his hands across the arm of the chair, leaning in toward me. For a split second, I flashed on a vision of him leaning in for a kiss. Weird. I must be channeling memories of the past.

He rubbed a spot on my cheek. "You've got dirt on your face."

I didn't like the tone of his voice—soft, like the velvet plush of the chair. His incessant human buzz reverberated in the back of my skull like the whine of a drill, giving me a headache.

I pushed his hand away and rubbed at the spot myself.

He rocked back on his heels and smiled. The smile had been another reason. It lit up his entire face. Made him almost pretty.

"Why were you locked in the prep room?"

"I went to fix a fuse. The lights went out as soon as I got in there. Then the damned door jammed."

Carlton laughed and stood up in one swift movement. "Are you sticking around?"

"No. I'm not waiting for Marty any longer. He can just talk to me tomorrow."

I pushed myself up out of the chair, and couldn't move anywhere. Carlton was standing too close to me. His body was less than a foot away. The buzz intensified, vibrating against my skin.

Automatically, I tried to step back, but the chair was in my way.

"Good." He spoke almost in a whisper.

"What do you mean by 'good'?"

Carlton stepped even closer, not quite touching me, but close enough that I could feel the vibration of his energy all over my body. Suddenly, I could scent him—a heavy musk smell clogging my throat with its thick sweetness. I swayed a little, nearly falling back into the chair. Holy Mother of all Holy Things. He wanted me. No doubt about it.

This was *not* going to happen. I forced myself back, pushed the chair aside, its legs screeching across the polished hardwood floor, and stepped around Carlton. I tried to ignore the sensations radiating from him. His lust didn't awaken an answer in me, more a panic response. Fight or flight.

I chose flight.

Even as a changeling—for that matter, even before—I was much stronger than he could ever be. But I didn't want to take the chance that he'd actually try something stupid. It was easier to just leave.

He stepped toward me again. "Keira, do you think—"

I held up my hand, stopping him.

"No, Carlton. I don't think." I couldn't let myself meet his eyes.

"You know I still care, don't you?"

His voice held a plea I didn't want to hear.

I couldn't do this. Not on top of everything else. I'd just spent hours locked in the Dead Zone with some sort of horrendous waking vision, and now my recently returned former boyfriend was making a pass at me.

"No, Carlton, stop it." I'd had enough and my voice was harsh. "This is not going to happen. What we had was a long time ago and it's long since over. You need to concentrate on the here and now. Like your wife, your family."

"Keira, please . . ."

"No. Go home, forget this happened. You'll be thankful for it later."

I turned away from him and hurried to the front door, pulling it open. It was still raining.

"Keira, please."

His plaintive words turned into an unattractive whine

as I let the door slam shut behind me in the wind. I'd had more than enough of Carlton, and of Marty's bedamned funeral home. I just wanted to get home. Maybe I could salvage what was left of the night.

As another clap of thunder drowned out the thud of the door, I realized my mistake. The only car out here was Carlton's truck. I'd parked behind the building. Damn. Now I'd either have to go back inside and deal with Carlton, or walk all the way around and get soaked.

I considered my options for less than a minute. Better water than whine. I started running for the back parking lot and the Rover, which I'd left unlocked. Thank goodness for life in a small town.

I scrambled into the front seat, tossing my pack into the back as I struggled to shut the door all at the same time.

"Ouch!" a voice exclaimed.

I jumped, hitting my head, yelping out a corresponding "ouch." I whirled, rubbing the top of my head.

There was a man in the back of my car.

CHAPTER FIVE

INSTANTLY, flashes of every urban legend I'd ever heard skipped through my mind: *Don't go back to your car, there's a man inside with a knife, a gun . . .*

I scrambled to open the door, my nerves having had enough for one day. My fingers couldn't seem to work the handle. All I could think of was running away as fast as I could, despite my training.

"Wait," he said, waving his hand in the air practically in front of my face. "I'm sorry. I just came in out of the rain."

He leaned forward. The front of the car was illuminated by the carport's overhead emergency light, so I could see the smile crinkling the corners of his eyes.

I let out the breath I'd been holding, letting the tension subside, the gathered energy fade as I collapsed back into the seat. I knew him . . . had known him. Not in the Biblical sense, but—

"Adam Walker? Damn." My heart was still racing, energy thrumming along my skin.

"Still eloquent, I see." He flashed even white teeth. Black hair set off a pair of deep sea-green eyes situated in pale skin. Oh. My.

I'd almost forgotten how good looking he was . . . almost. I suppose you could say I'd let myself forget.

My body responded almost automatically, a flush building inside me.

"It's been a while," I said, quietly, remembering the last time I'd seen him—a lot more recently than I'd seen Carlton. "What are you doing here?"

"Yes, it has been a long time," he said, ignoring my question.

I shivered, reacting to the sound of his voice. It always reminded me of chocolate. Not the wimpy, watered-down oversweet milk chocolate of commercial American candy bars, but the intense darkness of an 85% cocoa Lindt bar, flavor rich on your tongue, deceptively smooth until the tastes explode, capturing your senses, almost orgasmic in its intensity.

"Two years, London." He relaxed back into the seat and peered out at me from the darkness. "You haven't changed much."

"Someone else told me earlier today that I hadn't changed at all."

A rich laugh floated through the air.

"I said, 'much.'"

I narrowed my eyes and stared at him. "So I *have* changed?"

Another gleam of white teeth.

"It's not obvious, but there's something . . . different."

Yeah, different. You could say that.

"I can't say that I ever expected to run into you in my small corner of Texas," I countered. "So, what are you doing here?"

"Here in your car or here in this town?"

"Both, actually."

His shoulders moved slightly. A shrug? Hard to tell in the shadows.

"I ducked in here to get out of the rain. I'd forgotten you lived in this town. But I can't say I'm sorry I chose this car as my sanctuary."

He leaned forward into the light and smiled again, eyes twinkling, sending heat through my body. "Of course, it was the only one not locked."

"Locked or a hearse," I said, not totally facetiously.

"Or a hearse," he repeated, amusement evident.

I returned the smile with one of my own, finally relaxing a little. Despite the attraction, Adam had always been just a friendly acquaintance. No threat, no worries.

"So you climbed in the back?"

He shrugged a little. "It looked more comfortable."

The back wasn't *that* much more comfortable, but the seats did face sideways. More room for his long legs. Not that I was thinking about—

"Nice to see you again."

I extended my hand, not too sure how to act. I didn't think Miss Manners covered this particular situation in any of her etiquette books. *Chapter Ten: What to do when you find someone hiding in your car.*

Adam must have not read Miss Manners either. Instead of shaking my outstretched hand, as I'd expected, he bent his head and lightly kissed it, cool lips pressing briefly against my skin. He looked up, gave my hand a little squeeze and let go.

A thrill ran through my body; a rush of energy tingled up my spine. I slammed down my shields and pulled away, almost too abruptly. I could *not* have an episode right now. Damn it. Either my reaction to him had intensified since I'd last seen him, or my new and improved senses made me more susceptible than normal to his inherent charm. We'd played a game over the years, light, noncommittal, enjoyable. This was *more* . . . and eminently more disturbing, yet fascinating at the same time.

"So, Adam Walker," I said, ignoring my internal red alerts. "Can I drop you somewhere? I'm assuming you need a ride."

"Thank you," he said, "I'd certainly appreciate it. My driver was supposed to come back later. I hadn't expected the place to be closed."

"You still don't drive?" Amusing thought. He'd never driven in London, but that wasn't uncommon there. Of course, if he'd had a car, he wouldn't be hanging out in mine.

"Is that strange?" he asked, still smiling.

"Not strange, just different. Most folks around here do their own driving."

"I'm not most folks." The chocolate darkened; deep voice dropping a notch, sliding through the air, liquid and smooth, promising I didn't know what.

I shivered involuntarily. No, damn it, he wasn't. He'd never been. He'd been as conspicuous as Greg Brady at a witches' esbat and I'd been drawn to him from night one—a prissy fancy dress party in London thrown by a minor royal. Adam and I had never dated—and I didn't mean just "dating" as a virginal euphemism for sex. We'd never shared dinner, not even a movie. Our M.O. was to see each other at various parties and soirees thrown by other people, leaving separately, going our own ways. Safer . . . for me, anyway.

"I appreciate the offer of a ride, Keira. Before we go anywhere, would you mind terribly if I sat in front?"

"Oh, sorry." I felt my face turning red, something I'd thought myself incapable of doing. You'd have thought I was still in junior high. To cover my embarrassment,

I turned back to face the front and started the engine. "Please, come on up."

Adam maneuvered himself into the front, crawling between the two front seats and sliding into the passenger side. It's a pretty tight squeeze for a full-grown person, but he managed it with considerable suppleness.

His clothes were still slightly damp and clung to his skin, the cloth of his shorts outlining strong thighs and other parts I tried not to look at. Thick black hair swept back from a small widow's peak on his forehead, trailing over his collar and nearly halfway down his back, setting off his pale, smooth skin. Definitely not Greg Brady . . . more like a dark dream. Adam would probably fit right in at an actual full moon ritual. My thoughts kept going despite my intentions. Adam, skyclad. Oh, goddess. Not going there.

It wasn't easy, but I took a stab at forcing myself to stare straight ahead and not let my mind wander there . . . or to the other question in my muddled brain: "boxers or briefs?" I stole another glance. Silk boxers . . . if anything at all. He was definitely not the tightie whitie type.

His arm brushed my hand as he folded his body into the front passenger seat, grace in motion, contained energy in action, smooth, fluid, and elegant, but with a hint of controlled power hovering just below the surface. Almost like a shapeshifter. If Carlton was comfortable in his own skin, Adam was poetry in his. Poetry and a little music besides.

"Where can I drop you?" I said, my subconscious taking over and spouting the expected pleasantries. Thank goodness for social conventions or I might find myself babbling like an idiot.

"If it's not too far out of your way, could you take me to the Wild Moon?"

Somehow that figured. A fancy exclusive resort would be just the place for Adam Walker. But I was a little surprised he'd come all this way to vacation. I'd always pictured him in places like Marbella or Monte Carlo, not B.F.E. Texas.

"So what brings you all the way out here?"

"I came to talk to the undertaker, but the building was locked. Since my driver had left, I walked around the back to see if someone was here. Then the rain caught me."

"Why? Did someone die?"

Stupid questions. Embarrassing. I'd be happy to not totally turn into an idiot child before I could get him back to the ranch.

"No, nothing like that. I just needed . . . well, it's kind of personal, actually. Kind of a family obligation."

He hesitated a moment. "Were you here for . . . ?" He gestured, indicating the hearse.

"No, not me," I said quickly. "Just . . . you can say it was a family obligation, too. I'm sure he'll be back later. I can give you the number." I reached around to grab my backpack, meaning to get out one of Marty's business cards.

Adam put his hand on my arm, stopping my movement and sending another flash of heat through me.

"Thanks anyway, but I have his number. Now how about that ride?" His eyes crinkled as he smiled, briefly showing his white teeth.

I exhaled the breath I hadn't realized I was holding.

"Sure. Coming right up. Chauffeur service."

I turned to face front and started the car, promising myself to pay attention to my driving. I had to stop thinking about him, or I'd end up in a wreck. Nothing like a rampaging herd of hormones to ruin your concentration.

I KEPT my attention on the road, not saying much on the trip out to the ranch. Normally, I loved driving in the quiet shadows of the Hill Country, alone with my thoughts, wrapping the velvet darkness around me like a warm cloak, or a lover's voice. Tonight wasn't quite so silent. In addition to the unnerving presence of my passenger, whom I could feel so very solidly next to me despite my strong shields, the dark was full of the memory of the vision I'd had in the prep room.

These visions unsettled me. I couldn't let myself believe they were all true second sight. As much as I disliked Marty, I didn't want him dead. Not to mention the fact I was afraid that my talent would end up being true clairvoyance. No, not just afraid. I was scared—bone deep scared. The power exhibited during changing didn't necessarily have anything to do with our primary talent, but I was terrified of having to spend the rest of my prolonged life not being able to ever touch others, frightened of what I'd see, of the nightmares that could be generated by a single contact. The worst part was that I had no choice. Talent was inherited, like blue eyes or red hair. I could be fatalistic about it and hope my personal genetic symphony would be kind and the finale would be something I could live with, like shapeshifting or healing, but this particular overture wasn't at all comforting.

"We're almost to the gate."

His voice, still smooth, interrupted my train of thought.

My headlights flashed on a small square of wood hung from one of the horizontal posts that punctuated the fence lining the road. No lettering on the sign, just a stylized red circle cut by what looked like wisps of cloud.

"Nice logo," I said. "Not exactly obvious, though. Guess they're not much into advertising."

"You haven't come out here before?" He sounded surprised.

"Not exactly," I answered, not wanting to get into the whole happy clan hunting-ground scenario. "The place was abandoned for so long, we all trespassed on the Point at one time or another, but this part is a little out of my way. Out of most people's way, actually. I imagine that's why the owner bought it. No point in a private exclusive resort if you're in the middle of town."

"Touché."

Unlike most Hill Country dude ranches, the Wild Moon didn't have the usual arrogant wrought iron sign straddling the gate, proclaiming its status as a possession of someone with more money than sense. If I hadn't been watching for the entrance, I might have missed it. A single lamp illuminated the simple opening, throwing a weak pool of light over the road. I turned the wheel, steering the car up to what looked to be a state-of-the-art electronic gate. A keypad was mounted on the left, about driver's eye level.

I looked over at Adam who smiled, then pulled out a small remote control unit from his pocket and pointed it forward. The gate slid open and I pulled through. Handy. Don't make your guests have to remember anything as mundane as a password. Instead, give them a remote control.

Steadily increasing pools of water on the surface of the caliche road reflected the feeble light. Rain drummed on the roof of the Rover and showed no signs of slowing. In fact, it had gotten heavier over the last few minutes. I could barely see the path in front of me. It was like driving in some sort of weird otherworld, my headlights barely piercing the near-absolute darkness.

"Not so much into lighting around here, are they?"

"Guests pay for privacy here," Adam answered. "I give them what they want. At least most of the time."

"What do you mean 'you'?" I asked. "I thought you were here on holiday."

"Not exactly," Adam said. "Actually, I own the ranch."

A flash of something cut in front of us. I stomped on the brake and wrestled with the steering as we began to skid off the gravel. The rain-slick caliche didn't make it any easier to maneuver, but I managed to keep control as we slid to a stop bare inches from a cluster of live oaks. I could barely breathe. That had been way too close for comfort.

"Was it something I said?" Adam sounded amused.

I looked at my passenger, my hands still gripping the steering wheel. At first I couldn't speak, my brain warring with the hammering in my chest.

"Sorry," I breathed. "Something ran out in front of us. I almost hit it."

I peered through the windshield, but I couldn't see very far. My night vision was excellent, but tonight it was useless; it was much too dark and the rain completely obscured any view. If I hadn't known better, I'd have sworn I'd seen a creature that ran by on two legs, then four; a shapeshifter, one of my own clan. But it couldn't be.

"Did you see what it was?" Adam spoke quickly.

"It went by too fast," I answered quickly. "It looked pretty big, though, whatever it was. Maybe a wildcat. I'm not sure. I don't think it ran like a deer."

I wasn't quite lying. It hadn't run like a deer. It had run like a wolf . . . one that spent part of its life on two legs instead of four. But there aren't any wolves in Texas. Right? Not even were—at least not anymore, not that I knew of. At least not in the Hill Country. Maybe. Shit. I didn't really know. My family had cleared out, but that didn't mean someone else hadn't moved in without telling me. If that was the case, someone was going to be in for a world of hurt. This was still my family's acknowledged territory. As long as I was here, no other clan family could move in without permission. I almost smiled at the thought of having the chance to kick some supernatural booty. Playing Marty's babysitter for two years meant no opportunity to practice the fighting skills I'd learned. Even though I'd kept up my training, sparring at a dojo with a human who could get hurt was no substitute for a good confrontation.

Adam leaned forward and peered out into the rain-slashed darkness. "Is there something out there?" he asked. "Next to the road?"

I leaned forward and wiped the glass, trying to see. He was right, I couldn't see what, but something was just off the road, near a clump of mesquite bushes, a few yards away.

Oh, crap. I had to go look. As I opened the driver's door, a sudden gust of wind brought more than the smell of rain to my nose. Whatever was there was dead. Freshly dead. Predator, all right. But what kind?

"What is it?" His voice was terse, abrupt.

"I'm not sure."

Damn it, I needed to see what it was, whether or not it was another deer. If I could catch a sense of its killer, I might be able to figure out what was roaming around. I didn't think it would be dangerous out there. I'd put down some pretty serious odds that the predator had just crossed in front of my car, but I still didn't want to drag Adam into this. This may be his legal turf, but it was still my home turf. And someone was most definitely trespassing. Until I got closer, I wouldn't be able to identify it.

"Something's dead in those bushes," I finally said.

"Stay here, I'm going in to check." I stepped out into the rain, ignoring the fact that I was going to get soaked again.

Seconds later, a movement immediately to my right startled me. Adam appeared at my side, not a foot away. He must have gotten out when I did. I must not have been paying attention. I'd thought he was still sitting in the car.

"You didn't have to come out and get wet, too."

His answer was quiet, but forceful. "It's my land. I need to look. Although, it's probably just a dead armadillo or something." His nose wrinkled as if in distaste.

I shrugged. "If it's a dead armadillo it can stay there," I said. "But if it could be . . . something else."

"Human?"

His question startled me.

"What? No—I mean, it's too small."

I knew it wasn't a person. The smell was wrong, although I couldn't tell him that's how I knew.

I grabbed my Maglite from behind my car seat, shut the door and was already walking up the road, my hiking boots gripping the wet rocks. Adam walked to my left, his steps surprisingly sure and solid for a man walking in smooth-soled shoes on a slick gravel road.

The headlight beams didn't quite penetrate this far, so I snapped on the flashlight as I neared the clump of bushes. Lucky for me Mother Nature decided to cooperate just about then and turned off the overhead faucet. I blinked the last of the raindrops from my face.

Shit, I'd almost stepped on its head.

It wasn't a deer.

Glazed eyes stared up at the sky, a gash in the animal's neck spilled over with red-tinted water, washing out the blood that was once there. Orange-striped fur peaked in wet clumps around its body. Its mouth gaped open, exposing its pitiful little fangs. No match for whatever had killed it.

"A cat." Adam's voice had lost its previous warmth.

I nodded and looked at him as he stepped around me to stand on the other side of the carcass, carefully avoiding the animal's tail. It was a house cat. A big one, maybe eighteen, twenty pounds, but still, once somebody's pet. There was even a blue leather collar around its torn neck.

I braced myself and took a deep breath, trying to sort out particular scents underneath the reek of blood, death and wet ground. A few things came through, a touch of cedar, a hint of Mexican oregano as if the cat had brushed against a bush or two in its wanderings. The sharp bitterness of its maleness. An unneutered tom. Great. Some bozo hadn't bothered to fix his cat and it had either run off or had been dumped out here in the boonies, only to become prey for something bigger and nastier. Then suddenly, a scent I recognized. Shit. It couldn't be. We never hunted pets. I needed to get out of here and make a phone call.

"Do you recognize it?" I asked Adam, hoping it wasn't his cat.

"No." The once rich voice was brusque and flat. "We have a lot of strays abandoned around here. You really didn't see what ran past?"

"It went by too quickly. But from the looks of it, it could have been a bigger cat or other natural predator." I was lying, but I couldn't explain to Adam what I suspected. I could see where sharp teeth had shredded the cat's neck.

"Damn." The soft word spilled out almost in a whisper.

"Yeah," I said. "Not much like those deer."

Adam's head snapped up, eyes blazing green fire in the glow of the flashlight. For a split second, a trick of the light made it seem as if there was a real flame behind them.

"How did you know about that?" His voice rose, clipping the syllables.

"Hey, take it easy there, Adam," I said, backing up. "Everyone knows."

"Everyone?"

"It's a small town. Things like that get around. Look, there's no point in staying out here in the wet. Let's go back."

"I'm sorry," he said, calming down. "It really bothers me that someone could come poach on my land and hurt the animals that I spend so much time rescuing."

"Rescuing?"

"Most of our exotic stock comes from defunct hunting ranches," he said, ducking under a particularly vicious mesquite branch. "I couldn't let them go to another trophy-hunting place."

"Good for you." I meant it. I hated those places.

"You don't believe in hunting?"

"It's not that," I said. "Real hunting's fine as long as you eat what you kill." Okay, so the way I meant it wasn't exactly the traditional shoot, skin and butcher, but it was true. "I just want the prey to have a fighting chance. Not like these places that treat the game like pets, putting out feed and acclimating them to humans, then 'too bad, so sad'—it's now somebody's future wall-hanging."

I opened the back door of the Land Rover, and pulled out a couple of towels I kept in a gym bag in the back. I didn't explain that I mostly used them to wipe down the car. I'd just washed them and they were clean.

"Here," I said, and tossed him a towel.

He smiled as he swabbed the water from his skin, trying to sop up the worst of it. "That's better, thank you."

"You're welcome," I said and continued to mop water

from my hair. A losing proposition. My hair was still braided; in order to really dry it, I'd have to undo the braid and spend a good hour or two with at least two thick towels. That would have to wait until I got home. I peeled off my soaking flannel shirt, leaving me in a thin cotton tank top that was just as wet. But it was more comfortable than the sopping flannel.

Adam looked like he was a candidate for a centerfold, the kind where the model is posing in a pool of water, hair slicked back and clothes clinging to every muscle. He passed the towel over his hair and squeezed the ends.

I looked away, trying to maintain some semblance of control. I wrapped the towel around me and climbed into the car.

"Are you cold?" he asked, climbing in on the passenger's side, his voice once again full of the rich warmth.

"Not really," I answered, fumbling with the keys. It wasn't cold that made me shiver. I'd covered myself because I didn't want him to see how he was affecting me. At this point, idiot child was rapidly becoming slut puppy—and I was not happy with the whole idea.

"Let me start the car and see if I can get back on the road or we may never get out of here. It's all over mud."

As I put the Rover back into gear and inched until I felt gravel beneath the wheels, Mother Nature pulled another nasty trick. A boom of thunder heralded another downpour, this one stronger than before. I stopped the car and threw it in neutral, then turned off the motor and fastened the parking brake. It was impossible to see more than three feet in front of the hood. I wasn't going to try to drive anywhere again until it let up. The dash lights offered some illumination, so I left them on after turning off the headlights. I wasn't too worried about other traffic.

From the looks of this road, not even the guests traveled it very often.

"It looks like we're going to have to wait this out." I said. "Hope you don't have any major plans." As I said that, a little ping of memory registered in my tired brain. Shit. *Bea.*

CHAPTER SIX

I DIALED her cell, not sure where she'd be. She answered on the second ring.

"*Hola, chica,* what's shaking?" I could hear the sound of music in the background.

"Hey, girl, there's been a slight alteration in plans."

"What's up, Keira?"

"Well, I'm sort of stuck." I didn't quite know how to tell her what was happening. I didn't really want to get into all the gory and not-so-gory details until I could sort everything out. "Are you at my house yet?"

"Yep, just got here. I'm starting to fix some nachos."

"Great, but I'm going to be a little while yet." I glanced over at Adam, who, to his credit, was trying to pretend he wasn't listening to my conversation. I could see his head turned toward the front of the car.

"I'm giving someone a ride to the Wild Moon," I explained. "But the rain's coming down too hard and I can't see to drive. We're going to wait it out for a little while."

"Cool beans," she answered, mumbling over her chewing. "Who's the lucky passenger?"

"His name is Adam Walker. He was stranded out by the funeral home." I glanced over. He was still staring off into the dark.

I could hear Bea's gasp even over the rain pounding on the Rover. "No way, really? Adam Walker?"

"What do you mean?" I turned my head away from Adam and lowered my voice. He probably could hear me anyway, but I could at least pretend my conversation was private.

"Woo hoo, *m'hija;* you are so way lucky!" I could hear the grin in her voice. I started to flush again.

"What did you just say?" I wasn't sure if I'd heard her right.

"He's the owner of the ranch. Mm-mm, gorgeous and rich—two strikes for, I'd say."

I was startled. "You know him?"

"Sure," she said. "Well, not really know him. But I've seen him." She crunched in my ear. A nacho.

"I had to pick something up at the deli the other night after I closed and when I went in, there was this *guapo* over at the counter. Boris introduced me. Whew!"

She paused and I could hear a cork pop. Damn. She'd even opened the wine.

"Anyway, *m'hija,* he was something else. When he looked at me, I couldn't even remember my own name. Those eyes."

"Bea, uh, thanks. I'll get there as soon as I can."

Well, at least I knew I wasn't the only one who was affected by Adam. If I didn't hang up, I knew she'd go on to wax poetic about his physique, and then have me hopping into bed with him before the conversation was through. Beatriz Ruiz certainly had a fine appreciation for the male half of the species. Not that I was complaining, but no sense in getting even more embarrassed than I already was.

"No problem." She laughed into my ear. "See you when you get here, you lucky thing."

"Stop it! And don't eat all the food," I said as I disconnected.

There was a moment of silence that was more uncomfortable than not. I didn't exactly know what he'd heard of Bea's side of the conversation if anything. Adam spoke first.

"Everything okay with your friend?" I could swear I heard amusement.

I nodded. "Yeah, she's just dandy; she started the party without me."

He grinned, a flash of even white teeth that gleamed even in the faint light from the dash. "Sounds as if she's enjoying herself."

"That she is." I flicked on the headlights for a moment to see if the weather had improved any. It hadn't. I still couldn't see any further than a couple of feet past the hood.

"I think we're going to be stuck here a while," I said. I knew it wasn't exactly original, but I didn't know what else to say. I didn't know if I actually minded, but at some point, I still had another phone call to make—about that dead cat. It was a call I couldn't make with any chance of being overheard.

Adam didn't reply, but I could hear him shifting in his seat. The Rover was a great car, but it wasn't exactly the most comfortable vehicle in the world. This model was designed to be a working truck, not luxury transportation. Plus, it was getting a little chilly. I was probably more comfortable in my wet jeans and towel draped over my shoulders than he was in his wet shorts. My leather jacket was in the back, but his shoulders were much broader than mine.

"Are you warm enough? I might be able to dig up another towel or two." I automatically reached out to feel his arm. He'd turned in his seat and my hand touched his upper thigh instead. I snatched it back. His skin was cool and smooth to the touch.

"Sorry," I mumbled, glad that the darkness hid the multiple shades of red that I could feel blossoming on my face. Damn, I didn't want this blushing thing to become a habit.

"Don't be," he said, his voice soft. "Relax, Keira."

"I'm fine," I answered automatically. "I've just had a bad day." Or the mother of all bad days . . . and I had a feeling it was going to get worse before it got better.

"Do you want to talk about it?"

I turned toward the passenger seat. I preferred to face someone when I talked to them, even though I could barely make out the shape of his body against the darker background of night.

"Talk about it—why?"

"Why not? We're not going anywhere. We might as well chat for a while."

What I wanted to do was to change the subject. I didn't want to talk about me or my day. I'd never be able to explain any of it to him, so why even start.

"Nothing much to tell," I finally said. "Just one of those days." One that didn't seem to end.

"May I ask you a question?"

"Ask."

"You don't work at the funeral home, do you?"

"That is *such* a big 'no.' I went there to talk to my cousin, the owner. Not that he was even there."

"Your cousin is the undertaker?" Adam sounded surprised.

"Yes, unfortunately."

"Unfortunately?"

"Let's just say he's not my favorite cousin."

He laughed softly. "Sounds as if he were part of your rough day."

"Yeah, well," I said. "I can deal with him."

"I'm sure you can." I could definitely hear amusement in his voice.

"Hmmph." I wasn't sure if that was a compliment or not.

"So when did you get into town? My friend saw you at the deli the other day."

I could hear the smile in his voice. "A few days ago. Up until then, I made most of my arrangements via phone, but I wanted to introduce myself to the deli owner, Boris Nagy. He brings deliveries out to the ranch."

"So he said."

"He told you that?" He sounded perturbed.

I was quick to reassure him. "We weren't gossiping or anything," I said. "We were just talking about . . . oops, sorry. Small town again. I guess we were gossiping a little. Boris told me he was making a delivery when they found the deer. When Carlton came out to talk to you all."

"Carlton?"

"Carlton Larson, our Sheriff."

"You know him? I'd understood he was quite new."

"Only in the sense of being Sheriff. He grew up here. Just came back recently."

"What do you think of him?"

For a second, I thought he was being facetious, but then I realized he only meant what I thought of Carlton as the Sheriff. I'd never spoken about Carlton in England; hadn't needed to. I'd been happy to leave that part of my life behind.

"He's a good person," I said. "But I don't know much about his policing skills. I haven't seen him in a long time."

"You knew him before?"

In various manners of speaking.

"I grew up here, too."

"I hadn't realized you were a native. You seemed so at home in Europe."

"I'm not exactly a native," I said with a smile. "My father brought me to Texas as a child."

That's all I was willing to say. Native to me meant native Texan, native human. I was neither. I'd been born in my mother's homeland, deep below the faery mounds in a part of Wales still left to the wild.

Stayed there until I was nearly seven . . . just long enough for dear Mum to get tired of the idea of raising me. There weren't many children around the mounds. The Sidhe weren't known for providing a loving family life, especially for the few half-bloods around. Not much need for new generations when the old ones don't exactly die. Dad came to my rescue just in time to get me acclimated to the outside world and start school with Marty.

Mainstreaming, we called it now. Something Dad's generation pioneered years ago and what most of my contemporaries in the clan were trying to do. Hide in plain sight—at least, until the day came that we could live in the open and reveal ourselves. That was the plan, anyway. I hoped it would happen, but I knew it was too much of a pipe dream. Humans didn't take too kindly to "different." Even in our so-called enlightened Western culture, too many people were still discriminated against and they were all human. Imagine what would happen when people discovered that entire groups of beings existed outside of stories and movies. Plus, immortality: great idea, until you can't have it.

"So why did you decide to buy the Wild Moon?" I asked. "Last time I saw you, you were headed to Paris for some business deal. Why Texas?"

"I did go," he said. "But then my plans changed. I was looking for a place I could renovate or build into a resort. The Wild Moon was that opportunity. The first guests arrived a few weeks ago. This is the first time I've had a chance to come here and stay for a while."

"I remember when it was sold," I said. "But I didn't know it was you."

He sounded surprised. "You remember?"

"Yeah, I told you, it's a small town. I bought my place about the same time you bought the Wild Moon. Same realtor."

"So you're the one."

"The one what?"

"As you said, it's a small town. My estate agent stood me up one night. He'd been delayed by another client who'd just returned and was buying a house and some property."

I could feel him looking at me through the gloom.

"Small world." I stared out into the black night not wanting to think of things best left unremembered.

"Sometimes not small enough." Abruptly, his voice changed, the soft edges becoming a little sharper. "Why did you leave?"

"London?" I asked, knowing that's what he was asking.

"Yes." He watched me carefully. I could almost hear the implied "me" behind that "yes." He didn't have to say the rest. I never told him I was leaving. Didn't really tell anyone but the aunt I'd been staying with. I'd run away, but not from Adam. There hadn't been time for any good-byes, only a hasty scribbled note dropped in the post. Not that I'd owed him any explanations, but we'd both grown used to seeing each other at the endless rounds of meaningless parties . . . a comfort factor. Friendly faces in the frenetic pace of society's stupidity.

"The same reason I'd stayed in London for so many years. It . . . he . . . Gideon changed on me. Became someone I didn't want to be with."

"So you left without saying good-bye?" The mild reproach shamed me a little.

"I'm sorry," I said. "I never thought . . ."

"I know," he said. "I always knew. More's the pity." He smiled gently. "I suppose we never did have more than a . . ." He looked thoughtful, as if he was searching for the appropriate word.

"Flirtation?" I offered. "Friendship?"

"Yes. Both and neither."

He was right. It had been more than just a brief flirtation, yet not so much of a friendship. I'd felt a connection, an easy camaraderie that might have evolved into something more tangible, but there had been factors. My reluctance to involve myself with another human, plus I'd made the mistake of falling for Gideon.

Cousins only in the loosest sense of the word, Gideon and I were related, but no closer than a couple of generations. All clan were cousins, aunts, uncles, all connected. Clan blood begat clan blood. Our branch was particularly insular that way. Some connections were closer, some not so. Gideon fell somewhere in between. Tall, dark and devilishly handsome, he'd taken my heart and stomped that sucker flat, in the immortal words of an old country and western song. I'd been an idiot and too damned accepting. My family wasn't much into the concept of traditional Western marriage. When you live forever, that didn't exactly make sense. You could find all sorts of other hookups, though. Dad preferred serial monogamy. One of my brothers lived in a group home— two husbands, three wives and more kids than I cared to think about. It worked for them.

Me, I'd wanted to try this whole one-on-one thing, and chose Gideon. Bad decision. What I'd never told anyone is how much he'd scared me and that he'd done it on purpose. His power lay in darkness. He could speak to the shadows, call the shades. But that's not what frightened me. The dark is neutral; it just tends to hide a multitude of sins. Gideon not only flirted with power, he also toyed with evil. That's where I'd drawn the line.

He'd taught me much of what I knew today but, as is the rule with magick and power, there were always consequences.

I'd paid the price of naiveté. He'd convinced me we could never truly come together without removing all our barriers. I'd gone in like a puppy for a treat. When I'd touched his soul, the vileness inside him seared me and I'd scampered back to my aunt's to lick my wounds. Later, when I tried to confront him, his voice cut me with cruelty; words flayed my ego, slicing it like small sharp knives tearing away what had been left of my self-confidence. I'd run home with my metaphysical tail between my legs. I'd lost a lot of trust then, and I wasn't so sure I'd ever really gained it back.

I realized much later that he'd only been scared himself at his own potential for evil. He wasn't all that much older than me.

Before Gideon, the world had been mine. Now I was just happy to hold on to my little one-acre piece of it.

I closed my eyes against the memories and breathed in deeply. Mistake. I was sucker-punched by the warm enticing scent of nearby male, caught up by my supercharged senses, weakening my already shaky control. My belly clenched with want, my lips were suddenly dry. My eyelids flew open to meet Adam's steady gaze, the soft glow from the dashboard lights delineating his face, highlighting his glittering eyes, casting shadows underneath cheekbones sharp enough to slice your heart.

"Is he still a part of your life?" Adam's directness betrayed nothing, no sense of how he felt.

"Only in the sense of someone to avoid," I said, managing a weak smile and trying to turn the conversation back to a lighter tone. I forced myself to ignore the emotions raging through me.

"Avoidance? So that's how you . . ." His voice trailed off. "Never mind."

He'd pegged me in one. That was exactly how I coped.

"Yeah. I left. Came home, expecting comfort and what passed for normal in the bosom of my family. Except, surprise, so not."

Adam said nothing for a moment.

"Not?"

"Not normal, not comfort, not anything I expected," I replied. "Seems they'd decided to relocate. Bags packed, ready to go and all that."

Bea was there to help pick up the pieces when I flew home on the first flight out. I'd been only too willing to pay the exorbitant price to get back to my own turf as soon as possible. When I'd discovered my family had decided to leave and move to Canada, I freaked, electing to stay in Rio Seco. That's when my ever-loving great-great-granny lay down her version of the ultimatum. If I wanted to stay by myself and ignore my duties, the least I could do was watch Marty.

Home—warm, comfortable . . . and safe? Not so much

anymore. I'd sucked it up and taken Hobson's choice, figuring I could deal for a few years, until I figured out what to do.

Adam leaned toward me a little, his words a quiet counterpart to my agitation. "It looks like fate turned the other cheek," he said.

"I guess so." My words seemed a little loud in the silence of the night.

Silence. No more rain except for a few drip, drip, drips from the mesquite bushes.

"I suppose we should go," I said, almost reluctant to speak the words.

Despite the underlying tension, I liked sitting here with him, sharing the night with someone I'd always felt was somewhat of a kindred spirit. A relief after my earlier encounter with Carlton, even with the tremendous attraction. Adam and I had baggage, but it was definitely the small carry-on kind, not a burden. Carlton's baggage was more an overstuffed Pullman.

"I suppose," Adam echoed. He sounded as disinclined to leave as I did.

I sneaked another glance over at him as I turned on the headlights and started the engine. He turned to stare out the windshield, almost as if he could see through the darkness. There was an intensity about him that made me wonder if he was looking for something specific or just staring because he was thinking about something else. I figured I'd ask.

"What are you looking at?"

He turned to look at me. "Nothing," he said, his voice soft and quiet. "I think I prefer the view in here."

I ignored him, and hoped he couldn't see my face. I knew I was blushing again.

WE TOPPED a rise and I saw the lights of civilization or at least of the Wild Moon.

"Wow." My reaction wasn't exactly eloquent, but it was all I was capable of right then.

The complex of buildings was bigger than many small towns. A Victorian-styled inn sat on a small rise, its windows lit up by a soft yellow glow, giving it a cheerful appearance. From my vantage point I could see several outbuildings nestled around the grounds, and beyond those, a number of what could only be guest cottages, some more like full-fledged houses than vacation cabanas. Every cottage echoed the elegant styling of the main inn, down to its wraparound porches, gables and bay windows.

Without warning, Adam's hand was on my shoulder, a brand burning me through the towel. My heart began to pound, my breathing came faster. Every millimeter of my skin tingled as if I were filled with electrical energy. My mouth was suddenly dry.

"Nice view, isn't it," he said, the chocolate goodness of his voice melting over me, soothing the tension, but yet, at the same time increasing it with a subtle stroke.

At first I thought he was being facetious again, but I realized he was looking out the window at the lights of the buildings.

"It's lovely," I managed to squeak out.

This just had to be good old-fashioned sexual tension. If this were part of the symptoms of the change, it was most definitely not what I'd expected. A little magick, some clairvoyant nightmares, okay, but not this extreme sexual awareness and sensitivity, magnifying every bit of interest I'd ever had in him. Sure he was gorgeous, sure I'd always been attracted to him, but right now, I wasn't sure whether

I wanted Adam Walker to jump out of the car or just jump me—and neither seemed to be the appropriate choice.

I clamped down on my shields, and shrugged off his hand, trying to shut down the connection before I let myself act on my base instincts, no matter how much I wanted to. Reinforcing my guard didn't seem to help much. He was so *there*. No matter what I did, I felt him. Concentrate on driving, Keira Kelly, concentrate. If I stared straight ahead, I could force myself to ignore most of the sensations.

"Where would you like me to drop you off?" I was surprised that I could sound this normal when my entire body was humming.

"Go around the main building and to the cottages in the back. Mine is the first one on the left." His tone was pleasant and quiet.

I was shielding so tightly my nerves hummed with the effort. Controlling my emotions was my priority right now. Besides, I figured that Adam couldn't possibly tell how totally insane I was at the moment. His expression hadn't changed. A bland, but friendly, smile was still on his face.

I pulled to a stop in front of the house. No lights shone inside, but the front light illuminated enough of the porch and the circular drive for me to see that it was more than just your average two- or three-room weekend-getaway place. This mini-Victorian had some serious square footage. I'd guess at least a couple of thousand at the very least. Not too shabby. Guess it paid to be the king.

The other vacation cottages weren't much smaller. There were four houses in the little cul-de-sac, but each sat in its own small yard area, at least a hundred feet from its neighbor. Not bad.

He'd said the guests wanted privacy. I imagine they paid pretty dearly for it, too. Last I'd heard B&Bs in the Hill

Country were getting more than a couple hundred a night per room. A house this size must be at least triple that.

"This is nice," I said. "Not quite what I expected."

"What did you expect?" The teasing smile was back.

"A little more country cottage, a little less . . . house."

"It works for me," he said. He leaned over and planted a kiss on my cheek. The smooth touch of his lips left a trail of fire on my skin; I automatically leaned into him, wanting to feel more.

"Thank you, Keira Kelly." His voice was nearly as soft as a caress. "It was good to see you again."

I nodded and closed my eyes briefly, not trusting myself to speak. Holy shit. If I weren't careful, I would be following him inside and letting him have his way with me right this minute. I forced myself to pull away slowly, keep my voice steady and not look at his face. I was afraid that if I did, all my intentions would no longer be good, but very, very bad.

"Thanks." I finally forced the word out. "It was good to see you, too."

"I'd like to treat you to dinner sometime, if you'd like . . . as a thank-you."

I nodded again. "That would be nice."

"I'll call you, then," he said, sliding out of the seat. "Good night, Keira."

The words floated softly through the air between us, landing on my ear, a feather in the dark. It was as if he'd touched me again. Danger, Keira Kelly, danger.

"Good night, Adam," I said, turning the key and gunning the engine. I was having a hard time concentrating. My brain was telling me to leave now or damn the consequences. I pressed my foot to the gas and sketched a wave in his direction as I pulled away.

CHAPTER SEVEN

"**D**AMN IT, Tucker, answer." I swore at my cell phone. A click on the other line, a quick "leave a message" and a beep. My brother was either ignoring me, or really not at home. It had been *his* scent I recognized next to the dead cat. A scent almost as familiar as my own. Tucker was the brother closest to me, not in age, but in attitude. That aside, as far as I knew, he was supposed to be in Canada with the rest of my family, not in Rio Seco. Especially not killing a house cat. I pulled off the road for a moment to scroll through my phone's directory menu. I dialed his cell number.

"Didn't take you long, did it, little sister?"

His cheerful voice teased me on the other end. I could imagine his broad open face, blue eyes crinkling, accompanied by a wide grin. Damn him.

"Where the hell are you, Tucker?"

"I wouldn't call it 'hell,' exactly, sister mine, more like 'really uncomfortable.'"

"That was you, then, wasn't it? At the Wild Moon?"

A pause.

"Yeah, damn. I didn't expect you to be there. What were you doing there, anyway?"

I almost repeated his "really uncomfortable" phrase.

"Giving the owner a ride home. You didn't kill that cat, did you?"

My brother laughed. "Please, Keira, you know me

better than that. I was out at the ranch stretching my legs, getting in a good run when I found the cat. I had to stop to check it out." He didn't mean running as in "Just do it." Tucker was a 1,200-year-old hellhound, a Viking berserker with a touch of lycanthropy. He liked to run in the rain.

"Did you find anything?" I asked.

"Not much. Dead cat. Not sure what killed it. But it wasn't one of us."

I hesitated before I spoke. Telling Tucker about my nightmares might not be a good thing. He'd know I was changing. Then again . . .

"Tucker," I said.

"Yes, Keira?"

"Just why are you here?"

Silence.

"Tucker?"

His sigh echoed through the phone's speaker. Oh, crap. He didn't have to say it for me to know.

"I'll be damned if I let you play babysitter," I said, slamming my fist against the steering wheel. "You can just turn right around and go back to Canada."

"Be damned then, little sister." I could hear his grin. "Because here I am. You need me here. Besides, you know I'm your favorite."

"Favorite as in 'least obnoxious' . . . yeah, well, I guess." I still wasn't convinced. "I don't need someone to watch over me, big brother. I'm an adult. So I'm changing, so what?"

"So you're changing, that's what," he replied. "Look, Keira, I came because I knew you'd hate it less if I was the one doing this. Just think, it could have been Ciprian."

Oh great, Ciprian was almost as much of a prick as Marty. If I had to have someone around, Tucker was the least objectionable.

"All right, then," I said, capitulating. "You win for now. Do you have a place to stay?"

"I'm fine for tonight, Keira. I'm going to stay outside. I'll be by sometime tomorrow. If you need anything, just call."

"Thanks, bro," I said. "Really. I'm not pissed at you."

"I know." I could tell he was grinning. "See you tomorrow."

THE STORM still raged as I continued home, matching my own internal angst. I loved thunderstorms; their wild electric force resonated deep within me, answering some inborn restless need . . . for what, I wasn't sure. But the day's strangeness had been too much and the storm only increased my disquiet. In twenty-four hours, everything in my life had suddenly taken a turn. Not necessarily for the worse, but definitely for the different.

The power inside me was no longer dormant, but awake, restless, hovering on the edge of release. Ahead of me were a few weeks of my own internal stormy weather as my talent emerged and my ability matured. It was all so very unpredictable—the edgy tension, the feeling that I was suspended on the threshold, needing only a word or a motion to open the door still firmly shut in front of me. I couldn't go back, but I couldn't yet move forward.

Then there was that weird three-hour blackout and the weirder "vision" or whatever. Of course that might just be part of my "power surge."

To further complicate matters, my past, blameless as it had been, was catching up to me. In the space of the same twenty-four hours, I'd revisited an old flame, who, to my dismay, had kept that particular torch burning for the past fifteen years. Then chance had thrown another double and I'd re-encountered someone who'd turned my own personal burner up to "high." And let's not forget the lovely visions from hell: dead deer and a dead cousin. Finally, to top it all off, my brother was here to play babysitter.

Although I couldn't ignore the visions, I could try to avoid thinking about them until at least tomorrow, when I could talk to Tucker.

Since I couldn't offer Carlton what he wanted—more importantly, I didn't want to—I'd just have to ignore him.

As for Adam Walker, I just couldn't ignore him and didn't exactly want to. Neither my brain nor body would let me disregard Adam Walker. Suave, sophisticated and continental, he'd always struck me as the type that would accept a liaison as is, no strings, no regrets. I didn't picture him looking for a white picket fence. This I could do, and probably would have done before, except I hadn't seen him again after the last boring soiree we'd both attended. I'd figured that flirtation as part of the same past that was back knocking on my door.

I stared at the road in front of me, trusting to instinct to get me home safely, as I replayed my conversation with Adam Walker and added my own reality, one that involved Adam Walker in compromising positions. I took a deep breath and sent out a quick prayer to the powers that be. Trouble was . . . I wasn't sure what I was praying for.

THE REST OF THE NIGHT passed quietly, except for Bea's whoops and hollers when I explained I'd known Adam in England. I loved Bea, but she was not making my situation much easier. I'd arrived home, determined to forget about Adam, forget about Carlton, and not think about anything more than food and a bad movie, but Bea wouldn't let it rest. She was determined to make sure I was happy, whatever that meant. I wasn't too sure.

I read for several hours after Bea left and then fell into bed just before dawn.

IT TOOK a constant and very loud pounding on my front door to bring me out of Slumberland, where I was contentedly having tea and biscuits with Adam Walker, while Boris Nagy served and Bea and Greta watched. We'd just reached the refill stage and I'd raised a lace-gloved hand to Boris when the noise finally sank its way into my dreaming brain. Instead of sitting across from a morning-suited and gorgeous Adam Walker, I was staring into the brown eyes of someone all too familiar leaning over my bed, his hand reaching toward me.

"Carlton?" I sat up and scrambled to the head of the bed, quickly pulling up the sheets before all my assets were exposed to Carlton and the rest of the world, or at least to whoever else had let themselves into my house. "What the hell are you doing here?"

"You weren't answering the phone, Keira. Your door was unlocked, so I let myself in," he answered, stepping back and looking about as uncomfortable as only a more than six-foot, 200-plus–pound county sheriff can when confronted with a potentially embarrassing situation. He had his Stetson in his hand and was trying to talk and not look at me all at the same time.

"Of course I wasn't answering the phone," I said. "I was asleep. I don't normally answer the phone when I'm asleep. Besides, I unplugged it." I wasn't making a lot of sense, but I was still tired, still cranky and not too happy that Carlton had come into my house. "Why are you here?"

"Well, Keira, I . . ." He hesitated, turning his hat in his hands. If he wasn't careful, he'd ruin that precise brim roll he liked so much.

"Spit it out, Carlton," My mouth tasted terrible. I couldn't remember if I'd been awake enough for my normal brushing and flossing routine before I'd fallen into bed.

I wasn't all that comfortable sitting there naked except for a sheet, so I grabbed my bathrobe off the floor and tried not to flash my visitor as I wrapped it around me. My people didn't sweat nudity, but I'd grown up around humans and wasn't quite so open, especially with Carlton, and especially after what happened yesterday. I pushed past him to the bathroom so I could brush my teeth.

"Keira, I'm sorry, but I have to ask. Did you go back to the funeral home last night?" His voice was quiet but steady. Sounded like his official sheriff's voice.

"No," I answered, around a mouthful of toothpaste. I didn't like the way this was beginning to sound. I finished as quickly as I could and decided to skip the flossing when I looked at his reflection in the bathroom mirror. He looked as if he was ready to cry.

Fuck.

I came out of the bathroom, brushing my hair and pulling it back into a scrunchie.

"Come on into the kitchen," I said, "I'll make some coffee." I don't really know why I wasn't letting him talk. I suppose I knew that when I did, I was going to hear something I wasn't going to want to hear.

He let me go through the routine of grinding the beans, measuring the water and flipping the switch on the pot. I'd gotten out the mugs, sugar and cream before he spoke again.

"Come on and sit down, Keira." He pulled out a chair and motioned with his hat hand. "Please."

I walked over to him, my bare feet cold on the Saltillo tile. He took a chair at the other side of the hand-hewn mesquite wood table and set his hat down next to the place mat. He looked at me directly for the first time since waking me up.

"Do you know what time Marty got back?" he asked. He spoke slowly, as if choosing his words with care. Carlton had always spoken beautifully and deliberately, determined to lose the accent his folks had bestowed on him. He'd succeeded. Acting and debate classes in high school helped him speak more like a toastmaster and less like a hick country sheriff, which he wasn't.

"No, I pretty much just came back here after—" I stopped as I remembered my side trip to the Wild Moon. I didn't think he needed to hear that.

"Marty never called you or anything?"

"Not that I know of. If he did, he didn't leave any messages." My brain was trying to clear itself of too-early-in-the-morning fuzz. Had the place been robbed? It had happened once before, bored teenagers playing I-dare-you games, breaking into the funeral home to prove their testosterone.

I watched Carlton fiddling with his hat. His index finger pushed it, then reached and pulled it back. Push. Pull. Push. Pull. He didn't look up.

The drip of the coffee maker was the only sound in the room.

"Damn it, Carlton, what's going on? Stop beating around the bush."

He looked down at the table and cleared his throat. "I'm sorry, Keira, but Marty's dead."

I looked at him. Suddenly my hands were damp and my throat wasn't. I stood up and walked over to the cupboard for a glass and got myself some cold water from the dispenser. I drank it down and filled up the glass again.

"What happened?" My voice sounded unused and old.

"We're not exactly sure. Sometime last night, after we both left, someone, or more than one someone, got into the funeral parlor. Ruben Cortez found Marty this morning when he came in to do the cleaning." Carlton cleared his throat. "Could I trouble you for some of that coffee, now?"

My hands shook as I poured us each a large mug and brought them to the table. I could barely think. He'd meant *murdered,* not just dead.

Carlton took a long sip of the steaming coffee before speaking again. When he did, I had to strain to hear him. I'd never known him to speak so softly.

"Ruben went in and found all the lights on, as if no one had bothered to turn everything off after the electricity came back on. He said he didn't think too much about it and just went around doing the morning cleaning.

"When he got to the back, he realized something was wrong. The prep room door was open, something jammed in the doorway. When he went to check, he saw your cousin."

I looked up from my coffee when the words stopped coming. Carlton was staring at his mug.

"Tell me," I whispered, not wanting to know, but needing to. My hands wrapped around the oversize mug, as if to leach the warmth out of it and into the iciness of my body.

"He was laid out on the embalming table, nude. Blood completely drained from his body. One of those small drainage tubes—" His voice broke as he talked. We sat in complete silence; the only sound penetrating our awareness was an occasional drip of water from the kitchen faucet. I sipped my coffee, eyes closed, trying to not imagine exactly what Ruben must have seen and failing. I couldn't

erase the scene that had immediately been etched on my
mind's eye—the same exact scene I'd witnessed in my
damned-further-expletives-deleted nightmares. So much
for avoiding what my brain had viciously conjured up.

Looked like today wouldn't be any better than yesterday.
In fact, it was already worse. Was there some twisted
fuck sitting somewhere in the netherworld thinking, "I'm
going to screw with Keira Kelly's life now"? I gulped as
I realized how selfish that thought was. Marty was dead.

Carlton's fist slammed down on the kitchen table,
causing me to spill what was left of my coffee. "This
shouldn't be happening here! Damn it, I came back to Rio
Seco to get away from evil, from senseless killing—and
it followed me anyway." His head dropped into his hands.

I started to reach over to comfort him, but before my
hand touched his shoulder, he stood, slapped his hat on his
head and adjusted his Sam Browne belt. The lawman had
returned, leaving the emotion behind.

"I've got to go back there, Keira." He reached over and
took my chin in his hand, tilting my face to look at his. "I
only came over here so that I could be the one to tell you.
Now, I've got work to do." He dropped his hand and hooked
his thumb in his belt again. "You going to be okay?"

I nodded, still silent, still seeing my cousin's body
motionless and white on the table, blood dripping from his
body, just like the spilled coffee dribbled onto my floor.

"Go on, Carlton. I'll manage." My voice was quiet, but
steady. I had to manage. If I really stopped to think, I might
run screaming out into the day. "Do you need me to . . ."
I let my voice fade as I asked, but he knew what I meant.

"To ID him? No. But if you need to, I can arrange for
you to view the . . . him. Before the autopsy."

I nodded. I didn't want to, but I had to. In order to

convince myself this wasn't all part of the same bad dream that had started yesterday or the day before, or whenever the hell it had been. Whatever had happened, I needed to know for the clan's sake. They may have disowned Marty, but they would want to know.

"Take your time," he said. "It'll take us some time to finish at the mortuary. We don't have much in the way of up-to-date forensics here, but I called in a favor. A friend of mine is coming in from SAPD to help. I'll call you when we're ready for you." Carlton walked out the front door and turned as he reached the bottom porch step. I stood there staring at him, still not saying a word.

"Keira, until we find out what's happening here, please be careful. Keep all your doors and windows locked. We don't know who's done this." He adjusted his hat like some mockery of a movie cowboy and walked away.

I knew I'd have to try to reach Tucker to let him know about Marty, but not right this second. Before I called anyone, I wanted to think. I needed to put a little distance between what I'd just heard and talking to my brother.

I poured myself another cup of coffee and sank into my favorite easy chair. Who on earth would have wanted to hurt my cousin? Obnoxious? Yes. Annoying? Absolutely. But I couldn't think of why he'd been marked for death. Poor Marty, his life span was so short anyway. To have it cut even shorter was pure irony.

NIGHTMARE WAS NOT THE WORD for what I experienced during the rest of the morning. Bizarre phantasms and kaleidoscope horrors blended together with my mind's interpretation of what Marty must have looked like when the killer had finished with him. Maybe I shouldn't have gone back to bed, but since I'd gotten only a couple of hours of sleep, I'd figured that some rest was better than none. I wanted to be rested before having to face either my brother or looking at my cousin's dead body.

But rest was not what I'd gotten. Instead, my brain kept replaying my nightmare, only this time, every time I tried to leave, Marty appeared in front of me, miles of plastic tubing emerging from his body, filled with his blood and dripping on the floor. I'd try to push the table out of the way, but every time I grabbed the edge, Marty sat up and told me that I was trapped and I had to take the blood.

On the third or fourth round of this gruesome cycle, I woke up. A deafening clap of thunder knocked me out of dreamland and into the damp early afternoon of the same awful day. So much for a restful sleep.

I took my time showering and getting dressed. I didn't want to face the reality of being awake. Maybe if I stayed home and didn't talk to anyone, this whole thing would go away.

But the world intruded when I walked into the living room. My brother was sitting in my easy chair, a mug in his hand and an easy grin on his face.

"Hey there," he said. "Good coffee."

He nodded toward the answering machine, which was blinking malevolently on its small stand. "You've got messages."

"You listened to my messages?"

He shrugged. "Not exactly. I've been here for a few hours. I didn't want to wake you up. I heard the messages when they called."

I took the cup from my brother and sank into the couch across from him, slugging down a healthy dose of caffeine. He was right—it was good coffee.

"Who called?"

Tucker frowned. "Bea called, three times. Then your old friend, the sheriff. Did I hear him right? Is Marty dead?"

I nodded. "Yeah, Carlton stopped by earlier to tell me. The cleaning service found him."

"Dead how?"

"Murdered."

The word sounded so blunt, so final.

"Any ideas?"

I shook my head. "No, I was going to go over there, to—"

"Look at the body?"

More blunt words.

"Yeah."

"Good idea. Want me to come with you?"

I looked at him relaxing in the chair, all denim shirt, chinos and topsiders, a six-foot-four pale-faced pseudo-yuppie sporting a braid longer than Willie Nelson's and a history longer than most European countries. No one looking at him now would be able to guess his true nature. He really was my favorite brother.

I smiled a little. "Yeah, I'd love it if you came with me."

He smiled back. "Anytime you're ready."

I drained the remains of the coffee and stood up. "Tell you what, let's stop by Bea's first and get food before we go to the Sheriff's office. I need a little fortification."

Tucker grinned as he followed me out the front door. "Oh yeah, there was one more call."

I glanced over my shoulder as crossed the porch. My brother's grin widened.

"Adam Walker. Wanted to know about dinner."

Oh, great. Another complication I didn't need right now.

"Did he leave a number?" I asked, ignoring my brother's silent, but obvious question.

"I already programmed it into your cell phone."

He ducked as I swung my backpack at his head.

I GAVE IN and told Tucker about seeing Adam last night. Although he hadn't been in England while I was there, he knew about what happened with Gideon. Tucker had been the only member of my family to listen to me when I'd come back. It still hadn't stopped him from emigrating, though.

"I agree with Bea," he said.

"What?" I grunted as I pulled into the café parking lot.

"Go out with the guy, see what happens."

"Shit, don't you start," I said. "Besides, we need to find out what happened to Marty before I think about anything like a date."

Tucker smiled as he unfastened his seat belt. "That wasn't a 'no.'"

"It wasn't," I said. "But it wasn't an 'I'm going to jump his bones' either. Let's just get through today and worry about the rest later."

"Deal," he said.

Neither Bea nor Noe were out front, but Carlton sat at the same booth as he had yesterday morning, as if he'd never left. Piles of dishes and cups were pushed to one side. He was reading from a stack of papers. Well, shit. Didn't he have an office to go to? Or a murder investigation to conduct . . . somewhere else?

Without looking in his direction, I motioned to Tucker to follow me and walked past the cash-wrap and into the kitchen. The place was in chaos. Noe was up to his shoulders in dishwater and dirty plates in the sinks, while

Bea's elderly Aunt Petra sat on a tall stool peeling potatoes. Two equally elderly uncles were scurrying back and forth, various kitchen implements in hand, stirring pots of steaming food.

Bea appeared out of the storeroom underneath an industrial-sized sack of carrots. She hefted the bag onto the counter, whirled around and ran back into the storeroom, a bare nod of acknowledgement to us.

"Hey, Tucker, Keira, hang on a sec, 'kay?" she said over her shoulder as she rummaged through stacks of canned goods. "It's only a couple of hours until I have to serve the early dinner specials and I still need to make the carrot salad." The rest of her words were lost as she stuck her head between shelves.

"*Aqui, m'hija,*" said Tia Petra, patting a stool next to her. "You don't want to get dirty." She smiled and climbed back onto her own stool to peel more potatoes. Tucker followed and stood next to me. "Beatriz is worried. Those men never came to work today."

I looked at her with a frown. I opened my mouth to speak, when Bea came out of the storeroom balancing a large can on either arm. Petra's husband, Richard, took the cans from Bea and went back over to the stove. "Thank you," he said in his quiet, low voice. "I will begin the enchiladas."

Bea smiled her thanks at him then came over to me. "I'm so sorry to hear about Marty," she said as she grabbed me in a bear hug and kissed my cheek. "Are you okay? I was worried." She shot a glance at Tucker. "When did he get here?"

"Last night," I said. "I went to sleep after Carlton left. Nothing but nightmares. But I'll be fine."

She grimaced. "We've been pretty swamped all day,"

she said, starting to chop carrots. "The two idiots didn't show up to work and they're not answering the phone at their apartment." She chopped even harder. "I had to call in family to help."

So the Albrights had proven their reputation. I wasn't surprised.

Bea snorted, her knife hitting the chopping block with an audible thunk. Orange-colored slices flew off as her blade bit into the roots. "And *ese*"—she nodded toward her nephew, who was out of earshot—"decides to sleep in this morning and not show up until nearly ten. Petra and I handled breakfast rush. That boy is becoming worse than useless."

I watched Bea for a few more minutes, listening to the clanging of pots and pans and the normal kitchen busyness. I wanted to offer to help, but the last time I'd tried to help in the kitchen, Bea had thanked me and asked me to never do it again. I'd managed to ruin an entire night's special by mixing up tablespoons and teaspoons. Tucker stayed silent, observing the chaos.

Bea swept the last of the chopped carrots into a large metal bowl and handed it over to Aunt Petra. "Here, *Tia,* would you start the salad for me?" She wiped her hands on her apron then turned back to me. "Come on, you two, we need to talk," she said, and took off in the direction of her office. We followed her.

"Close the door," she said, settling into her chair. I did as she asked and sat down, Tucker settled beside me. "Tell me, what exactly happened? Sheriff-man out there isn't saying much even though he's been sitting in my café for the better part of two hours."

I wasn't sure where to start, so I told her everything. From the nightmares of Marty's death to what Carlton had told me. She was silent after I finished talking, her normally mobile face still.

"Damn, Sis," Tucker said quietly. "You dreamed all of this?"

Bea shook her head slowly from side to side. "I can't believe all of this," she said, her voice uneven. "Things like this don't happen in Rio Seco." She took both my hands in hers, pulled me over and grabbed me in a bear hug. "Are you okay? Really, okay?"

I stood up, pulling away from her hug.

"Okay? I have no earthly idea. I'm not sure what to feel. I don't feel like crying. I'm pissed off, at Marty, at myself for—damn it, I don't have any clue what the hell I'm supposed to do."

I felt as if I'd been set adrift in a bad *Twilight Zone* episode and if I looked closely, I'd see a skinny man in a dark suit standing in the corner, ready to announce the next episode. This was all too unreal.

"You're not supposed to feel fake feelings," Tucker said, his blunt honesty refreshing. "Keira . . ." He grabbed my hand and pulled me back into the chair. I hadn't realized I'd started pacing. "You never liked Marty and it's not your fault he died."

I leaned over and put my head in my hands, not wanting to hear him. Wallowing was better than having to deal with this guilt.

"It would be better if it was my fault," I mumbled around my hands.

Tucker's hand smoothed an awkward path down my back. He'd never seen me like this, not his all-together smart-ass sister.

"Damn, that really sucks," said Bea. "I don't know what to tell you. Marty was an asshole, but I know you didn't want him to be murdered. You had nothing to do with it. All you did was dream about it."

"But what if I'd told him?"

Both Bea and Tucker snorted at this.

"C'mon, Sis, you really think he would have listened?"

"He's right, Keira. Let's be honest here. Marty was about as fond of you as you were of him. He never listened to you about anything else, why would he have done so now?"

I shrugged Tucker's hand away and stood up again.

"I know, you're both right," I said. "But I was responsible for him."

"And you went over there," Bea said. "He wasn't there, was he?"

"No," I agreed. "He wasn't."

"There, then." Bea said it like everything was settled. I wasn't so sure.

"Now, if you want to do something, you should go talk to Carlton. I imagine that there's going to be a lot of red tape or whatever before you can even think about a funeral."

Oh, great, a funeral. I was going to have to plan my cousin's funeral. I looked over at Tucker who was trying not to chortle too audibly. He had another thing coming if he didn't believe I'd ask him to help with arrangements.

Bea stood up and glanced at her watch. "I'm sorry I can't be more help right, now, *m'hija,* but I've got to work the dinner rush. I can't expect my relatives to do it by themselves." She sighed and ran her fingers through her hair. "Damn it, Keira, I wish there was something I could do for you. Stuff like this is always too weird. I never know what to say."

I got out of the chair and gave her a hug. "Thanks, Bea. It's enough that you're here."

"You know I'll help any way I can," said Bea. "Just let me know if you need me. I'll be here until at least eight tonight, but then I can come over and stay with you." She shot a sideways glance at my brother. "Although, I think Tucker here has a handle on things." She smiled a brilliant smile and batted her lashes a little.

Tucker looked as if he'd been punched in the belly. His eyes narrowed a moment, then a thoughtful look crossed his face.

I grabbed his arm and pulled him toward the door.

"Thanks, girl. You know how much I appreciate it."

It was time to face Carlton.

CHAPTER EIGHT

I TOOK A DEEP BREATH and walked over to the booth where Carlton was muttering over a stack of papers. This could be awkward.

"Hey, Carlton," I began, not exactly sure of what I wanted to or should say.

"Hey, Keira," he replied, setting down the paper he was reading. He looked up at me, the expression on his face solemn, then puzzled as he saw Tucker.

"You remember my brother, Tucker?"

Carlton nodded. "Hey."

Tucker looked at me, then at Carlton, then disengaged my arm from his. "I'll just grab a cup of coffee, then go over to the deli," he said. "I need to pick up a few things. Take as long as you need."

I frowned at him, wondering what he was up to. "Okay," I said. "Meet me out by the car in about fifteen?"

"Sure thing. Carlton, good to see you." Tucker smiled a little and left the café.

Shifting a few papers and making room, Carlton invited me to sit.

I slid in across from him, clasping my hands together on the table, mostly to keep from fidgeting.

"That was sure quick," he said.

"What?"

"Your brother. He got here quick."

I smiled a little. "He was already here," I said.

"Oh."

Carlton toyed with his mug for a few moments.

"How you holding up?"

Suddenly, I wished I had a glass of tea or bowl of popcorn or something to keep my hands busy. I felt awkward and out of place. It was one thing to talk to Bea and Tucker, but another entirely to talk to Carlton. I didn't have to hide what I was from my friend and my brother. The sheriff was another story. He'd expect me to be the bereaved cousin. To feel human emotions I wasn't familiar with.

I'd helped so many cross the veil over the last dozen years. Performed the deed for clan members who'd had enough of eternal living and wanted to move on, watched as death sentences were carried out by my clan chief. Those deaths didn't bother me. They were part and parcel of my world. I really did know Death well. But he wasn't supposed to visit my human cousin, not yet. Marty should have died of old age or illness. He was an undertaker, for pity's sake. Not a mob boss or a drug dealer. His life was about as risk-free as a human life got—yet he'd been murdered and right under my nose. My mind was numb, empty, guilt still at the top of the confusing emotions. Marty had been in my charge and I'd failed.

"I just don't know, Carlton," I said. "This whole thing has been so bizarre. I keep feeling like someone's taken over my life and dropped me into a bad movie."

I started playing with a napkin from a stack on the table, folding and refolding it. "You know Marty and I weren't close. Hell, we were about as far apart as two relatives could be while still living in the same town. But, maybe if I'd stuck around until he got back, or—"

Carlton's hand landed on my forearm, sending a quick buzz along my skin. "Stop that thinking right now, Keira," he said in a stern voice. "What if you had been there and whoever attacked your cousin had attacked you, too?"

They'd have been dead instead, I thought viciously. I'm not only an Escort to the other side, but I was trained to fight, most of us were. I'd danced with Death daily until two years ago. But I'd left the mortuary and left my cousin to his doom, running away from something as intangible as a vision, not wanting to face it.

Carlton pulled his hand back and absently wiped the condensation from the side of his tea glass. "You could have been hurt or killed, too." He stared at his glass and wouldn't meet my eyes.

"I don't want to be the adult here, Carlton," I said. "I just want to go back to my house and pretend none of this happened." I wadded up the pieces of paper napkin that I'd torn into shreds. "I want to go back to yesterday morning."

"Keira, I don't rightly know what to tell you. I can't make time run backward. All I can do is to try to figure out this mess and find out who did this to Marty."

He looked up; his dark eyes showed both sadness and concern. As I met his gaze, something else flared briefly behind the worry. Damn it, even with everything that had happened, his desire was still there, a small flame behind the darkness. I dropped my eyes and stared at my hands. How much more convoluted could this all get?

"Keira, I talked to my friend a little bit ago. The forensics tech . . ." He hesitated, as if to make sure I was listening. I'd picked up another paper napkin and was folding it into a fan shape. When I realized what he was trying to tell me, I set it down and placed my hands flat on the table. I didn't look up though.

He paused and took a sip of tea. "She's pretty sure Marty was already dead when . . ."

I let out a breath of relief. I'd imagined the worst—that my cousin had been alive and aware when his murderer stuck the tube into his jugular to drain him of blood.

"Does she have any idea how he died?"

"Nothing obvious," he said. "No trauma to his body, other than the— We'll know more after the autopsy. Do you still want to see him?"

I nodded. "I really think I have to. Tucker's going with me. Where'd they take him? San Antonio or Blanco County?"

His face turned red and he looked down at his hands. After a moment, I caught the clue bus.

"Shit, Carlton, he's still here?"

"I'm sorry, Keira, but it's the only thing I could do for now. Both morgues are backed up. A bunch of staff are out sick. No one can come get him until sometime tomorrow morning. I'm trying to speed things up since it's a homicide, but no one's returned my call yet. We had to put him somewhere. It was convenient."

"Thanks, I get the picture." I changed the subject. "I imagine you have to come with us?"

"Yeah," he said. "I need to go through the place again, see if anything's missing. Take a look at his files, check financial records, you know. We did the obvious stuff, but I want to look for the not-so-obvious." He looked at me, trying to tell me something with his eyes. I wasn't up to reading eye language.

"What, Carlton?"

"I hate to ask you this, but would you be willing to help me dig through the files? Maybe you'll be able to tell if something's missing or different?"

Damn it. Even dead my cousin was dragging me into things I wanted no part of. I'd been planning to take a quick look at Marty's body and then get out of there. But this could take a while.

"Maybe," I said. "But honestly, I really didn't spend a lot of time there. I don't know how much help I'll be. Tucker would be more than useless."

"I'd appreciate it," he said, keeping his voice soft. His eyes stayed fixed on mine. I saw a mix of emotions whirling behind them. I stared back, letting the doubt I felt reflect in my own eyes.

He looked away first. "Look, Keira, I promise," he said softly, "this will be strictly business, routine."

I nodded. It would have to be. I wasn't about to let him get away with anything. Besides, my brother would be there.

THE BUILDING looked much the same as always. Quiet, secluded. A beautiful structure, two stories of red brick and soft gray-green shutters making it look more like a large comfortable home instead of a house for the dead. Marty's grandfather built it when the family had first settled in the area almost one hundred years ago.

Carlton parked his truck in the front. We pulled in directly behind him. He'd wanted us all to ride together, but I'd wanted an escape route, just in case things got . . . difficult.

One end of the yellow police tape across the door had come loose and the strip hung diagonally in front of the round stained-glass window, reminding me of an international "no" sign. All I could think of was "no death." Yeah, right.

"Do you have keys?" I asked, a little belatedly, already turning to go back to my car for the set I kept in the glove box.

Carlton nodded. "I got them from the janitor. You wouldn't happen to know which key it is, do you?"

I shook my head. "No. I have a set, but I've never had to use them. I didn't exactly come by here very often."

Carlton was having trouble finding the right key. Evidently, none of them were marked.

"I locked the door when we left this morning," he said. "After . . . there, I got it."

The lock clicked open and the three of us walked into the hush of the lobby. It seemed quieter than normal, if that was even possible. No sounds broke the silence, not even the hiss of the ventilation system. It was truly a house of the dead now.

Damn it. I really did not want to be here, even with my brother. Marty's body was inside, cold and still, decaying with every passing minute. If I were smart, I should just leave it all the hell alone. Let the medical examiner's office come in the morning and pick him up, cut him open and make the official determination. We'd find out in a day or two. Carlton didn't really need us, he could just as easily sort through files all on his own.

But some piece of the darkness deep inside me made me come here; some morbid curiosity or just plain need to regain control over my discombobulated life. I needed to know.

"Is the prep room locked?" I asked, my voice overly loud in the silence.

"Not exactly," he said. "I didn't know the combination to the door, so I left it propped open in case I needed to get back in there."

Oh, great. My perverse brain suddenly pictured the room wide open, police tape strung across the entrance like the velvet rope in a museum diorama. In this corner, the bloody table . . . at the far left, ladies and gentlemen, if you look closely, you can even see the body of the deceased. Step up now, don't want to miss the show.

Get a grip, Keira Kelly, I thought. Dead bodies weren't exactly unusual around here. Even if this one had been the proprietor.

A piece of duct tape was stuck across the locking mechanism of the prep room door; a small metal trash can kept it from closing. I started to step through and abruptly stopped. Carlton had followed behind me; he was so close now, I could feel his breath on the back of my hair. Tucker was behind the sheriff.

"I need to do this alone."

"I don't think you should go by yourself, Keira. I can—"

"Tucker can come with me, Carlton."

He stepped back. I didn't look at him. I couldn't.

"Are you sure?"

"I am." I'd never been more sure of anything.

"I'll be in the office."

I let him leave, then took a deep breath, trying to will myself to move across the floor. The air smelled dry, a touch of formaldehyde lingered, mixed with a slight scent of something I didn't recognize . . . not blood. My body hesitated, not wanting to make the move toward the stainless steel door at the far side, just opposite the no-longer-gleaming embalming table. There was the source of the odor. Smudges of black fingerprint powder smeared across the once shiny surface, dulling it. Everything was grimy with it, the work counter, the sinks and most of the equipment at that end of the room.

I stared at the table, wondering if Marty had felt anything when whoever began draining the life from him . . . and the blood. Carlton hadn't lied. There wasn't a trace of blood anywhere. Just the dirty black powder. But I was letting myself get distracted.

"I don't smell anything." My brother's voice echoed in the silent room.

"Anything like what?"

"Like what could have killed him," he said. "The place is so . . . sterile."

"Yeah, I know," I agreed. "All those chemicals."

I looked across the room. "Shall we?"

"After you, dear sister." He smiled and sketched a polite bow. Gee thanks, I thought. Let me go first.

After what seemed an eternity, we reached the heavy metal door that was the only barrier between me and the true Dead Zone—the refrigeration unit. Instead of wall cubbies with drawers that slid out bodies like loaves of bread on a proofing rack, this was a walk-in model. Four corpses, no waiting. The unit sat tucked into the far left corner of the prep room, its shining door hiding the fact that behind it lay the ultimate indignity of humans. The end of their sadly short lives, laid out like the daily butcher's special cut, $9.99 a pound, today only.

But this wasn't just any anonymous corpse. This was what was left of my cousin. A body now, not a person anymore, just a thing that had already begun breaking down into its essential elements, ready for the earth to swallow it back up and disintegrate into nothing more than molecules.

I took a deep breath before I opened the door. Strangely enough, the unit was bright, not intimidating in the least. For some reason, I'd imagined a spooky cavern, lined with shelves of the dead, kind of a cross between a restaurant's Sub-Zero walk-in and the Catacombs. But this was just a plain stainless steel room, a couple of shelves on the right wall, both empty. The room's sole occupant lay on a gurney in the center, wrapped in its very own giant economy-sized Ziploc.

Damn. This was for real now. What was in that bag wasn't the remains of the Jolly Green Giant's fried chicken lunch, but my cousin. Before I stepped over the threshold and committed myself to this foolishness, I double-checked the door. Good, it opened easily. I wasn't keen on the possibility of being locked in here, even though Tucker was here and Carlton was just down the hall.

I had to move, but felt as if I'd been dipped in wet cement that was now drying. My muscles didn't want to reach over there and do what needed to be done.

Tucker started to step around me.

"No," I said, putting out a hand and stopping him. "I need to do this."

He stepped back without comment.

Eons later, I allowed myself to pull down the zipper on the body bag, trying to be as careful as possible. As the plastic fell away from Marty's face, I cringed. I'd expected his skin to be discolored, but instead, it was white and waxy looking—unreal. He didn't even have enough blood left to turn him gray. At this point, he looked even less human than me.

Okay, Keira, damn it. You got this far. Now what? Had I hoped to have an automatic vision of who'd killed him? I wish. But that kind of power wasn't so easily tamed. Even if I did end up a clairvoyant, the likelihood I'd be able to control my farseeing was about as probable as Marty rising from the dead. Well, less likely. With the right spells and a powerful necromancer, the rising part could actually happen. A necromancer who could call up the dead. My uncle couldn't, but there was a woman I might be able to call.

She lived somewhere in Missouri—St. Louis, if I recalled correctly. But she was expensive and usually booked solid for days. I had no idea if I even still had her contact information. I suppose if I needed to, I could track her down.

I took another experimental sniff, but couldn't scent anything but me, the odor of the plastic around my cousin's body and a weak hint of blood, dried blood, nothing fresh.

"Tucker?"

"Yeah?"

"Something's not right."

"What do you mean?

I told him what I'd seen in my vision, blood dripping across Marty's body, along the drainage channels of the embalming table.

"Shouldn't there be more blood? A fresher scent?"

"Probably," Tucker said. "But are you sure the vision was accurate?"

"No, but even if I'm wrong, Carlton said they found Marty with a tube sticking from his neck. Again with the draining." I pointed. "Look. He's clean. Pale, but clean. No spilled blood."

The alarm bells dinged in my brain. Suddenly, the ante had been upped. Way up.

I leaned in to get a closer look at the wounds on my cousin's neck.

"Damnitalltohell and back again."

My brother leaned over me and saw the same thing I did.

The marks in my cousin's pale neck had absolutely not been made by any machined device. Those punctures were just the right space apart to have been made by a jaw. A human-shaped jaw with non-human teeth.

"Fuck." My brother was nothing if not succinct.

"My thoughts exactly, big brother," I said.

Now what? Was I going to go out and tell Carlton that my cousin Marty was probably drained by something that most people thought only existed in movies and novels? Not bloody likely. I was sure there was an end to Carlton's suspension of disbelief. Telling him that my cousin may have been murdered by a vampire was a little far-fetched.

"Vampire?"

I shrugged. "Maybe, I can't be one-hundred percent sure. They don't exactly leave little signs behind saying 'Vlad was here.' But I'll lay odds that it was."

"You're probably right, Keira. But let's not forget, some of us might go for a quick blood-suck instead of a traditional ripping out of the throat. Much neater that way."

"Yeah, but damn it, Tucker, it sure looks like a vampire bite. Look, check this out." I pointed to one of the wounds. "This hole is bigger, torn. That must be where they put the drainage tube. The other one's too neat. It's classic."

"Classic bite, yeah," my brother said. "But we can't exactly jump to any conclusions. Just because we think something supernatural killed him, we can't be sure."

He was right, we couldn't shut the gates of possibility on any other theory. Just in case.

"Keira? Tucker. Are y'all okay in there?"

I shot a look at my brother, who quickly pulled the plastic back over Marty's face and zipped up the bag. The door opened.

"I'm sorry," he said. "I was worried about you two. You've been in here a while."

"Thanks, Carlton, but we're fine. It's just . . . we needed a little time to digest this." I let my shoulders drop, trying to look dejected and sad. Tucker put an arm across my shoulders.

"We're done now. Thank you."

"Come on," Carlton said. "Why don't we go back to the office and y'all can help me sort through files."

I let him lead us out of the room and down the hall, wincing as each door shut behind me, so very final. Tucker walked behind me, his solid presence oddly comforting.

"What are we looking for?" I asked Carlton.

"I'm not really sure," he said, "We searched the rest of the place pretty thoroughly. Nothing but the usual mortuary supplies. Some of that stuff I didn't want to look at any closer. I'm just glad there weren't any bodies or anything."

"Did you search upstairs?"

"Marty's apartment?" Carlton looked at me as if I were a two-year-old asking useless questions. He obviously thought better of what he'd been on the verge of saying and nodded. "Yeah. We can go up there if you like, it's pretty messy."

"That's nothing unusual," I said. "Marty is . . . was a pig."

"Nice entertainment system, though," Carlton said.

I looked at him. "What?"

"The big screen TV, Surround sound and all that electronic stuff. Haven't you seen it?"

"Hold that thought." I took the stairs two at a time, Tucker right behind me.

Marty's rooms were just as messy and uninviting as Carlton said. Clothes piled all over the floor of the bedroom, unmade bed, stacks of junk mail and newspapers teetering on the edge of the secondhand coffee table I'd given him when I'd first moved to London some ten years ago. In fact, every piece of furniture was one of my hand-me-downs. Except, that is, for the giant sixty-inch big screen TV and brand-new entertainment center gracing the far wall of the small residence.

Curiouser and curiouser.

"What the hell kind of game was Marty playing?" I asked out loud.

"What do you mean?"

"This." I waved a hand at the room. "Fancy stereo equipment. Top of the line speakers, components. Bang & Olufsen? Marty could barely afford Kmart. I wouldn't be surprised if whatever he was up to was illegal."

Tucker grimaced and poked at one of the many remotes scattered across the cheap coffee table.

"Not too big of a leap, Keira. How much you want to bet Marty was playing with the big boys—vamps, predators or just someone not so nice? He probably did something stupid and got killed for it. Maybe he owed money?"

Now that made a kind of sense that shouted Marty's name.

Especially when my pity-poor-me, always-broke relative had somehow managed to outfit his shabby home with enough equipment to put the average household in debt for the next several years. All this in a twenty-by-thirteen living/dining room combo.

I was furious. Not at myself anymore, but at my cousin. Whatever he'd gotten himself into had gotten him dead.

"Carlton, Marty could not have afforded all that equipment up there," I said as Tucker and I came back down the stairs. "Especially not after doing all of this, too." I waved my hands around.

Carlton looked at me. "All of what?"

"This," I said, pointing things out. "New paint, new furniture, everything. This is all brand-new, Carlton. When I was in here yesterday I figured that business must be picking up, but I can't imagine there was enough to finance this plus the electronics."

"Shit," Tucker exclaimed. "He decorated, too?"

"That's what I want to look for," Carlton said. "Reasons he might have been killed. If he's suddenly been flashing cash, he's had to have gotten it from somewhere. Do you know what he was up to?"

I opened my mouth to say something about the phone call yesterday, but then thought better of it, remembering what Marty had said. Blood ties and family—not something to concern our Sheriff and most probably something to do with the vampire or whoever ended up killing him. Shit. Shit. Shit. He hadn't been exaggerating and I'd ignored it. But it was my business. I'd tell Tucker, but not Carlton. I just shook my head.

"No idea."

The three of us went into Marty's office and Carlton motioned to the desk. "Keira, why don't you sit there and look through the drawers. See if you think anything's missing. Tucker, can you sit here and help sort?"

My brother pulled a chair over to my left. Carlton scooted the other one close to my other side. I pulled away a little, already feeling the buzz surrounding him. Damn it, my shields should be better than this; he wasn't even touching me. Since being around Adam, it was like I was a little more sensitive to everything, a little more thin-skinned. Until yesterday, I'd have taken bets that seeing Carlton again wouldn't be any big deal, that he could no longer affect me. Now I wasn't so sure. I didn't feel any attraction toward him, though. I could just feel his energy against me, buzzing like a swarm of angry bees.

Tucker's elbow poked me in the side. I looked at him

briefly, making a face, then turned my attention to the contents of the drawers. "I never really kept up with what was here, but I'll give it a try," I said, ignoring my brother. I knew he could feel Carlton's energy, too. As a shapeshifter, he was better at it than I was. He also wasn't above a little teasing.

I started to pull out what I found, passing it over to Tucker so he could stack it next to the desk. Mostly junk in the first drawer, advertising fliers, office supplies, and trade show giveaways, including a black "gimme" cap stating "Any Day Above Ground Is a Good Day." I plopped the cap on the desk and continued to dig through the files. I wanted to take it home with me. For some reason, its dark wit appealed to me.

Carlton smiled when he saw it. "Gotta love mortician humor. Anything worthwhile in there?" His voice drawled out the question.

"Not so much," I said. "Mostly junk and blank forms." As I spoke, I glanced down at the handful of blue sheets I'd just dug out from underneath the pile of junk. "Wait a minute," I said. "Maybe I was wrong," I said. "From the looks of these, business really was pretty brisk."

"What are those?" Tucker asked.

"Looks like first-call logs and copies of contracts," I answered. "Marty filled out a log whenever he got a call to pick up a body. It opens the file on a service. Hmmm. A lot of these are fairly recent—from the last couple of months or so. Maybe he's just behind in his filing. Looks like a bunch of cremations."

I nodded my head in the direction of a two-drawer filing cabinet in the corner of the room. "We should really check those files out. I think that's where Marty kept the completed records for funerals."

The cabinet was unlocked. Carlton pulled out a stack of files and brought them back to the desk, piling them on the floor between us. None of us spoke as we sifted through the folders; the silence unbroken except for the quiet *whirr* of the ventilation system fan coming to life and the sound of us shuffling paper.

This was going to take a while. So much for tidiness and logic. Marty obviously didn't believe in it. There were thousands of pieces of paper in these files and not a whole lot of order to them. Bank papers were mixed in with advertising fliers for mortuary supplies and even completed funeral contracts. I wondered how his accountant could even stand working on his books. I'd begun sorting the piles into stacks, separating the obvious junk from the financial information. Both Carlton and Tucker were making their own piles.

"Okay," I finally said. "I think I've got it all sorted out." I pointed to a pile on the left. "Those are bank deposits by month, in reverse chron. Here's a printout of the last twenty or so funerals, just the bottom line stuff. Looks like an accounting report of some sort."

"Why don't we compare those to the deposits," Carlton said. "That might show us if everything matches."

Tucker stood up. "While you two do that, mind if I stretch my legs a bit and wander around outside?"

"Sounds like a plan, bro," I said, reading between the lines. Tucker needed to get out in the fresh air. He'd been cooped up indoors for too long. Besides, while he was out there, he could snoop around.

I smiled at him. "We shouldn't be too much longer." Tucker left the office and I turned back to Carlton. "Why don't I read off the names and amounts and see if you can match them to deposits?"

Carlton took off his Stetson and put it down on the floor beside him. "Shoot."

"Willner, total, $7,345.54. A deposit of $4,000 on April twenty-second, then a balance payment on May first."

"Check," he said. "Both numbers are here.

"Hinojosa, $2,000, then balance of $2,538.76."

"Got it."

"Tschirhart, $6,000, then $6,653.47."

"Damn, that's a lot of money," Carlton said. "Hell, my dad's funeral was way cheaper than that."

"Burials aren't cheap, Carlton," I said. "Plus, the markup on this stuff is outrageous and Marty was pretty ruthless about upselling. I may not have liked him, but he knew his business. Besides, didn't your dad buy a pre-need service?"

"He did. Between that and the allotment from the military, my brother and I didn't have to shell out any extra money. We bought a nice headstone instead."

"That's the point of pre-needs. The family doesn't have to worry about all that money or making decisions in the middle of grieving. Marty used to try to sell them everywhere he could. It was kind of upfront money for him. He even bothered customers at the café until Bea put a stop to it."

Carlton and I kept at it a while longer, matching each payment amount to corresponding amounts on the bank deposit tickets. Not a bad bit of change, but nothing outside normal parameters. About twenty funerals over the last four months. It sounded like a lot to me, but I recognized a lot of the names. Most of the folks had been rather elderly and their deaths were expected and these things seemed to happen in groups. Mr. Willner was nearly ninety, Honoria Hinojosa was seventy-eight. Ron Tschirhart was only sixty-three when he died, but I knew he'd been diagnosed with terminal cancer of some sort early this year.

But no matter the income, the outgo was pretty hefty, too. I saw receipts for caskets, urns, embalming chemicals and cosmetics, the usual expenses for a working funeral home, not to mention the standard building-type overhead: gas, electric and water. I didn't want to sit there and figure out the margins, but from the looks of it, money was as tight as it always had been for Marty. I didn't see any evidence of how he'd paid for the redecorating or the electronics. He hadn't asked me for the money.

I sighed. I was obviously not going to find the proverbial anonymous letter or "X" marking the spot. But a few minutes later, I found something even better.

"Carlton, look at this," I said, "This isn't Marty's regular business account. He's always banked locally." I handed him a bank statement from a Houston bank.

Carlton let out a low whistle. "Shit, that's a lot of money." The balance, from last month, showed a sum just under $100,000. I took a quick look at the transactions printed on the front: several deposits, each one for several thousand dollars, all in even amounts—$5,000, $5,000, $7,500 and $10,000.

"Where the hell did my cousin get that much cash?"

"That's what I'd like to know," said Carlton, as he carefully folded it up and tucked it into his pocket. He checked his watch. "It's late. I'll have to call the bank in the morning and see what I can find out. Money like this could easily provide a motive for murder."

"Don't you need a warrant or something?"

"Probably, but I'll call them first. Sometimes you get lucky."

He turned to look at me, a strange look on his face.

"You know, Keira, I'm beginning to think that if we keep looking, we may find a connection to the animal mutilations at the Wild Moon."

"Excuse me?" As I said that, I realized that maybe he wasn't so far off the mark. Until now, I'd forgotten what Boris had said to me yesterday. "Tell him," he'd said. Had he meant Marty? Damn. Could be. As far as Boris knew, there was no other "him" associated with me. He wouldn't have known Tucker was in town. Didn't know about Adam. Wouldn't put Carlton and me together since the Nagys hadn't come to town until after both Carlton and I had left. That only left Marty and my assumption that my cousin had been playing with the undead.

Would vampires hunt deer? Hmm, now that was a thought. I suppose they could. There were plenty of deer roaming around Rio Seco County.

"What makes you think the two are related?" I wanted to know what Carlton thought. I knew his theory couldn't even begin to touch mine.

"I'm not sure I know what I mean." He paused a moment then looked at me. "It's mostly a hunch. I told you those deer were completely blooded, like they'd been field-dressed. What I didn't say was that I didn't find a trace of spilled blood anywhere at the scene, just like here. Like Marty. I'm not a big fan of coincidence."

He looked down at the file in his hands, avoiding my gaze. Well, then, our sheriff might just be able to put two and two together. The fact that in this instance, two and two were more likely to make something closer to *pi* instead of the usual "four" would probably be his undoing. Hard to explain this kind of crime by ordinary means, motive, and opportunity.

I flashed back to my passenger of last night. Could

Adam be involved in any way? He had come out to the mortuary in search of my cousin, but that could have been for any number of reasons. Mundane reasons. Reasons that had nothing to do with the fact my cousin was dead . . . maybe. Damn it. Besides, Adam was human, and as far as I was concerned, this really was beginning to sound an awful lot like revenge. Revenge of a level of perversity that I could only attribute to clan, maybe not mine, but someone's family group. Creatures like us were the masters of warped payback, even more twisted than any human serial killer. When you lived nearly forever, you could spend time thinking of really sick things to do to your enemies, like treating them as if they were just another corpse to process.

"I think I need to go back out there," Carlton said.

"Out to the Wild Moon?"

Carlton scowled at me, but nodded. "Yeah, although I can't imagine why any of those rich tourists would have any reason to even know Marty, much less care enough to kill him."

I could give him a couple, but wouldn't. Complete privacy at an exclusive resort ranch could hide many things, even from its owner and including the supernatural. If my cousin had done something to piss off a couple of predators, this was family business. I'd let Carlton follow his leads and if he pulled out a rabbit, I'd applaud. If what I suspected was right, this might end up being an unsolved murder—officially, anyway. I'd be doing my own hunting down of clues, at least until I could discover whether or not this was something to pursue further.

"I can't rule anyone out, Keira. I do need to go out to the ranch before those tourists leave to go back to wherever they're from. Right now, I don't have enough reason to make anyone stay if they don't want to. People do tend to scatter when they hear there's a murder investigation."

"I'm sure you'll do your best, Carlton."

I started to gather up all the papers and stuff them back into the file drawer. He was going to do what he had to do. So was I. In the meantime, I was going to clean up the mess I'd made and then go back to my nice, quiet house, and figure out what to do next.

"Hey, Keira, did you know anything about Derek Albright working for Marty?"

Carlton had stopped filing away the papers and was looking at something that looked like a cancelled check.

"I saw him here yesterday," I said. "He told me he was working here. He's also working for Bea. He left right after I saw him. Why?"

"Check this out."

I looked where he was pointing. It was a check made out to Derek Albright for fifteen hundred dollars.

"Well, shit," I said. "Now, that's different. That's a hell of a lot of money for an errand-runner."

"That's an understatement."

Carlton stood up abruptly. Picking up his hat and jamming it on his head, he turned on his heel, pulled the door open and walked out.

"Wait," I called after him. "Where are you going?"

"To track down a pair of killers."

CHAPTER NINE

"WAIT!" I ran after him. "Do you really think the Albrights had something to do with killing Marty?"

I just knew he was going down the wrong path. It didn't fit. Those two were too stupid to orchestrate anything this devious. Crimes of rage, maybe, bludgeoning someone to death, running someone over in a car, I could buy. They may have been taking money from Marty, but killing him?

Carlton stopped and looked at me. "I don't know for sure, but I want to find out why your cousin was paying that much money to Derek Albright. Anything Derek's involved with usually means Dusty's right there with him." He turned and pulled open the front door to walk out.

"Wait," I exclaimed, "let me shut off some lights and lock up. I'll be right back."

I ran into Marty's office, turned off the lights and grabbed my backpack. Hurrying out the front door, I realized that Carlton was already in his truck and had started the engine. I flipped the lock, pulled the heavy door shut and brushed the yellow police tape out of my way.

I walked over to the driver's side. "You'll keep me posted, right?" Not so much for Marty's sake, but for my own. I wanted to keep tabs on what Carlton was doing.

He nodded. "Yeah, I'll let you know." He sounded

worried. "Look, be careful, Keira. If the Albright brothers are in any way part of this, it could be dangerous. I know those two are bad news. I think they've got some con or scam going, but I don't know what."

I almost laughed. I was pretty sure I didn't have anything to worry about from the Albrights, but they weren't the only ones in this equation. Somewhere, someone or more than one someone, was the victim of some scheme thought up by my idiotic cousin and maybe carried out by his ex-con minions. Whatever that trio had been up to, I was sure that it had ultimately cost Marty his life.

"A con I can believe, Carlton, but cold-blooded murder?"

"It's possible," Carlton replied. "I want to pick them up for questioning. Plus, I still have to get details from the bank in Houston about that account." He put the truck in gear, but then stuck his head back out the window. "Keira, please be careful, okay?"

"I will, Carlton," I said, as I stepped back. He sped off. I watched the car disappear around the bend.

"Where the hell was he going in such a hurry?" Tucker appeared from the side of the building.

I told him what we'd found, including what Boris had said yesterday.

"Hmm, Carlton may be right," Tucker said.

"Or he might just be chasing geese . . . or humans." I grinned at my brother. "I think we need to head in another direction."

"DAMN. He's not available."

"What does that mean?"

I'd tried to call Adam, but the phone clicked over to the operator at the Wild Moon.

"The operator said he wouldn't be available until later

in the evening." I shrugged. "He'll call back. Besides, it's still daylight. What we're looking for won't be up and about until after sunset. It won't do us a heck of a lot of good to go out there now. We can wait."

I reached over to turn the key to start the car. Suddenly, I fell back, a rush of energy washing over my body like steam rushing out of an overheated car. I gasped for air as the feeling on my skin turned from steam heat to shivers to a thousand fire ants crawling inside me, biting my skin trying to escape. The air felt too thick to breathe. This time, instead of the hyper-clarity of previous visions, it was as if layers of clear plastic surrounded me, blurring my ability to see.

I could make out the inside of the car around me, but all the edges were soft, vague. My ears rang as phantom bells echoed in my brain. The scent and taste of blood washed over me, nearly covering me in its rich thickness. But the blood wasn't the same as what I'd tasted before. This blood came from something more than a prey animal. I couldn't identify it.

Suddenly, just when I thought I was drowning in the thick blood-scented air, my ears popped as if I was in an airplane and everything was back to normal. There was nothing in my car but me and my brother.

I took a breath. I was back.

"Are you okay?" Tucker's voice was quiet, matter-of-fact. His cool hand pressed to my forehead felt good. "No fever. How do you feel?"

I took a deep breath and tasted the air—normal. No blood, no anger. "Okay, I guess. Just a little achy, as if I'd been running or exercising."

I could feel my tank top stuck against my back, dampening my flannel shirt. I must have sweated right through it. I wanted a shower and I wanted to figure out what the hell kind of vision that had been.

"Pretty standard reaction," he said.

"Reaction?"

"Hell, Keira, it's not exactly been a normal day, even with our twisted version of the word."

I grinned. "Yeah, guess you're right, bro. I'm just not used to this stuff."

"Look, let's just go to your house and chill for a while. You need the rest and maybe we can noodle out whatever was going on with Marty."

"Great idea," I said, reaching for my seat belt.

"Uh, Keira . . ."

"Yeah?"

"Maybe I should drive?"

TUCKER LOUNGED on the wide leather armchair, his legs crossed at the ankles, arms folded easily across his chest. I sat across from him on the matching couch, sprawled along its length, my upper body propped up by a pile of Indian print cushions. Bea, who'd shown up just as we arrived back at my place, sat on the floor, her short legs tucked underneath her. I'd poured each of us a generous glass of wine.

Bea was the first to talk. "I was thinking about something on the way over here. You don't think Marty tried to set up some weird witch cult or something again? Since he can't . . . ?"

Tucker laughed as I shook my head and sipped my wine. We both remembered the incident clearly. My great-great-granny had not been happy.

"Like in high school? I doubt it, not after what happened to him when he got caught. Gigi threatened to cut off more than just money. I think it's more mundane than that."

"Mundane, how?"

"Well, either Marty was probably selling something to the rich and shameless out at the ranch or he found himself a vampire lover . . . or both."

"I vote for the vampire," Tucker said.

"A what?" Bea spluttered over a mouthful of wine. Her hands flew up to finger the small gold cross around her neck. *"Madre de Dios,"* she squeaked. "You are so not telling me that vampires are real."

"I'm not?" I grinned at her, but then realized she was really freaked out. "Shit, Bea, yeah, sorry, I guess I thought you knew."

"How the hell would I have known that?" she asked. "Jesus, Keira, how many Tuesday nights did we both watch *Buffy* on TV? And you never bothered to tell me that vampires are real?"

"Nearly seven years," I answered the easy question first. "Look, I'm sorry, but it never occurred to me that you didn't know since you know all about my clan. Vampires are just another type of supernatural creature. They're as real as I am. Not like on TV with the foreheads and all, but real. I used to hang out at a club in London—vampires and the like."

"Great, a vampire club . . . why does this not surprise me?" Bea stopped fingering her cross and stared at me, then at Tucker. "Do you think Marty was killed by one of them?"

"It's a possibility," Tucker said and told her what I'd seen on Marty's neck.

"I'm thinking they might be what I saw in my nightmare," I added.

"But at the Wild Moon?" Bea's voice reflected her shock. "How would Adam not know?"

Tucker looked at me and grinned a little, no doubt remembering my phone message.

"Maybe he does, maybe he doesn't," I said. "Didn't exactly bring that topic up in conversation. Besides, it's not hard for them to mainstream. If they're staying out at one of those guest houses, people might just think they're eccentric—or from Hollywood. There are an awful lot of pretentious dweebs in L.A. and New York that dress in black, sleep during the day and listen to Marilyn Manson. Hell, I'm like that and I'm not a vamp."

"But you don't listen to Marilyn Manson. You're not human either." She looked at Tucker. "Neither of you."

He grinned at her and saluted with his wineglass. Bea grinned right back.

I ignored the interplay between them. "Point taken, girlfriend. Of course, there are a whole lot of other things out in the world besides vamps. We haven't ruled out Marty being killed by a human. Those were probably vampire bites, but they weren't necessarily fatal. Carlton's weighing in on the Albrights. I don't agree."

"The idiot brothers? Why?"

"Money, why else? Evidently, cousin dearest was pumping hundreds of dollars Derek's way." I told her about the canceled check.

"Well, shit." Bea took a big gulp of wine. "Could explain why those two skipped on work. I tried calling their apartment again, but there was no answer."

"Maybe they're history," Tucker said. "Could be they know what happened and took off."

"Tucker's got a point, Bea," I said. "Maybe you're better off with them gone."

"Definitely," she said. She took another gulp of her wine. "Keira, if Boris thinks there was a connection to the dead deer, do you think that Marty was just out at the ranch and saw something that he shouldn't? A predator that saw him back and wanted to silence him?"

My brow furrowed. "Unlikely. What do you think, Tucker?"

He agreed. "I'm not so sure that would be a motive for murder, a few threats or just lying low for a few days, maybe, but not killing. We pretty much tend to take these things in stride. We're good at hiding and keeping a low profile. Killing someone because they were peeping is not low profile stuff. There has to be another reason Marty was killed."

I shifted position on the couch, lying on my side, propped up on one arm. "Tucker's right, Bea. Low profile is the key, for vampires, too, no doubt. If there's someone at the Wild Moon we need to check out, I can take Adam up on the dinner invite. Give me a chance to sniff around a little, see what I can find out."

"Girlfriend, I'm not so sure you ought to go sniffing around that man for anything more than a good meal . . . or a good time," said Bea with a smile. "Leave the Nancy Drew-ing to Sheriff-man. If the idiot brothers and your cousin were involved, let Carlton deal."

I blushed and didn't want to look at my brother, who I knew was grinning bigger than the Cheshire Cat. Unlike me, Tucker didn't have any qualms about dating humans— of either sex. I was sure he thought my having a little hanky-panky with Adam Walker was just what the doctor ordered. But then again, Tucker had always been careful to stick to humans who cared little for permanence. Most of his real relationships had been with clan.

"Bea, Carlton's not going looking for the same things. I need to do this."

At this, my brother guffawed. I glared at him. He just smirked at me and drank his wine.

Bea scowled at Tucker. "Keira, I know, but look at what just happened to you just a little while ago. What if you start to freak out when you're out at the ranch? Maybe both you and Tucker ought to go to dinner. It's safer."

"No way. I am not going to drag my brother to dinner as a chaperon. Come on, Bea, you know me better than that."

I turned to my brother. "And don't you even get started on any of this. This is out of your territory, brother mine."

I shot him a look. It was bad enough that Bea was interfering, I didn't need my brother to chime in.

Tucker snickered and poured himself another glass of wine. "Far be it for me to interfere in my sister's love life."

Thing was, Bea was probably right. Considering what I'd been feeling toward Adam, if the opportunity arose, I might just start thinking with my hormones and not my head and who knew where that could lead?

My friend smiled. "Okay, go. Talk, eat dinner, get all couple-y." She tossed me the cordless phone. "But that's all, right? No matter how *guapo* that man is, you need to be careful. You can worry about getting laid later."

Her grin widened as she watched my brother's face. He was trying not to laugh. "Besides, this'll be a good chance for you to think about something other than Marty. Let Carlton do his job. You go out there and de-stress. Nothing better than a fabulous dinner, fantastic wine and something chocolate for dessert."

I felt my face turn red. All I could think of was Adam's voice, rich and dark and tempting as the finest Belgian chocolate. I knew that's not what Bea meant, but I blushed anyway. Okay, then, this would be an exercise in some serious self-control.

THE PHONE RANG twice before he picked up. His voice, still as smooth as the anticipated chocolate dessert, sounded a little fuzzy, distant.

"Hello, Keira Kelly," he said. "I heard you called. Does this mean I get to pay you back with dinner?"

Whoever said paybacks are hell was so very wrong. Then again, maybe their idea of hell didn't match mine.

"Yes, I'm taking you up on your offer of dinner," I said. "I'm sorry, though, did I just wake you up? Was that why you didn't answer the phone earlier?"

"You caught me out," he said, his voice clearing. "I was napping and asked not to be disturbed, but that's fine. I'm glad you called. If I remember rightly, you're a bit of a night owl yourself."

"You remember rightly. So . . . what's good for you?"

His deep laugh vibrated through the phone. "I'd answer that, but I'm sure it would get me in trouble."

Damn it, I'd meant the time for dinner. I felt myself turning red as I imagined the grin on his face. I couldn't even look at Bea or Tucker.

But Adam got me off the hook before I totally made a fool of myself. "Would tomorrow at nine be okay?"

"Sounds great," I answered. "Where should I meet you?"

"Just drive through to my house," he said. "You can park here and we can walk over to the restaurant. Hang on a second." He was back nearly immediately with the security code for the gate. "Do you have any preferences on types of food? I have an 'in' with the chef." I could hear the smile in his voice.

"I'm not that picky," I said with a laugh.

"See you tomorrow then, Keira," he said. "I'm looking forward to it."

"Yeah, me, too."

It occurred to me I wasn't just spouting pleasantries. I really was looking forward to this, despite everything that happened today. Tomorrow night, I could relax and enjoy a nice dinner out with a very attractive man. It would be a great chance to escape for a few hours, to forget, if only temporarily. Dinner with Adam Walker certainly had other possibilities. I could certainly contemplate enjoying a little more than just a meal.

Relief suddenly flooded my overstressed body. I let go the tension I'd been clutching like a not-so-comforting blanket, feeling it slip from me, taking my tightly held shields with it.

It was like a smudged film had suddenly been stripped from my awareness. I felt Bea's breathing across the room, a tangible current of air moving around me, the heat of her body nearly solid, as if I could see it, feel it. My brother's breath was heavier than hers, more solid, tasting of earth, of musk, of the woods and of blood. His energy burned red, gold, white with the changing swirl that was shapeshifter.

The leather of the couch caressed my skin, even through the thick fabric of my jeans; the nubbly softness of the chenille cushions stroked my back and sides. A burst of light and dark speared my eyes.

"Holy shit!" I fell against the couch cushions. The handset fell out of my nerveless hand to the floor.

"Keira, are you okay?"

"Bea, wait, don't—"

Before Tucker could stop her, Bea put a cool hand on my forehead. I cringed at the touch. Tucker squatted next to her, gently moving her hand off me. I felt the heat of his hand hovering above my face.

"I'm fine, just, please, don't touch me right now."

Bea scooted back to the easy chair Tucker had just vacated, curling deeper into the seat. "I'm sorry; I was just trying to help." Her voice was small and tight, holding in the hurt I knew she was feeling.

Tucker stayed next to me, concern on his face. He was careful not to touch me. He was too close.

"Tucker, please, move back a little."

He nodded, and moved back over by Bea, perching on the ottoman.

"I'm sorry," I said to both of them, struggling to keep the thin hold I had on what was left of my safeguards. "Something's happened. My shields are gone . . . everything's pretty raw right now."

"I felt them go," Tucker said. "What happened?"

"I don't know," I said. "When I hung up, I relaxed, then—"

"Your shields were gone."

I nodded. "Yeah."

Bea's eyes welled up with tears. I could feel her emotion brimming to the surface, empathy, pity, a little fear. I could taste her worry, rich on my tongue, her anxiety hovering just above the feeling of relief that I seemed to be okay. The heat of her body temperature flooded over me, covering me like a second skin.

I huddled into myself, pulling together the last shreds of my tattered barriers until I could block enough of her energy to speak coherently. Tucker had known how to react, he'd reinforced his own shields the second he felt mine going, blocking himself from me.

"I don't know what happened," I said. "I felt something,

power, maybe. I saw . . ." I didn't really know what. I'd
flashed on blood and death and hunger. I felt the need deep
inside me, clawing its way out, desperate for release. But
I couldn't tell if that was just remnants of my previous
vision, or if this was a new invasion of my sanity.

"It was like a rush of power," I finished, knowing it was
a lame answer.

It had been more than that. As I'd stupidly relaxed my
shields, they'd slipped completely away, leaving me raw
and open to everything around me. I'd touched the night
and it had touched me back. But it wasn't anything I could
explain. There weren't any words to give meaning to what
had happened. Like someone tripping on acid, I'd felt
colors and smelled light, felt the energies of everything that
ever hunted in the dark.

Bea sat facing me, both knees drawn up to her chin. Her
arms were wrapped around her legs.

"I'm sorry. I freaked you out, didn't I?"

"Yeah, you freaked me out, *chica.*"

She frowned a little. "Are you going to be okay?"

Before I said anything I took a deep breath and let it
out slowly.

"Yeah, I'll be fine. I wasn't careful." I mentally thanked
the powers that be that I hadn't done that in front of anyone
else. At least my friend understood—sort of.

"Damn it, girl," Bea said. "I thought you'd learned
that lesson." Okay, well, she was my best friend. She was
allowed to scold.

"Tell me about it." I was tired of complications. I was
beginning to feel that fate, or karma or whatever, was
stirring this particular piece of my life with a delicately evil
hand. Why the hell couldn't everything just stay simple?

"Keira?" Bea's worry echoed throughout the room.

Damn it, my shields were still too fragile. Her emotions still leaked through.

"Sorry, just trying to maintain."

"She'll be okay, Bea." Tucker's voice was soft and comforting. "It's just . . . a little unsettling."

Unsettling was a good word. Trying to maintain my stability was something that seemed to be getting harder and harder to do over the past day or two. My senses kept freaking out, my natural controls didn't seem so natural anymore, and it was way too easy for me to get sidetracked with emotion. I knew it was probably a side effect of my changing energies, but knowing it and being able to do something about it was altogether something different. Time to cancel my dinner date. I couldn't risk losing control while I was with Adam.

I picked up the handset, which had fallen between my feet.

"What are you doing?" Bea sat up straight.

"Calling Adam back and telling him the date's off."

Bea moved as fast as any human could and pulled the cord out of the wall before I could even dial. She hadn't had to move far. The main phone unit was on the table next to her. Lucky her. She'd caught me by surprise and done the one thing I hadn't expected. Damn her, she knew me much too well.

"What are you doing, *m'hija*?" she asked. "Are you nuts?"

"I'm not, I'm sane—totally calm and completely in control of myself for the first time since yesterday."

Who was I kidding? I was running scared. Scared of possibilities that were so vague they didn't even have a name. I wanted to see Adam, but I was afraid that all that emotion was what was loosening my control. I hadn't planned on having to deal with this kind of physical attraction to anyone, especially not with a human. But here I was and there he was and damnitalltohellandback. This was not getting me anywhere.

"Keira, stop and think." Bea was insistent. "You cannot pass this up. Isn't this an ideal situation for you?"

I stayed where I was. "What?"

"Adam Walker. He's gorgeous, rich, no complications. He's not Carlton and he's not Gideon. You don't need to worry about anything more than dinner. Just relax and enjoy, ask questions . . . you'll be fine."

"She's right, Keira." Tucker chimed in, having wisely kept his counsel until now. "Just say 'yes.'"

I glared at him for making with the stupid jokes. He was one to talk. After all, Bea had only seen me lose control once. Tucker was there both times in less than a few hours.

"Really, Keira, I think it's okay," he said. "You're just stressed. Too much happening. That's why you lost control. You have until tomorrow night. It'll be okay."

"All right, you win," I said, capitulating. "I'll go to dinner. I'll ask questions, but that's it. No romance, no strong emotions, no 'just getting laid'. It's not fair to Adam and I just can't deal."

I sure as hell wasn't going be so cavalier about shielding anymore. I'd gotten so used to being around nothing but humans, I'd let myself go a little. Let those metaphysical muscles get soft and vulnerable. I'd have to definitely do some serious work on strengthening my safeguards before tomorrow night.

"*M'hija,* look, I know I'm pushing you to go. You need to ask questions, maybe just even reconnect with someone who's a friend. But don't forget your cousin was killed by someone who meant it. It wasn't an accident. Whatever happens at dinner, whatever you discover at the ranch, don't forget. Whoever killed Marty might actually be someone with a grudge against your family. Please be careful."

My family saga was full of tales of vendettas and blood feuds, like some sort of supernatural Sopranos. Not all of those stories were ancient history. About ten years ago, a new feud had started between cousins in Spain over a piece of hunting land. Last I heard, they were still duking it out.

"But, Bea, this was Marty," I said. "He was human. That's backward. If there were a grudge, it would be against—" I stopped. The only one of my family around here with any powers was me—and Tucker—but as far as I knew, no one but Bea and Carlton knew he was here.

She nodded. "I know, he's the one that died, but what if it is family related? If there's a vendetta against your family, you're it around here, girlfriend, and no matter what you are, you're not invulnerable. You can still be hurt."

It might take the equivalent of a wrecking ball to really injure me, but the fact was that I could be injured, even killed. I hadn't thought of that. After all, how many women or even men were ever in real, life-threatening danger? Now, I might just be.

CHAPTER TEN

AFTER BEA LEFT, I turned to my brother.
"Well?"

"Well, what?" he asked.

"Know anything about any vendettas?"

"You know I don't keep up with that shit, Keira."

"Then how are we supposed to find out?"

Tucker took one look at me and said nothing.

"Damn," I said.

He grinned and shrugged. "There's no other way. She's the only one who'd know for sure."

"But if I call her, she'll know I'm Changing."

Tucker's smile turned into a belly laugh.

"You really think she doesn't already know?"

"What do you mean? She can't possibly know."

My brother came over to sit beside me on the couch. "Keira, sister mine, why on earth do you think I'm here?"

The realization hit me about the same time his hand took mine. I pulled away.

"Shit, Tucker. She sent you?"

He had the grace to look embarrassed.

"Yeah, pretty much," he said. "She's the chief, Keira, connected to each of us in more ways than you care to know. She knew you were changing before you did."

"Well, fuck me," I said. "So great-great-granny really did send you to babysit."

"I told you it was either me or Ciprian." He smiled. "I figured you'd be less pissed off if I came."

"You're right about that," I agreed. My brother Ciprian, although centuries younger than Tucker, was a dried-up old fart. He was the only brother who didn't enjoy the shapeshifting part of his nature. A numbers-cruncher at heart, he kept the family books and considered himself our prefect. Gigi let him play his little game because she hated dealing with the realities of modern financial considerations. Ciprian had increased the family fortunes tenfold in the last couple of centuries, meaning each of us was independently wealthy in our own right. We were grateful for his fiduciary talents, but Tucker was definitely an improvement over an immortal with the heart of an accountant and the demeanor of a Jesuit headmaster.

"Why don't *you* call?" I asked. "She likes *you*."

"She likes you, too, Keira," Tucker said. "I don't know why you don't think so."

"Maybe because I'm in fucking exile here," I retorted. "Think that's why?"

Tucker's voice was gentle. "Sister mine, be reasonable. You chose to stay in Rio Seco when we all left. There was nothing for you here except to rot and wallow in guilt and self-recrimination. So Gigi gave you an assignment."

I didn't want to admit it, but Tucker was right. I'd reacted out of confusion and stubbornness, refusing to take my family's advice. Too soon after I'd bought my house, the burning need to stay and lick my wounds morphed into an endless round of boredom and sameness. All I could see before me was the excruciating parade of endless nights/days/months turning into decades, into centuries. I'd been trained for and enjoyed action and all I had was inaction and ennui. Just last week, I found myself whiling away the hours pacing my own floors. Where does one go when the world stops being discoverable? When Paris, Rome, even Nairobi all have the same air of . . . sameness? Another city, another few decades. I'd felt the Change coming on, didn't admit it. Instead, I'd played the ostrich and look where it got me.

I looked at my brother. "I stayed in Rio Seco to get away from things, Tucker. It was easier then. I didn't have to think. All I had to do was to keep Marty out of trouble, and I couldn't even do that right. Damn it, I've pretty much fucked up what little life I do have at this point. I don't know what the hell to do."

Tucker handed me the phone then walked outside to the porch, closing the front door behind him. I knew I'd be fooling myself if I imagined he couldn't overhear. His hearing was better than mine, but at least he was pretending.

"DEAR CHILD, I knew you'd be calling soon." The honeyed voice was calculated to soothe and relax. It had just the opposite effect on me. I paced while I talked.

"Hello, Gigi." I tried to keep my voice steady and not let her hear my emotions.

Great-great-grandmother was too much of a mouthful, and I couldn't quite bring myself to use her given name of Minerva. Too personal. I'd started calling her Gigi as a child. "Grandmother" with two G's in front. For whatever reason, she'd thought it was cute. The name caught on and now even my brothers used it.

Her silvery laugh chimed in my ear. It didn't make me feel any better disposed toward her. I'd heard her laugh in the exact same manner after a hunt while she was blooding her kill. Not exactly calculated to put one at ease.

"You've come to your senses, then?" she asked. I could imagine her sitting in her opulently appointed sitting room decorated like some Arabian Nights fantasy. She loved her little luxuries. That was one of the reasons she never hunted now. Too much dirt and sleeping out in the woods for her taste. It was easier to have dinner brought in, even though she did prefer it still kicking. There were plenty of flunkies to cater to her whims.

"Come to my senses about what?"

I cradled the phone against my shoulder as I walked into the kitchen and poured myself a glass of wine.

"Coming home, of course," she said with the same infuriating self-righteous cheeriness that I hated so much. Some people called it "perky." I just called it annoying, especially in a woman who was my senior by more years than I cared to think about.

"Gigi, I don't have any clue what you're talking about," I said, being deliberately obtuse. I went back to the living room and curled up in the big armchair.

"Keira, I'm your great-great-grandmother and the chief of our clan. I know what's happening with all my people. I know you're Changing. I can feel your power even from here."

She sounded pleased, but she was also putting on her chieftain voice. The second-grade schoolteacher mixed with head librarian and Mother Superior all in one. I could even feel myself sitting straighter.

"Okay, so you know," I said. "And you know that I know, considering that you sent my brother here to spy on me. But let's not change the subject."

"Subject?"

"Gigi, I called to find out what's going on."

"What are you talking about, dear child?"

"Don't play games," I said. "Since you're so damned all-seeing, then you're bound to know that Marty's dead—murdered." As I spoke, I suddenly realized something. There didn't need to be a vendetta. I blurted out the words without thinking. "Did you do it?"

The silence on the other side was thick, nearly tangible. Not even a breath or a sigh escaped my ever-so-perfect granny. She was either trying to figure out an excuse, or a valid reaction.

"Do you really think I'd have him killed, Keira?"

Not the right answer. In fact, it wasn't an answer at all, only another question to deflect the truth. Damn her.

"I'm not going to pretend I'm stupid, Gigi," I said. "You're not exactly a candidate for grandmother of the year. I know how you felt about Marty. Did you have him killed?"

I was insistent. I wasn't going to hang up until she told me the facts.

"Do you really care?" She said it with the bald certainty that only our clan chief could have. Marty had been human and, therefore, not worth the paper his birth certificate had been printed on. A degradation and shame to our people who was better off dead.

"Yeah, Gigi, damn it. I care." I did. "Besides, you were the one who assigned him to me."

Gigi's light laughter danced over the phone. "You haven't changed a bit, Keira." There were those words again.

"Neither have you," I said. "You still haven't answered my question, Gigi. There were fang marks on Marty's neck. Which one of your muscle-men was it?"

She laughed even harder this time. "Darling child, do you really think that if one of my enforcers had been sent out there that they'd leave evidence so tacky as fang marks? Besides, why would I bother? You know the drill. You were trained in our ways. He was mortal. Eventually, we'd all just outlive him." I could picture the easy shrug and her dismissal of the topic.

She had a point. We almost never bothered with humans. Why kill something you'll just outlive? Survival is, after all, the best revenge. Gigi may tease, may skirt the issue, but deep down, I knew she really didn't care enough about Marty to inconvenience herself by having him killed. As long as he didn't affect the clan. As far as I knew, he hadn't.

"I take it you're investigating?" Now she was being sarcastic.

"Yeah, well, I wasn't," I said, "not really, just poking around a little. Then it occurred to me that there might be some sort of feud going on and Marty got caught up in it. Tucker didn't know anything so I called you."

"Keira, do you really think I'd forget to tell you if some family disagreement involved you or the human?"

"No, Gigi," I said, realizing she was telling the truth. "I'm just tired of this whole thing and punchy with no sleep."

"Hmmph. I imagine you're planning on finding out who killed him, then."

"I suppose so."

"Fang marks, you said?" The question was tossed out, casually.

"Two," I answered.

"Throat intact?"

"Yes."

"Doesn't sound like one of ours," she said. Another point to Gigi, since our brand of hunter usually ended up tearing out the throat of the victim, not just sinking fang and blooding the kill, but anything was possible, including killing him and making it look like a vampire kill. Why on earth had I not just stopped to think and avoided this call altogether? The only excuse I had for myself was that I was overly tired and not at my best.

"Any visitors lately?" she asked, meaning non-clan paranormals.

"No. At least none that I know of, but maybe."

"Maybe?"

I sighed. I told her about the visions and the dead cat. I could almost see the pretty frown on my granny's face as she pondered what I'd said. Gigi could pass for my sister—my younger one. It was her dainty size and delicate features that did it. I was far from dainty and delicate.

No matter that she was one of the most ruthless predators I'd ever known. Practical to a fault, her only raison d'être was the well-being of the clan.

"Use Tucker. He's a tracker, better than you. He'll help. Try not to get yourself killed." She hung up without further explanation.

My brother was back in the house the second I put the phone down.

"She told me to use you. You're a better tracker than I am."

"She's right," he said. "Centuries of practice." His grin took the sting away. "Tell you what, sis, why don't I spend some time roaming. Sniff around. See what I can find out? You can concentrate on the front end of things."

He meant the sniff part literally.

"Sounds like a plan, big brother," I said. "Let's keep in touch. If I hear anything from Carlton, I'll let you know."

"Or if you find out something from Mr. Walker." He was teasing.

"Yeah, whatever. I'm not giving you details of my date, though."

His laughter echoed as he walked back out and down the porch steps. Brothers. Sometimes, I wondered if they were worth all the trouble.

I PULLED the Rover up, hiding behind a stand of live oaks just in front of the entrance to the strip center. I'd finally managed to relax a little after Tucker left, whiling away the night by burying myself in a good book. I'd fallen deeply asleep sometime before dawn, waking up sometime after four in the afternoon. At least I hadn't had any nightmares, or any phone calls either, at least none that counted.

Carlton left a phone message about eight in the morning. Bexar County had picked up Marty's remains. He expected autopsy results in a few days. Odd word, remains. Made me think of scattered papers and bits of trash.

His message said he was headed for Houston to serve a subpoena for the bank records and one of his deputies was on the trail of the still missing Albrights. He'd be in touch. Sounded like he had it all under control. Bully for our man in brown.

Tucker hadn't called, but I didn't expect him to until later. He'd probably spent the night wandering the countryside, snooping around. Now that it was daytime, he'd sleep, hidden from prying eyes. I wasn't worried. I knew he'd done this more times than I could count.

My plan was to drive out to the ranch early, do a little snooping myself before I had dinner with Adam. With Carlton out of town for the rest of the day, I could poke around freely. Even if he hurried, it took at least three and a half or so hours to get to Houston, putting him there about noon. Then it would probably take a few hours to get the information he needed. If he left right after he was done, he couldn't be home any sooner than seven or eight. That meant I could go out to the ranch, do a little pre-dinner reconnoitering and not have Carlton mess up my plans by showing up unexpectedly. Planning was a good thing.

When I passed the deli, Boris was in front of the store loading the van. Precise rows of crates and boxes filled the inside. This *had* to be a delivery to the Wild Moon. If I hung out and followed him, I could watch from a distance, see who he talked to. Maybe the infamous mystery man would show up.

Boris loaded the last box and shut the van door. He mopped his forehead with his bandanna and placed it back in his pocket. He reached over to fiddle with the door handle as if to check he'd shut it properly, and then walked around the van and peered at each of the tires. He finally pulled keys out of his pocket, got in the driver's seat, and cranked the engine.

We drove through the silent, darkening evening in tandem; me keeping about a quarter of a mile back, trying not to close the distance between us. I wouldn't have followed so closely, but I wasn't completely positive he was heading to the Wild Moon. Sometimes Boris made deliveries to other outlying ranches.

The delivery van slowed as Boris approached the nearly hidden Wild Moon gate, his speed dropping automatically, with the assurance of someone who made this trip on a regular basis and didn't need to keep an eye out for the tiny sign. Even though I'd been out here just a couple of nights ago, I hadn't realized we were already approaching the entrance. The massive gate opened as Boris punched in a code.

The sun had nearly set, but I didn't want to risk turning

on my headlights and alerting him I was there. The night was clear and the moon still almost full, so even without lights, I could see nearly as well as if it were day.

I pulled over to wait on the side of the road to allow Boris to drive through to the main complex; I'd just drive in after. At that point, if he saw me, he wouldn't necessarily jump to the conclusion I'd been following him. Maybe. I wasn't sure why I really cared if he thought that, only that the whole thing was a little sordid. Me following an old man whose only crime was the fact he might possibly know something about my cousin's dealings at the Wild Moon.

I watched as the van's taillights faded beyond the first small rise. The sun had truly set, throwing everything into a weird graying twilight.

I'd always liked this part of the night. It seemed as if you were poised on the edge of something, a promise kept secret by the near dark. You almost lost the ability to see, but enough light still remained to turn even the most mundane shapes of bushes and mesquite trees into living things that hovered on the verge of movement. It was as if, with the right words or proper ritual, they would pull up their roots and slide out of the imprisoning ground.

I'd actually thought I'd seen it once—the trees shifting. But the night had been darker then, as had the company. I missed that feeling. The sensation that the night was endless and so were the possibilities. Maybe once I came into my own power I could experience it again.

I put the car in gear, banishing the mood, and drove forward, punching in the security code Adam had given me.

I drove slowly, letting my eyes adjust to the almost perfect darkness of the ranch property. A few streetlamps punctuated the black night, but those pitiful little spots of light did more to accentuate the shadows than to banish them.

There was an odd lack of life around the complex. At most inns and resorts, there were always people around, whether they were walking in between buildings on their way to dinner or to one of the scheduled events that were so common at these places—a movie, a dance, whatever— even just the common hustle and bustle of the staff going about their normal routine. But the Wild Moon was silent, as empty of sound as it was of light. I downshifted and pulled around the side of the main inn, toward the back, where I expected to find Boris.

Abruptly, a group of people appeared, walking across the road about thirty feet in front of me, causing me to slow even more. They all came into the pool of light by the road at once, as if they had materialized from the darkness. Each of them was tall, pale-skinned and dressed in dark clothes, like refugees from a Goth concert or bad movie. None of them paid any attention to the fact I was there.

I tapped the brakes lightly to stop. The flash of red light seemed to capture the attention of one especially young-looking man with paper-white skin and red-gold hair. He wore a black duster over an equally black shirt and pants. I watched him through the windshield as he came to a stop and turned toward me.

His skin was more than just pale, it was almost translucent in the reflected streetlight, and stretched over fine bones tautly as an artist's canvas over its frame. I couldn't quite make out the color of his deep-set eyes. There was something vaguely familiar about him, something that tickled my memory.

He stared directly at me, as if he could see my face in the

dark. He stood with the stillness of a mannequin; the only part of him moving was his long hair, which waved slightly in the night breeze, the ends lightly brushing his shoulders. Behind him, more people walked by, some glancing at the man, some at my car, but none of them stopped.

I stared back, not sure of whether I should honk or move forward or just stay where I was. The man was completely immobile, not a twitch or even a sign of breathing, a mannequin of flesh and bone.

My skin prickled, goose bumps raised on my arms and an odd thrill slid up my back. I felt power and it didn't feel the same as what I'd experienced before when I'd had visions—no overwhelming sensations or disorientation. Instead, I felt an odd expectation. Of what, I couldn't say. But it was as if, somehow, I knew something was coming; something I wanted more than anything else in the world, and it was just around the corner, over the hill, behind the curtain . . . I only had to find it. I edged forward in my seat, anticipating.

My jacket suddenly felt oppressive, hot, heavy and binding, but I wasn't able to move to take it off. A drop of sweat slid down the side of my face and down my neck. As it touched my collarbone, my entire body shivered as if an icy finger had slid down my back and caressed the base of my spine.

I tried to reach out, to feel what, who was out there, but it was as if my senses were wrapped around me, held in place like a cocoon, bound to my skin. Someone else was running this party and wasn't letting me dance.

The man's eyes narrowed slightly and then he smiled, flashing white teeth. Bowing quickly, he straightened up, smiled again and licked his lips slowly, wetly, as if savoring a particularly delicious thought.

I gasped. It was as if he'd reached in and grabbed me by the crotch. I could almost feel his hand caressing me; intimate in its knowledge of me, parting the fabric of my jeans and beyond.

As abruptly as it had begun, I was released. Another young man appeared behind the first one. The second man's white-blond hair framed a pale face set off by his black clothing. He laughed and grabbed the first man's arm, leading him away from the pool of light to join the others who were hovering at the edge of seeing.

I sat back in my seat and let out a deep sigh. I'd been gripping the steering wheel so hard it had made dents in my hand. All of my senses seemed expanded a little but not as severely as when I'd had an episode. The low rumble of the engine provided a counterpoint to my heavy breathing. Behind that, I thought I could hear whispers in the darkness. Sounds of shadows, tastes of—

"She's not for you. Mustn't frighten the locals."

I whipped my head around but saw no one. I knew it was the voice of the second man, humor still evident in the words. But where was he? Where were they all? The entire group of people had disappeared into the darkness, vanishing as if they'd not been there at all.

I got out of the car before I could even think. The soft breeze touched my face, bringing the scents of the night with it. But there was no scent of people. Nothing to corroborate what I'd thought I'd seen.

I peered down at the road in front of my car. Even in the dark, I could see that the dirt shoulder didn't show any footprints. There should have been scuff marks or something, some evidence that several people had just walked by.

I rubbed my eyes and stared toward where I'd seen the group vanish. But there was nothing but darkness and the shadowy shapes of trees and bushes sitting silently in the night, undisturbed by the passage of anything more than the night breeze.

Damn it. Either I'd had another hallucination or there were something other than just a couple of vampires hiding out at the Wild Moon. Well, not exactly hiding, more like hiding in plain sight. Ghosts, maybe?

"Miss Keira?"

I jumped, stumbling back against my car. "Boris, sorry, I . . . I was distracted."

"What are you doing here?"

"I . . . Did you just see a group of people walk by?"

He stared at me, his face expressionless. "There were no people."

Shit. It *had* been a hallucination. This was beginning to suck beyond the telling of it. If I was going to start having visions every time I turned around, I might have to sequester myself in my house for the duration. That wasn't an option I particularly liked. Even a well-appointed prison was still a prison. Besides, there was still the matter of my cousin's death.

"Come around to the dock. It is too dark here. You can sit there for a while."

I nodded and followed Boris around the side of the building. I really did need to sit down before I drove again.

"What's that you're holding?" I asked.

"Protection."

It looked like a cattle prod, but had some sort of extra attachment.

"Looks serious," I said.

He nodded. "I modified it. Added a taser attachment. Six hundred twenty-five thousand volts. Will take down an angry bear."

"Bear? There aren't any bears here."

"There are plenty of other wild animals."

The store's delivery van was backed up to a loading dock, obviously the rear of the restaurant. There wasn't a soul around. I started to move up beside Boris, when I stumbled and instinctively reached out, grabbing for support. My hand landed on the top of his hand, bare skin to bare skin.

A flash of light seared my eyes and a clap of thunder assaulted my ears. I cringed in the wet of the downpour, shivering in the cold. I huddled against the person next to me, trying to steal the warmth of his body. But there was none to be had. The man was no longer warm. Corpses don't give off body heat. I cried out loud, peering through the gray twilight, looking for my sister. She'd been next to me when the men had unloaded us from the train, but her hand had been torn from mine and we'd been separated.

A pair of worn black boots appeared in front of me. I looked up, blinking the water from my eyes. I cried again, this time with relief. It was the man from the village. His dark hat and high collar hid his features, but I could sense the Other about him, like the Mountain Lords that cared for us at home. I'd seen him before. He'd promised we'd stay safe. He was here to take us back. Not home, because home was only in a place of our memory, but back to the village that was our refuge.

I smiled and reached out, touching his black coat. He looked down at me and smiled back, patting my head with his elegant hand.

A rough voice made the man turn from me.

"Stop wasting time. You've done enough and gotten your money. We have what we need."

I peeked around the man's coat to see a soldier. One of

the cursed ones. Blond hair cut close to his scalp, a scar bisecting his left cheek. He held tight to his rifle as if it were a security blanket. Maybe it was. There were more of us than there were of them. But most of us were starving and near dead from the long train journey.

"Sir, sir," I said, tugging at the man's coat. "You are taking us home?"

The man looked down and me and smiled again, a sad smile on his thin face. "I'm sorry, little one," he said. "But home is not safe. You'll be staying here now."

I sank to the wet ground as I heard the first screams from the outer building. I knew I was going to die . . .

"No!" Boris screamed and stepped away from me, eyes wide in disgust. "How did you . . . it is foul . . . wicked." He pressed himself up against the side of the van as if for protection.

I shuddered as the vision let go of me and gaped at Boris. "I'm sorry, I can't . . ." I whispered the words, the horror of what I'd felt still wrapped around me like a filth-encrusted blanket that I couldn't remove. I wanted to wipe my hands on something, clean them off, but the evil was in Boris' memory and I'd shared his horror.

My body was still standing in the back of the Wild Moon's main restaurant at the loading dock, my emotions and mind still felt the agony of knowing that I was in a death camp, surrounded by enemies and barbed wire, hearing the screams of the victims of hate.

Boris turned from me and fumbled at the van door. "I must leave."

My faculties returned and I stepped forward, hand extended, then quickly drew it back. I couldn't afford to have that happen again. "Wait, I'm sorry, Boris," I said. "I didn't mean—"

"You have the visions. I saw. You are *chovexani,* witch," he said as he gave up trying to open the door with shaking hands. He leaned his head against the side of the van, and then turned toward me with a deep sigh. "When I was a boy, my mother saw evil coming. Her people had the gift of farseeing. She was afraid. So she sent us to live with my father's relatives in Germany at the beginning of the war. We were sent there to be out of harm's way."

Inadvertently sent *into* harm's way. Fate really was the mother of all bitches.

"For all her visions, my mother could not see the truth. That the Germans were taking Rom as well as Jews. None of us were good enough to be the 'Master Race.'" His bitter words tasted of acrid sorrow, ash and death.

"You aren't Jewish?"

He shook his head. "No, my sister and I are Rom, gypsy. They took our people to experiment."

"And the man I saw?"

Tears flooded his eyes, not yet spilling and he looked away, unable to meet my gaze. "He traveled with us. One of the landowners, the Mountain Lords, that my family worked for in our homeland. Brought the children to Germany and stayed there. He promised he would take care of us, keep us safe. Instead, he turned us over to the filthy bastards."

A lone teardrop rolled down the old man's face. His voice grew bitter, the sound tasting of dust, dirt and blood. "He betrayed us. Like cattle they took us into the compound. Like cattle they did experiments on us, tortured us, fed—my sister and I were the only survivors from our *kumpania,* our tribe." He scuffled his feet on the gravel and wiped his eyes. "I cannot tell you more. I am very sorry, but you would not understand. It is dangerous. Please. Promise me you will be careful here."

"Here—the ranch?"

"Yes, at this place. Everything is not as it seems. Now, please, let me go. I need to go back to the store. It's already late."

"No, Boris," I said. "Why are you so spooked about the ranch?"

He looked around. There was still no one in sight. "He is here. I do not wish for him to recognize me. Your cousin came, spoke to him. I think . . . he was the reason—"

"Marty?"

"Yes, he was here. Talking to—"

"Good evening."

The resonant tones cut through Boris' words like a Learjet slicing through a fog bank.

I whirled to see Adam standing behind me, backlit by the area lights, a dark avenging angel come to the rescue. All he was missing was the flaming sword and wings.

"Hello, Keira Kelly."

The soft words and smile nearly made me smile back in an instant reaction to his presence. But I resisted that, too. I wanted a little distance. All these visions were wearing me out. But it was difficult to disconnect when just the very sight of this man made my pulse race.

He was dressed in a well-cut pair of sleek black slacks and what looked like a raw silk black dress shirt. The long sleeves were loosely rolled about halfway up his forearms and the rest of the shirt billowed around him as he moved to stand closer to me. It looked great on him.

"I'm sorry, did I interrupt something?"

I shrugged and forced myself to smile at him. "Not really," I said, unsure of what to say.

I couldn't see Boris, but suddenly, I could feel his tension like a shimmering wall behind me. My hackles rose as a cold frisson danced up and down my spine, strong enough so I almost dropped to the ground to avoid whatever threat I felt in the air. My lips drew back instinctively, as if I were getting ready to growl and let out the claws I didn't yet have.

"I brought the wine order."

Boris' soft words shattered the pressure and I let out a long breath, releasing the strain in my body.

Adam walked past me to stand next to Boris and reached for the clipboard that Boris still held loosely in his hand.

"Thank you." He scribbled a signature across the papers that Boris held out, then turned back to me and smiled again. "It's good that Boris helps us out," he said. "I don't know what we would do without his regular deliveries."

Boris shrugged and slid past me to climb into the driver's seat. "It is my job."

I watched as Boris pulled the door shut and nodded, not daring to look at me. He started the engine and put the van in gear and drove away.

"So, you accept every delivery?" I turned to face Adam.

He laughed, that wonderful sound that was nearly as tempting as his voice. "Not in the normal course of events," he answered. "But I saw you."

"Everything okay, Mr. Walker?" A voice behind me made me turn around.

A man stood on the dock, dressed in a red tuxedo shirt, black pants and suspenders. He dangled a bow tie from his hand. His short blond hair, blue eyes, and square shoulders should have been accompanied by the loose-limbed attitude and golden tan of a California surfer boy. Instead, his skin was nearly as pale as mine and his bearing was rigid, almost absurdly militaristic—the proverbial poker up his cummerbund.

"Thank you, Evan, everything's fine." Adam stepped over to him and handed him the copy of the receipt that he still held. "I signed for the delivery."

Evan nodded sharply and folded the paper. I'd halfway expected him to salute. No wonder Boris kept reliving his childhood. This guy was definitely a candidate for Master Race-hood. All he lacked was the uniform and jackboots. He turned on his heel and went inside, no doubt to whip the other restaurant flunkies into shape.

"So . . . what now, Keira?" Adam's voice was like a veil of chocolate. "If you're here for dinner, you are rather early. Not that I mind."

Suddenly, the attraction was back, and with a vengeance. What now indeed? I took a deep breath, my mental equivalent of a step back.

"Don't take this personally, but . . ." I paused. This was awkward. Technically, I suppose I was trespassing.

He smiled at me, one eyebrow raised in question. He'd crossed his arms and looked relaxed and utterly delicious.

I kept talking, trying to concentrate. "Look, this is kind of strange, but I needed to come out and check out the place."

I shut up as a couple of young men came out of the restaurant then and began to pick up the cases of wine still stacked on the dock. One of them grinned at me, lifting two cases at once, as if to show off.

I glanced over at them and then back at Adam. "Maybe we should talk about this later."

He waited until the men had disappeared into the back of the building.

"Come into my parlor?" He grinned and gestured with a hand. Yeah, said the spider to the fly. Problem was, I wasn't sure which one of us was the spider.

CHAPTER ELEVEN

"Y OU OBVIOUSLY want to talk about something, Keira, so why don't we go somewhere comfortable and sit down?"

Adam gazed at me, the quizzical look on his face vying with the weight of the seriousness in his eyes. The sea green had darkened, flecks of gold danced in their shadows.

"Come, follow me."

He held out his hand, but I didn't take it. Not that I wasn't tempted, but after what had happened with Boris, I didn't want to risk the possibility of another unintentional vision.

We walked down a tastefully lit gravel path, small landscape lights illuminating the wide walkway. A few minutes later, we were approaching the same cluster of small homes that I'd driven him to the night before last. We were almost to the bottom of the steps that led up to his porch when I stopped walking.

"What is it?"

"There's someone there."

"Where?" He didn't sound concerned.

"On the porch swing."

Adam looked at me, his eyes narrowing with a silent question. The small path lights cast shadows on the angles of his face. For a split second, he looked almost inhuman, then he smiled and the angles softened just a little.

I shrugged and looked back at him. What could I say? I hadn't actually seen the person, since no light penetrated the shadows in that corner, more that I felt a presence.

"She's good."

The lush contralto made me turn my head. A tall woman stood just at the edge of the light. Slender to the point of skinny, I could still see that she was strong. She wore a tight-fitting jumpsuit of some kind that emphasized the muscle cuts on her arms. Her pale blond hair was pulled back in a tight ponytail, emphasizing her well-defined cheekbones and piercing blue eyes. Her aura fairly screamed *predator.*

"One of your guests?" I turned back to Adam, still keeping her in the corner of my sight. Turning your back on a predator wasn't a good idea. I couldn't tell what she was, what place she held in the ranks of the preternatural, but I'd bet a not-so-favorite body part that she fed on blood and terror. The scent was just there, just beyond the obvious, underneath the normal smells of the night.

"An employee," he said, looking at me with an odd expression on his face.

"Muscle?"

He nodded. "Security."

"Makes sense."

"I think I'll be going now. I don't think I'm needed." The woman looked at Adam as if for permission.

He nodded his head slightly, still staring at me as if he'd seen me sprout fangs and a lumpy forehead.

The woman slipped down the steps without a sound, silent as a shadow on the face of an ice slick, and disappeared down the path.

I went to the swing and sat down. Adam perched carefully at its opposite end. I got the feeling he was trying to be very careful to not make any sudden moves or disturb me in any way. I smiled despite myself. I guess I'd freaked him out a little by spotting her.

"I'm speculating here, but I'm going to have to assume you have a reason to hire . . . non-traditional security?"

"I do."

Okay, now how to put this delicately. "I'm also guessing that you know she's not quite normal."

He nodded slowly, watching me, curiosity mingling with something else in his expression. "Andrea said you were good. I don't know if she knew how good."

I took a deep breath. Immediately, I felt the rush of heat, of desire traveling up my skin. This man exuded pheromones like an asphalt road gave off heat waves in the middle of summer. If I concentrated, I could almost see the energy rising from his skin.

"Adam, stop," I breathed. The distraction was too much.

In an instant, he was standing in front of me, all pretense gone. His eyes burned with intensity, silent pools of green fire flickering in his pale face, lips red against the pallor. My heart began to beat faster in response. He leaned in to me, one hand reaching to touch my cheek, the other on the arm of the swing, supporting his weight.

"Are you so sure you want me to stop?" It was almost a whisper, soft, seductive.

The answer to that was simple.

"No."

My own voice was hoarse, my throat almost too dry to speak. This was not going the way I'd expected, but at this point, I didn't care. I should have, but I didn't.

His face neared, his body moving even closer. A breeze sprang up, brushing a lock of his hair across his face. I automatically reached up to move it away, my hand grazing the cool skin of his cheek. His hand came up to cover mine, pressing my palm to his skin. A slight turn of his head and his lips rubbed against my hand, smooth, enticing. His gaze locked with mine, and I shivered, seeing the promise behind his eyes. I let myself get lost in the sensation of the softness of his mouth moving against my palm.

Adam's face turned to mine, leaning in, his lips relaxing into a smile. His even white teeth were no longer even. The delicate points of his canines teased his bottom lip. Those had not been there before. I would swear to it.

I reached up with my free hand, putting it on his chest and pushing. "Stop. Now."

He pulled back with an obvious effort.

I stayed silent, my heart still pounding, unable to speak.

"Well, I guess I'm not good enough," I finally said. "I should have guessed. The attraction, the fact that I completely lose track of my train of thought when I'm around you. It wasn't just me, was it?"

I wasn't really asking. I didn't need to. Add in the fact of Andrea and the point was beyond moot. But was that all it had been—my attraction to the dead, his power calling me? Or was there truth behind the glamour? I studied his face for a clue.

The humor in his eyes faded, only the seriousness remained as he squatted down in front of me, hands on either side of my thighs, not touching, just resting lightly on the wooden slats of the swing.

"You recognized Andrea. You know us for what we are?"

I nodded. "I felt her presence."

He stood, a movement so liquid it was like quicksilver, and went back to sit on the other end of the swing.

"You felt her, you didn't see her?"

I nodded, my hands gripping the chain of the swing. Even now that I knew that what I'd been feeling might only be him, I still couldn't trust myself. Even knowing what he was and what he'd probably done to me, I still wanted to run my hands over his body.

"Keira, just so you know, I have not used any glamour on you. I swear." He watched my face intently, as if he were searching for more than a verbal answer.

"Well, then." Now that was certainly interesting. No glamour. Was he telling me the truth? At least he hadn't said he swore on his own grave. That would have been pushing it.

Small muscles twitched in his jaw, betraying the tension he was feeling. But his eyes remained steady on mine, open and guileless. Maybe he was. I wanted to touch him, to get more of a sense of what he was saying, of whether he was telling the truth. But I was afraid to. Afraid that if I lowered any part of my shields, I'd lose them altogether.

"You're not the first ones I've met." I said it with a kind of defiance, and more than a little humor. Now let's see his reaction.

His brow furrowed a little. "You've met other vampires before?"

There. The word was out in the open, hanging in the cool Hill Country air like an odd scent or wisp of fog. It couldn't be taken back now.

"Does that bother you?" I asked.

He looked a little startled at my question. I guess he hadn't quite been expecting my response. I kept my own gaze steady now, wanting him to realize that it didn't matter that he was a vampire. Not one bit. How could it, when I was just as inhuman? Although I guessed he still hadn't picked up on that. Well, there was time enough for explanations later.

Something else did matter now and I needed to find out the answer before I went any further with this.

"I need to ask you something, Adam."

"I'm still trying to assimilate the fact that you'd met vampires before. You're serious?"

"I am completely serious." I almost said "dead serious." It was getting to be too easy to find the jokes.

"Where?"

"In London. In a club in Soho." I'd gone there before and during Gideon. Not information I intended to share. That was old news and not relevant.

"Not at Night Moves?" So he knew the place. Somehow that figured.

"You know it, then. It's a popular hangout for the not-human. But really, I need to ask you something."

"You mean whether or not I actually died?"

"No, that's not important," I said.

It really wasn't. I just wanted to find out if he or Andrea had had anything to do with Marty's death. Until then, everything else was moot, including my total fascination with him.

"What I want to know is about the other night," I said. "When I took you home from the mortuary, you were looking for my cousin. Why?"

"Sorry, it's personal." His voice was curt.

"Not anymore," I said. "It's sharing time, bucko. My cousin had a perfect set of fang marks on his very dead neck. I need to know if you had anything to do with it."

Adam moved nearly too fast for me to see. He grabbed both my arms, his face inches from mine.

"What do you mean?" His anger swept over me, washing heat and pain across my body in those four small words.

I stood nearly as fast as he had, slid out of his grasp and backed away to stand at least five feet from him.

"Back up," I warned. "I'm not in the mood for playing games." At least not anymore.

"How did you do that?" He sounded amazed. He'd probably not imagined that a human woman could have moved that quickly or removed herself from his clutches quite so easily. Surprise, surprise, surprise, Mr. Adam Walker. You aren't the only one with a closet to come out of.

"Never mind that now," I said, crossing my arms to put more distance between us. "Why did you need to see Marty?"

"I didn't kill him. I didn't even know he was dead." He sounded angry. "You think so little of me you believe I'd kill your cousin?"

I frowned, my eyes narrowing. "I don't know what to think." I said. "Hell, I just found out you're a vampire and I've known you for years."

"We don't exactly have vampire pride parades, Keira. Waving banners and wearing little ribbons is not our style."

I almost had to laugh at this. But I didn't.

"Okay, then," I said. "If you didn't kill him, then why does a vampire need to talk to the local funeral director?"

Oh, shit, I thought, as the words spilled out of my mouth. I just thought of a dozen reasons. Coffins. Any style in the catalog, no doubt. What if all he'd needed was to buy a new place to sleep or something? That could explain Marty's sudden riches and his ties to the ranch.

He sat back down at his end of the swing before he answered me. One pale hand grasped the chain. He motioned with the other one for me to sit. I did, but cautiously. I wasn't going to give him another chance to grab me.

"I wasn't seeking him out because of his profession," Adam said. "There have been some strange things happening around my ranch. My investigations led to your cousin."

"Strange, as in what?" Don't be stupid, Keira. Mutilated deer . . . duh.

"I had evidence leading me to believe your cousin was involved with a couple of locals of the not too savory variety."

"The Albrights."

"You know them?"

"They've been minor criminals around here for a while," I said. "I'm pretty sure the two of them were mixed up in some scheme or something with my cousin."

"'Or something' is close to correct," Adam said. "My wildlife manager caught the Albrights trespassing. He thought they were poaching, but there was no proof. We had to let them go."

"You have a wildlife manager?" I smiled a little.

"Is that so unusual?" he asked.

I shrugged. "Guess it's so . . . mundane." I wasn't really sure what I meant.

He laughed, throwing his head back and obviously enjoying himself. "My life is less exotic than you might think, Keira. I run a business—an inn, restaurant, a game preserve. I do what it takes. My wildlife manager is as dedicated to the health and welfare of the stock as I am."

"Is he like you, too?" I asked.

"An environmentalist? An animal lover?" His eyes danced as he teased me.

"You know what I mean. Vampire."

"He is," Adam said. "We came here together. Niko takes care of the property and wildlife, I handle the rest of the business. We've known each other a long time."

"Great. So, I'm guessing here, but I'm betting the Wild Moon is a home away from coffin for vamps?"

"In a way." He laughed. "I offer a place for my kind to stay."

"So why did you all think the Albrights were poaching?"

Adam lost some of the humor in his eyes. "Niko found evidence of hunting, field dressing, remains of dead animals in various areas of the ranch. The Sitka deer were just the last in a long string. It's been happening over the past few months. We were able to keep it quiet, until now. I'd hoped it would stop after the guests arrived. But it didn't.

"The other night, while patrolling, Niko ran across the Albrights, driving around on ranch property, outside the private fenced area. Their truck contained several guns, a scent of blood, but no actual animal parts. He followed them to the funeral home."

"I'm pretty sure Marty was paying them for something," I said. "But, come on, Adam, this is the Texas Hill Country. Every good ol' boy with any self-respect has a truck full of guns."

Adam shook his head. "The guns had recently been fired. Niko could smell the gunpowder. The blood scent was fresh."

"You knew this and you let them go?" I was a little surprised. If this had happened on clan territory, the trespassers would have just vanished. Forever.

"What would you expect me to do with them?"

I shrugged. "I guess I thought your kind of justice might be a little less . . . average?"

"Making them disappear?"

"Something like that."

"We may be vampires, Keira, but we're not the mob. That kind of vengeance doesn't happen anymore."

It does in my family, I thought. "So you let them go and tracked them back to my cousin."

Adam nodded. "I meant to confront him. Glamour him if needed. Find out what they were doing with the animals . . . and why my ranch."

"Oh, shit," I exclaimed.

"What?"

"It just occurred to me. The mortuary's a great place for stashing dead meat. Big walk-in refrigerator, totally too much for the place, nearly always empty. Who's going to go in there besides Marty?"

"You think it's a possibility?"

"Anything's possible. Marty wasn't the brightest bulb in the lamp. He always needed money. I imagine they thought they could make quick bucks from city boys who could pass off a poached deer as their own kill. Hunting season doesn't open for another couple of weeks. They probably couldn't care less about buying a hunting license."

"It makes a twisted sort of sense," Adam said. "The only thing I don't understand is this last kill. I don't understand it. Why a couple of young Sitka deer? Not much in the way of trophies or even meat there. They didn't even take the bodies, just the heads. There are more exotics wandering around here that would fetch a premium."

Now it was my turn for a little truth or consequences.

"They didn't kill those particular deer," I said, watching him for a reaction. "At least they didn't do the hunting down part. But they might have come by afterward and taken advantage."

Adam started to say something but stopped abruptly as he looked at me. I think he realized he needed to be quiet and let me speak. Good choice.

I couldn't look at him and stared down at the even wooden floorboards of the porch. "I had a vision, a nightmare."

My voice was quiet, but even.

He responded in the same low tones. "Does this happen often?"

I didn't quite answer. "I saw the hunt in a dream, Adam. It wasn't the Albrights."

"Could you tell who it was?" he asked.

"No, I never saw their faces. But they were something that hunted for food, for blood, not for pleasure. Whoever took the heads came much later."

"You're sure about that?"

I nodded. "Positive. Believe me, I remember every detail." I looked at him and asked the question that had crossed my mind as soon as I'd realized what he was. "So, I guess it wasn't anyone you know."

His face set in a grim scowl. "We care for animals here, Keira. We don't hunt them."

"Sorry, just asking," I said. "No offense, but it did cross my mind. I didn't mean to imply anything."

"None taken," he said. "I must admit that I'm a bit touchy about this. I suppose I'm more than a little tired of the stereotypes, of these horrible movies, and novels that presume to know us."

"Evil cruel vampire, bloodsucker, killer, seducer of young virgins." As soon as I'd said the words I wished I could take them back.

But Adam had a sense of humor.

"Exactly that. Some things are real, some aren't. Some

are just open to interpretation." He grinned. "Like that last one."

I blushed, the heat rising from my boot-clad toes to the top of my head. I was not going there right now. I also wasn't going to mention the fact that my dream-self had fed on those deer, too. Although, I suddenly realized, of all people, he might understand the need I'd felt for the blood. That certainly opened up another door of possibility. I guess Bea had been right, damn her. This would make things easier—that is, if he really hadn't killed my cousin. Time to talk about different things.

"Look, Keira. I can't say for certain no one here hunted those deer. It's not likely, but I need to talk to Niko. There are some things I can't share with you yet, but I promise if it has anything to do with your cousin's death, I'll tell you."

"You'll tell me and not the Sheriff?" I smiled again.

"If I'm right," he said, "this is personal business . . . and deals with things that our eager young Sheriff only has nightmares about."

I met his eyes and knew his meaning. Matters of the dark needed to stay in the dark. Matters of power, blood, and the hunt weren't to be shared with any human, not even the law.

But there was something else I had to tell him. "Adam, just so you know, I do have another theory about Marty."

"What's that?"

How could I explain without actually going into too many details? He'd revealed himself to me, but I wasn't ready to share all my family angst. I was still trying to figure out how to tell him about my own personal little secret . . . the difference he'd seen in me.

"You never actually met Marty, right?"

Adam nodded and I continued.

"He was always kind of a geek, an outsider, never actually fitting in with any group. He hated it. The possibility occurred to me that somehow, Marty met up with a vampire and let him, or her, drain him on purpose. Thinking it was cool, or that he'd come back powerful or whatever." That should work. I didn't want anyone to suffer consequences if Marty had asked for it.

"He knew about our kind?"

I shrugged. "Maybe, he could have. I don't know. I only saw the marks after he was dead, not before. If someone was chomping on Marty's neck on a regular basis, I wouldn't necessarily have noticed."

"He was your cousin. You wouldn't have noticed?"

"We weren't exactly close. I'd never had any reason to go pulling down his collar. Adam, really, I kept out of Marty's life as much as possible."

"Keira, let me do some investigating. I'll try to find out for you. On both issues."

"Also . . . the only thing I can be sure of is that the hunters weren't human," I said. "Is there anyone besides vampires around—shifters, maybe?"

"What do you mean by 'shifters'?"

He sounded puzzled, but I was just as puzzled at his question. Admittedly, the two groups didn't exactly hang out together on a regular basis, at least not that I knew of, but if, as I'd finally realized, he was running a resort where vamps could vacation, why not shifters, too? It made sense to me.

"You know, shapeshifters," I explained. "Maybe you call them something else?"

He burst out laughing, the sound slid over me, bubbles of mirth rolling off my skin, almost tangible enough to touch. Damn, he'd been holding back on me. I suppose now that I knew what he was, he wouldn't hide his power. But that still didn't make the laugh any easier to take.

"You're laughing at me?" I sat up, my body stiff, already feeling the resentment.

He turned in the seat to face me and I could see the realization creep across his face. "You're not joking."

"Of course I'm not freakin' joking," I said, letting him hear the anger in my voice. This was hard enough to do without being laughed at.

"Keira, I'm sorry," he said, "but I don't know how much you know about the supernatural world. Vampires can't shapeshift. Werewolves and such are all part of the myths and legends that get mixed up in our reality." I started to speak, but he held up his hand. His voice was kind, but just this side of condescending.

"I suppose I should have explained before you leapt to any conclusions—"

"Conclusions, my ass!" I jumped up, furious at the implication. So he was Mr. Know-it-all, was he? Just because his personal belief system was flawed and he couldn't accept the truth. I was *so* out of here. This was worse than being gay and coming out in a family of homophobes. However distasteful to them, at least no one told you your kind didn't even exist.

I turned on my heel and stalked across the porch, flying down the steps.

"Keira, wait." He was standing in front of me, blocking my way on the path. I hadn't seen any movement. He definitely wasn't hiding his abilities any longer.

I pushed at him but he didn't budge.

"Get out of my way," I said.

"I'm sorry, I didn't mean to insult you," he said. "It's just that, well . . ."

He shrugged and smiled at me, his fangs peeking out just a little. I supposed he could retract them when he wanted since I'd never seen any evidence of them before . . . and we'd spent many an evening talking, flirting and laughing together.

But damn it, at least I admitted I didn't know much about other species of supernaturals, why the hell was he being such a jerk about it?

"Well, what, Adam?" I said. "I'm not insulted, I'm angry. You have absolutely no idea what you're talking about."

"I suppose you do?"

His sardonic tone matched the clever arrogance of his pose. Damn it, he looked so good doing it, too. He stood with his arms loosely crossed over his chest, the pure black of the silk contrasting with the clear pale skin, green eyes smoldering at me in the dark. But I wasn't going to let a little lust distract me. Okay, a *lot* of lust.

"Yes, I most certainly do," I said. "I have every idea of what I'm talking about. Did you not even begin to wonder why I was so quick to accept the fact that you're a vampire?"

"I'm sorry, I don't follow your reasoning. You said you'd met vampires before, in Soho."

I was getting exasperated. "Did you ever actually go to that club, or had you just heard of it?"

"I'm not much for nightclubs," he admitted.

That's why he didn't know. If he'd spent any time at all there, he'd have met several of my London relatives who tended to consider the club their home away from home. At Night Moves, no one bothered hiding who or what they were. Normal humans couldn't even find the place because it was so well shielded. I should have realized he hadn't been there when he hadn't been surprised I had, especially since he thought of me as a human.

Unless, of course, this was all some macho bullshit game and he was just playing me.

I climbed back onto the porch and sat down on the swing. Later was turning out to be now. Adam followed, sitting next to me, saying nothing.

"Adam, about me, my life," I began.

His gaze didn't waver, fixed on my face as if he were memorizing it.

"There's so much I need to explain." I tried to keep my voice even and steady.

He stayed silent, watching me with a measuring gaze. I wondered what he was thinking.

I placed my hands on my knees. Words weren't going to be enough. How did I tell him about the physiological and metaphysical changes I was going through? About the power that was in me and that I could neither control yet nor identify?

The palms of my hands weren't exactly sweating, but I could feel them buzzing a little with the contained energy that I was holding back with a great deal of effort. I couldn't find the words to explain but I could definitely give him a taste of what I was. Share the possibilities.

"Hold out your hands, Adam," I said, my voice husky. He did as I asked. I took a deep breath in preparation and then took his hands in mine. He jerked a little, as our palms touched, but I gripped harder. He hadn't seen anything yet.

I held his gaze and smiled a little, trying to reassure him with my expression. He smiled back, but still kept silent. I closed my eyes and consciously relaxed my muscles, hesitating a little before taking the final step. In a rush, I lowered all my shields, allowing my power to travel down my arms and across to the man sitting next to me. It wasn't the full measure of what I'd be capable of in a few weeks, just the untapped potential of a Changeling, but I knew it would still be rather impressive. I'd always tested fairly high.

Adam trembled a little but didn't let go of my hands. I poured out everything I had, reached out with every iota of my ability and energy, letting it completely loose for the first time since I'd been with Gideon. Adam's eyes burned at me, shadows and flickering fire dancing behind the glittering green. His hands convulsed on mine, sliding up to grip my wrists as if my hands were no longer safe to touch.

I grasped his wrists in return, swallowing as the craving built in me, a need stronger than the darkest hunger, more powerful than the overwhelming and totally absolute drive that I'd felt during the hunt. Was that my hunger or his? I couldn't tell.

Adam growled and pulled me closer, lips pulled back, fangs bared, extended. I felt desire engulf me as my need merged with his. I crawled into his lap and embraced him, both of us fighting for control. I wanted to sink fangs into him, drink the hot blood pulsing beneath the skin of his neck, knowing that was the only thing that would satisfy my thirst. I could feel the same yearning echoed in him.

Saliva collected in my mouth as I bent my head, my knees straddling his thighs, my hands on his shoulders, my teeth straining to reach, to tear, to taste.

"No!" Adam roared and stood, pushing me away. I fell, my head hitting the wooden planks with an audible crack. As I passed out, I felt the connection between us break.

CHAPTER TWELVE

M Y NOSE TWITCHED, the smell of waxy smoke reached me, teasing me awake. I blinked a few times, trying to figure out where I was.

The soft glow of a pair of Victorian-style wrought-iron floor lamps created the perfect ambience, the purple watered-silk shades diffusing the glare of electric light. I was lying on a soft overstuffed couch covered in a matching purple, cushions piled under my head and my feet. The couch sat just under the front windows and facing a doorway that must lead to a bedroom.

In front of the couch, a rustic wooden coffee table just a few shades lighter than the polished hardwood floor displayed a varied array of candles surrounding a handmade ceramic bowl filled with an assortment of individually wrapped chocolate truffles. One of the candles had just extinguished; its gray-white plume of smoke rising to the ceiling like an unnaturally thin ghost. A bottle of wine stood in front of the bowl, flanked by two wine stems. Adam must have brought me into his house.

An afghan covered me. The pain in the back of my head was a dull ache, nothing I couldn't handle, but still annoying. I shuddered as reality washed over me and the memory of what I'd almost done returned. I'd been a scant second from tearing out Adam's throat. Definitely not a way to win friends and seduce a possible lover. I turned my head and scanned the room, not moving from my supine position. No sign of him. Had he completely freaked and bolted?

After a few moments, I realized I was hearing something other than the normal creaks and groans of a country house. Voices. Outside on the porch.

I struggled to sit up without hurting. That wasn't going to be easy. Every muscle ached as if I'd been beaten by an expert. Trouble with channeling raw power was that you paid for it, usually in spades. I'd known that going in, but figured the risk was worth the effort. Now I wasn't so sure.

I carefully swung my feet to the floor, waiting to see if I was dizzy or disoriented. I wasn't, but I realized I was in stocking feet.

I walked to the front window, moving as slowly as if I were driving a Ferrari through a school zone. My engine wanted to rev, but my body said "no way."

The blinds were drawn and I couldn't see a thing. I slid over to the front door, which stood slightly ajar. Through the two-inch space, I could see the screen door was closed. I put my eye to the gap.

Adam stood to my right on the dark porch, his back to me, hand to his ear. He was on the phone.

I strained to hear, but the words were muffled as if I were listening through a thick wall. I rubbed at my ears and tried again. Nothing. I couldn't be sure if there were even words.

This was stupid. I swung the door open. Adam turned without a sound.

I started to say something, then thought better of it. I shook my aching head and just went back inside. I needed to sit down.

"Keira?" The word floated softly on the air, almost tangible as it reached my ears. "Can we talk?"

"Maybe."

I went back to the couch and curled up in the corner, wrapping the afghan around me. I wasn't really cold, it just felt safer that way. As if the blanket could protect me . . . from myself, mostly. I was afraid if I let Adam Walker get close again, my body would betray me and I'd forget about the fact that he'd just dumped me on my ass—literally. Not to mention the fact that both of us had come a hairbreadth away from feeding on each other.

He walked toward me, slow and careful, as if nearing a pit full of hot coals, or maybe a rabid dog you weren't sure was restrained. If I were him, I'd have definitely thought of the dog analogy.

"Are you well?" he asked as he carefully sat down in the armchair. Good choice. I couldn't have handled him sharing the couch, being so close again, at least, not right now.

I nodded, not yet sure of what I wanted to say.

His face remained neutral, expectant, as if he'd sit there patiently and let me take my own time about talking. His posture was loose but not quite relaxed, more the not-quite-tension of an animal waiting to see if the noise it heard was predator or fellow prey. At this point, I wasn't sure which one I was—or wanted to be.

"Who was that?" I said, my voice a little hoarse as if I'd not spoken for days.

"Where?" His wasn't any better. He sounded as if he'd been silent for centuries, voice rusty with disuse. Nothing like a little discomfort to change our normality. Oh yeah, none of our communications had exactly been normal.

"Outside, on the phone," I said. "Who were you talking to?"

"Andrea." He fixed his gaze on me. "Before I explain—what the hell happened out there?"

I met his eyes, the weight of his expectation fixing my gaze. "I guess I could ask you something similar. Why did you throw me off?"

He looked down at his feet, hands smoothing the fabric of his slacks over his thighs. I heard him swallow. The tip of his tongue flickered out, fast as a serpent's, and licked his lips.

"I'm sorry," he said. "Something happened that frightened me."

His voice was nearly a whisper in the dark room.

"I scared you?"

"I haven't been tempted to feed from a person in years—more years than you've been alive, I'd wager. Do you know how close I came? I nearly sank my teeth into that lovely neck of yours."

I'd have let him.

"No kidding?" The words burst from me in surprise as I realized what he'd just said. "You don't take blood from people?"

"Not since . . ." His gaze burned with that hidden flame again. "I've seen too much death and destruction in my life, Keira. I won't be a part of it anymore."

"Wait," I said, sitting straight up and letting the afghan drop. "You're serious. Don't tell me . . . a vampire with a soul, helping the helpless?" So I was making a very bad joke. Sue me. I didn't know what else to say.

"I am completely serious, Keira. This isn't some B-movie or a cult television show," he said. "We're lucky now. Modern science is a wonderful thing. We don't have to risk discovery by feeding on people anymore."

"But someone fed on my cousin."

"That is why I told you I'd investigate. It's against our laws."

"Even when it's consensual? If Marty had wanted it?"

He didn't answer. I watched his face in the shadows, a multitude of expressions flickering across his features.

"Adam?"

"It's not against the law if it's consensual." The words held no expression, but behind the syllables, I sensed the weight of something else left unsaid.

"Why does this bother you, Adam? Isn't this your nature?"

A heavy sigh escaped him. "Yes. Our nature and our need, driving us to first seduce and then to bleed our victims, our prey. There's a fine line between glamour and consent. It's easy to glamour, to seduce an all-too-willing victim, but this kind of thing is distasteful to most civilized vampires. The difference between rape and seduction is salesmanship. If the ability to make a choice is removed, if 'no' isn't an option, then it's rape, pure and simple."

He had a point.

"But surely some of them seek you out?"

"Always. Perhaps your cousin was one of those. But if he wasn't, then whoever fed from him crossed a line, especially if they're responsible for his death. I will find out."

I had to ask. "Don't you miss the hunt?"

I'd felt his need when we'd merged—the same thrill of the chase, the stalking of the prey, the capture and finally the taste of the hot, fresh blood as it filled your mouth.

I knew that somewhere inside Adam Walker, reformed vampire, the crude, yet powerful, drive to hunt still lurked.

"What do you know of the hunt?"

His comeback was nothing if not timely. I wanted to bring up the truth I'd been skirting: the fact Adam and I had shared power, merged psyches, whatever that had been. I'd only meant to lower my guard and let him feel the hidden energy. It had never occurred to me that my plan might backfire. I'd been trying to prove a point. In this case, the point had been just a little too sharp.

I let the darkness show in my eyes as I caught his gaze again. I knew what those shadows looked like. I'd seen them in a mirror just a couple of days ago.

"You may have wanted to feed from me, Adam, but you're not the only one. I felt the need, too. The hunt is a part of who I am. I'm a Changeling. In a few weeks, I could be hunting for real. You felt it, you know the truth."

He shook his head as if in confusion. "What I felt was something more than hunter, Keira. You're not a vampire. You're not human. What are you?"

"I'm me, Adam. I don't know what else I am anymore. Hunter, shapeshifter, clairvoyant, I could be anything. In the meantime, I'll exhibit varying symptoms—most of which I don't have a whole lot of control over."

He stood, a rapid jerky motion, as ill-fitting on him as an Armani suit would have been on Marty. Without a word, he strode to the window and opened the blinds, to stare out at the night. He stood still as a rock in a stream, one hand still touching the wooden rod, one loose at his side. I sensed no movement from him, not even the slight exchange of air from breathing. Did he have to breathe? Another question.

"We're not all the same, Adam," I continued, talking to

his taut back. "My father, my brothers are mostly shape-shifters, predators. Some relatives are weather-talents, seers, sorcerers, necromancers . . . many other things. We lived here for decades, until the Hill Country became the playground for rich assholes with more money than sense. Then they all left. But I stayed."

"Tell me of your cousin Marty. Was he a necromancer, then? Was that why he was dealing in dead animals from my ranch?" The bitterness was evident.

I shook my head, even though he wasn't looking at me. "No. Marty, to his eternal shame, was human."

Adam turned and strode back to the couch, crouching in front of me so his face was even with mine. His eyes glittered in the dark. "You swear he was human?"

"Completely," I said. "He was some sort of throwback. The family disowned him."

His sigh proved to me that he did have breath in him. I felt the current of air brush my cheek. To my embarrassment, I could feel my body reacting to his presence. I grasped the blanket closer to me, as if to keep the barrier.

"So your cousin was a human playing at death," he said. "Didn't he know how dangerous that was?"

"Evidently not," I retorted. "Whatever he was doing, it obviously got him killed."

Adam rocked back on his heels, his hands resting on his knees. For a brief moment, I flashed on Carlton in nearly the same position when he'd made the pass at me at the mortuary.

Adam reached out and touched my cheek with the tips of his fingers. "You've changed my world tonight, Keira Kelly," he said. "In more ways than one." A smile curled his lips as he leaned in toward me.

"Stop." I put a hand up. "Wait. I'm not so sure . . ."

I let the words trail off as I saw the heat in Adam's gaze mirroring the fire that I knew was in mine. Damn.

Whatever had gone between us, whatever the psychic merge had been, had created a link that hadn't been completely broken. My hand dropped as I leaned forward, a hungry fish to a shiny lure, my eyes captured by his, my lips already aching for the taste of his mouth on mine.

"Adam, are you ready?"

Andrea's voice fell between us, cutting off the connection like a razor through paper.

Adam pulled away, with visible effort.

"Damn it," he whispered. "I'll be there momentarily, Andrea."

She looked at me, then at Adam, shrugged and left as silently as she had arrived.

"Sorry. Duty calls."

"Duty?" I asked, as I tried to dismiss the whirl of emotions clouding my thinking.

"I need to meet with my security staff, take care of some internal business," Adam replied. "That's where I was headed when I saw you at the loading dock."

I nodded and fumbled around looking for my boots. I needed to leave right now. Go home, clear my head, process everything I'd learned.

Adam touched my cheek, a tender smile on his face. "Go on home, Keira. I'll take care of my business and then see you later for dinner?"

Dinner. I'd actually forgotten.

"What time is it?"

"Only seven. Would you meet me here at nine?"

"So, what's with the wine and the chocolates?" I asked, inclining my head toward the coffee table as I pulled my right boot on.

"Nothing," he said. "At least—not yet."

I turned to look accusingly at Adam. "You were going to set me up."

The soft sound of his laugh sent a tingle shivering up my spine. "Let's just say I was planning to optimize a situation."

"Optimize?"

His grin grew wider. I felt myself flushing.

"I asked you over for dinner at the restaurant. There's no rule that you couldn't have an appetizer here . . . or come back for dessert," he answered with a come-hither smile that sent a shiver up my spine.

Damn. Well, maybe a couple of hours at home, a hot shower—no, make it a cold one—and a little distance would let me deal with him on a more reasonable level. Besides, I needed to keep in contact with him if I were to find out more about Marty's death. I couldn't just go barging around the place trying to dig out vampires who might know something . . . pun intended. Adam was my best chance of finding out.

"Fine," I said, "I'll be back at nine . . . and it better be damned good."

He laughed quietly, his voice dropping into the seductive tones that matched his smile. "I promise, I'm always very good."

That was precisely what I was afraid of.

CHAPTER THIRTEEN

A S I TURNED UP THE ROAD that led to my house, I pulled out my phone and dialed Carlton's cell phone. I didn't know if he'd known about the Albrights having been caught trespassing at the Wild Moon. Even though other things might be personal matters, this could put our Sheriff on the path to arresting those two clowns. Hell, they might have been the ones to kill Marty. Just because he'd had fang marks, didn't mean that was what had killed him. Delusional? I didn't know. I preferred to think of it as keeping my options open.

The rings gave way to voice mail as I pulled into my driveway. I didn't know if Carlton's phone had service that reached to Houston, but if he wasn't already back he should be fairly soon. Even if he'd left when the banks closed, it only took a few hours to drive home.

The beep sounded and I began to speak. "Carlton, hey, it's Keira. Listen, I found something out that I think you should— Holy mother fucking hell." I dropped the phone to the seat next to me and stared at my porch.

I got out of my car, smelling it before my brain processed the reality of what I'd seen in the flash of headlights.

The soft glow of the porch lamp lit up the thing that had once been part of a Sitka deer. There was enough of the hide left to see the telltale white spots. Most of the lips were gone and I could see there were no front teeth. Wasn't I glad I knew so much about this species? Yeah, right.

Of course, since it was only a head, there wasn't much more to see. It had obviously been dead for a while. Most of the skin and underlying muscle tissue was gone, chewed away by whichever animals and insects had gotten there first. No blood, except for what had been used to write the words on the porch next to the decomposing head.

STAY AWAY BITCH. THIS COULD BE YOU.

I stood there staring at the thing on my porch. I was fully in the thrall of rubbernecker's syndrome. The sick part of you that makes you look, even though you know it's going to be really, really bad.

Great. Abso-fucking-lutely dandy. Just what I wanted as a before-dinner appetizer. My brain tripped a switch and slid into dead calm overdrive. This was just one step beyond sanity for me today.

I jumped, crouching into a defensive stance as a shadow moved to my right. As I realized who it was, I relaxed.

"I'm not sure I like your idea of a present, bro."

Tucker came into the light, laughing, only the underlying growl giving away his discomfort.

"You think I put this here?"

I shrugged. "You've done worse."

"That I have."

"If you didn't do this, who did?"

"That, dear sister, is a question for you. What have you been up to?"

I sighed, leaned back against the porch rail and filled him in on what I'd found out at the ranch. I even told him about Adam. Not the sharing power part, though.

"So, Mr. Mysterious is really a bloodsucker," Tucker said with his trademark grin. "This could make things really interesting. My sister dating the undead."

"Laugh it up, Cujo," I replied. "As if you've never dated

outside the family. C'mon, let's go inside. The smell of this thing is making me sick."

I took another look as I passed the gruesome present. There wasn't much there. Most of a deer head and a good part of the neck, as if it had been either torn from the shoulders of the living animal or hacked inexpertly from the recently dead. No sign of what had killed it, there were too many rips and tears in what was left of the skin. It was far from fresh. I was sure if I concentrated hard enough and squinted, I could see maggots crawling in what was left of the flesh. I didn't squint.

Before I could open the front door, the lights of a car swung in behind me and distracted me. Bea scrambled out of her compact, already talking.

"Hey, *m'hija,* shouldn't you be pampering yourself for your date? I came over to— *Madre de Dios!*" Bea crossed herself and stepped back up against her car.

"Don't ask," I said. "This is just gross." My voice sounded tired.

"Come on, girlfriend," said Bea, climbing up the steps and grabbing at my arm. "I came so I could help you get ready, but we're going to my house for the rest of the night. You need to get out of here."

"No," I said, turning to face her. "Thanks for the offer, but I need to clean this mess off the porch before it's harder to scrub off the blood. I will not let these bastards chase me out of my own house."

"I don't want you staying here by yourself. Come on over to my place and we'll come back tomorrow morning and I'll help you."

"I won't be by myself," I said. "Tucker's here. Besides, I doubt that whoever did this will come back. Somehow, this reeks of the Albrights."

I opened the front door and Bea scrambled to follow me. Tucker followed at a more leisurely pace.

I took a deep breath before I flipped on the inside light, halfway expecting the room to be in a shambles. Nothing. The living room looked just as I'd left it: newspapers stacked on the floor by the couch, junk mail in the trash. I dropped my backpack on the recliner as I went into the kitchen.

"How about I pour us each a big glass of wine?"

"Sure," Bea said, perching on one of the kitchen stools. "But aren't you going to call Adam Walker and tell him you're going to be late to dinner?"

"Yeah, Keira, aren't you going to call?" Tucker smirked at me, his eyes dancing with humor. One of these days, I was just going to—aarrgh. Brothers—no matter how powerful, how supernatural, they were still all the damn same.

"Shit, I was just there, too. Here." I tossed Bea the opener and reached for the phone. "You open the bottle."

"You were just there?"

I shook my head at her and put a finger to my lips as the phone began to ring. He picked up almost immediately. I could hear some talking in the background, but couldn't make out any words.

"Hey there," I said. "Sorry to bother you."

"Did you change your mind?" He sounded disappointed.

"No, I didn't change my mind. It's just that I seem to have had a visitor at my house. Someone left behind a really nasty present." I quickly described what had happened.

There was absolute silence at the other end of the phone. "Adam?"

"I'm here, Keira." He voice was brusque and commanding. "Look, you wait right there. As soon as I'm finished here I'll bring dinner to you. Don't go inside, you don't know if it's safe."

"Too late," I said, "Already inside. Adam, really, I'm fine, my friend is here and the house is okay. I'm sure it was just some sort of sick joke by the Albrights."

"You think it was them?"

"Who else?" I asked. "Unless you know something I don't."

"I'd still like to come over and bring you dinner," he said. "The chef was already putting together a great meal. It won't be any trouble to bring it to you."

I could hear the promise under the words as his voice worked its magic. My body started to respond almost instantly, as if he were already in the room with me. Despite the frustrating anger I still felt, I blushed and glanced over at Bea, who was pretending not to listen while pouring the wine.

"Your friend can wait with you until I get there," Adam continued. "I won't be long."

Bea put a glass of wine down in front of me. She whispered, "Things are looking up. Let him come over. He can help with the cleanup."

I made a face at her and turned away, gulping my wine. It was as if he and I were speaking intimate, suggestive words in front of strangers. But we were only talking about dinner.

I nearly capitulated, half kicking myself mentally for giving in so easily. "No, please. Don't. Let's just reschedule, okay?"

There was no sound on the other end of the phone.

"Adam?"

"If you insist, Keira," he said. "I'll respect your wishes and reschedule dinner."

"Thank you," I said. "Why don't we plan on dinner tomorrow night?"

"Certainly," he said. "I'll see you."

He hung up without additional fanfare.

Well, hell's bells, after all the emotional waltzing we'd been doing, I expected a little more protest from him.

"Boyfriend not coming?" Tucker was definitely enjoying this way too much.

"No," I said, "and he's not my boyfriend."

"Stranger things have happened, *m'hija*." Bea joined in on the teasing.

"Great, you're both too damned funny for words," I growled. "Now who's going to help me clean up the mess?"

Bea reached over and tapped the glass of wine in my hand. "Let's drink up before we even think about that."

I did as she suggested, glaring over the rim of the glass at the two seeming co-conspirators.

Maybe after some more wine I could start seeing the humor in all of this. My new suitor, a vampire, didn't believe in werewolves or shapeshifters. My girlfriend, who was scared by the fact that vampires existed, was pushing me to date one, with my brother's help. Of course, I wasn't exactly planning to spill the beans about Adam's little secret to Bea. That was probably a little more than she could handle right now. Talk about complications.

Tucker gallantly dragged the deer head into the woods behind my house and the three of us had made a decent dent in the bottle of wine when I heard the gravel crunch under a new set of wheels. Oh, fucking hell. Now what? Probably Carlton. That would just be dandy.

A black SUV was just pulling out of the drive as I

reached the front door. I caught a glimpse of pale hair on the person at the wheel: Andrea.

Adam stood at the edge of the porch, a look of disgust on his face as he stared at the bloody warning. He looked up and saw me.

His eyes held something new. Not the insides-twisting clarity that had intrigued me since we'd first met, but instead, a subtle darkness clouding the crystalline green. It was as if someone else was looking out from the inside, someone whose purpose and intent was much grimmer.

But this darkness wasn't tainted like Gideon's had been. I didn't feel contaminated. It was like a breath of shadows and night whispering behind the sea green.

"I thought I told you not to come."

He smiled at me, the darkness vanishing as if it had never been there. "I said I would respect your wishes. Tell me you don't really want me here."

I couldn't say a word. Bea shoved a full glass of wine into my hand, which I then automatically held out to Adam.

He paused a moment and I held my breath. Oh, crap. Had I committed a faux pas? The vamps at Night Moves had always carried around flasks of blood, I never really paid much attention to what else they'd been drinking—if anything.

He reached for the glass, grinned at me and went for the obvious.

"I really like . . . wine."

I grinned back like a fool, trying not to giggle, conscious of Bea and Tucker behind me.

Adam walked across the letters, being careful not to step on any of them, and stopped just short of coming inside. I stayed where I was, up against the open screen door. The night had gotten cold; a chill slipped up my right arm, raising goose bumps.

"Hello."

He was so close his breath teased my hair, drifting across my scalp. Suddenly, I didn't feel the cold anymore. It was as if there was some sort of fire arcing between the two of us, a space heater at full tilt, the warmth of it wrapping both of us up in its electric hum. I'd always assumed that vampires would be cool, lacking the normal energy and temperature of the living human body. I guess I'd been wrong. Or maybe this was something else entirely. Something I'd started by sharing with him earlier, opening up the barriers between us. Once you cross that line with a person, it's almost impossible to completely close yourself off again. But I didn't want to close off.

I stood transfixed, reveling in the sensation of power. He'd relaxed a little and let go some of his shielding. His was one of the strongest auras I'd ever sensed. I could feel my own power starting to stir, responding to him, the heat building between us.

"Aren't you coming in?" Tucker's voice cut in like the slap of a cold wet towel.

I startled and almost dropped my own wineglass, which had been hanging loose in my left hand. I was glad it was almost empty. Small drops of wine splattered the porch, red liquid glistening in the light, their color redder than the now-brown words scrawled so cruelly across the wooden flooring.

Adam looked at Tucker, then at Bea, then turned back to me with an enigmatic smile. He gave a brief nod, almost a half-bow. For a fleeting moment, in my mental haze, I flashed back and instead of Adam, I saw a tall, pale young man with red-gold hair. The guy in the hallucination. I gasped and stepped back away from the door. Déjà vu all over again.

Adam whipped around to peer out at the darkness beyond the porch. "Did you see something?" His voice rang, a steel trapdoor slamming shut, cutting off our connection. All the energy I'd felt from him was gone, giving way to a complete blankness, smooth and featureless like opaque glass.

"No, nothing, it was just something . . . else." I stammered out the words, disconcerted that anything about Adam had reminded me of that uncomfortable vision. "Please, Adam, come in. Let's go inside."

He turned back to face me, smiling.

"Are you sure?"

So, was that part true, too, then? Could he not come in without my invitation? I wondered, but didn't hesitate.

"Please, come in."

My brother took a step back to let us enter, but stared at Adam with a slight smile, lips pressed together carefully. No baring of teeth here. I knew he was being careful.

Adam spoke first, still staring at Tucker. "I didn't realize you were so . . . well protected. In fact, I'm beginning to think there's a great deal you haven't told me, Keira."

Adam's expression mirrored that of Tucker's. They recognized each other as predator and were both treading lightly, assessing each other, trying to figure out where each of them fit in my life.

The silence stretched out, both men silently appraising, Bea's gaze darting between the two, not sure of what to do. I just stood there, wineglass in hand, wondering what would happen. I began to feel a surge of power, of energy, emanating from my brother.

"Interesting," Adam finally said, backing down, his

expression relaxing into a gentle smile. "To borrow a phrase, I suppose you have a reason to hire . . . non-traditional security?"

"Hire? Not exactly," I said, laughing a little with relief. "Adam Walker, meet my brother, Tucker Kelly."

"Your brother. Hmmmm. Definitely not traditional, then."

"Not," I agreed. "Right now, though, he's basically a babysitter. My granny is a little too overprotective."

"My ass," Tucker exclaimed.

"Such a nice one, too." Bea's sotto voce remark wasn't meant to be heard by anyone. She didn't count on all of us having preternatural hearing ability.

Tucker grinned widely and turned to my friend, a silent question on his face. Bea matched his grin, staring at him, frankly appraising. This was most definitely getting interesting. From Bea's expression, she was thinking the whole idea was pretty nifty. Well, at least I wasn't the only one whose hormones were taking over.

"Look, Tucker, why don't you take Bea home?" I didn't want Bea to have to deal with Adam. She'd already been put through enough weirdness on my behalf. Besides, from the looks of things, my brother wouldn't mind in the least.

"Keira, are you sure?" Bea frowned, looking first at me, then at Adam.

"I'm sure, Bea," I insisted. "You need to go home and get away from this."

Tucker came to me and gave me a hug. He whispered, "You'll be okay?"

I nodded, answering him in the same low tone. "I'll be fine, really. Take her home. Keep her safe. I don't want her involved in this."

He kissed me on the cheek. "I'll keep her safe. She'll be okay with me . . . ?"

I giggled, knowing what he wasn't exactly asking. "She'll be just fine. She's not into commitment, either."

He grinned and kissed me again. "Take care, little sister."

"I will, bro. And thanks." I squeezed his arm, grateful he'd taken me at my word. He didn't know Adam from, well, Adam, and I was afraid he'd insist on sticking around. Unlike some of my other brothers, though, Tucker did tend to trust my judgment. Most of the time.

My brother took Bea's arm and headed out the door. Before he reached it, he paused and turned.

"Oh, by the way, you should ask your boyfriend about the blood."

"Blood?"

"The writing on the porch. It's not deer blood."

Adam stared at my brother for a long moment, but said nothing.

Tucker ushered Bea out the door. With a smile and a nod to me, he let the screen door slam behind him.

Adam and I both watched the little red sedan speed away. My best friend and my 1,200-year-old brother off for a night of what I hoped would be full of fun and unbridled sex. Of course, I wasn't sure where she was taking him, since her aunt and uncle lived with her and I didn't see them going there, but I didn't worry too much about it. They were both grown-ups. They'd figure it out. And I hadn't been kidding when I'd told Tucker that Bea wasn't into commitment. She'd been married once, to someone who treated her poorly. I didn't know the whole story as she hadn't wanted me to know. I hadn't found out until after it was over and I'd come back to Rio Seco. Since then, she preferred to keep things simple. No commitments, no risks.

After a few moments of watching the empty night, I asked the question that still needed an answer.

"So . . . when were you going to tell me?"

"About the blood?"

"Well, yeah."

"I'm not sure."

"What about it?" I asked.

He spoke without looking at me. "It's human."

I turned to look at him, didn't say anything for several long beats, just stared at his face, wondering what this meant.

"Were you planning to tell me?" I finally asked.

Silence.

"You weren't, were you?"

He still said nothing.

I shut the front door and stepped around him into the house.

"Damn it, you're all the fucking same."

"All?" Adam's voice was quiet, as if he were afraid to say much of anything.

"Men," I said. "Human, vampire, whatever the hell you are doesn't matter. You all act the fucking same. My family sics my older brother on me, under some ridiculous notion that I can't take care of myself—"

His soft words stopped my tirade in midstream. "It's because we . . . care for you. Nothing more."

My head whipped around. "Well then stop it, damn it."

"Stop caring?" Adam followed me into the living room. Before I could stop him, he picked up the wine bottle, grabbed my empty glass from my hand and refilled it.

I took it back from him and took a big gulp.

"Stop patronizing me," I said, exasperated at his cool smoothness.

"That, I will do," he said, smiling back at me.

I flopped onto the couch, glaring up at him, not really knowing why I was angry.

"That was your . . . brother, you said?"

"Yes, half-brother, actually," I said.

"He's a predator?"

"Hellhound," I replied. "Shapeshifter, whatever you want to call it."

"I see." He watched me, his face expressionless as if he were processing the information.

"Some more wine, then?" he asked.

"Sure." I was relieved. He seemed to be accepting all this new information.

Adam pulled a fresh bottle from my small wine rack, then came over to join me. He sat to my left, putting the bottle on the coffee table, then lit the candles I kept there. I reached over and turned off the table lamp. He smiled as he caught my eye but said nothing.

I watched as he opened and poured the wine with the efficiency of an expert. He'd chosen a Syrah and its garnet-red glowed in the ivory light. I let my eyes narrow to enjoy the play of the candle flames on the shimmering liquid jewel of the wine. I sipped it slowly, savoring the flavor. I'd always preferred a full-bodied red over the sharper whites.

"So you think the Albrights left the deer head?" His question certainly broke the mood.

"Yes," I said. "It wasn't the head that bothered me much in itself, but the fact it was so intensely vicious and nasty. I'm positive they were trespassing on the Point that night and took advantage of the situation. They probably realized their mistake later when they took the heads to

Marty . . . he would have known he couldn't sell them for trophies."

I took a sip of wine. "And the blood, Adam?" I asked. "Human?"

He nodded. "The blood used to write the words, yes."

"Marty's?"

My memory called up an all-too-clear image of the decomposing head as it lay against my front door, superimposing it with an image of my cousin's lifeless body lying pale and bloodless in the mortuary prep room. Behind that was my dream memory of stalking the beings that had hunted the deer.

I was curled up in my favorite corner, cradling the wineglass stem in both hands. Adam sat at the opposite end, staring straight ahead, as if captivated by the candles. Neither of us spoke as we enjoyed the wine. It was odd, but I felt completely comfortable sitting with him this way. I'd always felt silence was much more intimate than conversation. I'd never been able to sit this quietly with anyone else, not Carlton, not Bea . . . not even Gideon.

"I don't know, Keira," he said softly. "I never met your cousin."

"Oh," I said. "True."

"You couldn't tell?"

I shook my head. "No, I'm not . . . well, it's complicated, but I'm not exactly like my brother. I can't distinguish scents that well."

"Could your brother not recognize the scent?"

"I doubt it," I said. "He'd have said something. Marty wasn't . . . well, he wasn't close to anyone."

"I see," Adam said. He fell silent again, sipping his wine, watching me watching him.

He had a strong face marked by experience, not age. I

had no idea how old he was, but he could pass for thirty-five, maybe thirty. High cheekbones set off a nose that didn't quite make a straight line, but was well defined and matched his square chin and finely cut lips. Black hair waved back from his forehead and fell well past his shoulders. Taken separately, none of his features were particularly remarkable, but the whole was definitely greater than the sum of its parts.

I could hear Bea in my head. "This is a good one, *m'hija.*" I shifted in my seat and reached for more wine. He was there ahead of me, his hand closing around the bottle as mine closed over his.

"Let me." He spoke softly, not quite a whisper.

I pulled my hand away, reluctant to break contact with his skin. It was smooth and rough and everything in between and held the heat I'd felt earlier.

Our long-term flirtation was finally coming to a conclusion; an inevitability I would once have questioned. But tonight, I knew as unquestionably as I knew the sun rose every day and set every night, as surely as I knew at least once a month my father and most of my brothers would change into four-legged furry animals—I knew something more was going to happen between Adam and me. For the first time in a very long while, I felt the possibility of something that might just work, if I gave it half a chance.

"Here," he handed me my now-full glass. I felt the warmth of his skin brush mine once more as our hands passed. Again, I'd expected cool skin, but Adam's hand felt almost as hot as that of any shifter. I made a mental note to sit and have a long talk with him, one day, soon. Now was not that time.

"Will you come with me to the funeral home?"

"What?"

I blinked a little, trying to wrap my brain around the extreme change of subject. Suddenly, I knew exactly what he was getting at.

"He's . . . Marty's not there anymore. They came to pick him up this morning."

He nodded. "It won't matter. If there's any blood left, I'll know. I want to do this for you, for me."

I didn't hesitate. I stood up and grabbed my keys from the counter. "Let's go."

CHAPTER FOURTEEN

THE DOOR WAS LOCKED when we got there, a fresh strip of police tape across the entrance. Adam pulled it down, impatient as I fumbled with the keys, opening the heavy door, turning on lights so I could see.

He brushed past me to stand in the foyer, eyes shut, suddenly still as the silence within. What passed for humanity in him was lost at that moment, all I could see was vampire, scenting, sniffing the air for something, some clue.

"There is death blood here," he said. "Much death."

I put my hand on his arm. "It's a funeral home, Adam, there's always death. That's kind of the point."

He shook his head. "Maybe. Show me the embalming room."

We walked through the darkened building, only a few lights illuminating the corridor.

When we reached the security door, I punched in the code, swung it open and reached in to flip on the overhead lights. Adam stopped me, a hand on my arm.

"No light, not yet."

"Does the light bother you?"

He smiled. "I work better in the dark."

I ignored the double entendre and stepped back, away from the blackness of the room.

"I'll wait for you in the storage room . . . down the hall and to your right."

I couldn't stand there with him in the dark. My senses could still feel Marty's death, the vision I'd had, the dream become reality. I couldn't be there in that room right now.

"Keira." Adam gripped my arm again, stopping me. "Is something wrong?" The light from the hall cast shadows across his face. He looked worried.

"I'm okay, Adam," I said. "It's just . . . this room. It's too soon."

"Be safe," he said, leaning over to kiss me lightly on the forehead. "I'll be through shortly."

I nodded and left him there.

The storage room didn't look any different from the other day, when I'd confronted Derek. Mini-fridge in the back, shelves full of cremains boxes and cremation urns above it, a battered desk on the left, piled with old *Mortuary Management* magazines and *Funeral Monitor,* flanked by a couple of old file boxes bursting with paper. A cupboard on the right was closed and locked. I knew that's where Marty kept his back stock of embalming chemicals.

I cleared a space on the desk and sat there, waiting for Adam. It didn't take him very long.

"There's been blood here . . . recently, if my senses are correct. But nothing I could pinpoint."

I knew what he was thinking, part of me did, anyway. I was sure he suspected one of his people of having hurt Marty. It wasn't so much the blood he was looking for, but evidence of one of his own having been there. He hadn't found it. That was good news . . . for him anyway. It still didn't get me any closer as to why Marty was killed. In fact, all it meant was that if the killer was indeed a vampire, that he or she hadn't killed Marty here. He could have just as easily been drained elsewhere.

I said as much.

"I know," Adam said. "I was hoping it would be cut-and-dried. That I'd know immediately. But the lack of evidence doesn't clear any of my people. All I could scent was a faint trace of blood."

"Marty had an upswing in business recently," I said. "At least, according to the paperwork. More bodies equals more blood—and more money. Check out that shelf. He even ordered extra urns. Carlton and I were looking at the funeral records and discovered Marty was paying the Albrights."

Adam frowned as I filled him in on what Carlton and I had found out the day before.

"That could be it," he said. "I'm still hesitant, though. Something doesn't seem quite right." He tilted his head and sniffed. "I keep smelling . . ."

He squatted down in front of the mini-fridge, swinging open the door.

"What was in here?"

I peered over his shoulder. The shelves were bare of anything but a few crumpled condiment packets and a couple of jars of jam.

"I'm not sure," I said. "I imagine food. Derek was in here taking stuff out and putting it in his cooler. You smell blood?"

Adam shut the small door and stood up. "I can't tell," he said. "Not conclusively. Someone's washed the shelves, used a bleach cleanser." He shook his head. "I'm sorry, Keira, I can't be more sure. This is turning out to be a wild goose chase."

I sagged against a stack of magazines. "I'm not even so sure what kind of goose we were chasing, Adam."

"I'm not that sure myself," he admitted. "I might have been jumping to a conclusion."

"Doing a bit of that tonight, aren't you?" I smiled at him, taking the sting out of my words.

"I suppose I am," he said. "I'm not used to having to believe so many impossible things before breakfast. I may have jumped the gun a little." He smiled at me, a little sheepishly.

"I guess you did," I said. "It's okay, you know. We're all, well, not human, but not mistake-proof." I smiled back at him.

He leaned up against the cupboard, his features relaxing.

"Has the mortuary been in business long?" Adam's voice was quiet, respectful.

"Not quite a century," I answered. "My great-uncle built it. You can feel it, then?"

"Death is something I know intimately. There have been a great many dead things here. So you feel it, too?"

"It's part of what I am. Kind of a natural pull, a draw."

I sighed, grateful my shields reduced the effect of his relentless aura. "I've been an intimate of death for a great many years, Adam. My job, before the Marty babysitting gig. I . . ." I let out a breath, trying to figure out how to explain myself. "We don't die. Unless we choose to. I help escort people across."

"Across?"

I didn't look at him. Even though my work was perfectly acceptable in my family circle, having been brought up with humans made me look at death a little differently. Kind of seeing both sides of the coin, in a way.

"Until two years ago, I helped clan members die. Fed them poison—a potion of herbs and death magic concocted by those who know how. My job was to be there to greet Death when he came to get them. Make sure they took the trip. My people don't do death well, even when we choose it. So, yeah, I kind of know a lot about it. I've learned to shut it out, not let it affect me."

His laugh surprised me, echoing off the silent walls.

"My love, I don't know who you think you're fooling."

"Fooling? About what? I mean— Shit."

Red-faced, I picked up one of the magazines and riffled the pages. Not that I was in the least interested in its contents. I needed a moment to collect my thoughts.

Adam remained where he was, still leaning, arms crossed over his chest. Damn if he didn't look almost exactly the same as the first time I'd met him. Thick dark hair cascading past his shoulders, touching the middle of his back, framing the rugged beauty of his pale face. His long, lean body relaxed, yet underneath the façade, energy, something that I now knew was power contained. I'd felt the pull of him then, just as now.

He was wrong. Even though I could feel death in here, it was just another aura to avoid. That's all.

The other shoe dropped.

"Is that a British thing?" I snapped.

"What?"

"Calling me 'love.'"

I watched his neutral expression turn to what could be amusement.

"Yes . . . and no."

"What do you mean, 'no'?" I was beginning to feel a little queasy.

"What do you think it means?" he countered.

"Adam, you don't even know me, how can you begin to think you love me?"

"Know you? How could you possibly say I don't know you?"

He pushed himself away from the cupboard. "For more

than eight years I watched as you pretended to avoid me, tried to pretend you didn't feel anything toward me. But here we are and things have changed."

I looked back down at the magazine, not seeing what was on the page. "We never even exchanged so much as a kiss, never went on a date."

"You can't deny you feel the same." His voice remained even, almost amused. He was playing games with me; he had to be. "You can't possibly deny that you felt me, felt the pull . . . knew I was something different."

"I don't know what I feel—felt." Just call me the Queen of Denial. I didn't really know why I was avoiding this, whatever it was. Attraction, lust, the power of hormones.

"Keira." Adam crossed the small room and stood in front of me, taking my hands in his. I tried not to watch.

"Keira," he repeated. "Eight years ago, when you first walked into that silly soiree, I felt you. From across the room, I recognized something kindred. I know you did, too. You spent all that time coming to the same events, deliberately never spending too much time around me, but at the same time, making sure you were close by. Close enough to talk, to flirt, to make sure I knew you were there. But you never crossed that line. Yet, I knew."

"I thought you were human. I couldn't cross *that* line."

No matter how much I'd wanted to, I thought. He was right. Despite my then on-and-off again relationship with Gideon. I'd instantly been attracted to Adam—and just as instantly put the brakes on my feelings.

"No, you couldn't," he agreed. "But as surely as I'm dead, I knew. I still know . . . love."

"Lust," I said. "Not love."

He laughed softly, his hand reaching down to stroke my

cheek. A thrill ran through me, heat tracing down my skin where he'd touched me.

"Lust . . . love . . . in me, for you, they blend. Keira, you're how old?"

"Thirty-seven," I answered, my mouth almost too dry to speak.

"I was older than that when I died—too many years ago to count. I know what I feel."

I watched his face as he drew closer. Close enough to feel the breath of his words against my lips, but not touching, not quite. Shimmering energy danced across my skin. My pulse quickened, as I drew in a breath, and with that breath, his scent followed, assaulting my senses, flushing me with desire. The stillness of his being washed over me as I felt a great well of cool darkness inside, deep within him.

"Why is your skin hot?" I asked, breathing my words against him.

"It's not," he answered. "Feel . . . " He placed the palm of his hand against my cheek, the soft skin of a man to whom manual labor is only a concept. I started to tell him he was wrong as heat pulsed against my face, on fire from the warmth of his hand.

But then, suddenly, I realized he wasn't wrong. If I concentrated, I could tell that his skin temperature was no hotter than the room we stood in. It wasn't him. The heat was coming from me.

"And you still think you can shut out the dead."

I closed my eyes against the truth, pulling away from his touch. "Is that all this is then? An attraction to the dead?"

I stood, pushing him away, then turned, not able to face him. My hands gripped the side of the desk. I wanted to ground myself, to swallow the feelings that threatened to take over my rationality.

A pulse of power, an angry red aura from behind me was my immediate answer. It dissipated almost immediately, only to be replaced with a thick tension, a silence almost tangible in its heaviness. Then words, at first almost too soft to hear.

"That's the way it started," he began. "You could lie to yourself, keep it neutral. Pretend that it's the draw of power, of the magick that makes me live, of the death that makes me who I am. But we both know better. It's moved beyond that. You're not drawn to Andrea, to any other vampire the way you're drawn to me. Just as I'm not drawn to anyone else."

I stayed still, unmoving, not trusting myself to say anything.

The soft voice continued. "I lied to you, Keira. About the ranch. About why I chose to settle here. I've always known where you were."

I turned at that, needing to see his face, needing to know that what he spoke was truth.

He stood silently, watching me with the same need on his own face.

"Always?" I could barely get the word out.

Adam nodded. "I came to find you. To find out why I couldn't forget you."

"But . . . you've only been here for a couple of weeks."

"More than that," he said. "I've been traveling back and forth for the better part of two years. A great deal of construction was necessary before we could live here. Construction and preparation took more time than I anticipated."

"The other night, did you know I was here . . . at the mortuary?"

A smile crossed his face. "That was pure serendipity,

my love. Fate playing her twisted little game. I really had come to talk to your cousin. I wasn't ready to see you yet. I wasn't yet ready to play my hand."

"Your hand?"

He stepped closer, reached out tentatively, stroked my hair. I shut my eyes again, reveling in the sensation, almost not hearing his next words.

"I wanted it to be perfect. I wanted to make it so perfect that you couldn't say no. I was going to throw a soiree, a masquerade ball for Halloween. Invite the townspeople, invite you, especially. The Inn would have looked beautiful. The perfect setting. I had a plan."

My eyes opened, catching his gaze. "Then you had to get caught in a rainstorm and so much for the perfect setting."

His thumb brushed my cheek as he drew even closer.

"But that didn't matter quite so much, after all, did it?"

As his lips met mine, I knew I didn't have to answer . . .

A thousand years later, we pulled apart, my mind hazy, whirling with the possibilities, but knowing if this was going anywhere, it wasn't going to happen here in the storeroom of the funeral home. I could think of a lot better places.

"Adam," I croaked, barely able to speak.

He stared at me, unseeing, the clear green of his eyes as dark with craving as they had been earlier in the night, when I'd shared my power with him. He blinked, once, twice, then a shudder went through him and he settled, once again the suave sophisticate that I knew. His hand caressed my cheek again, a smile on his face.

"I think we have a dinner date, love. You still haven't eaten and it's still early."

"Dinner. Goddess, you made me forget again."

His laugh made me smile. "I distract you?"

"Totally," I said, and stroked his hair. "You are a complete and utter distraction."

"There are so many things I want to do with you, Keira Kelly. But you need to eat. Then we must talk to my staff about your cousin." A sigh, then a slight scowl. "Business before pleasure, my sweet. Time enough."

Damn. I couldn't argue with him. The sooner we found out who killed Marty, or at least whether or not it was a supernatural kill, the sooner Adam and I could get down to our own business—the business of finding out what was next with us.

CHAPTER FIFTEEN

I DROPPED ADAM at the ranch, then promised I'd be back in a flash. There was no way I was going to dinner in worn jeans and a flannel shirt. After a lightning-fast shower, I checked my voice mail. One message from Tucker. He didn't say much. Just that Bea was safe, he'd be in touch, he knew I could take care of myself and not to do anything stupid. Girlish giggling in the background explained the rest. Wherever they were, they must certainly be enjoying themselves. I didn't question my luck. I loved my brother but, so far, all he'd done for me was get in the way. I could work much better on my own, despite Gigi's warning.

After tearing through nearly everything in my closet, I finally realized it was more than useless. When I left England, I left most of my fancier clothing behind, not imagining I'd need it here in Rio Seco. Shortsighted as I was, most of my wardrobe consisted of more of what I was already wearing. I settled for a pair of plain black slacks, black silk tank and a dusky purple silk jacket, one of the few items not in my standard palette. Ankle-high black suede boots finished off what would have to pass as an ensemble. Not exactly a symphony of color, but my wardrobe always tended toward the monochromatic. It wasn't so much about the Goth look, more about the fact fashion wasn't my raison d'être. Black went with everything else and I didn't have to think about it. I debated on whether or not I should pack an overnight bag. I did it anyway. I'd always been a good Girl Scout.

I DIALED Adam's number as I climbed into my car. I didn't want him looking for me and thinking I wasn't coming. I'd started to leave several times, each time thinking I was forgetting something important. The last time had been to leave my brother a note. Just in case.

The phone rang in Adam's cottage only once.

"Adam Walker." The two words came through the speaker dispassionately.

"Adam, it's Keira."

"Keira, are you all right?" The tone changed, to the smooth chocolate voice I'd been used to.

"I'm fine. I just wanted to let you know I just left and I'm on my way. I'll be there in about twenty minutes."

"Good. See you soon."

I shivered as I disconnected. Those words held a world of promise. Damn it, Keira Kelly. I scolded myself.

I *had* to concentrate on shielding better. If I was going to make it through dinner and a meeting with the staff before anything else happened, I couldn't let myself get distracted by just his voice.

I started to turn down the main farm-to-market road that led to the ranch when I noticed the gas gauge. Wonderful. I was almost out of gas. There was no way I'd make it out there and back on fumes. I'd have to double back to the deli and fill up at their pumps. The only other gas station was nearly ten miles in the wrong direction and I wasn't sure I could make it that far.

I stood by the car, shivering as I pumped. The wind was picking up and we were finally getting a true cold front.

My silk jacket wasn't going to be warm enough. After I'd filled the tank, I switched it out for the black leather coat I kept in the car. Greta was alone in the store when I entered.

"Hello, Keira," she said.

"Hello, Greta."

"Is there something I can help you find?"

"Just paying for gas," I replied.

"Going somewhere?"

"To dinner."

"Going to town? A little late, isn't it?" She smiled at me and gave me my change.

"Nope," I answered. "I'm heading out to the Wild Moon."

Greta gasped a little, pursed her mouth, then closed the cash register drawer with a bang. "Is that all?"

"All what?" I was genuinely puzzled.

"The gas. Will that be all?"

"Yes." I looked at her. "Anything the matter, Greta?"

She shook her head, her lips still pursed together as if holding back words she didn't want to say.

I shrugged and left, not wanting to stop to psychoanalyze Greta. As I tossed my backpack in the back of the Rover and started to climb in, a movement out of the corner of my eye made me stop. A hand motioned from the side of the building, just around the corner. I couldn't see him clearly but I was sure it was Boris.

I glanced through the store window and saw Greta with her back to us, on the phone. Sliding out of the driver's seat, I walked around to where Boris was standing. Damn it, now what? I wasn't up for another round of whispered allusions and suggestive remarks. I could ignore him, but it might be easier to see what he wanted.

"I heard what you said to my sister in there," he said in

a near whisper. His hands were twisting his red bandanna. I said nothing.

He looked up at me. I'd never seen his face like this. Anguished, tortured, as if someone were beating him.

"You are a good person," he continued. "Please do not go back out to the Wild Moon. It is a place of the dead."

I started, surprised at his words.

"What do you mean?"

"The deer, the blood, there is evil. There is someone there."

"Boris, this is getting damned tiresome." My words snapped like bullets. "Who the hell are you talking about? Adam?"

"No!" He nearly shouted, but then dropped his voice again. "It is the other. Your cousin was talking to him, working with— Keira, you mustn't go out there. He is dead now and I am afraid."

"Look, Boris, I don't understand. Who was Marty talking to? Did someone at the Wild Moon kill my cousin?"

His hand whipped out in a blur and grabbed my arm. "Here, take this." His other hand pulled something from his jeans pocket and put it into my coat pocket, then patted my hand. "Here. Take it. Use it to keep safe."

A thrill of fear and anger skidded through me, starting at where my hand touched his. I pulled out of Boris' grasp and stepped back, afraid to be near him. I didn't want to risk another vision. The man was a seething mass of raw emotion.

"Go. Go now." Greta dashed around the corner and grabbed her brother's arm. "Go away and leave my brother before he— You and yours have caused enough trouble already."

"What? Are you talking about Marty?"

Boris dropped to his knees and started to shake.

Greta whispered to her brother, stroking his head, speaking in a language I didn't understand.

"Greta, what is going on? I'm sorry, I—"

"Go." Her hoarse whisper cut my words off.

I just wanted to help, to find out who Boris was so afraid of. But not only could I take a hint, I could act on it, too. Whoever was Boris' own personal boogie monster was at the Wild Moon. Since that's where I was headed, I could discover his identity without further terrorizing a sick old man.

Greta watched me walk away, eyes narrowed in anger. At me, maybe? She probably blamed me for this. She was probably right. Every time I was around Boris lately, he started to freak out. It wasn't really my fault, but it's hard to be actively angry at something that had happened more than fifty years ago. I was convenient.

As I climbed into the Rover, Greta spat in my direction, then threw up a hand, middle fingers tucked under, her index and pinky finger pointed outward. The sign against the evil eye.

I slammed the car door and started the engine, needing to get away. What the bloody hell was going on now? Boris, I could understand; everything he knew, everything he saw, was filtered by his version of reality and his hold on that seemed to be slipping. Greta's reaction simply spooked me. She was the sane one in that dysfunctional family, the one who kept the business going, who hauled her brother to the doctor once a month, made sure he took his sedatives, tried to keep him calm.

Was she starting to believe her brother's rantings, or had it been just a loving sister's automatic response to something she couldn't control? I didn't know. I'd like to think I didn't care, that I could divorce myself from their obvious pain, but I couldn't—because I had a horrible suspicion that some of what Boris said was fact and that something my cousin had done helped trigger the old man's descent.

As I drove down the main road, I reached into my pocket and pulled out what Boris had given me. It was a silver cross, plain with no decoration. A black cord, probably silk, was threaded through a jump ring at the top. It was obviously meant to be worn as a necklace. Damn it. That clinched it. He definitely knew about the vampires. Greta's reaction now made sense and Adam was not going to like this one bit.

Crap, crap, crap. What the hell was I going to do?

Of course, there was the possibility that Adam already knew and had hired Boris as some kind of Renfield or something. Some of us did. Have Renfields, that is, or personal assistants who were human. Not many, because in most cases, our natures weren't as obvious and we could pass. We didn't have to stay out of the sun or whatever. But, for example, a group of distant cousins, all clairvoyants, always had someone human to handle the outside world and help minimize their contact with humanity. In most cases, our human assistants were completely trustworthy and posed no threat. In a few rare cases, they did. Then the threats ceased to exist. That's what I was afraid of. Even if Adam was aware of Boris and Greta's knowledge, he might consider them to be a threat. In this case, the "threat" was two people I knew and were friends.

Either way, this evening at the Wild Moon would provide more than I'd originally bargained for.

CHAPTER SIXTEEN

I PULLED INTO THE DRIVE in front of Adam's house, wheels crunching on the gravel. A soft light illuminated the windows, spilling out past the sheers, leaving most of the porch in shadow. I got out of the car and leaned back in to pull out my backpack.

"Good evening."

I yelped as I banged my head on the door frame. "You have an uncanny way of sneaking up behind me, Adam Walker."

A soft chuckle made me smile. "I'm good."

I shot a glance in his direction, but it was too dark to see his expression.

He stepped even closer and took my hands in his and looked into my eyes. "You look fabulous."

I swallowed hard, my mouth suddenly dry, my breathing quickening with the surge of heat that rose, enveloping my senses. My brain told me to rip my hands out of his and regain control, but I couldn't, didn't want to. His thumbs stroked the back of my hands. He continued to look into my eyes, his own sea-green ones darkened to a dusky olive. I felt as if I were drowning, melting into his gaze. Was I imagining things or could I see my reflection in those depths? I felt no magicks, no power other than the pull of my own craving and the answering hunger of his, appetites that no ordinary dinner could satisfy. Second verse, same as the first.

Damn. I was well and truly hooked, and I didn't care.

His head bent to mine, a movement so slow, I could almost see each individual molecule of air moving aside. His breath brushed my skin, a touch delicate as the lightest silk, smooth against my cheek. My ears began to buzz and grow hot.

Soft lips reached my forehead as his hands squeezed mine. My skin tingled in an electric hum. As he gathered me even closer, a growling noise interceded and broke the mood. It was coming from somewhere in the vicinity of my belly.

"I think we should go have dinner."

A sigh left me unintentionally. I nodded wordlessly, my hunger for food waging war with another appetite. If we didn't eat soon, I'd most certainly be skipping the meal entirely and heading straight for dessert. I wasn't sure that I was quite ready for that yet.

THE MAIN RESTAURANT at the inn continued the Victorian theme, albeit with a uniquely Texas stamp. Where in most ranch resorts, you'd see bandannas, denim, and the obligatory antler furniture, here were plush lamps and purple velvet draperies, adding a lush softness to the carved cedar furniture and wrought-iron accessories. It shouldn't have worked, but somehow it did. Of course, who was I kidding? My idea of decorating was to buy furniture from a catalog.

Adam led me to an arched doorway that led into a dimly lit smallish restaurant. The place was packed. Groups of patrons sat in tables of two or four, at first glance typical diners, then not, as you began to realize that things were a little different. Everyone was wearing black, a sea of no-color, broken only by ghostly faces and hands, the soft flickering of multiple candles on every table emphasizing the contrast. An undercurrent of power filled the room, like water in an aquarium, staying just below the threshold of normal awareness, a roomful of vampires.

I snickered as the words *I see dead people* danced through my brain.

"What's so funny?" Adam asked.

"Nothing," I said, shaking my head. "Good thing I called ahead for the dress code. Guess I'll fit right in."

"Excuse me?"

"Never mind," I answered. "Just being silly."

"Good evening, sir." A tuxedoed maitre d' approached, looking just like any other attendant at a fancy hotel, despite the fact he was as much vampire as Adam—well, maybe not so much. His power was more of the 40-watt level. Adam's was more along the lines of a klieg light.

Menus in hand, perfectly polite, yet obsequious, smile on his face, the maitre d' bowed slightly. "May I show you to your table?"

Adam gave a small nod. "Good evening, Gerard. Keira, shall we?"

So what was for breakfast at Vampire Central? It really wasn't all that late, despite everything that had happened. I imagined that everyone here had just gotten up. Although I didn't think the vampires would be noshing on bagels and lox, I was curious as to what, or if, they did eat. Blood sausage? Bloody Marys? Weetabix with a blood chaser?

My curiosity didn't get satisfied, though. The maitre d' swiftly led us around the outside of the dining area via a secluded hallway to a separate room at the far back of the restaurant. When we entered, I realized we could have gone through the dining room to get here. An arched doorway opened between the two rooms directly to the left of the entrance I stood in. I don't know if the maitre d' had taken us this way because Adam wanted privacy, or because the other diners wanted theirs. I suppose it could be a bit of both. Either way, I could deal. I understood the concept of privacy and, despite the connections to the other areas, this room still seemed intimate.

To the right and centered against an oak framed floor-to-ceiling window, a small table set for two stood in solitary splendor. The window gave a view of the heavily wooded terrain outside. At least it would if it were daylight. Right now, all I could see was the dark mass of a tangle of live oaks. No floodlights illuminated the outdoors. I suppose vamps didn't need the false comfort of lighting the night. Well then, neither did I.

Our reflections mirrored our movements as we walked to the table, both Adam and me, and that of the maitre d'. Another myth bites the dust. I had always wondered. Never could figure out that whole mirror thing. Vampires may be dead, but they were definitely corporeal. (Now ghosts and shades, that was entirely different story. No bodies, no reflection.) A few stereotypes seemed to hold though, the love of elaborate surroundings for one.

A low centerpiece placed in the precise center of the beautifully set table spilled red and black rose petals across the immaculate white linen. Aside from the spillover from the other rooms, the only light in the room came from a pair of intricately wrought black candelabra bearing crimson candles. The entire room continued the theme—walls lined in dark red velvet, the matching carpet thick and luscious at our feet—making me feel as if we stood inside a luxurious jewelry box. It was nearly overwhelming.

Adam pulled out my chair and I sat, murmuring my thanks, then he rounded the table and took his own seat.

The maitre d' performed the standard napkin, menu and water ritual in silence, bowed and left.

I studied the exquisite menu, wondering if there were a standard version and a vampire version. Mine showed more than five pages of gourmet treats, from appetizers onward, but nothing you couldn't find in any expensive eatery in any large city. As I skimmed the selections, my thoughts turned to other things: the other reasons I was here.

"Adam?" I began, hesitant to say anything to ruin the mood, but I knew that we needed to have this conversation.

"Yes, Keira?"

"We need to talk."

"About dinner?"

"No, about—"

"Later, love," he said, interrupting me. "We have all night. For now, let's just enjoy."

Our gazes met over the tops of the menus, and held. All night. We did, didn't we? I looked away, not wanting to get lost again. Lost in emotions too intense to deal with in public. I glanced through the menu again, now restless, wanting this dinner to be over.

As I turned the page, I couldn't help notice that a large group seated in the dimly lit bar reminded me of the people from my vision. Tall and slender, each seemingly blonder than the next, laughing, talking and drinking, obviously enjoying themselves.

The only one I recognized was Evan, the man from the loading dock. He was behind the bar serving drinks. His Nordic good looks weren't out of place among those others. He glanced over at us, and caught me watching him. A shadow of something crossed his face, then quickly turned into a smirk. He saluted me lightly with the glass he was polishing, then turned to one of the other men at the bar. A gust of laughter exploded from the second man.

"Have you selected a wine yet, sir?"

The maitre d's voice interrupted my thoughts. He was back. I hadn't noticed that he'd given Adam the wine list.

"Red or white, Keira?"

"I prefer red."

Movement at one of the tables just inside the main restaurant caught my eye. A man was pouring a glass of a dark deep red. The bottle was the same brand of wine that Boris delivered last night. I'd never heard of it, but I couldn't go wrong with a good robust red.

"How about a bottle of the same wine that table's having?" I said.

"What they're having?" Adam's voice sounded peculiar.

"It must be good, right?"

"Why do you say that?"

I looked at him. "Because I've seen Boris Nagy delivering a van load of the same wine here. You must sell that a lot of it, ergo, it must be good."

Adam smiled. "You could say it's one of our most popular labels, but, if it's all the same to you, tonight, I'd rather have something else." A slow smile crossed his face as he spoke, a look in his eye telling me he wasn't only talking about the wine.

I blushed a little, remembering the heat of our earlier kiss and the implied promise of more to come. I concentrated on the wine. Safer that way.

"Do you have a Llano Estacado Cellar Select Merlot?"

"We do. A '96, one of the best." Adam nodded to the hovering maitre d', who scuttled away, hopefully in direction of either the wine cellar or the wine steward.

"Any idea what else you'd like?"

"Else?"

He motioned to the menu, grinning a little, enjoying our nonverbal interchange. "For dinner, love. You need to eat."

He flustered me so easily. Damn him. Oh yeah, too late, if you subscribed to popular theory. Vampires were damned already.

I glanced over the menu again. "I'm not sure yet," I answered, "But it's definitely going to be beef. I am in serious need of some meat."

A deep chuckle came from the other side of the table. "That could be arranged."

More innuendos. This time, I tried to ignore him.

"Might I make a suggestion?"

I took a deep breath and risked looking at him. He was smiling a Mona Lisa smile. He was enjoying himself far too much.

"Okay, I asked for that," I agreed. "Suggest away."

"Our chef makes an exquisite mesquite-grilled rib eye. Would that work for you?"

I looked him square in the face, keeping a neutral expression. "I love my meat grilled."

Our waiter, a golden-haired, chubby-cheeked youngster whose name tag identified him as Travis, hovered nearby. He was obviously new and unsure of whether he should go ahead and approach us. I grinned. Evidently Adam Walker could unsettle more than just me.

"I think the waiter is trying to get our attention."

Adam looked at Travis and motioned for him to come closer. As he approached, I realized the boy didn't exude any power or feeling of otherness. Could he be human? Odd. He didn't even look like the typical Goth-wanna-be, more like the nerd next door. Maybe Adam did employ humans.

The young man cleared his throat and had barely started

reciting the litany of specials when Adam raised his hand.

"Thank you, Travis, but I believe we already know what we'd like."

Adam looked at me as he paused, the enigmatic smile back on his face. The heat rushed to my face and I looked down at my place setting. He was going to have to stop this or we'd never be able to eat dinner. I was likely to grab him and drag him out of here.

"May I take your order then, sir?" The young man, eager as a puppy, was either better at ignoring the byplay than I was or just completely clueless.

"I'd like the mesquite-grilled rib eye," I answered, disconcerting the boy, who'd been addressing Adam.

"I'm sorry, yes, of course." He nodded, his hands clasped behind his back. "How would you like that prepared?

"Bruised and brought in. Blood on the inside. Barely warm."

"Yes, ma'am."

He didn't miss a beat. There was hope for the boy yet. "That comes with garlic mashed potatoes and baby grilled vegetables. Would that be satisfactory?"

"Garlic?" I looked at Adam.

"Afraid I'll stay away?" He grinned, barely flashing a glimpse of fang.

I closed my eyes and counted to ten before I spoke.

"That would be fine, thank you, Travis."

Travis turned to look at Adam.

"Your usual, sir?"

Adam closed his menu and handed it over. "Yes, my usual."

Travis nodded and with relief, collected the menus and made himself scarce.

"How old is he?"

"Why do you ask?"

"Only because he's human and I want to make sure he's of legal age."

Adam grinned. "No worries, Keira Kelly," he said. "Travis looks rather young, but he's legal. He's the son of my daytime manager."

"Good." I wasn't sure what I'd have done if the boy had been as young as he looked. It really wasn't my business. But it would have bothered me.

The sommelier arrived then. Adam played his part in the customary wine ritual, examining the cork, swirling the ruby liquid in the glass, and taking a small sip. He nodded his head and the man poured and left.

I tasted the wine. "This is fabulous."

The oaky plum flavor burst on my tongue and teased my palate. The start of what I hoped would be an excellent meal, that is, if Adam could rein back his impulse to tease me. Not that it really mattered, his very presence was enough to fluster me if I didn't concentrate on other things.

"It is a most excellent wine," Adam agreed. He lifted his glass in salute. "It's only made better by the company."

I stared down at my wine stem and played with the edge of the glass. He was so very good at this and I was too long out of practice. I'd forgotten how to flirt. Maybe it was because now it wasn't a game anymore.

I changed the subject. "So, what's your usual?" I asked. "Not . . ."

I didn't really want to say the word out loud, it was just too open, too not-hidden. The idea of speaking about things like this in public was a little more than I wanted to handle. I'd spent too many years being raised in the so-called normal world, spent too much time mainstreaming in human society. My instinct was to hide who I was, to play the I'm-only-human game.

Adam smiled, leaning forward a little in his chair as if to whisper to me. "I can eat many things." The smile broadened into an even white grin.

The words flowed like rich honey over me and I felt the heat sliding up my face. This was going to be a very long dinner.

ADAM'S USUAL wasn't a bucket of blood, but turned out to be a gorgeous filet mignon, delicate as a rose and served as rare as my rib eye. He'd dispensed with any of the side dishes, instead, the little jewel of a steak sat precisely in the center of the plate, commanding all the attention.

I took a bite of my own steak. The tender meat was exquisitely flavored, the woodsy taste of the mesquite complementing the beef. As I picked up my glass to take a sip of wine, Adam captured my gaze with a look and another one of his enigmatic smiles.

I watched him, wondering what he was up to. He lifted his knife with a bit of a flourish, and cut through the seared outer layer of his steak, parting the interior, revealing the tender red center, glistening with juices that ran across the pristine white china, staining its snowy perfection, red mixed with clear, enticing.

He speared the slice with his fork, and, still staring at me, transferred it to his mouth and chewed slowly, lips working sensuously, tongue flicking out to taste the full flavor as he swallowed. I'd come to a full stop and couldn't look away, captivated by his movements, catching a glimpse of extended fangs, prey captured by her predator. I watched, fascinated as a drop of the steak's bloody juices landed on his lower lip. I had to force myself to keep my hands still and not reach over to wipe the drop from his mouth, or worse, lean over and lick it off.

He smiled again, a wicked, knowing look in his eye. Instead of dabbing at the blood with his napkin, he ran his tongue slowly across his lower lip, licking it clean, leaving it shiny and wet. I shivered and found myself leaning forward, mimicking his gesture as my own tongue flicked out and gingerly touched my own lips.

"Well, looks like you two are having a great time."

Talk about freakin' interruptus. I couldn't even look at Adam. Part of my brain cursed whoever it was, the other part breathed a silent "thank you," knowing that I'd been so very close to losing control.

I turned to look at the man who'd spoken and was almost sorry I had. My skin flushed even hotter and I lowered my eyes in embarrassment, recognizing the young redhead of the other night. The one that stood in front of my car in my vision. The one who— Bloody hell. It *had* been a vision, right?

"What do you need, Niko?" I could tell from the tone of Adam's voice that he wasn't happy to have been interrupted.

So this was Niko the wildlife manager. Different. While Adam's power was completely contained, otherness surrounded this vampire, clinging to his skin, his clothes, his very self, a shimmering bubble of energy, a bubble that had weight and substance, almost tangible. Still not as powerful as Adam, but the potential was there.

Up close he didn't seem as young as he'd looked in my vision. The face was unlined and, at first glance, he'd pass for twenty, but there was a heaviness of experience behind the luminous blue eyes that only came with years. His pale skin shone against the deep black of his velvet pirate shirt floating untucked over equally black leggings tucked into low boots. A blood-red brocade vest embroidered with black traceries topped off the Goth ensemble. Long reddish-blond hair swept just past his shoulders, set off by the rich dark colors of his clothing. Niko was so definitely not trying to pass. The words "barnyard rooster" came to mind.

Niko's eyes flickered over to me momentarily, then back to Adam. "Just being courteous and greeting our . . . guest."

He turned to me and smiled broadly, flaunting a hint of fang. "But now, I'm sure the young lady here would like to finish her meal. Perhaps indulge in some dessert?" I could sense the intended double meaning behind his so polite words. Niko was as much of a tease as his boss, if not more so. I hoped this wasn't typical behavior for all vampires. One teasing bloodsucker I could handle, and wanted to, but all of them? Not even a consideration.

"Go away, Niko," Adam did not sound amused.

Niko's twinkling eyes crinkled at the corners. It didn't take a genius to know he was very well aware of just what he'd interrupted. I was convinced he'd done it on purpose. I already didn't like him much. Niko grinned again, and then snapped a small bow before leaving.

"Did he just interrupt us to be rude?" I asked, spearing a slice of meat on my fork.

"Niko can be a little impulsive," he answered. "I think he wanted to check you out."

I raised an eyebrow. He'd done more than check me out in my vision, damn it. Even though it hadn't actually happened, I definitely got the feeling Niko was fully capable of playing the glamour ticket. His arrival alone had been a calculated act of passive-aggressiveness, intended to disrupt our meal and our rather heavy flirtation. Jealous? Or just too damned curious? I wondered what exactly his and Adam's relationship had been over the years. Employer and employee, friends, more? Niko definitely gave off some interesting vibes.

"He should remember what curiosity did," I said and turned back to my meal.

Adam laughed out loud. "My sweet, you are undeniably an interesting dinner companion." He grinned at me and raised his wineglass in salute.

I smiled and shrugged, raising my own glass in answer. Look who was talking.

"Well, isn't this just ducky?" The scathing sentence dropped between us, a biting chill of frost crashing into our intimate mood.

Carlton stood in the doorway of the bar.

I put my wineglass down as Adam turned and stood in one movement, smooth and graceful.

"Sheriff Larson," he said, his voice neutral.

"Why are you here?" I wasn't quite so neutral.

Andrea pushed past Carlton, apologizing. "Sorry, Adam, I asked him to wait in the lobby until you were—"

"No worries, Andrea," Adam waved a hand, dismissing her. "We were nearly done with dinner. Sheriff, what brings you here?"

Carlton scowled at Adam, then at me, then back at Adam. "I came to talk to Walker about the deer. I didn't know you were here."

I glared at Carlton, whose body language held all the hurt and defiance that only an old boyfriend could have when finding his former lover is now dating someone else. I could say something totally untrue, like "it's not what it seems," but it was exactly what it seemed. It just sure as hell wasn't any of Carlton's business.

He sauntered into the private dining room, a little bit of a strut in his walk. He was playing jealous ex-boyfriend for all it was worth.

"I just got back from Houston and figured you'd want to know what I found out at the bank. Besides, you left a rather interesting message on my voice mail. Went by your place, you weren't there. Left a phone message. Then I came on over here." His drawl was pronounced and as artificial as Fresca. He hadn't talked that way since high school. "I was going to go back by your place after I came to the ranch. I didn't realize you'd be here."

"I don't file my plans with you, Carlton," I said, trying to keep calm. "So what part of what you found out was so all-fired important you had to talk to me this late?" I glanced over to the clock on the wall as I stepped forward, in front of Adam. "At nearly ten-thirty at night?"

Adam rested a hand on my shoulder. A show of solidarity? Possessiveness? I ignored it as best I could and made an effort to keep calm.

The Sheriff frowned. "I have news about what I found out in Houston. About your cousin Marty."

"So, talk," I demanded.

Carlton looked down at the ground and didn't speak.

I may have lost some self-control, but surely I hadn't lost my common sense. Why didn't he just tell me? I was getting impatient with him.

"I think that your . . . friend . . . doesn't want to talk in front of me." Adam's silken voice sounded amused, superior and smug.

Damn this male posturing, anyway. Was Adam going

to start acting the jealous possessive date now? Shit, did vampires still have testosterone to throw around? I certainly hoped this wasn't going to disintegrate into a "whose is bigger" game.

"Why don't the two of you go into the parlor," Adam continued, "and discuss your personal matters. Then the Sheriff may speak to me in my office."

"Is there anything I can do, Mr. Walker?" Evan's voice came from behind Carlton. He stepped to the side, wiping his hands on a bar towel, looking like nothing more than a concerned bouncer.

"Nothing, thank you, Evan," Adam said. "The Sheriff is here to talk to Ms. Kelly. Everything is fine."

The tall blond frowned, but nodded and tossed the bar towel over his shoulder as he left. I looked back at Carlton, who had the grace to look embarrassed.

Adam closed in and lightly brushed a kiss on my forehead, his hand caressing my cheek with a wisp of a touch, his look smoldering a promise. Stepping to the side, he turned and sketched a slight bow to Carlton, who stood rigid as a steel beam.

"Go, speak to the Sheriff," Adam said. "We'll talk later. The parlor is just through the lobby to the left."

"Let's go," I said, and walked out, hoping Carlton would follow. I noticed Evan watching us as we crossed through the bar.

Before I reached the main area of the lobby, which was suspiciously empty of guests, Carlton's voice stung me.

"How touching." The acrid harshness of the words warred with the sleek softness of Adam's tone.

I whirled, anger coloring my own words. He wasn't going to wait until we got to the parlor. He was planning on having this out right here. That was fine with me. I had nothing to hide.

"What right do you have to comment on anything that goes on in my life, Carlton Larson?"

He approached me, stopping only when I raised a hand. "I did once."

"Not even then," I said, moving away from him. "Besides, it's long since over. We've had this conversation."

"Yeah, I noticed you're conversing with someone else."

"And you're married. For twelve years, is it? How is Carol, anyway?"

Carol, the petite blonde bombshell whom he'd run to after our breakup. Okay, I was being mean. He'd run to a new job. She'd only been a fringe benefit. An oilman's daughter, she'd been temping as a Citizens On Patrol liaison at the San Antonio PD when they'd met. I'd heard the whole story in great detail the one time I'd called him in San Antonio, not long after he'd left Rio Seco. I'd tried to extend a hand of friendship. He'd metaphorically slapped it away.

His laugh spilled anger and frustration into the air. It was the "I have to laugh before I cry" kind of sound.

"Married. If that's what you want to call it. My so-called wife decided that life at her parents' mansion in Conroe was infinitely preferable to life in Rio Seco with me."

He sat down with a heavy sigh, pulling his hat off his head and running his hand through his matted-down hair until it stood on end. It made him look more vulnerable somehow, not the in-control lawman.

I sat on a chair across from him, far enough away so I didn't have to work so hard at blocking the emotion that was pouring off him in waves.

"I put up with years of city politics, of gang-bangers, of innocent dead children for her. She hated the fact I wanted to stay a cop, she wanted me to get promotions, make captain, get a desk job with a little prestige. So I suffered." He stared down at his hands, clenching and unclenching them.

"The last case I had, these hands had to touch the bodies of three dead kids. All of them were under the age of five. They'd been playing in the living room when a group of gang-bangers shot up the wrong house. One little girl had no face left. The bullets ripped through her skull like it was a birthday piñata. Her brains were scattered across her mother's brand-new white couch."

He looked at me through unshed tears. "I quit the next day. Carol left me before I even moved back home, Keira. It wasn't just that I'd quit my job. She always knew how I felt about you. That you were the reason I came back here instead of moving somewhere else. I stopped in Conroe on my way back from Houston. Wanted to see my kids. Tried to convince Carol to come back with me."

I couldn't speak. His heartbreak was more than I could take right now. Part of me wanted to comfort him, as a friend, as someone I'd once cared about, but I couldn't. This was too much for me to handle. I was afraid that if I let down my guard, he'd take it the wrong way.

"I'm sorry. But I can't. What we had was years ago, Carlton. It's over. I can't be the reason you came back home."

"I'm not good enough for you anymore, is that it?" The nastiness returned.

"Stop it, Carlton. Do *not* make this about me. What happened in your home life is your business, not mine. What I do with my life is my business, not yours. Now what did you come here to tell me?"

His glare matched mine. But he got the hint and changed the subject.

"I got the bank records," he said. "Your cousin was in deep with the Albrights. For every deposit he made, he wrote a check to either Derek or Dusty for a good chunk of money. The last check he wrote was a couple of weeks ago."

"And this is news because—?" I was livid. If he'd come over here just to play pity poor me and to tell me information I'd already figured out for myself—

"The money came from someone you know, Keira. From here. From the Wild Moon."

"You're lying." My response was automatic.

"I am not. Why would I lie about this? I had no idea you were seeing that guy when I came over here. When the hell did you meet him anyway? You didn't say anything the other day when I saw you at Bea's."

"Again I ask the question. Why exactly do you think this is your business?

"Because if that money came from your new boyfriend, then maybe he had something to do with your cousin's murder."

"How do you know the money came from the Wild Moon anyway?"

I didn't know much about banks, but unless someone had been stupid enough to write out a check to Marty, there'd be no way to know this. My bullshit detector was screaming.

But Carlton had an answer that I couldn't argue with.

"I sweet-talked a young clerk who remembered your cousin. She was more than willing to talk about the creepy little bald guy who tried to pick her up. She said he kept talking about all the money he was making from this rich jerk at the Wild Moon. She remembered thinking the name was odd."

"How convenient," I said. Two could play the sarcasm game. "She just happened to remember all of this."

Carlton looked at me as if he couldn't believe how stupid I was. Maybe he was right. But before I went off accusing Adam of anything, he'd have to give me more to go on than some bank clerk's memory.

"I imagine you'd remember, too, if someone kept coming in person all the way from Rio Seco every month."

I slumped back into the chair, staring off toward the bar. The place had nearly emptied. I was sure Adam had asked the patrons to leave. Either that, or even the vampires weren't amused by our antics. Evan and his friend were the only ones there. As I stared, the two of them looked at me, looked away, then walked out. Great, they probably didn't want to deal with us, either. Neither did I for that matter.

But I had to stay and listen. Carlton was right. If I were a bank clerk, no matter how many transactions I'd process in a day, I'd remember somebody that came that regularly and from that far away. Knowing Marty, he'd been flirting with her, making sure to wait until she was free to help him. He may have been stupid, but he'd always been tenacious.

Damn it all. I would swear on all my future talent and all the talent my family possessed that Adam was innocent of anything to do with Marty's death, but I was still confused. I was sure Adam never knew Marty, but he had to know each one of his guests and one of them must have been paying Marty for something, although I couldn't think what. Had Adam known it was happening? I didn't think so, but until I could talk to him, I wouldn't know the truth. I so didn't want to deal with this while Carlton was here.

"There's more, Keira."

"More? How could there be more?"

"I'm sorry, but this is a murder investigation. What do you want me to do?

"Go home, Carlton. Leave me alone and talk to Adam tomorrow." I said, suddenly tired.

I was beyond exhausted. Bone deep weariness flooded my body, making me want to do nothing more than sleep. I was tired of this nightmare that was now my life. I didn't want to deal anymore, didn't want to have a dead cousin, didn't want to think about any of this. All I wanted was to be left alone to try to figure out what I wanted to do next. How was I going to confront Adam about all of this?

"You want me to leave?"

"Don't sound so surprised." I looked over at him. "Did you think I'd ask to you to take me home, rescue me, stay the night?"

He shook his head. "I don't understand you, Keira, I wonder if I ever did. I tell you—your boyfriend may be involved in your cousin's murder and all you can say is 'go home, Carlton'?"

"What do you want me to say? Oh, gee, I've seen the light and I want to get back together with you?"

"You made it perfectly clear that wasn't an option."

"It's not."

"Fine."

"Fine."

Okay, now we both had resorted to junior high verbal sparring. What was next, stomping off in a huff and not sitting together in the cafeteria? Shit.

"I have to question him." He said it as if it were a dare, a challenge.

I shrugged, pretending indifference. "What's stopping you?"

"Nothing."

"Let's go." I sprang up from the chair, just as suddenly reenergized. Damn Carlton Larson anyway for bringing all his personal baggage into this.

As I turned to look for someone who could take us to Adam's office, Andrea walked through the bar and approached us. Great. Vampires who appeared on cue. Of course, she'd probably heard every word.

"Sheriff, would you care to accompany me to the office?" Her melodious voice was subdued. I'd bet Adam had told her off for having let Carlton in.

Carlton hesitated, then tucked his hat under his arm and followed the lithe security guard.

My interesting night just got more than interesting.

CHAPTER SEVENTEEN

A DAM CAME UP behind me and took my arm. "Everything all right?"

"Yeah. I'll live." I smiled at him.

"Good. Now let's go to my office and see what the Sheriff wants."

He led me out through the lobby and down a small hallway to a door marked "Private." Before he opened it, he turned to me, a serious expression on his face.

"Keira, I don't mean to pry, but before we go in . . . I need to ask you something."

"Yes?" I braced myself. What could he possibly need to know right now?

"Just what is the connection between you and our Sheriff?"

Oh, crap. Even with the lovely little scene out front, I'd forgotten Adam wasn't familiar with all of my past. I drew in a breath, then let it out slowly. How to explain in a few words the confusion that was Carlton Larson.

"On my part, what there was of a connection, is in the past, way past. We were lovers once. About a dozen years ago, for a very short time."

"And that's over?"

"Completely."

"Odd," Adam said. "I don't think the Sheriff knows that."

I snorted a little. "Knowing and accepting—two totally different things."

Before he could turn the knob, I stuck my hand out and placed my palm on the door.

"The reason he's here . . . is not me." I hesitated. "Did you hear any of the argument?"

"I deliberately didn't listen. I know it's hard to keep things private in a building full of vampires, but I promise. I wasn't listening."

I thought for a moment, then just blurted it out.

"Money. Someone from the Wild Moon was paying Marty money. Lots of it."

"How does he know this?"

I filled him in, gave him the short version, explaining the regular deposits and the payments to the Albrights.

"He said there was something else, too, but I don't know what. I didn't let him finish."

Adam grabbed my hand and pulled me away from the door, strode down the hall, gently dragging me along, and ducked into a small recess which held two chairs and a table. A typical off-the-beaten-lobby alcove, ripe for a romantic tête-à-tête. A grim look on his face made me doubt romance was on Adam's mind right now.

"He was sure the money came from here?"

"As sure as he can be, being human and getting the story from a bank teller. He's a good man, Adam. Despite everything."

"Damnation." Adam's curse was soft, almost silent. "That means one of my staff or my guests . . ."

"He thinks it's you," I said, putting my hands on his.

"Do you?" He studied my face intently.

"No."

"But someone here did give him money."

"I'm sorry, Adam. It looks like it's more than just Marty having had a vampire lover, doesn't it?"

"I'm afraid so."

"Any ideas?"

He closed his eyes, as if trying to collect his thoughts. "Perhaps. Let's go speak to your Sheriff."

"He's not *my* Sheriff," I protested.

Adam smiled, a pale echo of his earlier sensual expression. "I know."

THE OFFICE DOOR OPENED onto a spacious reception area, decorated in the same dark purples as the main hotel. A large aquarium filled with exotic-looking fish dominated the wall directly opposite the door. A modern Euro-styled desk and chair sat in front of the aquarium, as if guarding it. A plush couch lined the right wall, facing two luxurious chairs in a dark violet suede on the left.

Carlton sat uncomfortably in one of the chairs. Andrea sat in the other. I nodded to Andrea as we entered, acknowledging her power. She smiled slightly and nodded back. Both she and Carlton stood as the door shut behind Adam.

"Mr. Walker, Keira. Have a nice chat?" Carlton's smirk was evident in the tone of his voice.

"We did," I answered, just as smugly and took Adam's arm. Two could play this game.

I saw the answering grin on Andrea's face. Her senses were probably as acute as mine. She could smell the jealously on Carlton as easily as a human could pick up strong cologne. Adam stayed quiet beside me, his muscles still. I couldn't look at him now for fear of breaking into laughter. This whole posturing thing suddenly struck me as being terribly funny.

"That's nice," Carlton drawled. "Now, Walker, if you have time?"

Adam gently disengaged my hand from his arm with a slight caress. "If you'd care to accompany me into my office?"

He walked over to the right side of the aquarium and pressed against the wall. A hidden door swung open and revealed a glimpse of a sumptuous room inside, decorated in the same color scheme as the reception area. Adam turned and held the door open, motioning for Carlton to enter.

Adam looked at me and smiled. "Keira, if you wouldn't mind waiting out here, I'm sure this won't take long." He then looked at Andrea, who nodded and left through the main entrance. Adam and Carlton disappeared into the office.

I sat on the couch, prepared to wait as long as it took. I could try to eavesdrop—now that I was changing, my hearing would probably be more sensitive—but I didn't think it was fair. Adam would probably tell Carlton exactly what he needed to hear and nothing more.

I'd barely gotten a chance to look around the reception room when the main door opened again and Niko walked in. Well, maybe "walked" was too tame a word. The man's movements reminded me of a shark's—smooth, deadly and ready to strike at the slightest provocation.

"Well, well," he said, a grin spreading across his face as he sprawled in one of the chairs. "If it isn't Ms. Land Rover in the flesh, so to speak. I didn't recognize you at first."

Well, hell. Wasn't he the suave one? I wasn't about to cut this guy any slack. Any powerful talent who used it to spellbind others was breaking the code. At least my own personal code.

I met his gaze, keeping my eyes fixed on his. The clear blue of his irises began to darken. The power surrounding him began to swirl, building intensity, thickening like the clouds before a sudden summer storm. His gaze bored into mine, trying to pull me down, capture me in their glittering stare, a cobra mesmerizing its prey. But I wasn't prey and I wasn't all that easy to catch, at least not when I knew what was happening.

His smirk became a frown as he realized it wasn't working.

"That's enough, Niko," Adam said.

The power died down like a transformer drained of electricity. I looked over at Adam, who was holding his office door open. I hadn't heard the door open and I'd bet neither had Niko.

"We think it would be a good idea for you to come in and hear this."

Niko stood up in preparation to walk into the office. Adam stopped him with a gesture. "Just Keira right now, Niko."

I resisted the urge to turn and stick my tongue out at him. There had been enough childish blustering around here tonight. I didn't need to add to it, no matter how much I felt like it. Adam's sidekick brought out the worst in me.

The office was a magnificent study in modern Renaissance revival decor. Whereas the public areas had encompassed hints of Victoriana, Adam's private room glorified the lush style of a previous era. The mahogany desk commanded attention as I entered, its dark wood polished to a satin sheen. Quatrefoil medallions adorned all four walls in between tapestry hangings, while pseudo-torch sconces provided the ambient light. I looked around for the requisite suit of armor, but saw only a couple of mahogany bookcases set into niches. At least the wide leather armchairs looked fairly modern and comfortable. Adam's own chair was a tapestry-covered version of the standard high-backed executive model.

"So are you going to come in and sit down or just stand at the door?" Carlton smirked at me, making me feel like a tourist ogling the big buildings and fancy cars.

"Stop it, Carlton," I said and crossed the room to sit in the chair next to him. He still looked as uncomfortable as he had in the reception room, except this chair seemed to be a better fit.

Adam moved around to sit behind the desk, pausing for a moment to touch me briefly on the back of the neck. I shivered involuntarily as a wave of heat flushed my skin. Carlton's expression turned from a smirk to a glower as he stared at me.

"Keira, I explained your theory to the Sheriff, about the poaching and about the deer head on your porch. He believes that someone here at the Wild Moon was paying your cousin money. Perhaps selling poached animals."

Adam's voice remained smooth as the polished crystal paperweight on his desk, and about as expressive. I got the sense he was holding something in. I thought I understood the subtext. He was asking me to play nice.

He continued. "Sheriff Larson tells me they found a knife in the Albrights' apartment."

I shot a glance at Carlton, who nodded. "I bagged it and sent it to Bexar County along with some other bits and pieces. But I'm pretty sure the knife had blood and bits of hair."

"From the deer?"

He nodded. "I think so. I've got a deputy following up with all their known relatives—here, in Medina, a couple in San Antonio. I'm hoping they just holed up in the area and didn't head for Mexico."

"You still think they killed Marty?" I asked.

Carlton shrugged. "They're my only lead right now. The knife wasn't the only thing we found. They had a lot of electronics in their apartment, too, like Marty. New stuff, some of it with price tags still on it. I found a few receipts where they paid cash."

"So they were poaching?"

"More than likely. Walker tells me that he and the wildlife manager saw the Albrights on Wild Moon property."

He avoided looking at Adam and me.

"It's possible that someone here was working with Marty and selling the poached animals or buying them off or something. That's why the money. It doesn't really click for me, but that's all I've got. It would, though, make more sense the other way round."

"What do you mean?" Adam asked.

"If the Albrights were poaching on your land, don't you think they, or Marty, would be paying someone here off to keep quiet? To keep it from you? Not someone paying them money?"

"So you don't think Adam had anything to do with it, then?"

Carlton played with his hat a moment, then sighed. "No, Keira, I don't think he had anything to do with it."

He had a sick look on his face. I caught his gaze and a flash of anger and sorrow explained it. I knew that look. It wasn't because of Marty's murder. It was me. Specifically, me being with Adam and him having to do the decent thing and be a good cop and admit the truth.

I turned away from him, feeling only pity mixed with

sadness. He didn't understand and I couldn't explain. I was sticking with my own kind. Well, not exactly, but close enough. Carlton would never get this picture, because he'd only ever see the surface.

"In my experience, Sheriff," Adam said. "Money exchanges hands for a variety of reasons."

"I'm aiming to find out exactly what those reasons might have been," Carlton said, a touch of anger coloring his voice.

"We will help you," Adam replied with equanimity. I could see he wasn't going to allow Carlton's emotional response to affect him. I smiled at Adam, looking at him across the expanse of the desk. The clear sea-green intensified as our gazes met and held, each of us allowing ourselves just a fraction of a moment to recognize the other, to acknowledge the connection between us. I could get lost in those eyes, I thought. So easily lost and I'd enjoy every second of it. Adam's quiet smile echoed mine, his expression a mirror of what I was feeling. I'd never meant to let myself become entangled with anyone else, so soon after Gideon. I'd meant to spend the next few decades alone. But I suppose that Fate, or whatever, had other ideas.

Adam stood and walked over to me, crouching down, taking my hands in his. "I promise, Keira. I will find out for you."

I nodded, silent in the knowledge that he would do exactly what he said, even if it meant betrayal of one of his own.

Carlton's voice, acid with anger, broke the spell. "I hate to interrupt this love fest," he drawled, letting himself fall into the Texas cadence of his childhood, "but there's still a murder to solve here."

I blinked, tearing my gaze away from Adam. I felt him

doing the same as he took his hands off mine and stood in an elegant movement. He didn't go far, though, remaining standing next to me, a hand resting lightly on the back of my neck. I barely heard Carlton's next words.

"The problem is, we still don't know why the Albrights would have killed Marty. They had means and opportunity, but what's the motive? He was helping them out. It doesn't make any sense. We won't know any more until we catch up to them."

"You haven't gotten any leads?" I asked.

Carlton shook his head. "We're looking. They could be anywhere. This is a big state and they had a pretty good head start." His expression turned from grim to worried. I almost knew what he was going to say next and I really didn't want to hear it. I was right.

"In the meantime, Keira, you need to take care of yourself and stay out of trouble. I don't think they'll come back to this area, but just in case, don't go wandering around. Don't even go back home, at least not for a while. I mean it."

He'd seen the automatic stubborn look on my face.

"When it was just a few poached animals, I wasn't too worried, but I'm damned sure they left that head on your porch and the threat. It's probably just posturing, but what if they decide to keep messing with you? I'm sure Bea would be happy to put you up."

I scowled even more. He made a certain sort of sense. Damn it. I hated this. I didn't want to have to hide out, like a weakling, like prey. I wasn't a predator yet and might never be, but I was far from powerless. I opened my mouth to speak but, right then, Carlton's mobile rang, interrupting me. I stayed quiet as he listened to the call for a few minutes and then mumbled something into the receiver.

"I've got to go, Keira; that was the dispatcher. We've found the Albrights' truck. It's been abandoned out near the old limestone quarry. I'm needed back in town." He got up, his movements slow and deliberate. "I'll call you later to check in. Can I call you at Bea's?"

Before I could say anything, Adam broke in. "You may call her here. I have round-the-clock security. She'll be safe."

Carlton glowered, not liking the answer. Without a word, he walked out the door, letting it slam shut behind him.

Adam squatted back down and placed his hands on the chair arms, keeping his eyes steady on mine. His right hand lightly touched my cheek. "He really does think he still has a claim on you."

"Yeah, well, you're not far off the mark," I admitted. "He's married now, but can't seem to remember that part."

"You're not exactly forgettable, Keira Kelly."

I blushed, remembering his admission to me at the mortuary.

"You're not very forgettable yourself," I said. "But I need to ask you, do you think Carlton is right about Derek and Dusty? You met them, you think they were up to killing Marty? Or was he drained by someone from here?"

His eyes got that haunted look. "I don't know, Keira. I wish I did. You know that's what I was looking for. What I was afraid I'd find."

"I know, Adam. Is there no other way to tell?"

"If I could have seen his body, I could tell. There would be a sort of latent potential."

"So he could become vampire?"

Adam nodded. "Yes, if fed from often enough and then

drained to the point of death. He'd have to feed from one of us, as well."

Oh yeah, the whole big sucking thing, guess that wasn't a myth, either.

I shook my head. "I saw his body, Adam. I don't know if . . ."

"You saw it?"

"Of course I did, both Tucker and I were there. That's why I know there were fang marks and no blood," I said. "I didn't just take Carlton's word—and he didn't recognize the marks."

Adam looked thoughtful. "Earlier, you were able to sense Andrea on my porch. Can you perceive all power?"

"I've always been pretty good at scoping out others, except . . ."

"Except what?"

"In England, with you, even here, before . . . I never clued in."

"I've been at this a very long time, Keira. Most vampires don't bother to shield their power here at the ranch. I still do. There were a great many years where my life depended on my passing as human, even to other vampires." He took my hand. "Had I known sooner what you were, I might have . . . Never mind. Time past. You're here now."

I shut my eyes briefly and let out a small sigh. No regrets. It wouldn't have made sense to fret about what could have been, what might have happened years before.

Adam continued. "I was wondering if you would have been able to sense if your cousin had been turned."

"Good question. Maybe." I tried to remember the sensations I'd felt when I'd viewed Marty's body. I'd felt uneasy, and tense, but nothing specifically supernatural. Even if I'd known my cousin was playing fang hag, we were never close enough for me to ask him if he reciprocated the blood suck.

"I didn't feel anything unusual. But that doesn't mean it wasn't there. I'm not too sure what I'd have to sense. We'll just have to wait, I guess."

"And find out when he rises at the morgue?"

"Damn." I hadn't really thought of that. "He's at Bexar County and they're backed up because of a flu outbreak among the staff. They're not going to be able to do the autopsy for a few days yet, and that means they won't release the body before—"

"I'll take care of it," Adam said. "I'll send out one of my people tonight. If your cousin has been turned, we'll bring him back. If not, we'll leave him be."

"Your people?" I asked. "You keep making that sound less like *employees* and more like, you know, *minions*."

"Minions." He laughed a little. "Well, to borrow a phrase, you're not wrong, exactly. That's, well, that's part of everything I want to talk to you about, the reason I've had to pretend, to hide my power. I was going to tell you, Keira—"

"Yes, *do* tell her." Niko's voice floated through the now-open door, derision coloring the words, the "I double-dog-dare-you" implicit in his tone.

Andrea stood next to him, saying nothing. She turned her head and stared when he spoke. The two of them came into the office, Niko striding over to the desk and perching on its edge. Andrea standing just behind him, ever the bodyguard.

Adam flinched a little, his muscles tightening. He ignored Niko for the moment.

"Andrea, where's Evan? I need him to take care of something."

"He's gone out. Said he needed to do something. I suppose he's patrolling."

Adam nodded. "Fine. When he comes back in, tell him I need to see him."

"Patrolling? What's up with that?" I asked. "He hunting vampire slayers?"

The three vampires ignored my facetious question. Niko stared at Adam, the look of challenge still on his face. Adam simply stared back, his own expression neutral, but wary.

"She already knows," Andrea said. Niko glanced at her but kept his comments to himself. He still wasn't able to keep the quizzical expression from his face.

Adam stood, watching Niko but addressing me.

"I'm the leader of my people, Keira. We've been a community for a long time. Since long before the war that changed everything."

"Could you be a little more specific? Which war would that be?"

I wasn't being flippant. I might only be thirty-seven, but my father, my uncles and my elder half-brothers had personally witnessed several human conflicts and had even fought in some. None of them looked much older than me, or even Adam. To my brothers Duncan and Cullen, "the" war meant the First Opium War. Ciprian tended to think in terms of the Restoration. I wasn't even considering what other members of my family considered their "Great War," I didn't want to.

"I suppose that's a fair question," Adam said. "The Second World War."

"Was that when you . . ." My voice trailed off. I wasn't exactly sure how to ask the question. When he died?

"No, I've been around for longer than that." He shook

his head, his hair hiding his expression. I could hear the pain in his voice. "That's just when the blood and the killing became too much. When I vowed to make changes in our lifestyle. It wasn't my first war, just my last."

"Why that one?" I asked. "What makes it any different from all the others?"

I tried to see his face behind the curtain of hair. I thought I knew the answer but I wanted to hear it for myself.

He looked at me, a film of misery sliding across his eyes, echoes of horror reflected in their depths. "Wars had come to be all the same. Only the weapons changed. All I cared about was the survival of our people, no matter what I had to do to ensure it. But this time, this war . . . it was more than even I could take." He paused, swallowing hard, as if the words hurt his throat. "I saw things there that no living or dead soul should ever see. Even when our people hunted humans, we were never that cruel."

"That would be my point," Niko broke in. "We aren't cruel. We simply hunt for food. We can hunt animals, not humans."

"But we still follow the laws, Niko." Adam warned.

"Whose laws, Adam?" Niko's derision sliced through the tense atmosphere. "We've always had our own laws."

Adam's expression hardened as he stood and looked at Niko.

"We still do, Niko. We still do. You'd be wise to remember that." I heard the underlying threat in Adam's voice.

"I remember who—what—I am, Adam. Do you?"

"Enough to remember I am master here. I set the laws. We. Do. Not. Hunt."

I got up to stand between the two men. Damn it, I was doing way too much of this lately. First Adam and Carlton, and now these two. Were all males perennially twelve years old?

"Stop it," I said, "What in hell is going on here? Some sort of vampire politics?"

"In a way." Andrea's drawling voice held amusement. "We've been having a little difference of opinion lately."

"This ranch is an experiment, Keira," explained Adam. "I bought it so we could set up a lab, do research. I wanted my people to be able to exist in the normal world, without having to hunt, to feed from humans. To stay safe."

"Okay," I said. "I have to ask now. I know you can eat regular food, but surely, that can't be enough."

"It's not," replied Niko. "We have to have blood to live."

"We're attempting to develop synthetic blood proteins," Adam said. "Right now, we mix natural animal blood extracts with wine, which substitutes . . ."

He didn't have to finish the thought. Substitutes for the real thing. I wondered if it was like trying to convince yourself that you were eating chocolate when, in fact, it was only carob. Not a nice idea. Commendable, maybe, but as far as I was concerned, neither satisfying nor sensible.

"Where do you get blood?"

"That's why the animals," he said. "We draw blood humanely."

"He doesn't even let us hunt them, do you, Adam?" Niko asked. "Not even to thin the herd. Even your little human girlfriend here thinks that's stupid."

"You think I'm human?" I was amused at the idea. So Niko couldn't tell.

"You're not one of us," Niko sneered.

"Well, you are right about that," I agreed.

"So, what are you then?" I could tell he didn't believe a word I said.

I shrugged. "I'll tell you in a few weeks."

His eyebrows rose.

"I'm not being facetious," I said. "I won't know for sure until then. But you can rest assured, I'm not human."

Niko laughed. "If you believe this, Adam, then you're more of a fool than I originally thought."

The redhead turned his gaze back to me, his grin more a leer than anything else, as his eyes traveled from my face, down my body and back again to catch my gaze. It was a slow, lingering appraisal; the lewdness was nearly tangible. As he'd done on the dark road in front of my car, he grinned and gave a brief bow, then turned back to look at Adam.

"Not that I blame you, Adam," he sneered. "Ms. Land Rover here seems to be a pretty tasty treat."

In a motion nearly too fast for me to see, Adam sprang forward and gripped Niko's neck, lifting him from the floor with ease.

"Never speak like that again, Nikolai. You forget yourself."

The growling words rolled throughout the room with a rumble of power, thundering in every corner and echoing in ricocheted sound. Andrea had unobtrusively slid to one side, putting herself between me and the two men, as if to shield me.

"Don't move," she whispered. I stayed where I was, stunned into immobility by the sudden attack.

Electric power rose from each vampire, waves of color, light and force crashing together, building, merging and knocking against each other with the force of a hurricane-tossed sea. Both men remained preternaturally motionless, the struggle for dominance concentrated into this silent battle of wills, the redhead still dangling from the other man's grip, Adam still holding Niko at arm's length.

"We've got to stop them," I whispered to Andrea, trying keep from drawing the men's attention.

"Be quiet. You don't want to get involved in this."

"In what?"

Andrea didn't answer me.

The tension hummed and sang with energy, building layer upon layer, wrapping the room in power, rising from the floor, covering the walls, pressing against the carved tiles of the ceiling, looking for an outlet, only to crescendo with a nearly audible crash as, with a flick of his wrist, Adam tossed the other man across the room. Niko's limp body smashed into the dark wood panels, coming to rest in a huddled heap at the base of one of the tapestry hangings.

The thick silence hung heavy as a nun's veil, as if the very air muffled even the sound of our breathing. Andrea remained standing in front of me, but I could still see Adam clearly. He stood staring at the crumpled bundle that was his wildlife manager, lips set in a straight line, eyes still flashing brilliance. All pretense of humanity had left his face. Instead of looking like he'd put on a mask, it was as if an obscuring film had been erased, allowing the unearthly beauty to shine. His fists were clenched so tight that his fingernails cut into his palm, drops of blood beginning to drip between his fingers.

I started to move, but Andrea moved with me, still trying to shield me. I grabbed her arm with all the strength I was capable of, and shoved her out of the way. With a look of surprise, she stumbled, then caught herself.

"What are you?" she asked.

I could have made some sarcastic remark, but decided to skip it. Right now, I wanted to go to Adam and see if I could help him. I didn't waste a lot of thought on Niko.

He was a vampire, it was unlikely he was dead or even seriously injured.

Adam's face was frozen in a stare, his eyes unfocused, his expression set in a grim look.

"Adam?" I moved a little closer. "Can you hear me?"

"He's fighting it." Andrea's voice came from behind me and low down. I turned for a quick look. She'd crossed the room and was squatting next to Niko, who'd begun to stir.

"Fighting what?"

"The hunger, the bloodlust," she answered.

Niko groaned and stretched, moving with a slow jerky motion as if making sure everything worked. His voice hissed from his broken mouth. "Even he can't stop it now."

Before I could say anything, Adam's body convulsed in a shudder and he dropped to a low crouch, his hands covering his face.

I knelt in front of him. "Adam, are you all right?"

He groaned, shaking his head. "I can't . . ."

I reached for him, laying my hand on his. A rush of energy slammed into me, stronger than I'd ever felt before. The roiling hunger ate at my belly, bloodlust screaming to be released. Adam shuddered again and dropped his hand, his eyes widening as he leaned in toward me, needing to feed. I tried to scoot back, to stand, but in a flash of movement, his hand whipped around and grasped my wrist. I couldn't break his hold. Our gazes met again and I froze.

I took that gaze, let it capture mine, called to whatever power I had inside me, and let Adam's need sink into me. His head lunged forward, fangs bared, reaching for my neck. Ripping my hand from his grip, I grasped the sides of his face, holding him back, pressing my forehead to his, whispering calming words. If I could divert him, channel that energy into something else, maybe I could soothe him.

Flashes of scenes skipped across my brain, my memories mingling with his . . . my first sight of Adam standing solo at a party . . . the unparalleled sweetness of fresh blood pumping out of a soft hairless neck, filling my belly . . . the taste of Gideon's death magic and my own fear . . . emaciated living human skeletons behind razor wire, clinging to what was left of their humanity, eyes dead in breathing faces, skin stretched over brittle bones like old canvas. Then the overwhelming hunger. I watched as my hands, his hands, filthy, skin cracked and peeling, reached out, grabbing the scrawny neck of the woman and feeling my fangs sink into her throat. As we let her dying body drop to the dirty floor, her eyes blinked, gratitude at her release replacing despair. Hot tears ran down my cheeks as I saw what Adam had seen, felt the anguish, the guilt. He'd been there, inside the death camp, feeding on the already condemned. Adam's tears merged with mine as the thrumming energy subsided, the hunger easing, draining away, replaced by grief and sorrow.

We sat huddled together, clutching each other, rocking back and forth. I let some of my own tension go, my arms encircling him, holding on as he leaned into me. I closed my eyes and let my head drop to his shoulder, relaxing into his body. How ironic my life had become. The peace, the predictability, everything that I'd stayed in Rio Seco for, had been shattered, and the only safe haven seemed to be in the arms of a dead man. A dead man who still mourned for the atrocities he'd seen and himself committed. It was no wonder that he'd turned from the hunt.

CHAPTER EIGHTEEN

W E SAT ON THE COUCH in the reception area, Adam silent next to me, Niko leaning against the far end, not yet completely healed, but nearly so. Andrea perched on the arm of the couch, watching all of us.

"I'm sorry." Adam sounded hoarse, his voice rough and broken.

"No, Adam, don't," I said. "There's nothing to be sorry about. You stopped it, didn't you?"

"Barely," he whispered.

"Barely counts," I answered. "You owe me no apologies, Adam Walker."

"I almost—"

"Again, you didn't." I leaned into him and he automatically put his arm around me. "If you had, it wouldn't be the end of the world. Don't worry about it. Let's move on to another subject."

He smiled, a weak imitation of his usual seductive grin, but it would do for now. He'd had more than a mild scare. He'd lost control and I knew what that meant to someone like Adam. Control was everything. He was master vampire, king of the undead, or whatever passed for that around here, and had established a no hunt, no kill policy. I might not agree, but this was his playground, not mine, and I had to accept that. Obviously, from Niko's behavior, not everyone was as compliant. But if the vampire community worked anything like my clan, Adam's word was law, and

I'd definitely gotten that feeling here tonight. Niko could argue and complain all he wanted, but Adam was in charge. I'd never known a preternatural clan or community that could operate any other way. Too many predators do not make for a good democracy. Hell, even the smaller covens had only one leader. I didn't have any clue as to how one became the vampire king, but I'd bet it was not an elected position. I was definitely going to ask for a primer at some point. After all of this was settled. Whatever that meant.

I figured I could at least ask the question that was poking around in my brain. Since I didn't believe in coincidence, this was as good a time as any to find out the connection.

"Is that how you know Boris Nagy? From before?"

Adam looked puzzled. "Boris? He works for me. Handles all our deliveries so we don't have to expose ourselves to the public."

"You don't know him from the war, then? From the camps? He knows what you are."

"I don't understand, Keira," he said. "Boris would have been a young boy then. I only met him a few days ago. How could he know us?"

I searched his face, trying to determine if he were telling the truth. But all I saw there was confusion.

"Boris and his sister Greta were imprisoned in a death camp, Bergen-Belsen. He's been warning me about the Wild Moon since the deer were found. Earlier, when I stopped for gas, he gave me a silver cross for safety." I spoke bluntly. The time for games was over.

A gasp from Andrea made me turn and look at her. She wasn't looking at me, though, but at Niko. The redhead remained silent, his face set in a neutral expression. The cuts on his face were gone. If I hadn't just seen him thrown up against a wall, I'd have never guessed.

"Did you know Boris Nagy, Niko?" I asked. Adam stared at me, then at Niko.

A shrug and a grunt were the only reply.

"Niko, answer Keira," Adam commanded.

Andrea's eyes flicked over to me, resentment in her expression. Was she partnered with the other vampire? Is that why she was staring daggers at me?

Niko shrugged again. "I don't know," he answered, his voice quiet. "A human of older years isn't the same as a child. I knew many people, many victims. It's possible. There were so many then."

No inflection, no emotion colored his answer. I couldn't tell what he was feeling. Maybe the absence of sentiment that comes from seeing too much death and evil up close, of having to forget. Adam had said that he and Niko had been companions, partners for a long time. They'd probably experienced the war together, too.

"Does Boris say he knows Niko?" Adam asked me.

"I don't know," I said, not taking my eyes off the pair next to us. "Boris keeps trying to warn me about someone here he recognized from the camps. Someone who was talking to Marty."

"You think this person had something to do with your cousin's death?"

"Death?" The question came from Andrea.

"Yeah, as in drained of blood, fang marks on his neck. Left on his own embalming table like one of his own clients."

"I do not kill humans," Niko said, staring steadily at me. "*We* do not kill humans. Not even when we feed from them."

I stared back at him, meeting his gaze. He didn't flinch or look away. How could I tell if he was telling the truth?

He was a vampire of power, and could probably tell me bald-faced that he was directly descended from Vlad Tepes and I'd have to believe him. Of course, he might just be.

I scooted even closer to Adam. I wanted to sit nearer, to touch him, a little for reassurance, a little to reestablish the connection we'd had before. A small thrill of energy ran up my arm as I touched his hand. I glanced at his face, and he smiled, but the emotion didn't reach his eyes. Instead, a deep sadness welled up behind the clear sea-green, tingeing them with gray.

I started to say something to him, ask him what was wrong, but Andrea's voice broke in.

"Your cousin was the undertaker?" She sounded surprised.

"What do you know?" Adam fixed his gaze on Andrea.

She glanced at Niko, then looked back at Adam. I could have sworn I saw a flash of defiance instantly replaced by the same neutral look that she'd had earlier.

"I saw him," she said. "He was here, talking to John."

"When?" I asked.

She shrugged. "A week, two weeks ago. Before the security gate began working. Before most of us were here. I'm not sure. Our nights tend to blend together."

I looked over at Adam, who shook his head in a small gesture. "John is our day manager and human," he said. "He's been with us for more than twenty years, but he's only in his late forties."

I slumped in my seat. "So he couldn't be the one Boris was talking about. Too young and too human."

"Yes, John would be too young," Adam said. "But not the rest of us." He looked over at Niko and Andrea, his face set in grim lines. "I'll talk to John later, but there must be someone else here, someone who knew Boris, who conspired with the undertaker. We need to find out who was in residence when Marty came."

"I'm on it, Adam, but conspired how, and for what? What would we need from an undertaker?" Andrea spoke with distaste, as if the thought of a mortician was beneath her. Guess that crossed her off my list of potential Marty mates.

I answered what was probably a rhetorical question. "Coffins?" Three pairs of eyes turned and looked at me. I shrugged. "Well?"

I hadn't really meant it, but if there was one thing I knew about my cousin, he wouldn't have stopped at poaching animals.

Adam smiled and kissed my hair. "We don't buy retail, my sweet. Besides, I prefer a nice canopy bed with curtains and a Sealy Posturepedic. Infinitely more comfortable."

Niko and Andrea weren't quite smiling. I got the feeling I'd definitely committed a faux pas. Well, sue me. How the hell was I supposed to know?

"Fine, but my cousin was getting paid by someone here for something. Plus he was obviously someone's dinner, at least once. You people are the only vampires in the area, so, hello, get a clue? I don't give a crap about your politics or—sorry, Adam—about whether or not someone's hunting your game and breaking laws, or even if Boris Nagy is just having hallucinations or there really is a former Nazi at the ranch. All I really want to know is if Marty was actually murdered by the Albrights or if he convinced some bloodsucker to drain him, planning to come back in three days."

I stood up, frustrated by all the talk. I'd been willing to listen, to find out the lay of the land, so to speak, but now that the cards were on the table, it was time for someone to shut up and start dealing.

"Nazi?"

"She's right."

Adam and Niko spoke over each other. Adam looked at his wildlife manager and nodded. "You first. Why is Keira right?"

"I was coming to tell you," he said to Adam, his voice quieter than before, the cocky attitude gone. "But the Sheriff showed up just then."

"Tell me what?" The danger was back in Adam's voice.

"I found out the two humans, the Albrights, were collecting money from someone here at the ranch."

Carlton was right after all.

"How?"

Niko stood, shaking off Andrea's hand. "After we saw them the other evening, when Andrea dropped you off at the funeral home, I followed them to find out where they lived. This morning, I broke into their apartment just before dawn. No one was there, but I found a couple of envelopes with cash still stuffed inside. Our envelopes."

Adam rose and faced Niko. "What else did you find?"

The redhead shrugged. "A couple of hunting knives, some guns and too much beer. The knives had blood and hair on them, from deer. The place was a pigsty, spoiled food, pizza boxes, piles of filthy clothes reeking of animal and human blood."

"Human blood?" I asked, immediately thinking of Marty.

"No large amounts," Niko answered. "Just spots, like if you cut yourself and wiped it off on your shirt."

"Oh." I slumped back into the couch.

Adam perched on the arm of the couch, his hand stroking my hair. I was beginning to think this was a nervous habit of his, something tactile to do while his brain was ticking.

"Cash, in envelopes from the Wild Moon," he said. "We know they were poaching. Could one of my guests be hunting?"

"Adam, that has to be it," I said. "Hunt, feed, let the humans clean up after so you don't find out. Easy and safe and points the finger at the Albrights. Too damned easy if you ask me."

"She's got a point." Niko leaned against the wall, now relaxed; his natural arrogance again evident. "In fact, it's not a bad idea, Adam," he said. "Leaving out the cleanup part, anyway. It's not like hunting humans. We could set up regular hunts of the native fauna, leave the exotics alone. Hunt the weaker ones. Kind of a supernatural natural selection."

"No. We've barely begun to live without hunting. We can't go back now."

"We have to do something, Adam," Niko argued. "You asked me to manage the stock, to take care of the animals. A good wildlife manager knows when it's time to cull. It's getting to that point. We've been building the herds since you bought this place. Between the rescued exotics and the local whitetails, the deer population is going to overtake the natural resources soon. Do you want idiots hunting them from deer blinds? Or would you rather let them starve to death?"

"How soon?"

"Months, maybe by early next year."

"Damn it, Niko, why didn't you tell me sooner?"

"Because you weren't here," Niko replied. "When you finally arrived, you were too damned busy working on your plan. You didn't want to talk about livestock."

"I don't want to now," Adam said. "That can wait. Right now, it's important we find out if Keira's cousin was killed by one of us."

"But you will consider it?"

Adam looked at Niko in silence, his gaze steady, as if weighing the consequences of what he was going to say. The seconds stretched into a long minute, then he finally spoke.

"I'll consider it," he said, quietly.

Niko nodded, acquiescing the point.

"Andrea, we need to make sure the ranch is secure. If the hunters are my guests, I need to know. If there's a rogue around, I need to know that as well. There could be someone here out to undermine my power base."

Andrea moved swiftly and was almost out the door before Adam stopped her.

"Wait, have one of Evan's people go out to the Bexar County morgue and find out if Keira's cousin was turned. If he was, he'll know what to do. Have Evan come see me. Niko, make sure the lab is secure. I'm taking Keira to my place. When you get back, Andrea, assign someone to watch the house. Until we find out what's going on, Keira may be in danger."

Andrea left without a sound, like a good little minion. Handy. Niko stood, much more slowly, and looked at both Adam and me, as if he wanted to say something, to make a parting remark. But instead, he said nothing, then turned and walked out the door.

Adam came back over to me, and kneeled down in front of the couch.

"Can they do that?"

"Do what?"

"Undermine your power base."

"Yes. Our culture is fairly Darwinian, my love. Survival of the fittest and all that. Another reason I moved out here. No other vampire enclaves for hundreds of miles. I thought we had this place to ourselves."

"You don't?"

"I don't know. If your cousin was killed as some sort of payback to me . . ."

"But he may not have been."

"Exactly, and we won't know until we can find the answers. That's why I asked Andrea to get one of Evan's crew to go to San Antonio and get your cousin."

"You just sent a barback to check out my cousin's body."

He laughed. "Not a barback. Evan's not just a bartender, either. Think of him as Andrea's counterpart. He takes care of the Inn while she handles the outside security."

"Has he been with you as long as the others?"

"Not quite. He came to me after the war, escaped from Germany, changed his name, his apparent nationality. A little rough around the edges, but good with security. Makes a mean margarita, too."

"So all those people in the bar, the blond brigade. Were they lackeys or guests?"

"If you're talking about who I think you are, they're employees. Evan's security staff. Although I think I like 'blond brigade' better."

"They don't like me," I said, remembering Evan and the other man laughing.

"I'm not so sure it's you they don't like," he said.

"You?"

He nodded. "Quite possible. They were unhappy in Europe. Evan convinced them to come to the Wild Moon. They're fairly new to us and still adjusting to my way.

Most of them prefer to take human companions. I've told them not to while they live here. They have to obey me, but they don't necessarily have to like me. I can tolerate a little dissension behind my back as long as my orders are followed."

It was just like my own clan. I had to obey direct orders from Gigi, but I sure as hell didn't have to like it. A major reason I was living apart. If I wasn't in her immediate radar, I was fairly safe.

"I don't know how long it's going to take to find out," Adam said. "The drive to San Antonio is at least an hour and half, and there's the matter of getting inside and finding out. I imagine he'll call after that. If he has to wait long, it could be early morning."

"Damn. Then he'll have to bunk down somewhere and you'll be asleep."

"Not necessarily," Adam said. "I prefer to sleep and need to sleep at least a few hours, but I can stay awake during daylight if I try. I just can't go out in direct sunlight."

"You don't poof into dust or anything, then?"

He took my hand in his and grinned again. "No. No dust, no glowing flames. But, if we're weak, it could be fatal. If we've fed and are strong, it's more like an extremely bad burn."

Adam's tone sobered. "I promise you, Keira, I will find the answers. The 'blond brigade' do come in useful. If someone here killed your cousin, they'll help me find the truth. In the meantime, you will be safe."

"I'd be safe at home," I protested. "That's not why I agreed to stay here." I leaned a little closer to him, concentrating on his face, letting my emotions and desire show in my eyes. "I think here could definitely be a lot more interesting."

"Definitely," he whispered.

He closed the small space between us, his lips brushing mine, a soft feather touch, a promise of more to come.

"Does that make it more interesting?"

"I'm not sure."

"Well, then, I think I can do better."

And I let him.

Eons later, we broke apart, mostly because I needed to breathe. This whole undead immortal thing could come in handy, except when the undead in question forgot that his partner was living and needed oxygen.

He smiled at me, sheepish. "Sorry, got a bit carried away."

I smiled back and traced my finger across his cheekbone. "No worries. I kind of was a little carried away myself."

I rubbed my thumb over his lower lip, feeling the points of the fangs that were now fully extended. "You do distract me, love."

He playfully bit at my thumb, grazing the skin slightly, then ran his lips across the palm of my hand. "I distract you, do I?"

"What do you think?" I closed my eyes, letting myself get lost in the sensation.

"And you called me 'love.' Was that a distraction, too?"

I blinked and started to pull my hand away, but he grabbed it and pressed it back to his mouth, placing a careful kiss on the palm. Shit. I had said that, hadn't I?

"Does this mean you share my feelings, Keira Kelly?"

His eyes blazed green fire at me. I knew I wasn't going to get away with anything. I'm not so sure I wanted to, but I wasn't quite ready to admit to love. I'd done it so easily in the past, and gotten so very burned.

"I . . . I don't know."

"Liar," he said, smiling. "You know."

"It's just everything that's going on, Adam," I protested. "Marty's death, Carlton, Boris flipping out . . ."

Adam dropped my hand and rocked back on his heels, then rose to his feet. "Damn."

"What's wrong?"

"Distraction goes both ways. I asked Andrea to send Evan to me for a reason."

"Why was that?"

"The thing you said, about a Nazi . . ."

"Yeah?"

"I think I know who that might be."

CHAPTER NINETEEN

T HE PHONE RANG. Adam answered, listened and began to scowl.

"Find him. Bring him back here."

Adam hung the phone up with a curse.

"Bloody hell."

"What's the problem?"

"That was Andrea," he said. "Evan's vanished."

"Vanished, as in 'poof'?"

"As in cleared out, taken his car and hit the highway." The anger in his voice frightened me. Adam ran his fingers through his hair and began to pace. "Andrea says she never found him to send someone to the morgue. One of the other guards says Evan didn't make patrol, so they just went on without him. She's at Evan's house now. Everything's gone."

"But why—"

Adam dropped into the chair next to me. "I think Evan was the man Boris was talking about."

"The . . . oh, shit, the Nazi?"

"Yes. I told you he came to us from Germany."

"You said he escaped," I accused.

"He did, Keira. But he was a member of the party, just like everyone else who wanted to survive. Eventually, it was too much for him. That's why he escaped. He and several of the others who came with him hid out in the north of England for many years, afraid to go back to Germany."

"Even if that's true, then why disappear?" I asked. "What kind of threat could a poor old guy like Boris be to someone like Evan?"

I didn't understand. It was possible that Boris had recognized Evan, but who knew? Just because Evan had been a Nazi, didn't mean he hadn't reformed. Some of my own relatives had to hide in plain sight as members of the party, as horrible as that was to contemplate now. They'd had no choice, maybe Evan hadn't either.

Adam shrugged and leaned back in the chair, his tiredness evident. "I don't know. But Evan may well have been the one talking to your cousin. He's the only one here that fits the description. That's why we need to find him and bring him back." He sprang from the chair and headed toward the door. "Wait here, I'll only be a few minutes."

I started to get up to go after him, but thought better of it. He needed to calm down and my following him wouldn't make it any better. If I guessed right, Adam was feeling guilty. He'd brought Evan here and Evan may have just been the one to kill Marty.

After no more than a few minutes, the door opened. A thin middle-aged man stood there, holding a white paper bag. He was dressed in brown corduroys and a white button-down shirt, sleeves rolled up to his elbows. He didn't look like a waiter. But the bag he was holding was obviously food. I could smell it.

"Were you bringing me food?" I was a little confused, since I'd eaten not that long ago, but my stomach growled in reaction to the delicious smells. Maybe Adam had gone to order us something to eat.

The man gave me a sheepish grin and shook his head.

"Sorry, actually this is for me and my wife. I was just looking for Mr. Walker. I'm John, the day manager." His clothes might be working class, but his educated accent could have come from Oxford or somewhere just as plummy.

"Oh, hello. Adam just stepped out, he'll be back in a few."

I expected John to either leave or sit down, but he just stood there, his thin arms holding the bag of food. A lock of his graying brown hair fell into his eyes, as he shuffled his weight from one foot to the other. It was obvious he wanted to speak.

"I'm sorry to hear about your cousin," he finally said. "Niko told me what happened."

"Thank you," I said, wondering what he was getting at.

"I saw him one day, you know. Late evening, really. Just before dusk. Your cousin, I mean. He came looking for the owner."

So that was it.

"Andrea said something about that," I said.

"Your cousin wished to leave information about preneed funeral services. He was rather persistent." John's homely face lit up with a grin. "I couldn't exactly explain why no one here needed them."

I joined in his laughter. My poor cousin.

John sobered. "I'm sorry. I had to have Lise escort him out."

"Lise?"

"One of the security staff," John replied. "She followed him out to the mortuary to make sure he left. As far as I know, he never came back."

No doubt. Marty didn't like conflict. He'd never have

come back to a place that had him escorted out by security.

"Were there many people on premises when Marty was here?"

John thought a moment, then shook his head. "That was before the main hotel staff even arrived," he said. "I believe it was only myself and my family, plus a few of the senior staff—and security, of course. I believe all the laborers had gone by that time."

"Senior staff?"

"Niko, Andrea, Evan," he replied.

Evan. That figured. Maybe when this Lise had taken Marty away, Evan had seen them and stopped them and that's how he'd hooked up with my cousin. I wondered where Lise was. I asked John.

"She's gone back to Europe," he said. "Just left last night. Didn't like it around here."

"Does Adam know about this?"

"About her leaving? Yes."

"Did Adam know about Marty coming around?"

"No. I didn't know it was important until now. We had various other trespassers try to get on property until the gate was installed. Lise or someone else would usually take care of it."

Made sense to me. Lise was probably nothing to worry about.

"You've been with Adam a long time," I said. "How do you like it?"

John's answer was instant and unambiguous. "He's an excellent employer. I've been with him most of my life. Working for him since I was twenty-two."

"What made you decide to work for . . ." I hesitated, not sure how to phrase my question. "Or maybe you had no choice?"

John smiled. "To work for vampires? It's not a dirty word, you know. I did have a choice."

"I know," I replied. "I'm just not used to talking to other people about stuff like this."

"Not the kind of conversation one can have over billiards and a pint at the local pub," he agreed.

"Too true. So you did have a choice?"

"Absolutely. Even though my family has been with Adam's tribe for several generations, we may choose to stay or to leave. I left for university. Studied hotel management, then came back to run his place in London. Now I'm here. He's a good employer. Takes care of his people."

"Tribe? Is that what they call it?" I laughed. "I suppose that's no worse than 'clan.'"

A muffled sound came from my pocket. The phone again. I pulled it out and glanced at the display, but I didn't recognize the number on the screen.

"Hello?"

"It's Carlton," he said without preliminary.

John smiled, mouthed a good-bye, then disappeared out the door. I turned my attention to the phone.

"What's up, Carlton?"

"Still at the ranch?" he asked.

"Is that why you called?"

"Not really."

I waited, unwilling to get into it again with him. If he had a legitimate reason for calling, he'd better be telling me in the next few seconds, or I was going to hang up.

A sigh came over the other end of the phone. "I just got to the truck."

"Any sign of the Albrights?"

"Not a one, but there were a couple of coolers in the bed."

"Coolers? I don't understand."

"Beer coolers. Smeared with what looks like blood. There's a couple of broken mason jars, too, also stained. I'm going to send them off for testing. Just thought you'd want to know."

"How long do you think you'll be?"

"I don't know, a couple of hours or so," he said. "But Keira, we won't know the results of the tests right away. I'll have to send them to Bexar County."

"Thanks."

Before he could say another word, I hit the button to disconnect the call. It had taken a second for the clue bat to hit me. Beer coolers. Igloo coolers, no doubt, just like the one that Derek was carrying when I'd seen him in the mortuary. The day Marty was killed.

I dialed a number. There was one person I knew could help me out.

After a couple of endless rings, a voice answered. "Wassup, little sis?"

"A lot. Put your pants back on, bro, I need a favor."

I quickly ran down what Carlton had said.

"They're at the old quarry?"

"Yeah," I said. "The one out near the county border. Hurry, Tucker. If they send off those coolers, we may never know."

"Don't worry," he said. "I'll take care of it."

I hung up. Now, there was only one thing left to do.

I was halfway out the door when Adam and Andrea arrived.

"Where are you going?"

"To the mortuary," I said. "And you two are coming with me."

Adam took my arm and stopped me. "A moment, Keira. What's going on?"

"I need to look at something at the mortuary. I need you to go with me; Andrea, too."

"Andrea is going to San Antonio to check your cousin's body."

"Well, whatever, but I still have to go and I need a vampire to go with me."

"You still haven't told me what's going on, Keira."

I blew out a breath in impatience and quickly told him about Carlton's call.

"Tucker's going to go out to the scene. See if he can 'accidentally' check out those coolers. See if they have human blood on them. If they do, then I can safely assume it's Marty's and they—"

Adam grabbed me again, and pulled me around to face him. His eyes glittered and his voice was quiet. "Keira, wait. There's something you need to hear."

I stopped trying to move, frozen by something that ran through me, suspiciously close to fear. I wasn't afraid of Adam, but afraid of what he might be about to tell me. I don't know how I knew. Maybe it was the undercurrent I heard when he spoke, the trembling energy I could feel him holding back.

"Let's go back to the office. I'd rather not talk about this in the hall."

I let him lead me inside, this time we sat on the couch in the reception area. Andrea walked behind us and shut the door after she entered.

"When I went out, I met Andrea at Evan's house."

"And?"

I waited in silence, not saying anything because of his expression. The look on his face was one of defeat, of sorrow and anger and frustration.

"We found something."

I'd never heard him sound so very tired. The rich goodness of his voice was gone, replaced by an emptiness that scared me.

Blood. I sensed the word more than heard it, the memory of the visions I'd had racing through my mind. They were always about blood.

"Jars, some empty, some not. I smelled it before I even opened the refrigerator door."

I looked over at Andrea who stood against the wall, every inch of her the bodyguard. She stared steely-eyed into the distance, as if unwilling to look at me, or even at Adam. Her arms crossed below her breasts, legs slightly apart in a ready stance. Muscles bunched below the knit fabric of her slacks, her thighs slim, yet strong. I could feel the tension radiating off her, energy storming just below the surface of tightly held barriers.

"Not deer blood, then." It wasn't a question. I knew.

"No, it's not."

In contrast to Andrea's barely controlled energy, Adam's aura was preternaturally still. He sat only ten or so inches away from me, but I felt nothing, an utter blank, all emotion swallowed inside of him, into a blackness so deep, I couldn't touch him. Not physically, but psychically. It was if he'd cut himself off. He stared down at the carpet, his face smooth and expressionless. I reached for him, but he slid away.

"Do you think it was Marty's blood?" I ventured the question, almost afraid, but more afraid of not knowing.

Adam didn't react at first, then, when I was sure he hadn't

heard me, he began to turn his head, a movement so slow it was as if every muscle in his head, neck and shoulders fought the very air. I looked into his expressionless face, all expression, all life had drained from his eyes.

"No." The word was barely a whisper of agony. He shuddered, taking in a breath he didn't need, his head dropping into his hands.

"Adam, what?" I slid across the couch and wrapped my arms around him, cradling his head to my shoulder. I snapped at Andrea.

"What the hell happened out there?"

She broke the unseeing stare and looked at me. "It was human blood. From many different humans."

"Holy shit," I said. "Many? As in more than one?" I knew I wasn't making any sense but I didn't want to let it sink in.

Andrea nodded. "Many."

Adam sat up, pulling away from me, staring at the opposite wall.

"Many as in at least ten, maybe more."

What the—? "Adam, how? Why?"

His voice was harsh, bitter. "The 'why' I know," he said. "It's what we do, isn't it? Feed. Bleed others to sustain ourselves." He turned haunted eyes back to me. "When Niko told me about the animals, I didn't like it. I wanted to stop all hunting. Cold turkey as it were. But I understood Niko and can even see where it might be beneficial. But this—not this. Not here."

"Shshh." I reached over to him and took his hand. "You couldn't have known."

"I *should* have known," he snapped. "I am the master here. I should have known and been able to stop it."

I couldn't answer. He wasn't wrong. A good leader should always know what his troops, or minions, are doing.

Even if you don't, you're ultimately responsible. Part of the raw deal.

A terrible thought occurred to me.

"Adam," I began, hesitant to bring this up, but seeing no other way around it. "Where did Evan get all that human blood?"

"I don't know," he whispered, voice raw with pain.

"There have been no humans here at the ranch." Andrea spoke quietly, but with conviction. "No outsiders. He must have been hunting in town."

I snorted, almost a laugh. "In this town? I doubt it. There's fewer than a couple of thousand people in the entire county. I think someone would have noticed Evan. I think your boy was ranging farther out. San Antonio maybe, Blanco? Wherever. He wasn't feeding from this local trough."

"He was here every night," Adam said. "At the bar, patrolling, somewhere on property."

"How do you know?" I asked, allowing a little of the sarcasm to leak through. I was sickened by this new revelation, but not surprised. Predators will hunt and feed. Adam had just made a bad mistake with Evan, assuming he'd accepted the local master's rules. Evidently not.

"I know, Keira," Adam said quietly. "Evan may have been chief of inside security, but I never trusted him completely. There was always someone watching him."

"Except tonight."

Adam grimaced, guilt washing over his features. "Except tonight," he admitted. He stared at me, his eyes both sad and tired. "Distractions, you see."

I gulped. Damn. It did work both ways, didn't it? He'd been my distraction, and I'd been his.

"Then how—?" I stopped as the realization hit me. "Marty."

Adam's expression immediately changed. The weariness left with a startling suddenness, replaced by horror and the terrible knowledge that was beginning to dawn in my own mind.

I could barely get the words out. "It wasn't just the poaching," I said. "No one would pay that much money to simply remove a few dead animal carcasses. Not even your not-wanting-to-get-caught vampires, Adam."

I stood up and began to pace, my fury mingling with guilt and embarrassment. "I don't know if you know this, but in Texas, when a body is prepared for embalming, the blood is pumped out, washed down the drain."

Andrea shuddered a little, the distaste showing. "Into the sewage system?"

I nodded, not sure if she was upset because it was gross, or because of the waste of all that food.

"There was no scent of fresh blood in the mortuary," Adam said, standing and crossing the room to join me. He put his hands on my upper arms, his gaze searching for mine.

I dropped my head, not wanting to see the accusation I expected in his eyes.

"Yeah," I said. "The only blood you smelled was old. There should have been more. Even though the place is washed down all the time. You should have smelled fresher blood in the pipes. Tucker didn't smell anything either. 'Too sterile,' he said."

Adam took my chin in his hand and raised my face, forcing me to look at him.

"Can you . . . can vampires eat blood from the dead?" I asked.

He nodded, still holding my chin. "As long as it's not too old," he said. "It begins to decompose immediately, but if we drink, or refrigerate it within a few hours, it's usable."

I closed my eyes against the tears I felt building. This was my fault.

"You didn't know, Keira," Adam said, gently. "You couldn't have known."

I pulled away from him and stalked to the other side of the room, brushing at my eyes, angry at my tears, angry at my dead cousin.

"I should have known. Just as you should have known about Evan. Marty was my responsibility. My burden."

I didn't want to think about it. If we were right, my cousin had gleefully packaged up blood from the recently deceased and just as cheerfully sold it to Evan. I'd bet anything that the Albrights and the poaching were only an afterthought. Another way to eke out some cash from the vampire group.

"I'm sorry, Keira," Adam said. He was right beside me again. I hadn't seen him move. Handy trick that.

"Sorry, Adam? Why are you sorry?"

He stroked my hair, then cupped my face in his hand. "Because I caused all of this. Because I wanted to be here so much that I brought death and danger to your life. If I hadn't come—"

"Stop it," I whispered, already lost in his gaze again. I could see the anguish, the guilt written all over the clear green eyes, the chiseled planes of his face. "It wasn't you. It wasn't me. It was Marty. His greed. His need to be more than he was." I reached up and touched Adam's cheek lightly, tracing the angular curve of his cheekbone with my thumb.

"If it hadn't been Evan, it would have been someone else," I said. "Some other squeeze-money scheme cooked up by my cousin."

"I promise we'll find Evan," Adam said. "He will pay for this."

Andrea cleared her throat. I'd forgotten she was there. For a few moments, my world had shrunk again, only me, only Adam. Two people with more than human lives twisted together by Fate, by circumstances and by whatever made us need each other. But Andrea made me remember there were others involved.

"The rest of Evan's crew is waiting, Adam," she said, as if reading my mind. "We'll need to speak to them."

He nodded, still staring at me. "Niko's sent a group out to track Evan," he said to me. "I need to question his staff."

I allowed myself a small smile and a final caress of his cheek. "I understand," I said. "Why don't I wait at your place?"

Adam smiled back, a little of tonight's earlier fire back in his eyes. He leaned forward and brushed a brief kiss across my lips. "I won't be long."

I TOOK MY TIME walking back over to Adam's house. I wanted to think, to process everything. We had no proof, but it was the best explanation I could come up with. It fit all the evidence. Evan, rebelling at Adam's no-hunt, no-humans policy met up with my stupid cousin, who'd visited the ranch only to sell pre-need funeral contracts. No doubt the recently departed Lise had something to do with Marty and Evan hooking up. I'd bet anything that she'd been his vampire lover and Evan had taken advantage of the situation. In fact, knowing my cousin's nature, I wouldn't be surprised to find out he'd been the one to approach Evan with the plan. That's something none of us would find out until Evan was caught.

One thing bothered me, though. What had Marty done

to get himself killed? If he was supplying Evan with fresh human blood, why would the vampire kill his only supply? This was the same question Carlton asked about the Albrights. No one kills the cow while she's still producing milk. Unless Marty had done something stupid. Maybe he'd threatened Evan, tried to hold out for more money.

No. Marty was many things, but he wasn't that stupid. He'd found a ready source of cash with the vampires, he wouldn't have jeopardized that. Now, on the other hand, the Albrights were stupid. Maybe they'd been the ones . . . but then again, they weren't the dead ones here.

I rubbed my forehead trying to scrub away the confusion. Until Evan was found and questioned, we'd never know why Marty was dead.

Rain began to fall as I rounded the corner of the back of the Inn and stepped onto the gravel path leading to Adam's house. I hurried my pace, but as I started down a small incline, my boots slipped on a wet patch and I fell. My right knee slammed into the gravel, skidding across the small stones. My right hand scraped across the ground, searing a fiery path across the palm. Damn.

I got up slowly, testing my knee. It ached but was okay. There would probably be a heck of a bruise in the morning, unless my super healing kicked in. I knew that was part of my great good fortune in being who I was, but I hadn't had a chance to test it out since I'd begun to change. I could have cheerfully waited to test my healing abilities for a long time. At least my slacks hadn't ripped.

My hand was in worse shape, oozing blood and stinging, but I could clean it when I got to the house. Since I was already as wet as I could get, I'd walk the rest of the way. I didn't want to risk slipping again.

The light overhead flickered as I walked by it. There,

again. All the outdoor lamps were flickering. I turned to look at the Inn. Dark windows stared back at me in mute acknowledgement of the fact the power was out. As I stared, the outdoor lamps joined in the outage. A few breaths later, a few of the low pathway lights came back on. I could see a gentle glow from some of the previously darkened windows. Someone must have cranked on an emergency generator.

I stood there in the rain. Should I go back to the main Inn to what was sure to be minor chaos? Or I could pick my way back to the cottage and spend the power outage in relative quiet, waiting for Adam, waiting for any news. I chose the quiet. Besides, there were plenty of candles.

The few pathway lights faded to none by the time I reached the outskirts of Adam's house. I walked slowly, shuffling my feet and feeling my way past the edge of his porch. My great night vision wasn't of much use in this misty rain. My foot found the cobblestones that marked the boundary of the path up to my porch steps. I walked a little more confidently, intermittent flashes of lightning in the distance illuminating enough of the path and making it easier for me to walk a little more quickly—a mistake. I misjudged the distance. My right foot hit the bottom step, the impact reverberating up to my sore knee. "Shit!" I said aloud.

Another flash of lightning silhouetted the pale hair of a figure standing near the porch swing. I scampered up the steps as quickly as I could.

"Hey, there," I said, as I stepped onto the porch. "Sorry about that last, I banged my knee." I heard the person come closer. "Andrea?"

Just as I realized I couldn't possibly be her, a big hand clamped over my mouth. A flash of pain seared the back of my skull and then I felt nothing.

CHAPTER TWENTY

"**Y**OU THINK you're so fucking smart, don't you?" The rough voice matched the gritty feel in my mouth, the pounding in my head. My knee still throbbed, the bloody scrape on my hand less so, but still uncomfortable.

I was tied up, duct tape binding my hands behind me, my knees bent awkwardly. I was on the floorboards of a car, stuffed into the space in front of the passenger seat like a bag of old laundry. I winced, a bruise on my head making itself felt as I tried to ease the cramping in my knees. He must have used brute force to cram me in; I was too tall to fit into the small awkward space using anything less.

Evan laughed, making me realize he was definitely no match for Adam. His voice, his laugh were no more powerful than mine. Maybe I did have some natural immunity or something. Or maybe my connection with Adam negated the natural vampire mojo. I didn't really care. I just hoped that Adam would soon find out where we were.

"Don't play games with me, little girl," Evan said. "I know you're awake. Felt you. Don't try to hide."

"Not hiding," I muttered, clenching my teeth to keep from screaming at him. "Just not wanting to look at you."

He chortled again. "Whatever. Adam thinks he's the smart one. Taking up with a stupid human chick, not hunting, not living."

I croaked out a laugh. "Last time I looked, you're not so much the living one yourself."

"At least I'm still a vampire," Evan said. "Not some poor excuse for one. Some king. He didn't even know your stupid cousin was selling pints of human blood right under his very nose."

"You like that word, don't you?" I shifted my position a little.

"What word?"

"Stupid."

He laughed again, this time I felt the car slowing. Were we there yet? Wherever the "there" was he was taking me. I somehow didn't think we were going on an outing to Sea World.

Evan put the car into park and reached down toward me. His hand grabbed the back of my shirt and he heaved, forcing me out of the enclosed space and onto the passenger seat beside him.

I grunted as my bruised head came into contact with the bottom of the dash on the way out.

"Sorry," he said, an evil grin crossing his face. "Well . . . not really."

He shifted back into gear and eased the car back onto the road. I looked around. No lights, just the jutting beams of the car's headlights stabbing through the darkness, illuminating the stretch of narrow Hill Country road. We could be anywhere in Rio Seco county, or anywhere else within a two-hundred-mile radius. There were so many quiet little back roads in the Hill Country, roads that rarely saw humans pass over them. Of course, not seeing that now, since neither of us were. But he didn't seem to know that part . . . about me, that is. He'd called me human. Maybe I could use that to my advantage.

"I repeat, why are we stupid?" I asked.

"You, your cousin, those ridiculous brothers, all of you wandering around in your own little worlds, no one knowing the full truth of the others."

"By that you mean—?"

He laughed. "If I tell you, I'd have to kill you."

Okay, not going there. Not that I had any doubts about this little road trip. I doubted he was taking me somewhere for my health. I was pretty sure he meant to drain me and dump me.

I stared at him, trying to get a clue from his expression, but there was none. None at all. With humans, you can always tell something, even from professional killers whose faces don't reveal emotion. Vampires—most beings like us—can shut down, become blanks, emotion swallowed like so much light swallowed by a black hole. Evan wasn't leaking anything. Not fear, not even the glee of a criminal who'd gotten away with something. Of course, he probably didn't think of himself as a criminal. He really wasn't. He'd just taken advantage of a situation to provide himself with food. Jean Valjean of the vampire set. Well, maybe not. He'd killed Marty. Even though humans were prey to him, that was still unforgivable—at least in my book.

"Where are we going?"

He didn't answer, just kept driving in silence, the only sound a small under-breath hum that I doubted he even knew he was making.

Some time later, we pulled off the main road and drove through what was once a gate. The quarry. We were at the old abandoned limestone quarry. Where Carlton had found the Albrights' truck. Not good. I saw no sign of the truck, nor of any police activity. They were probably long gone. I didn't know how long I'd been unconscious, but if Evan had put

me in the car directly and driven here without detouring, I'd
estimate it to have been about an hour or so. Long enough for
our dear Sheriff and his crew to have towed away the truck
and gone away themselves. I wondered if Tucker had ever
made it out to the scene. Not that it made any difference now.
Now that . . . shit. I should have called him when we found
out about Evan. He might have . . . Oh well, no use crying
over calls not made. I'd have to figure this out on my own.

Evan drove through the gate and onto the quarry
grounds as far as he could without driving the car into the
quarry itself.

A raw hole in the ground, the pit reached nearly
a hundred yards across and about fifty or more front to
back, kind of like an unfinished football field. The place
had been abandoned about twenty years earlier when the
cement company declared bankruptcy and couldn't unload
the business.

No one ever came out here anymore, not even teens
in search of a quiet place to neck. It was just a little too
creepy, even for the I-dare-you types. Especially since
that girl had died out here. Lots easier to trespass on Wild
Moon grounds and hang out at the lake.

He pulled me out of the car. "Walk," he commanded,
forcing me in front of him and poking me to get me started.

"You really think you can get away with this?" I asked,
trying to sound sure I'd get rescued. It didn't work. I wasn't
even fooling myself. That didn't stop Mr. Macho Vampire
Man from bragging, though. I guess there was a reason for
the old cliché. Bad guys really did like to hear themselves
talk. Egos are us.

"You think you're so fucking smart. They all did.
We were doing this right under your eyes, under Adam's
eyes. Your greedy little cousin was selling us blood."

"Blood? I thought he was helping you all hunt in secret. The animals?" Okay, so I already knew this but I figured the longer I kept talking, the more time I'd have for someone to come find me.

"Hunt?" Evan laughed. "That wasn't my game. Why the hell would I want animal blood if I could get human? Newly dead. Almost as good as fresh from the living cow." He licked his lips, an obscene gesture coming from him.

"How much could that get you?" I snapped at him, too tired to watch my words anymore. "C'mon, a human body can only produce about five and half liters, not exactly much of a feast. Besides, it doesn't last long, does it? I mean, being dead and all."

I lost my attitude as he returned my stare, an evil grin widening across his face. "Do you think we bothered to wait?"

"Son of a bitch," I whispered as the truth sank in. Why wait when you could provide your own supply, laundering it like the mob laundered drug money? In this case, laundered through the county's mortuary, the logical place for human bodies. So logical, in fact, that no one ever clued in to the recent upswing in deaths.

"Yeah, it wasn't hard to convince those two that keeping a steady supply coming to us would be worth their while. They were getting tired of the whole animal scam. Too messy."

The Albrights. Of course. It made sense: rope in two ex-cons as tired of Rio Seco's limitations as I was, but a hell of a lot more willing to cross the invisible line. Poaching wasn't enough anymore.

"But how? No one ever knew."

He smiled, confident in his cleverness. "Your cousin sold a lot of those pre-need contracts. All Derek had to do was get the list. From there, it was easy to help them along on their way."

So Marty's ability and salesmanship made it happen. This was too logical. That's how he hooked up with Evan's group in the first place. He'd gone out to the Wild Moon, hoping to increase his pre-need funeral services income, and Evan (via the missing Lise, no doubt) had latched onto a sure thing.

Evan laughed again. "No one ever noticed. All those humans, so pleased that Uncle and Auntie didn't suffer anymore. Helped that we only chose the weak and already dying. Too easy."

Culling the herd—just like Niko wanted to do with the deer. I suppose it made a creepy kind of sense, especially if you didn't consider yourself human. Evan was a predator, like my brothers, like my father, like me or even Adam. Except we'd chosen to keep our predatory habits humane.

My family only hunted four-legged beasts, and only the natural way, chasing them, selecting the weakest . . . Oh, God, he was right. It was the same thing. If you didn't consider yourself to be part of the same species, then what was the problem? I swallowed hard, my mouth suddenly dry again. Was this what I would eventually become? Vampires were once human, but me, I wasn't, not one bit of me.

No. No matter what, I thought of myself as equal to my human friends. They were people, not prey.

"Did he know . . . did my cousin know about this?" I had to know.

Evan's laugh relaxed me a little. "No, he was as stupid as Adam. He thought that he'd just gotten lucky, all those people starting to die on cue. What an idiot."

Well, yeah, he had a point there. Marty was—had

been—the king of ostriches, ready to ignore evidence he didn't like, too easily swayed by promises of easy money, riches without effort.

"C'mon." Evan pushed me down the path, my feet sliding along the slick gravel as I tried to keep my balance. The way was steep, meant for strong work-booted men to travel in the bright sunshine of a dry Texas day, not for a still-bound non-human in the wet stillness of a dark night.

When we reached bottom, I stumbled, staggering forward a few steps as I avoided falling and scraping my already bruised knees. Evan caught up to me, and caught me under my arms as I began to lose my balance.

His kindness lasted only a few seconds. Leading me a few more steps, he shoved me to my knees, up against the west wall of the pit, directly across from where we'd descended, right next to a small white cross surrounded by plastic flowers.

This was where Antonia Garcia had died more than fifteen years ago, a dare gone bad after a night of drinking too much Boone's Farm Strawberry Hill and smoking far too many joints. She'd tried to climb the wall of the pit, avoiding the footpath on the other side, avoiding the small road once used by the workers to get the heavy equipment to the quarry floor. A bet, a rite of passage of sorts, but she'd slipped near the top and had fallen more than thirty feet, her sixteen-year-old skull no match for the stony ground. The Garcia family planted the cross the next week. It remained there as a silent tribute to the stupidity of teenagers. That was the last night anyone had used the quarry as a trysting place.

This was not where I was going to die. Not if I could help it.

I groaned in pain and rolled onto my side, scrambling

away from Evan and trying to sit up. There was a slight depression there, almost like the entrance to a natural cave, except this one was most definitely man-made, scooped out by equipment meant to dig the once-lucrative limestone out of the earth. I tried to scoot back against the wall, but something was in my way. Something soft, something that smelled.

"Watch out for the garbage," Evan sniggered.

Garbage? That didn't feel like . . . My bound hands brushed something behind me. Cloth, flannel, skin. Holy fuck. I craned my neck and strained to see. A large irregular blob, darker than the surrounding shadows resolved into two distinct shapes. Not Tucker. I'd have known. He hadn't come back from his earlier reconnaissance of the quarry, maybe he was still poking around. The whole area around the pit was undeveloped. A great place to hide evidence. Of course, I was here with the person that killed my cousin. Too bad I wasn't telepathic. The only thing I could hope was that Tucker would come back. If he were snooping around in wolf mode, he'd have had to leave his clothes and car somewhere hidden. I was hoping that "somewhere" was near here.

"Who is it?" I whispered.

"Who do you think?" I couldn't see the sneer that I could hear in his voice. "After your cousin died, the Albright brothers stopped being useful to me," he said. "I couldn't let them just leave."

"But the police were here earlier, my . . . friend, the Sheriff." I'd almost said "my brother," but stopped in time. I didn't want Evan to know that Tucker had anything to do with all of this.

"Don't be any stupider than you already are," he said. "I hid while they were here. Then I went back to get you."

Clouds scudded across, revealing the moon. Not full, but close. The wind picked up a little. I could tell the weather was changing. I could see a smile beginning on Evan's face.

"Okay," I said. "So I'm here. What do you want with me?"

"You're an inconvenience." His words were calm, matter-of-fact.

"I get that." I tried to stay as calm as he was. "What do you plan to do with me?"

"I thought about that a long time," he said. "I could take you, drain you, turn you." He licked his lips, a smacking sound both hungry and lustful all at the same time. His eyes glittered in the darkness. "But that would be a problem."

I didn't say anything. I knew where this was going, but I wasn't about to put words in his mouth.

"I won't turn you, but I can take you."

Take. Did he mean . . . ?

"I bet your blood would be sweet. I haven't had living human blood for too many years to count. Your cousin only let Lise drink. Wasn't much of an equal opportunity whore."

Again, I could see that, too. Sharing blood was too much like sex. *Was* sex, for all intents and purposes. Marty didn't do same-sex partying. But I wasn't going to let out one of my smartass comments. No way. No point in tempting fate.

"So why'd you kill him? Jealous?" I asked, my good intentions lasting long enough for my brain to make the words form on my tongue.

"Are you crazy?" Evan screamed at me. "Whoever killed him totally fucked up my life." He started toward me—and the unmistakable ringing whine of a ricochet echoed throughout the quarry pit, a split second before the pain of the bullet tore through my side. My bruised knee smashed into the dusty ground, making me scream in agony. As my head hit the gravel, another bullet ripped into my thigh . . .

In a haze, I watched as Evan landed slightly in front of me, his body shielding me from whoever was firing.

I doubted he was doing this out of the goodness of his shriveled vampire heart, especially since his head had hit the ground with an audible thump. He'd been shot, too.

Can vampires die from a bullet wound? Bloody hell. This hadn't ever come up in any of my conversations with Adam. Not that I cared so much, considering that whoever shot Evan was bound to be on my side of things, but I needed to know if he could die because I didn't want to be stuck down here with a wounded vampire getting more and more pissed off. He'd already threatened to drain me, this would probably just make things worse.

I was able to scoot around, gradually leaning my head out, still not allowing myself to get too close to him. I needed to see where the shots were coming from. My injuries throbbed, but I ignored them as best I could. They weren't life-threatening, at least not yet.

Silence. No more shots. No. Wait. I could hear someone scrabbling down the side of the pit, loose gravel tumbling ahead of him or her. It wasn't Tucker. He didn't do guns. He'd just have shifted into wolf form and jumped Evan.

I scooted back a little and then lay still, hoping whoever it was couldn't see us in the pitch dark. The person kept moving, slowly, as if testing the ground ahead, a smart move, considering the slippery path.

The smell of blood began to seep into my nose, rich, fresh, recently spilled. Not mine. Evan was bleeding. A lot, I hoped. If I were lucky, he'd bleed out and I'd be safe, at least from him. I tried to avoid the thought that I could bleed out, too. At least I was still conscious.

A flash of light behind me made me cringe. I could barely move. Superior strength notwithstanding, I hurt and I could be hurting a heck of a lot more if my mystery savior turned out to be another bad guy. It was most definitely possible that Evan's enemies were not necessarily my friends.

"Miss Keira." The words slid quietly across the gravel, riding the air as lightly as a piece of down fluff escaping a battered jacket. "Miss Keira?" The whisper came again, almost too soft to hear.

"Boris?" Thank goodness. He probably hadn't seen me when he was shooting.

"Yes, it's me," he answered.

"Thank—" I started to say.

"Is he the only one?"

I nodded.

"How did you find me?"

"I followed you. I was at the ranch."

Boris set his flashlight down, tucked his rifle under his arm, took something out of his pocket and leaned over Evan. A flash of metal, a swift jab and the hypodermic needle sank into Evan's exposed throat. The vampire convulsed once, twice. A tortured groaning sound escaped, shuddering past his lips, then all was still. He was dead. True death. I held my breath, waiting for the disintegration, the dusting. It didn't happen. He didn't conveniently vanish in a cloud of dust with special sound effects. He just lay there, just another corpse. But I could tell he was gone. The energy that had been there, unnoticed until it didn't exist, left an empty space. Whatever animated the vampire was missing.

"Silver nitrate." Boris watched me as I struggled to my knees with a gasp.

"Effective," I said, not wasting time mourning for Evan. "Boris, I'm hurt. Can you help?"

"Not so fast," he said.

"What?" I sank back down.

His expression never changed. His eyes, flat as the darkness behind him, reflected no light, no hint of compassion.

"Evil. All are evil. Your cousin, the other one, they betrayed me, my sister. They work with the evil ones."

"What the—?"

Boris' head began to shake, slowly at first, back and forth, his body trembling. "Evil, they are evil . . ." His words faded to a soft mumble, the words unchanging.

"Boris," I began, not sure if I should try to reason with him, to talk to him. But I had to. I needed him to cut my bonds, bandage me, to help me get out of here. I could worry later about his thinking Marty was evil.

"Boris. Please, help me." I tried to make my tone even and reasonable, as if I were talking to someone who hadn't just obviously flipped his last lid.

He wasn't listening, or maybe he couldn't hear. He just kept trembling and muttering to himself.

I started to scoot a little closer, but froze as he swung the rifle in my direction.

"No. Don't move," he said, his face suddenly clearing and his voice firm.

"Boris, why?"

"Be quiet." He moved a step closer. "Do not move. I have something I need to do."

He seemed to be considering something, looking at me,

then at Evan's body, then back at me. A moment later, he sighed loudly, then stepped a bit closer.

I let my own held breath escape, figuring he'd decided to do the kind thing and let me go. As the stock of the rifle connected with the side of my head, I knew I was wrong.

I WAS REALLY BEGINNING to hate this. I was alone now and my head felt like ten thousand monkeys were tossing coconuts at it. My thigh and side still burned from the bullet wounds. This was not what I'd had planned for tonight. A nice quiet dinner, a little snooping around, not confrontations with my ex-lover, being kidnapped by a rogue vampire and wait, there's more, being shot and then knocked unconscious and left in a pit by the kindly old store proprietor. What the hell was wrong with this picture? Or better yet, what the hell else could go wrong with this picture?

The sound of gravel skittering made me perk up. Someone was coming. Someone—

I sighed in relief as I saw the store van pull up, headlights off, running only on parking lights. Greta must have figured out where her brother was and come looking for him. Not that I knew where he was right now, but that didn't matter. She could untie me, get me back to town. Both Boris and I needed help and here it was.

Boris opened the car door, the inside light flashing on. Oh fuck. So much for the rescuing. He must have gone to get his sister.

He climbed out of the van and fumbled with the latch on the sliding door.

"I'm sorry you had to get dragged into this, Keira," he said, not looking at me, not sounding at all like he meant it. "But you're here now and we can't leave any of you."

"What do you mean, 'any of you'?"

Boris opened the sliding door, never letting loose his gun.

The overhead light in the van flashed on and I could see two huddled forms inside. All I could see was part of two men's backs, arms tied together with some sort of wire. Their heads were hidden in the depths of the van.

A second later, I knew it was Adam. Possibly Niko, but definitely Adam. I'm not sure how I was so certain.

The old man moved slowly, but with purpose. In a few minutes, he'd dragged the two men onto the ground. I was right. Adam and Niko.

CHAPTER TWENTY-ONE

B OTH VAMPIRES WERE UNCONSCIOUS—at least I hoped they were when I saw their limp forms thump to the ground like so many pounds of potatoes. A breath, then two. Shallow, distant as a cool breeze in a Texas summer, but they were still alive. The wire around their wrists and ankles looked like silver, like that cheap by-the-inch type that you can buy at any flea market or jewelry kiosk at the mall. Cheap or not, it seemed to be doing the trick.

"What did you do to them?" I asked, my voice surprisingly steady. I could feel my blood pressure rising as anger flooded me.

"Nothing that shouldn't have been done sooner." Boris' expression grew hard. I'd never seen him like this before. So determined. So harsh.

He dragged both vampires toward me, first Adam, then Niko, depositing each of them next to me, up against the memorial marker. Great. Here I was with two dead humans, a dead—really dead—vampire and two unconscious vampires. Somewhere in the surrounding woods, my werewolf brother was still prowling around, looking for clues. If it weren't so damned serious, I'd be laughing at the whole ridiculous scene.

"Now what?" I asked. "More deaths?"

"It started with death, it will end with death." He looked at me, then away. "I didn't want to involve you. You've always been . . ."

His voice trailed off, his head slowly shaking from side to side as if in denial. He looked at me again, the sadness in his eyes evident. "You shouldn't have. I never meant . . ."

"Then let me go, Boris," I said, trying to keep my voice calm and soothing. "I promise to help—"

"No. It is too late."

"I don't understand, Boris. Can you explain?" I hoped that by keeping him talking, I could buy time and figure out a way to get us out of this. How, I wasn't sure. This whole thing was resembling some really bad movie-of-the-week plot. This old man had managed to subdue two powerful vampires, kill a third and wound me.

"It was easy, really," he said. "Told them Andrea was in the van, hurt. That I'd found her. No one ever paid attention to me at the ranch. No one cared." He smiled a little then. "I knew they'd never . . ." His eyes narrowed. "Cattle prods work on two-legged beasts just as well."

Oh, Christ. That's how he'd done it. His ultra-special modified cattle prod/stun gun—625,000 volts of electricity. Useful for self-defense in more ways than one. He was damned resourceful, all right.

"It was easy to bind them, then. Silver wire, duct tape. Bring them here."

Why?" I needed to know. Why not just kill them if he'd meant to rid the world of vampires?

"Here." He motioned with the rifle, indicating the small white cross. "A place of sanctity. Too far to take to the church. Too public. Here is holy enough. A girl died here. There is a cross." He looked directly at me. "I only wanted the one, you know. Not the other. But they both came and now they both die. Like you."

His matter-of-fact delivery chilled me. This was Boris 2.0, no longer the quiet, haunted man I'd known. This man had a mission and was ready to carry it out. I had to do something, but what? I wasn't in much better shape than the two vampires. The bullets had gone through me, and my healing ability should take care of the wounds, but it wasn't instantaneous. I was weak, tired from all the stress my body had taken over the past few days.

"Why, Boris, why kill us?"

"They are soulless creatures, already dead," Greta climbed out of the back of the van, wiping her hands on a small towel. Yep. Definitely not going to be the one rescuing us. She stepped closer to me. "It is just a matter of degree."

She had a point, but not one I was willing to concede. I knew death—the real version, the I'm-never-coming-back version—and vampires weren't that. Whether or not they had souls, or whatever, was a subject for theological debate. I didn't care. What I did care about was the fact that Adam and Niko were about to die.

"I am sorry," she said. "I did not want to involve you." Greta squatted down, eyes seeking mine. "I hoped that Boris had warned you away, kept you away from these people."

"Why are you doing this? Maybe they hunted animals, but the ranch is private property. What they do there is none of your business. They weren't involved with—"

"It has always been my business," she spat at me as she stood up. "It is not for what they do now, but for what they have done and will do."

"What did we do?"

Adam's voice was hoarse, a croak of a sound. I turned my head. He'd managed to sit up; his mouth was raw, cracked. It should have been bleeding and evidently, it had a little, but only a trace of dried blood showed at the corners. A scrabbling sound behind me made me turn the other way, Niko had also struggled to a sitting position.

"You, move over there." Greta pulled out a small pistol from her pocket and waved it at Niko. "Do not speak. Move over there with the other monster."

Niko glared at her, his eyes speaking the words he didn't utter. His lips were as cracked as Adam's, blood dripping slowly from the corner of his mouth. He slid across the gravel, ending up on Adam's right. Except for the difference in hair and eye color, the vampires looked more alike than ever. Glittering eyes stared daggers in Greta's direction, finely chiseled lips pressed together, holding back words I knew they needed to say.

"You, Keira, please move over there." Greta motioned to her left. "You do not need to be near them."

So she didn't automatically class me in with the monsters. That was a mistake I might be able to use—if I could figure out how. I wasn't good at this. I was still a changeling, not fully empowered. Damn. I needed my brother to show up. But neither of us was telepathic.

I could, however, work on loosening the duct tape on my wrists. Muscle against the miracle of polyethylene-coated cloth and adhesives. It might work. My strength was more than that of a human. Suddenly, I realized my wounds weren't as bad as they should have been. I still hurt, but not as if I'd just gotten shot. I sneaked a glance at my thigh. The bullet had only grazed the top of my leg and the deep scrape was filling in. Hooray for super healing.

"What did we do?" Adam asked again.

"You ask? You dare to ask?" Greta snorted and pointed

the pistol at Niko's head. "Why don't you ask your man there? Ask him what he did during the war."

I stopped working my wrists at this and looked over at Niko, then back at Greta. What was she talking about?

"Why Niko? It was Evan who was a Nazi," I said.

Greta laughed, a curt bitter sound. A small smile danced across her lips like a ghost, then the solemn look reappeared. Boris stood quietly behind her, looking at the ground.

"He was a Nazi? How appropriate." She laughed again, this time with a bit more humor.

"You didn't know?" I was puzzled. "I thought that's why . . . Boris said he recognized someone at the ranch, someone from the camps."

"Not him." Boris began to shake again.

Adam slowly turned his head.

The silence grew thick with the waiting, but Niko remained silent, his head bowed to his knees.

"Niko?"

"He is a coward," Greta said. "As much of a coward as always. So much the lord of the mountains, the caretaker of his people—this monster sold our village to the Nazis. Sold us to the death camp."

"I only came to the ranch in the daytime," Boris said. "One day, I was delayed. A flat tire. I came after dark and I saw him there, with a group of others. I knew him." Boris turned to look at me, eyes brimming with tears. "Then you saw him. They walked in front of your car. You asked if I saw people. They are not people."

My "vision" that wasn't.

Boris turned to Greta. "Keira saw. She knows. She had a vision and saw the day we were brought to the camps."

I gasped as the memory came flooding back—the vision I'd had when I'd touched Boris' hand. The man in the cloth coat and the hat was Niko. Niko had been their betrayer.

"Why, Niko?"

Tears rolled down my cheeks as the memories I'd tapped into that night returned, all thousand and more days spent in the confines of the camp. Knowing that tomorrow, my sister and I might be the next ones to be tortured, raped. Watching as day after hellish day, the unrelenting hell of every night began; hunters crawling through the fences, aided by the Germans, coming for their nightly feast of blood and horror. Even our dreams weren't safe. The dreams came back night after night to haunt us.

"She sees, Greta," Boris whispered. "She sees the truth."

Greta's voice droned on behind the scenes flashing in front of my mind's eye. "He was supposed to take care of our village. But he turned us over to them, to be tortured, to be food for others of his kind. In exchange, he gave the Germans samples of blood."

Adam's eyes closed, his head drooping. He turned his anguished face to his companion.

"I saved you, Nikolai. When you were a boy, you were selling your body on the streets to survive, to anyone that would have you. I found you and saved you. Gave you life, wealth. Yet you did this?"

"I didn't know." The words were a wail of despair. Niko's face was wet with tears, tinged pink, streaking his dusty cheeks.

Greta screeched at him. "How did you not know, monster? You watched as they tried to take me, to rape me. Only my little brother saved me, offered himself up in my place. They took him. One fresh young body was the same as any other to them. I was too skinny for the ones who liked the women."

"I thought . . . I thought I was keeping you safe," Niko whispered, the words almost too soft to be heard. "They promised me you all would be safe in the camp. Safe from the SS troops. The only way I could keep my people alive."

"Your people, Nikolai?" Adam growled. "They have never been your people."

"I did what I could, Adam. You were gone, taken to the other camp. I couldn't find you and the Germans came to the village. I did what I could. I didn't know until it was too late and they would have taken me, too."

"But you did not stop." Boris spoke softly. "Even now, here, you helped the brothers set up the hunts, to hide."

Adam's head dropped, lolling for a moment as if he'd lost consciousness. Then with an obvious struggle, he raised it again.

"It never ends with you, does it, Niko? Is he telling the truth?" His voice was only a whisper, as if it were a terrible effort to speak. I closed my eyes and breathed in, trying to reach out to Adam, to sense his status. We'd shared power, we'd shared our bodies and we should still have enough of a connection to let me probe his physical state.

I leaned into him and felt the fading power. Something was in his bloodstream, something that made him groggy and weak. He needed to feed, and soon. He looked at me, briefly, as if he could feel my metaphysical touch. His eyes fluttered and he forced them open again.

"Niko?"

The younger vampire shuddered and turned his head away, speaking to the empty air. "We are hunters, Adam. We shouldn't live like humans. The hunt is who we are, what we are. I did nothing wrong."

"You are monsters." Greta approached them both. "Monsters who hunt and who kill. Today you hunt the deer; tomorrow, you will again be hunting us. I cannot let you do this. For this, and for what you did to us in the war, you will die."

She stood next to me and looked down. "I am sorry, Keira, that you became involved, but it was fate and it is necessary. I will leave you all out here to die when the sun rises. They will suffer and burn."

"We should take Keira back with us, Greta," Boris said. "She is not a part of this. She needs a doctor."

"That is not possible, Brother," Greta replied, her voice softening as if speaking to a small child. "She is a part of their circle now. She is with the monster. I see this now."

"But she can be saved. She is still human. Please, let me take her with us."

"No, Boris, it's not safe. She will tell the Sheriff we killed them."

"Take her, Greta," Adam said. "She is innocent. Our bodies will burn in the sunlight, no one will know."

I glared at him. If they took me back, there was no chance for Adam and Niko. If I remained behind, I might be able to do something.

"No, no, no." Boris began shaking his head. "No, you are monsters. It does not matter if we kill you. But they will find out about Mr. Nelson."

"Marty? You killed Marty? I thought—"

"I would do anything to help my brother," said Greta, a vicious look in her eyes. "But your cousin was an accident."

"Accidentally drained of blood?" I didn't bother to hide the sarcasm.

"It was an overdose," she explained. "My brother was only supposed to sedate him so I could question him; find out about the monsters. I drained him of blood after I saw the marks on his neck."

She started to laugh, the kind of laugh only heard in bad horror movies and on the soundtracks of cheesy Halloween CDs: a high-pitched cackling that gave way to the gasping sobs of the truly disturbed. All these years, we'd been careful around Boris, knowing that he suffered from these terrible nightmares, when in reality his sister was the one on the edge, her darkness hidden behind the façade of a simple shopkeeper.

"It didn't work, though, did it? You had to get involved."

"They're going to find us." Niko finally spoke. "The others at the ranch."

Greta laughed again. "You think so, do you, little monster?"

"What did you do, Greta?" I asked, a cold fear sinking into me. I'd pretty much counted on Andrea to round up the troops and envisaged the vampire cavalry coming to the rescue. I hadn't really started doing really serious worrying until just now. There was no way in holy hell that I'd be able to keep both these guys alive for any length of time once the sun came up and began to fry them. Adam was weak and I wasn't sure about Niko, but I couldn't just trust that he'd be okay. I didn't know how much sunlight they could take before becoming truly hurt or even dead. Permanently dead. Now was not the time to ask, not in front of the people trying to kill them.

"The other monsters will be just as dead, just as burned as the two of you. Boris drugged the last shipment of wine with holy water and hemlock to burn them from the inside out, and set incendiary devices to burn the buildings. He learned many things during the war. The place will burn and take the evil with them as the sun will burn you."

"Greta, what are you going to do with Keira?"

Boris' voice contained an unspoken plea. He must still be having second thoughts about hurting me. Awfully human of him.

"She can stay here and die from her wounds." She shrugged. "I don't care. She stays with the monsters. She can die with the monsters. I'm sure the animals will come soon. Come on, Boris, we need to leave now."

"Are you leaving Rio Seco?" I had to ask.

The laugh floated back as Greta didn't even bother to turn around. "Leave? We have no reason to leave. You will all be dead. They will think you died in the fire."

CHAPTER TWENTY-TWO

A LOUD GROWL from above our heads was the only warning. A blurred shape passed over us and landed on Greta, knocking her into Boris and taking them down to the ground. I scooted back, intending to protect the vampires from whatever this was.

A groan escaped Adam as he slumped down, rolling to his side. I could see the effort of remaining upright had taxed his waning strength. I struggled to loosen the tape around my wrists.

Greta screamed words I couldn't understand as she struggled with the dark shape. Boris scrambled to his feet, pointing the rifle with trembling hands.

"Tucker, watch out!" I'd recognized my brother's wolf form.

With preternatural speed, the wolf leaped to one side, barely escaping the bullet.

Boris dropped the rifle and screamed, a howl that echoed off the walls of the pit, heartbreak and agony in every note. He sank to the ground, hiding his face in his hands.

"Greta." The soft whisper barely made it to my ears.

Greta Nagy lay on the rocky ground, a pool of blood spreading underneath what was left of her head.

The wolf nudged the rifle with his snout, bringing it close to me and away from Boris, who was crouched next to his dead sister, rocking and keening. The old man's head was buried in his sister's side, his hands clutching at hers.

"Boris . . ." I started to speak, wanting to feel sorrow, wanting to feel something, but I couldn't. I was numb.

The old man took a deep breath, shuddering through the sobs that racked him. He pushed away from Greta's body, hands coated with her blood. Glittering eyes accused as he stared at us, still on his knees, a supplicant. In a movement nearly too fast for me to see, he reached down and put Greta's pistol to his own head and fired.

A fine spray of blood spattered my face as Boris Nagy slumped across the body of his sister.

I buried my head in Tucker's furry side, suddenly beyond tired. This was not the kind of death I was used to seeing. People, broken beyond repair due to the violence in their lives, meeting an end just as violent. My brother nuzzled my thigh, a questioning look in his wolf eyes. I looked at him, grateful for his presence. It was over.

"I'm fine, Tucker. Nothing a little time and distance won't heal. Shift back and help me get these guys into the van. It's getting pretty close to dawn."

"Keira, the ranch . . ." Niko's quiet plea reminded me. It wasn't quite over.

I'd forgotten about the Nagy's little love gifts to the vampires at the ranch.

"Adam, Niko, does what Greta said make sense? Are they all dead then?"

"Holy water?" Adam groaned, as if even speaking was too difficult. "Myth. Rumor and legend."

"But the fire, Adam? The hemlock?"

His voice was ragged, tired. "Hemlock maybe . . . sedate them. Won't kill them. Slows down motor centers.

Humans . . . stop breathing. Don't need to . . . breathe. But fire . . . destroy . . ."

The words trailed off, as he drifted out of consciousness. Damn it.

I explained the situation to my brother, who cocked his wolf's head and whined a little, nudging my still-bound hands.

"I can handle this, Tucker. I'm not sure when the bombs are set to go off. You can get there faster cross-country. I'll take care of things here."

The wolf nodded once, licked my face, and took off across the quarry. It wasn't the best we could do, but it would have to be our answer for now.

"Hurry, bro," I whispered. I hoped he'd make it in time. I'd already seen too many deaths.

Now I had to get myself free.

I worked my hands against the tape, pushing with all the force of the muscles that were stronger than human. My back strained, shoulders heaving with effort. Drops of sweat rolled down my face as I worked, pulling my hands apart, feeling the tape starting to give, to tear just a little. With a final effort and a yank, the bonds tore with that distinctive fleshy ripping sound. I pulled the rest of the tape from my wrists and just as quickly removed it from my ankles.

I crawled over to Adam, touching his head, his face. "Adam?"

His muscles were limp, slack, as if no life remained in his body. But I knew better. Below the imitation of death was a spark that lay dormant. Just touching his skin let me know that whatever made him Adam Walker was still there. Call it what you will, soul, magick, necromancy— it wasn't gone. But I also felt the change in the air, the lightening of the breeze that announced that dawn was just about to tap me on the shoulder.

I pulled the duct tape from both Adam and Niko, but couldn't break the wire that still bound them. It was heavier than the jewelry-making wire I'd first taken it for. It seemed to be some sort of cable coated in silver.

"Niko, damn it, can you help?"

He shook his head.

"I'm afraid that silver does make us weaker, Keira. That's how Boris was able to keep us unconscious in the van. The cattle prod weakened us, but the van's lined in sheets of silver foil. I fed yesterday, so I'm not as powerless, but Adam hasn't."

Damn it all to ever-loving hell and back. I'd been hoping to drag them inside the van, to escape the sun's rays. I looked around, trying to see if there was any sort of shelter at all. Nothing. We were on the west side of the pit, maybe if I were able to get them to the other side, away from the first rays of the sun . . . I said as much to Niko.

"I'll do what I can, but I'm still pretty weak," he said. "Keira, Adam hasn't fed in a while. He may die if the sun rises."

"That would bother you?"

I couldn't help myself. I was angry and tired and not choosing to be nice.

"Whatever our differences, I don't want Adam dead," he said. "He's my friend, my sire, he's—we can work out the problems."

"He said he'd saved you."

I tugged at the cable—a futile gesture but I had to try. There was nothing else I could do right now, nowhere to drag them to safety.

Niko looked down at the ground.

"He saved me from a life you can't begin to imagine. I was a whore. I was beaten nearly dead by my master, left on the streets to die. Adam found me and fed me, let me grow up to be a healthy man. When the plague came, he turned me. I'd contracted it, was dying."

"What Boris and Greta said?"

"They were right, but I swear to you on all that's holy. I believed the Germans—that the children, the people would be safe. It was the only way I could see to save them, save my own people from extinction. The Nazis had attacked a nearby village and burned everyone, including the small tribe of vampires living below the church. After they looted the treasures, the Germans burned the building."

"They lived under a church? But I thought—"

"We are as religious as we ever were—or not," he answered. "Holy symbols, belief in God, that never changes, at least not because we're vampire."

"Handy."

I turned my attention back to Adam. What I felt about Niko would have to wait. There were more important things to worry about right now. If the vampires survived this, then we could discuss the morals and ethics of his actions of more than half a century ago. I had to admit, the reason I'd asked was selfish. If Boris had been right, I might have just been tempted to leave Niko to die.

Adam groaned slightly, his eyelids fluttering. I'd helped him to lie on his back, slightly leaning to one side off his bound hands.

"Adam, can you hear me?"

He nodded, slowly, as if even this slight movement hurt him.

"Can you feed?"

"Feed?"

The words were no more than a gruff croak.

"Adam, it's nearly dawn. There's no real shelter. Derek and Dusty are here, at least their bodies. Maybe I can slide you closer—"

"No." I felt instead of heard the internal turmoil that came with that word.

"Dead too long. Can't feed."

Okay, let's try door number two. Not a choice I'd wanted to give, but it was available.

"Boris—"

"No! I will not feed from the dead."

That only left one option.

"Then you're going to feed from me."

I scooted over closer, trying to figure out how just to place myself. I didn't know if I should try to offer my neck or my wrist, or what. It wasn't as if I'd ever done this before.

"No." Adam closed his eyes and turned his head away. "Won't."

"He won't feed from you, Keira," Niko explained.

"I get the point, Niko," I said in exasperation. "Damn it, he needs blood. I can't keep the sunlight away; can't stop it from rising. But I can offer this."

I touched Adam's forehead, the connection between us opening up even more. I stretched my senses, trying to reach in and touch his awareness. With that extra clarity that comes with psychic perception, I realized that my own wounds were nearly healed, surprisingly quickly, even for one of my kind. But almost as quickly, Adam was vanishing, slipping from my mental touch.

I pressed my wrist to his mouth. "Feed, damn you," I insisted. "Adam, come on."

"Can't you just magick us out of here?" asked Adam, rousing enough to try to make a joke.

"It doesn't work that way."

"Why not?"

"You think I can just wiggle my nose like *Bewitched* and poof, we're gone? Why the hell don't you just turn into a bat or mist and escape?"

"I get the point."

"The only chance we have is to have someone notice we're missing. Maybe Andrea." I could hope. Andrea seemed strong enough. If she couldn't come herself, she could send someone. Maybe she hadn't drunk the tainted wine. Maybe my brother could run faster than a speeding bullet, save the other vampires and get back to us before Adam and Niko fried. There were a hell of a lot of maybes floating around here.

"It's too close to dawn," Niko reminded me. "They'll all be hiding, sleeping. If they haven't been drugged into insensibility with the hemlock. John will make sure they get into their coffins."

If they're not all already permanently dead. We didn't say the words. We didn't have to.

"I though you said you preferred a bed?"

"A coffin is the only sure safety, my sweet. In an emergency, we hide belowground." Adam gave me a weak smile.

"Then we're stuck here."

"You can leave. You should leave."

"And leave you—the two of you—to die? Not an option. Even if you scoot to the far back of this overhang and I try to cover you, we're still facing east. The sun is going to spill in here with a vengeance and you're going to become a crispy critter. I can tell how weak you are. You're fading, Adam. You've got to feed."

"I won't feed from the dead, Keira."

"I'm not talking about the bodies, Adam," I said. "I'm not dead and I'm right here, full of blood. You can feed from me."

"No."

"This isn't a matter for discussion, Adam Walker. I am not going to let you die because of some ridiculous principle."

"Would you ask an alcoholic to drink wine? A junkie to shoot up just one time?"

"It's not the same thing," I argued.

"Nearly enough," he said. "Human blood is more than a drug. It took decades for me to kick the need. I am not going back now. I'll take my chances."

"I'm not asking that you shoot up a speedball, damn it! Drinking blood is what and who you are."

This nobler-than-thou attitude was going to result in his death and I wasn't about to accept that.

"Need I remind you, vampire king, that I am as much not a human as you are? The only difference between us is that I'm not the walking dead. You'll be the extremely not-walking-dead if you don't bloody well do something about it. Feed from me. I doubt that losing a little blood will hurt me. After we get out of here, if you want to go back to being a fucking vegetarian, then fine. But in the meantime, feed."

With a visible effort, he turned his face away from me.

Niko had kept silent through this exchange, watching me, lost in his own thoughts. I didn't need to ask him his opinion. Annoyingly, I realized that both he and I were of one mind on this matter. Principles be damned, survival was the key. Martyrdom was for, well, for martyrs. That particular job description held no interest for me. I preferred to be a live lion, as I was sure did Niko.

Our gazes met and held. For a brief moment, I saw the

truth behind the cocky attitude—the determination to live. He had been telling the truth about his deal with the Nazis. With the perspective that can only be found after several lifetimes, he'd realized that to save his people, he had to make a bargain and had danced on the edge of a very sharp sword to keep both the vampires and the villagers alive during a hellish time. But the knowledge of failure also lurked behind those bright blue eyes, that the sword turned out to be sharper than he could ever have imagined. Niko hadn't counted on the fact that human men could commit acts of such pure evil as the Holocaust.

"You'd stay here to save me?" Niko finally asked, sounding unsure.

"I do what I have to. No matter what you did in the past," I said. "I don't pretend to understand. All I know is that you made a terrible error in judgment and only you and your own conscience can live with that. I won't be your judge or your jury. What Adam does with you is his decision. He's your king. I'm not." This wasn't easy. I couldn't get the images of those small children sacrificed to the Nazis out of my mind, but being who I was, and who my family was, I'd grown up learning that every story has several sides. I was in no position right now to make any kind of moral decision about this. No matter what, I still had to help him.

Niko bowed his head and remained silent. Sometimes punishment was not death, but eternal life, living with the guilt of unintentionally sacrificing dozens of people to torture and evil.

The pressure increased, the day had just about arrived. The quality of the air changed, a slight breeze arose, bringing the scent of morning with it.

The first fingers of light crept over the horizon, slid

across the ground, snaking closer. Threatening. I spread
my body across the front of them, trying to block as much
of it as possible. But the light was as inevitable as the day,
and it pushed past me, almost as if to mock me, a ray
catching first the body of Derek Albright, then alighting
on Adam's cheek.

He winced, a gasp of fear escaping him, a hiss of pain
as the light touched him. I moved to cover his face, but
there was too much, light spilled over and around me as
the sun rose above the edge of the quarry. I couldn't stop it.

Niko curled into a small ball, trying to cover himself.
He wasn't complaining, but he was healthier, had fed
recently, and could probably stand the burning for a time.
Adam hunched into a fetal position, up against Niko's side.

I couldn't stand this. No matter what happened later, the
recriminations, the guilt, I was not going to let Adam die. I
forced my wrist against his mouth.

"Feed, damn it, feed." His nostrils flared, I could
imagine him taking in the scent of blood, of life as it
pumped just below my skin. I grabbed the back of his head
with my other hand, pressing his head to me.

"I can't let you die, Adam Walker."

He clenched his jaw, muscles straining, lips pressed
together tighter than a reluctant virgin's legs. Fear and
longing ruffled through me, a discordant riff of emotion,
counterpoint to the thumping sound of my own heart,
heard as if from the outside; the rush of blood pumping, the
remembered taste of glory filling my taste buds. Adam's
hunger surrounded me. His weakness colored the need and,
below both of those emotions, I felt the buried imperative
that he so desperately tried to ignore. The one that both
his second-in-command and I embraced so thoroughly: the
need to endure, to survive, to live, no matter the cost. If I

could reach that need and force Adam to acknowledge it, maybe then he could accept my blood and the fact that it was part of his nature.

I moved away momentarily, trying to figure out how to accomplish this. A moan escaped him, and a pang of craving flavored with panic stabbed through me. The hunger flared higher, stronger, overwhelming the apprehension as the reality of another shaft of light reached in to touch his face, sapping his energy. The connection faded as I felt him lose consciousness. I reached over to Niko, thrusting my wrist in front of him.

"Do it, Niko, bring the blood."

"Do you know what you're asking?"

"Yes, now hurry."

Niko's eyes met mine as he strained his head forward, wincing in the light. His fangs extended and I pushed my wrist into his face. His jaw muscles tensed and then he struck.

The pain was instantaneous and sharp. Small needles sinking into the sensitive skin, then just as quickly, numbness. A quick sucking motion and the blood began to flow. I started to pull my wrist away, when Niko's tongue gave a quick lick.

"Couldn't help myself," he said, a slight grin crossing his face.

Ignoring him, I moved over to Adam's side, and rubbed the bloody wrist against his too-still mouth. He wasn't breathing, but that didn't mean anything.

"Drink, damn, you," I said, cradling his head again. "Come on, Adam, drink."

His throat convulsed, and his lips twitched, tongue flicking out briefly as he scented the blood on my wrist.

"That's it," I encouraged. "Drink, save yourself, damn it."

Another sharp pain as Adam's own teeth took the place of Niko's. He began to swallow, mouth working, throat gulping, drinking in the only thing that could save his life . . . or undeath. Sensation washed over me, searing dark longing and passion swirling with the metal heat flavor of the fresh blood filling my mouth, fighting off the burning of the sun. My own passion rose, matching the intensity of Adam's rising energy. I took a deep breath and tried to dampen down the connection enough to concentrate. He continued to drink, tongue licking my wrist like a cat's, lightly flicking, teasing, as his eyes caught mine in their gaze. I shuddered and closed my own eyes as the image of the two of us locked together, bodies straining, sweaty with—

"What are you doing with my sister?"

My brother stood just above us on the edge of the quarry, all six-foot-four, shrieking Viking stature of him glistening nude in the increasing light.

"Interesting choice of wardrobe," Niko said with a bit of a leer.

"No facetious comments from the bloodsuckers," Tucker answered, a lascivious grin splitting his face as he eyed the attractive redhead. My brother dropped down into the pit. "Come on, Sis, help me with them."

Tucker grabbed Niko under the arms and hoisted him up into a fireman's carry. Even with my wounds healing fast, I couldn't have managed that. I helped Adam stand, my arm around his waist. He threw his right arm around my shoulders. After his breakfast snack on my blood, he was strong enough to hold on and stumble with me to the far side of the quarry, out of the direct path of the sunlight.

"The ranch?" Adam asked.

"All safe and tucked into their coffins for the duration."

"You did *not* have time to go all the way to the ranch," I accused.

Tucker shot me his trademark grin. "No, before I got too far I remembered this." He tossed me his cell phone. "I'd been carrying it in my mouth, but dropped it when I smelled your blood." He shrugged. "I should've thought of it before I went racing off, but hey, I remembered soon enough. Called the ranch, woke up a guy named John. They'd already found the fire starters. Someone named Andrea sniffed them out earlier in the evening."

Adam gave a weak laugh. "I should have figured."

"We can't stay here long," I said. "They need to get into the dark." I looked at the sky. "I think maybe an hour, no longer, bro. Then this whole pit will be in sunlight."

"Not a problem, Sis. If you all can chill here for a few, I'll see what I can do to get you all out of here. My van's not far." He shot a smile and looked back over to Niko. "I'll pick up my clothes along the way."

"Pity." Niko smiled back.

This was certainly interesting. Tucker might have been playing with Bea most recently, but his tastes often ran to both sides of the sexual fence, and Niko was damned pretty. Whatever, *not* something I needed to be thinking about right now, especially since my brain was finally putting two and two together and getting a very interesting answer about the nature of Adam and Niko's partnership, at least in the past. I'm not saying that it bothered me, but it was something to consider. It certainly explained a few things.

Tucker clambered up the side of the quarry and was gone before I could say anything else.

Adam was beginning to look more like his usual self now that he was out of the sunlight. I sat across from him, my legs bent at the knee, my toes touching his side ever so lightly. I half expected him to move away, to not want to touch me. I'd broken his taboo, forced him to feed from a living person.

He smiled at me, as if he could read my thoughts, then moved a little, scooting so he could lean against my shins, his arm wrapping around them, his chin leaning on my knees.

"You're not mad?" I asked.

"Angry at myself for falling into their trap, yes. But mad at you for doing everything you could to save us? No. I would have done the same in your place."

"But—the blood?"

He closed his eyes and sighed.

"You felt it as much as I did, Keira," he said. "I almost died, the real thing, the forever kind, like Evan. When you gave me the chance, I think part of me realized I might do almost anything to survive and I was happy doing it. I've spent the last several decades fighting my need for blood and winning. But this, this scared me. Scared me into thinking I needed to do more thinking. Reevaluate things. It's been a long time since I had to think about—"

"Survival?"

"Not exactly on the modern vampire's menu," he joked. "Mostly I worry about making payroll and making sure my guests are comfortable."

He got serious. "Nearly dying changes things, even for us, for me." His breath skittered across my legs as he sighed, eyes closed against whatever he was thinking.

"Keira, I can't change how I feel about things, but today I risked losing my life, exposing my people because of my stubbornness." He raised his head and looked me directly in the eye. "That's not a price I'm willing to pay. Not now, not ever."

Niko just sat across from us, the small smile on his face widening to a grin. I could almost imagine what he was thinking. If Adam's viewpoint could be altered, maybe they'd get to start hunting. Can't say that I blamed him.

"Don't jump to any conclusions, Nikolai," Adam said, glancing over at him. "I'm not changing overnight. I'm just willing to reexamine my policies, not throw everything out the window."

"As long as I get a fair shot," Niko said. "This is progress."

Adam shook his head and smiled, as if ignoring an indulged younger brother. I started to smile. Things were definitely looking up.

"Maybe we should all have a long talk," Adam said, shaking his head. "After we deal with—" He cocked his head in the direction of the store van and the bodies beyond it.

"With Boris and Greta." I interrupted him. In my delight at being rescued and not losing Adam, I'd almost forgotten the carnage across the pit.

"No worries." My brother, now clothed, dropped back down into the pit.

"What do you mean?" I asked.

"We can take care of them," he said. "Bottlecap Curve?"

I nodded, getting the gist of his suggestion.

"And Evan?"

Adam looked at me. "He's in the path of the sun. There won't be much left soon."

"All in a day's work." Tucker smiled. "Now, let's get you all out of here. My van's just beyond the curve of the path. No direct sunlight." He bent down to offer Niko a hand. The redhead took it with a smile.

CHAPTER TWENTY-THREE

T HE NEWS CAME the next day. Swiftly, on the wings of
the fall breeze, as most news does in a small town.
Whispers around a corner, behind doors, in the chairs
at the beauty parlor. No one really knows who heard it
first, but by the time Tucker and I hit Bea's for coffee
and breakfast at three, the entire place was abuzz with
excitement.

"Well, that didn't take long," I said, rocking back in
my chair and taking a long sip of the hot coffee. I was
sitting in Bea's office, watching her rearrange the work
schedule one more time. Tucker had stayed out in the
café, knowing I wanted to speak with Bea alone.

"The news?"

I nodded. "Funny how people see only what they
want to see."

"Yeah," she mumbled and leaned forward to peer at
the computer screen as if looking at it more closely would
make it make more sense. She was cutting her hours again,
only opening Thursday through Sunday, and then only for
brunch on Sunday. Noe was still reluctantly working for
her, as was one of his former school buddies who had lost
his job in San Antonio. Tia Petra had bullied one other
nephew to pitch in, but he was only able to work weekends,
since he was attending school at UTSA full time.

"Carjacking," she said, finally leaning back and
reaching for her own giant coffee cup. "Guess the

Albrights were more desperate than we thought. Too bad they had to carjack Boris and Greta. Heard they went over the cliff at Bottlecap Curve. The bodies were so badly burned it was hard to ID them."

"Yeah."

"Hmmmm." Bea took a long sip from her mug. "Good coffee, even if I do say so myself."

"Yep."

We sipped in silence for a few minutes.

"So you going over to visit your bloodsucking boyfriend?"

"After a while," I said. "It won't be dark for another few hours."

"Your brother still here?"

I nodded. "Out front. He'll be staying for a while. Seems he's my penance."

"For what?"

"For starting to Change too damned early and for not coming home."

"You *are* home."

"That's what I told Gigi. Good news is—she agreed to leave me alone if Tucker stayed."

"Any chance of chick flicks and munchies anytime soon?"

"You bet," I said. "Next week maybe? If I can shake Tucker. Maybe he can go into Austin or San Antonio or something." Or go hang out with Niko. Not that I was going to let Bea in on that particular development.

"Let him stay," Bea said. "He can make the popcorn." She looked at me. "He can even invite Niko over if he wants."

"Excuse me?" Was she saying what I thought she was saying?

She grinned. "Yeah, you can't be the only sibling interested in creatures of the night."

"You *know*?"

"No worries, *m'hija*. Tucker and me—you know that was just flirting. He told me about Niko last night. I can deal. Besides, who knows what could happen?"

I laughed. "I am so not going to go there, girlfriend. You're all adults. Your choice. No advice from this corner."

She stood up suddenly. "Well, then, I guess I'd better go out front."

"Why?"

She nodded in the direction of the door. "You've got company."

Carlton was walking through the kitchen, toward the office.

"You can stay, you know," I told her.

"Yeah, but I won't." She grinned and tossed her hair back. "Later, *chica*."

I grimaced. "Hmmph."

"I guess you've heard." Carlton's tone was non-committal, just like his expression remained neutral.

I nodded. "About a dozen little birdies told me. Dead on impact?"

"DPS is running the accident investigation, but they're pretty sure it's cut and dried. A carjacking gone wrong." He fiddled with his hat.

"We found a bunch of money in that abandoned car out at the quarry. Walker says it was one of his employees." Carlton turned to face me, his expression serious. "What was Marty doing, Keira? Not just poaching, was he?"

"Trust me, you don't want to know. Someday . . ." I shook my head. Someday would never come. I couldn't tell him.

"I'm taking a short leave of absence."

"Oh?" I raised my eyebrows at him.

He shrugged. "Family business."

"Carol?" The little birdies had been very busy. At least three people had told me this juicy tale before I'd made it back to Bea's office.

"She called last night. Wants to try again."

"And this is good, right?"

"Yes." He looked down and began to shuffle his feet against the tile floor. "I guess this is good-bye, then."

My smile was sad, echoing the emotion I felt inside. Even after everything, he still didn't get it. "It was good-bye twelve years ago, Carlton. Please, let it go." I stood up. "Are you coming back?"

"I'll be back," he said. "With my family."

"Good."

He inclined his head toward the incongruous metal container on Bea's desk. It was ugly, but serviceable. I'd brought it inside because I hadn't actually been sure what to do with it. I needed to wait until sundown, but didn't feel comfortable just leaving it sitting around in my car. So here I was carting it around like a bad piece of luggage.

"Marty?"

"Yeah."

Marty hadn't turned. He was just dead, not undead.

Bexar County had completed the autopsy and ruled the cause of death to be an overdose of sedatives, a bottle of which they'd found in the Albrights' car. They'd released my cousin's body to me, next of kin and all that. We found a willing funeral home that would cremate him right away. Tucker had gone over to pick him up.

"What are you going to do with the ashes?"

"Scatter them out by the lake."

"Special meaning?"

"Sort of."

Carlton looked a little puzzled. As well he should be. The place did have meaning, but not to Marty.

AFTER THE SUN went down, when the last light of the sun had faded and the first light of the now waning moon illuminated the night sky, I stood with my lover, the local vampire king, and tossed the ashes of my poor dead cousin on the spot where the two Sitka deer had been killed and where these days of blood had begun. Seemed like weeks.

"What are you going to do now, Adam?"

"Keep trying, that's all we can do."

"And the blood?"

"I can't deny it. It was a rush, but I can't let myself . . ."

I put my hand on his arm. "Adam, I can't say I understand it, but I accept it. It's what you want."

"And us?"

"There's an us?" I smiled, letting him know I was kidding.

"You'll stay with me?"

I nodded. "Yes, if you can stand it." I stepped away from him, not wanting to feel the intimacy just now. "I'm still Changing, Adam. There's no telling what's going to happen."

"I can live with it."

"Or not live," I joked.

He smiled and reached out for me. "Or not live."

"One of these days, you're going to have to fill me in on all these convoluted vampire politics of yours."

"One of these days, I will."

Here's a "sneak peak" at
Blood Bargain
Book Two of the Blood Lines Series
by Maria Lima

CHAPTER ONE

T HE SOUND was more than a thought, less than a whisper.

Here . . . come . . . here . . .

I don't know how, but I heard the insistence behind the words and I knew they were meant for me.

Sis . . . sis . . . sis . . .

The sound faded, even less distinct than before. I strained to hear more.

Sissss . . .

The last hissing sibilant was drowned out by the sound of a door shutting upstairs. I heard a shuffle of movement then muffled steps descending the thickly carpeted staircase.

"Tucker?" My own voice sounded overloud to my ears.

Adam appeared at the bottom of the bedroom stairs holding two open bottles of wine in his left hand, each suspended by the neck. His right hand cradled two wine stems, each two-thirds filled, the red liquid gleaming in the low light.

He was dressed in his usual casual elegance—black silk dress shirt, sleeves rolled back to reveal muscular forearms, collar open to show a small V of pale skin at the neck, shirt tucked into finely woven custom-tailored black slacks. His feet were bare, owing to his habit of removing his shoes at the front door. Adam told me once he liked to feel the textures of the carpets, the fine grain of the hardwood floors, the cool of the tiles as he walked.

Occasionally, he'd spend entire nights free of footwear, even outdoors.

He paused on the final step, giving me a small nod and a smile, lifting both hands. "I'm sorry I'm a bit later than I intended," he said, stepping down. "Did you—"

He slipped, stumbled a little, holding his elbows out as he tried to regain balance without spilling the wine. He seemed to waver a moment, then stilled and sank slowly to his knees, sitting back on his heels, arms held carefully in front, keeping the bottles and glasses level.

"Adam!" I scrambled toward him. I'd been reading in bed the past couple of hours, having decided since he was working late, I'd skip my usual meal at the Inn's restaurant, have a snack at the house and just curl up with a good book. "Are you okay?"

"I'm fine, Keira. Seem to have slipped on the last step." With the liquid grace endemic to vampires and other non-humans, he rose to his feet, still holding bottles and glasses. There was no evidence of spillage, except for a single blood red drop of wine sliding down the side of one glass. We both watched its slow progression as it followed the curve, went down the stem, then slid across the pale skin of the back of his wrist.

Adam caught my gaze and, without a word, extended his wrist to me, the dark drop of clear red poised, shimmering on the pulse point against the outline of blue veins beneath. I reached to cup his hand, two fingers extended underneath the offered wrist, holding it steady.

I held Adam's gaze as I bent my head, inhaling the wine's bouquet, deep notes of darkest red-purple woven through with hints of smoky oak and cedar. The scent of Adam's skin lay beneath, soft spice and coolness, with a hint of nutmeg and—

Something else.

My nostrils flared. Mingled with the wine, underneath the liquid—blood. Not Adam's, not the living rich scent of life, but concentrated, a heavier weight of *ironmetalcopper* infusing the liquid. The aroma of Adam's own blood lurked under this, just beneath his skin, pulsing, heat growing as I drew closer. My own pulse quickened as the scent reached the back of my throat.

This wasn't my wine that spilled, but his. Wine laced with blood extracts. Animal blood, not human, drawn from living donors, the procedure inflicting no more pain than a veterinarian's blood test.

Inhaling the rich fragrance, I closed my eyes, confused, not certain of his intent.

"Are you sure?" I whispered, opening my eyes to look up at Adam, watching his face.

He held my gaze, expression frozen in a neutrality held by the strongest of wills. A test then? A challenge? What was he doing?

An eternal heartbeat, two, then the briefest hint of a nod as a word I barely heard escaped his lips. "Yes."

I closed my eyes again, letting myself get lost in the heady scent, then licked the crimson globule from his wrist.

The taste expanded in my mouth, stronger than a single drop should be, dark red *oakironblood* flavor exploding, catching me off guard. I swallowed and straightened, opening my eyes to look at Adam.

"Not what you were expecting?" He'd dropped tight neutrality for a composed amusement, any hint of emotion still hidden behind the mask.

"Not," I answered, stepping back, letting go his wrist and taking the correct glass from his hand. I had to force myself to imitate his dispassionate detachment. We obviously weren't going where I thought we were with his little display of whatever it was.

I took a sip of my own wine, to mask my confusion. The once heady Torre di Pietra petite Syrah, a favorite, now tasted flat, less real by comparison. I'd never tasted the special blood-laced wine before.

Ever since I'd moved in, our nightly wine had become a ritual; Adam would either return from his office up at the Inn with a couple of bottles, one for each of us, or—if Adam had elected to stay in and work from home that night—one of the Inn's waitstaff would deliver the wine. The ritual never varied. The bottles would already be decorked and ready to pour. Adam would pour a glass for me, then one for himself. We'd clink a wordless toast then enjoy, usually sipping in silence.

I'd come to think that Adam drinking his blood wine with me was his way of letting me in, letting me be a part of his life, part of the private side of Adam Walker.

"So what was that in aid of?" I asked, finally gaining enough control to speak.

Adam set the wine bottles down on a small table, then took a sip from his own glass before he spoke. "A thought," he said. "Simply that." He sipped again. "You called out for Tucker?"

Avoiding the subject, Adam Walker? I thought. So that's the way he's playing this. A thought, indeed. More like a whim that turned out to be less whimsical than he'd expected.

"I did," I answered. "Before I heard you upstairs, I was reading and I thought I heard a voice calling me. It said 'come here,' then I heard it say 'Sis.' Tucker wasn't here, was he?"

"He was not."

"I don't think I dozed off," I said, "but maybe . . . no, I'm pretty sure I was awake. Maybe I should call Tucker and see if something's wrong."

Adam's hand on my forearm stopped me. "I wouldn't do that if I were you."

"Why?"

"I don't think your brother would appreciate the interruption."

"I'm sorry—what?"

Adam's expression, accompanied by the raising of his right eyebrow, could only be called a smirk.

"Inter—what? You *know*? How could you possibly know?" My mind zoomed to a place I didn't particularly want to go—to where my brother and his lover were doing things I wish Adam and I were doing. Except Adam and I hadn't been doing *anything* in that area for more days than I cared to count, which is one of the reasons I'd been so confused about the whole spilled wine thing.

"Niko is tied to me by blood and bond," he answered. "When you called Tucker's name, I instinctively—"

"Holy crap, you can read Niko's mind?"

He laughed. "No, not exactly. I can sense many things, strong emotion being the . . . shall we say, 'loudest.' I don't think either Tucker or Niko would welcome your phone call."

"Huh."

Chalk that up to Vampire Lesson #694. I'd only been with Adam for a few months. Some days, I felt as if I knew everything there was to know about him; evidently, this wasn't one of those days.

Of course, learning about each other was par for our particular course. When Adam found out last year that

I was as supernatural as he was—more so, actually, because I'd been born that way—he'd been as interested in my abilities as I was in his. Problem was, I wasn't sure what those abilities were quite yet. Like a child entering adolescence, I was beginning my own Change, moving into what would eventually be my nature: weather witch, healer, shapeshifter, necromancer. Odds were, since my father and all six of my elder brothers were shifters, I'd be joining them, but that wasn't a given. My own experience remained completely out of the realm of the usual. Six months ago, I started having visions and feeling the power surges that heralded Changing— some twenty years ahead of schedule. My omniscient double-great-granny and matriarch of our clan figured it out long before I did and sent my brother to watch over me. So far, my body failed to follow any sort of normal pattern. By now, I should be Changed. But, six months after onset, I still experienced the odd surge of power at random times, but nothing much more. No wonder I was hearing things.

"Okay, well, I guess I was just dreaming then," I said. "I sincerely doubt my brother is calling for me when he's . . . busy."

"I'm quite sure of that." Adam smiled and took another sip of his wine as he walked toward the bed. He picked up a copy of this week's edition of the *Hill Country News* from the nightstand, set the wine down and, as he started reading the paper, unbuttoned and shrugged off his shirt, then climbed onto the bed—the picture of domestic bliss— still reading.

"Hey," I said, walking to the bed, setting my own glass on the other nightstand. I crawled across the mattress, settling in at his side. "The night's not all that old yet and

I've still got a few hours before I need to meet with the Realtor guy about the mortuary sale."

"The estate agent, yes. He sold it quickly, didn't he?" he said absently.

"Well, now that Marty's dead and my family's moved, no one really wanted to deal with it. I just let the realtor do what he thought was best. It's not like the family needs a funeral home. I'll sign the final paperwork, around eight A.M. or so. Evidently realtors don't work at night."

Adam nodded, still intent on something he was reading. I had no idea what it could be since most stories in the small-town weekly were along the lines of what the week's school menu items would be and discussing area bond voting issues and what not.

"So . . . you want to?" I snuggled closer to Adam. Hey, it didn't hurt to try. I wasn't sure why the recent lack, but I thought it was time to end the dry spell and, from his action earlier, maybe he'd thought about it, too.

Adam looked at me over the newsprint, folded it carefully, took a pen and circled something before placing both on the bedside table on his side of the bed. "His side" . . . when had we chosen sides?

Six months ago, this thing between us was all "What the heck are you doing in my very obscure little redneck corner of the world"? Now, evidently, we had sides—both of the bed and philosophically. We'd agreed to disagree on whether he should hunt for his blood fix—especially since I mostly sided with his second-in-command, Niko. I held the opinion that hunting was fine as long as you ate what you killed, and in Adam's case, and most of the vampires at the Wild Moon, they didn't even need to kill their prey: local fauna, carefully managed by Niko in his role as wildlife manager. Vampires might not need human blood, but they did need blood to survive. Adam refused to hunt, but continued to subsist on the blood extract–laden wine, which I thought was a poor substitute. We managed to sublimate our difference of opinion most of the time. Tonight had been a bit fraught already, so I figured a little closeness couldn't hurt.

"What did you circle there? In the paper? You seemed so interested."

"Nothing . . . well, perhaps something," he corrected himself.

I made an attempt to emulate the slightly sardonic raised eyebrow that came so naturally to him. I failed miserably and probably looked somewhat demented. My eyebrows had never learned independent movement.

"It's a ranch," Adam said.

"Excuse me, a what?"

I sat up from my semi-recline and reached over him to snag the paper with my fingertips. I had a long reach, but it was a very big bed.

"Actually, it's an advertisement for a ranch for sale. I wish to buy it."

Again I tried for the raised brow. Again I failed.

"Ha, funny. You own a ranch—well, more of a fancy haven for vampires to hang out. You thinking of going native? Working cattle, riding horses?"

Now *that* was a picture indeed. Adam Walker, undead king of the local vampire tribe, long black hair, green eyes and pale skin, all decked out in faded jeans, Lucchese boots, western shirt and . . . oh my ever-loving overactive imagination . . . *chaps*. Jesus. I seriously needed either a cold shower or a hot vampire. Ten guesses as to which I preferred and the first nine don't even come close to counting.

I tossed the newspaper to the side and ran my hand up Adam's leg, the fine weave of his trousers smooth to my touch. I dropped my head to his shoulder, tasting his skin as I murmured, "What say we talk about ranch ads later? Let's spend the next couple of hours doing something a hell of a lot more interesting."

My shoulder kiss turned into a neck nuzzle. I moved my hand further up his thigh, across his bare belly and up his chest. Under my touch, his skin was cool at first, his natural temperature heating up as the energy between us built. I wasn't sure if this was magick or something else. It didn't matter.

We'd only started having sex a couple of months ago. I'd been willing to go for it right away. My initial reluctance when I knew him in England had been due only to the fact I'd thought he was human. When I discovered differently, I was ready to act on the attraction.

But Adam was old-fashioned. He'd wanted to woo me, to court me. So, for four months following Adam's arrival in Rio Seco and my cousin Marty's brutal murder, Adam played the suitor.

He'd started with traditional standards—a single rose, elegant dinners at fine restaurants in Austin or San Antonio—and then, bit by bit, upped the stakes, no pun intended. I'd enjoyed every decadent minute of it.

By week six of the sweet onslaught, I'd been ready to lay down an ultimatum to get laid, but then he pulled out all the stops and handed me an envelope with tickets . . . tickets to a three-week holiday in a remote vampire encampment at the Arctic Circle during the height of polar night. We'd spent the greater part of the time in bed . . . not sleeping.

When we got back to Rio Seco, I hadn't even bothered to go back to my own house. I'd taken all my luggage and went straight to the Wild Moon Ranch and Adam's place. When I asked for closet space, he'd looked at me, seemed about to ask a question, but then shrugged, smiled and bowed to the inevitable. I'd been there ever since.

The sex was great, the company even better. Adam would spent a few hours a night doing ranch and other vampire business. I'd amuse myself, something I'd already managed to do for two long years babysitting my cousin Marty. Compared to that, this was cake . . . with sprinkles on it.

I smiled against Adam's skin, remembering how hard he'd worked, how earnest he'd been to make a good impression. He was definitely different from any of my previous liaisons.

My neck nuzzle turned into a kiss, deep, intense and oh, yes, most definitely a prelude to much, much more. I slid over, moving on top of Adam, letting my hands, my body, show him just how much he'd come to mean to me. How much I wanted . . .

Our skin heated with the contact, the energy growing, building, generated by two supernatural people letting down all their walls. Adam reciprocated, his hands skimming my sides, wrapping around my back, his legs twining with mine. Yes.

I needed more—more skin, less clothing. I sat up with a moan, hands scrambling to take off my T-shirt. Adam's hands tangled with mine as he pushed my hands to the side, grabbed the neck of my cotton tee and ripped it down the middle, pushing the pieces off me. We were both sitting up now, my legs wrapped around his hips, only the thin cotton of my panties and his trousers keeping us apart.

I bent my head to his, losing myself in another kiss, taking, demanding, needing to connect. I threw my head back as the heat rose, gasping with the need to breathe.

A low growl issued from Adam's throat as he bent his head, lips to my neck, mouthing, nuzzling, tasting, then nipping a little, teasing me.

"Yes." I arched in pleasure as I hissed the word, palming the back of his head and pressing it to me.

His lips moved against my skin as he licked me again. I felt a sudden scrape, then a sharp pressure/pain.

Finally, I thought. *Finally.*

Adam's fingers dug into my back, slid into fists as a huge shudder gripped his body. He froze then, every muscle stone. He didn't pull away, didn't continue.

I kept silent, waiting. I knew what he'd nearly done.

After a moment . . . an eternity . . . during which the only sound in the room was our mutual harsh breathing, Adam lifted his hands from my back, placed them on my biceps with a gentle stroke. His head dropped to his chest with a huge exhalation.

"What?" I whispered. There had been a word buried in his sigh.

I pulled away a little, brought my hands up to cradle his face.

"Adam, what?"

With a visible effort, he dropped his hands to his thighs, shuddered again and with a deep intake and release of breath forcibly relaxed.

"No." The word hung out there, bald and blunt.

I blinked, not sure I understood.

"What do you mean, 'no'?"

Adam slid back and off the bed, moving about three feet away. His erection was still visible through the thin fabric.

I scrambled to join him, to confront him. I was sure

we looked a sight, both of us half naked, still flushed with arousal, except mine was quickly turning to anger. Damn it all, I was going to get to the bottom of this. He could not just keep ignoring me.

As I opened my mouth to speak, the not-so-dulcet tones of my cell phone rang.